INTERZONE: The 5th A

As a race, we are about to find out what kind of breed we are, what sort of game our nature's up to; the vote may be cast before the century turns, belly-up or dawnwards; but maybe not for a while longer. There are at least three choices. We may find we're a swarm that eats its host and dies, or a swarm that sets up housekeeping, or a swarm that migrates. Most American science fiction published in the last decade assumes – tacitly or explicitly – us to be the kind of swarm that migrates, which to many Britishers is just what one might expect from Frontier addicts stuck to a ball. British science fiction, on the other hand, has always tended to vacillate between the first two choices, which to many Americans is like trying to choose between death and taxes (or no choice at all).

INTERZONE: The 4th Anthology

'This compilation . . . keeps the faith with a regularity which never betrays our mouth-watering anticipation: the best of British'

The Times

'The *Interzone* selections . . . are, quite simply, the repositories of some of the finest short fiction to be found anywhere. Oldsters like Ballard and Sladek are in fine form . . . but as usual with this fine imprint, the big names get more than a run for their money from the young bloods'

Time Out

'Fuses logic and fancy into genuine and appealing fiction'

The Independent

INTERZONE: The 3rd Anthology

'*Interzone* strides over the frontier and well on to a summit of art'

New Statesman

'A selection of stories that combine the grim and the glorious with an audacity that recalls *Dangerous Visions* . . . it should not be missed at any cost'

Locus

INTERZONE: The 2nd Anthology

'Its best stories are quite enough to be heard even among the mindless roar of the big guns; they are pockets of clarity like soft sensible dialogues'

City Limits

'They have the quality of going right to the edge of ideas which can chill as well as warm'

The Times

INTERZONE: The 1st Anthology

'Science fiction is supposed to be a backwater, albeit a commercial one. But *Interzone* strides over the frontier and well on to a summit of art!'

New Statesman

'A must for science fiction enthusiasts'

Cosmopolitan

Also available from NEL:

INTERZONE: The 2nd Anthology
INTERZONE: The 3rd Anthology
INTERZONE: The 4th Anthology

Interzone:
The 5th Anthology

New Science Fiction and
Fantasy Writing

Edited by
John Clute, Lee Montgomerie
and David Pringle

With an introduction by
John Clute

NEW ENGLISH LIBRARY
Hodder and Stoughton

First published in Great Britain in 1991 by New English Library Paperbacks

A New English Library Paperback original

British Library C.I.P.
Interzone V.
I. Pringle, David II. Clute, John
823[F]

ISBN 0-450-54063-4

Printed and bound in Great Britain for Hodder and Stoughton Paperbacks, a division of Hodder and Stoughton Ltd., Mill Road, Dunton Green, Sevenoaks, Kent TN13 2YA. (Editorial Office: 47 Bedford Square, London, WC1B 3DP) by Clays Ltd, St Ives plc. Typeset by Hewer Text Composition Services, Edinburgh.

Contents

Introduction 1

BRIAN ALDISS A Life of Matter and Death 5
PHILLIP MANN An Old Fashioned Story 31
WILLIAM KING Visiting the Dead 43
IAN R. MACLEOD Well-Loved 58
CHERRY WILDER Looking Forward to the Harvest 69
KIM NEWMAN Twitch Technicolor 100
IAN LEE Once Upon a Time in the Park 111
RICHARD CALDER Mosquito 128
DAVID BRIN Piecework 146
IAN MCDONALD Listen 179
KAREN JOY FOWLER Game Night at the Fox & Goose 201
IAN WATSON The Eye of the Ayatollah 215
NEIL FERGUSON One-Way to Wap Wap 224
BARRINGTON J. BAYLEY Light 244
NICHOLAS ROYLE The Sculptor's Hand 258

Notes on the Authors 275
Acknowledgments 279

JOHN CLUTE

Introduction

P. G. Wodehouse almost said it. Peace which did something which had slipped our minds to the something sleeve of care (he almost said) poured over us in a healing wave. The world, in other words, with a great heave of the winds, has changed its tune, and the 90s began, and once again history's march-time could be heard (rataplan, rataplan), like a beating of human hearts. No longer need we fear the dread zero of millennium (said the likes of Herr Kohl); no longer would the *Titanics* of our dreams sink ozone-sickened nightly into acid-poisoned icefloes choking gong-tormented, torn-dolphin seas. Time said tick, the Wall is down, Time says tock, the walls dissolve, the armies melt, the politicians waken from their funhouse slumber and serve their masters (us); tyrants cave, elections come, sages whose scars have begun to heal tell tales of the world's great age, which begins anew.

Poo (as A. A. Milne once almost said). We may have taken a first step or two, we may have survived the alpha male stinkpot of Iraq, but who knows if we're crossing a tightrope to haven, or clinging to a loose hawser at the whiplash end of its tether. The planet continues to bald, eczemas slur the bared scalp of the mother, who seems (from the safety of satellite cameras) increasingly inimical to life. But the species which dominates the scalp is continuing to breed, and the skull of the mother crawls with itch. It looks as though the dominant species is about to *swarm*. Wave.

As a race, we are about to find out what kind of breed

we are, what sort of game our nature's up to; the vote may be cast before the century turns, belly-up or dawnwards; but maybe not for a while longer. There are at least three choices. We may find we're a swarm that eats its host and dies, or a swarm that sets up housekeeping, or a swarm that migrates. Most American science fiction published in the last decade assumes – tacitly or explicitly – us to be the kind of swarm that migrates, which to many Britishers is just what one might expect from Frontier addicts stuck to a ball. British science fiction, on the other hand, has always tended to vacillate between the first two choices, which to many Americans is like trying to choose between death and taxes (or no choice at all).

For the writers who contribute to *Interzone*, and some of whose best work has been assembled in this Fifth Anthology (wave), there is some tendency to eschew the final option. Most of them stick to the planet; even Americans like David Brin, many of whose novels range through interstellar venues far from the vale of tears (and death, and taxes), sets 'Piecework' on Earth. Though it reads with the dashing clarity of his larger tales, 'Piecework' is in fact a remarkably complex positive prognosis of the nature of life in the next century. Much of the cognitive beauty of the best American hard sf glows through the narrow polished facets of the story, a sense of the ineluctable reality of the world, its populousness (in the best sense), its variety and grit and confluence; and perhaps most important, a sense of the *momentum* of things. Time is an engine.

In 'A Life of Matter and Death', Brian Aldiss conveys a similar sense that world history must be defined as things happening, even though his protagonist (the tale is couched as a confession made long after the events marked) cannot begin to tolerate the transformations to which he has paid shocked witness; hints and slews of implication proliferate throughout the deft and effortless dramatic ironies of the tale, compacting family romance and history and heart-death. Beneath the semiology jokes and the world-historical staging of Neil Ferguson's

'One-Way to Wap Wap', human beings can, once again, be witnessed in their fret and torture, the shoulder-shrugging sang-froid of mere survival, which counts. Here, and in Ian Watson's utterly sane morality tale, 'The Eye of the Ayatollah', the planet itself seems to have only a bit role (that of Stage), but this is a trick of the pen. Both stories are in essence parables of planetary survival, writ small. In each of them, human protagonists bound to historical cusps make (or attempt to make) sense of lives that will only make sense if the world does. In the Ferguson, sense does not abide; in the Watson, precariously, it may do so.

Neil Ferguson's tale is very funny; Ian Watson's is urgently swift; Kim Newman's 'Twitch Technicolor' shudders from data-noir overload, though it comes sharp and clean in the end; Karen Joy Fowler's 'Game Night at the Fox & Goose' unfolds into its savage denouement like a chess-trap that begins to close with the first words of the tale, so that the whole tale is trap, exquisite and loaded; and Barrington Bayley's 'Light', here published for the first time, similarly closes into cul-de-sac as its illumination grows, its darkness shivers into light. From hilarity (however torn) to the actinic glow of Bayley at his most undeviating, these stories (most of them recent) show something of the variety of work authors have been publishing in *Interzone* since the first issue in 1982. Never, however, have we been able to publish enough of them; even though the journal has grown steadily in issue size and in frequency, and we have gradually been able to increase our frequency, from quarterly to bi-monthly, and since April 1990, when editor/publisher David Pringle, felt we could make the next move, monthly. Perhaps we'll be able to keep up.

It will be a task. Like Fowler and Ferguson, Phillip Mann shapes a cunning DIY trap for the dissection of sexism in 'An Old-Fashioned Story', very nasty, very funny: like a mirror. William King's 'Visiting the Dead', like the Brin story, posits and populates a complex ongoing world whose effect is to *enable* the intimate workings at the heart of the tale. Ian R. MacLeod's 'Well-Loved' traverses mean streets, turns off them, looks back with a child's eyes. In 'Looking Forward to the Harvest', which is also original to this anthology, Cherry Wilder weds serenity and conniption in her telling of a world that has precariously survived the closure of our own. 'Mosquito', by Richard Calder, might be described as a Dynaflow contortuplication of Cyberpunk, and reads with astonishing potent smoothness (it is his second published story). In 'Listen', Ian McDonald glosses the hard and utterly clear implications of his post-catastrophe story with a subtle (and rather cunning) lacquer of Dunsany. 'Once Upon a Time in the Park' by Ian Lee ties postmodernist surreality and wordspin (fleetingly reminiscent of Guy Davenport) to a strict and telling genre context. And in 'The Sculptor's Hand', Nicholas Royle similarly transforms guignol conventions into a most significantly hilarious assault upon the hospital-visiting habits of one very strange politician. Wave.

It is a full hamper. It is the best of our latest year. It is full of the things we all say together, wise folk and fools, on the raft of Earth. If talk can help us steer, let us talk. Let us never stop.

BRIAN ALDISS

A Life of Matter and Death

A Novel in One Chapter

Very well. Here I sit looking out over the sea, on this little rag of an island, Uskair. I may as well tell the story, though a new generation, growing up since the Odonata arrived on Earth, will find it incredible.

Do you wonder why I have hesitated until now? Because it isn't really my story. It's my brother's.

Yes, my brother Alec. The Man Who Changed the World, damn him.

Last year, before I decided to settle here for keeps, my business took me to one of the great northern cities, chief among those of the prosperous world. From the air, it seemed a place of beauty, from ground level often horrifying. From the city's government and economic centre, the destinies of billions of people round the globe were decided, yet the population was still not under control. The problem of the living remained, though the problem of the dead had been solved.

To the man who had solved that problem, a statue stood in one of the main squares. On the plinth were the simple words:

ALEC GREYLORN
1985–2036
He Brought a Cleansing Force
To Human Affairs

My brother's figure stood in bronze, and on his shoulder was an Odonata.

Many cities have erected similar memorials. All his fortune went to institutions; only the island came to me, the younger brother he spurned as a liar.

All cities have changed their appearance in the last decade. Even villages and hamlets have changed. Odonatist towers stand everywhere, glass towers resembling translucent vases. They say that such towers stand in Alice Springs, in Cove, Oregon, in Timbuktu and Petra and downtown Samarkand. The vase towers bring beauty to the ugliest place, and have altered human perceptions of what is sublime. Sometimes as the light of the sun catches them, you see the Odonata fluttering down into them to receive the gifts that mourners leave there.

It is not only the landscape that has changed. So have religions. It is laughable now to imagine a single one of the world's multitudinous dead being burnt by fire or buried in earth.

Much has changed for the better, thanks to Alec's discovery. All the same, there's no glass tower on Uskair.

The Odonata themselves are pretty splendid, I admit. Another generation will grow accustomed to their beauty, and no longer marvel at them. I take a shot at the odd one that flies over Uskair – strictly illegal, I know. In general, their irridescence, their startling speed, remain a joy. It is easy to see why a new religion has grown about them. Besides, people will worship anything.

But the Odonata are not spirits. They scarcely resemble the order of dragonflies after which they were named. Some have been sighted more than thirty feet in length, cruising almost a kilometre above sea level. Wing-spans are recorded of up to forty feet.

They are intelligent, although it is an intelligence unlike humanity's. There's no aggression. Odonata have never attacked a living human being. They avoid planes and helicopters. What they do is basic: they fly, feed, breed sparingly, and look beautiful. They do good. They inspire musicians. They make me sick.

And it was Alec who let them loose.

Alec took after my father. He was a man of action. And a boy of action.

He was two years older than I, taller, more handsome, better at sport. On his fifth birthday, he climbed a tall tree until he reached twig level, where he sat contentedly as the wind rocked him to and fro. On the ground far below, father applauded while mother cried for him to come down. I stood and licked my ice-cream.

Later, I asked Alec if he liked being perched so high.

'Oh, no,' he said.

It was an irritating answer. I believed him to mean that he climbed trees not for enjoyment but because he felt danger was his natural environment. Perhaps he did it to hear mother scream.

While I was always told I talked too much, Alec was quiet. That was because he was athletic.

We used to go sailing on the estuary when we were boys. Father taught us everything. He taught us how to ride out a storm. That was when my sister drowned. Father wanted her to be buried at sea; mother did not. They quarrelled terribly over that. I'll never forget how they quarrelled.

Alec liked sailing more than I. I got seasick. Fortunately, we spent more time mountaineering than sailing. Father was a mountaineer; he made his fortune from the ski resorts on a mountain grandfather had bought cheaply in Colorado. So we were for ever heading for the rocky interior of continents, to regions of crags and barrenness. Father was at his most hearty in places where there was an echo. Alec liked solitudes too.

Father was a big square man, very freckled and covered with sparse sandy hair. He perspired a lot, he enthused a lot. He liked to sing hymns as he worked his way up cliff faces. He was a schoolboy at heart – as I realized later in life.

He used to tell us that on our expeditions we were 'confronting the Unknown'. The phrase gave him satisfaction; he used it a lot. Mother – another sandy person, with pretty green eyes – would nod to herself when she heard the phrase, as if in recognition, and smile a little secret smile.

Personally, there were things other than the Unknown I would have preferred to confront. But there's no doubt this activity stood Alec in good stead when he finally came across the truly Unknown.

When we were not at school, we were under canvas, often as not, and far from the crack-crazed cities of Europe. In the nineteen-eighties and nineties, there were still remote places, and if there were remote places we found them. Although I was no linguist at school, I could still say a few useful words in Spanish, Nepali, Urdu, Carib, Slovak, and Bahasa Malay. We often slept under the stars. I knew the word for *star* in about twenty languages.

So it was that, just before my sixteenth birthday, I found myself with my parents and brother at the foot of an unprepossessing mountain called locally El Jocoso, The Jocund. I had tried many lies and devices to avoid this mountain, including a realistic limp and stories of leg cancer. To no avail. Even my bloodcurdling tale of the Curse of El Jocoso had not prevailed. There I was, there the mountain was.

We were camped amid the little-visited Calaste chain in southern Bolivia. The mountains are no great height, but the ascents are steep, the country wild, and the snakes prolific – all plus factors as far as my father was concerned. Another irritating item was that the place was swarming with tortoises, clashing against each other in their anxiety to mate. One can only question the wisdom of a god who gave shelled creatures a sex life.

We had experienced great difficulty in procuring bearers and mules, since a small war was raging in valleys and hills. Several rival revolutionary armies were challenging the central government and each other. Father dismissed all this as typical South American ferment, and believed that all would be well as long as we sang a hymn before breakfast.

The fact that we had ventured into disputed territory meant nothing to my father. Guerrillas warned us that the CIA were about to spray the area with a new defoliant and anthrax contaminants. How often have I heard father, after listening impatiently to similar warnings, exclaim, 'Oh, don't be an idiot – let's get on with it, man!' and stride ahead, swinging a machete.

Men thus instructed often found it easier to get on with it than to try and explain the danger all over again.

So it was that – ill-equipped, ignoring all warnings, and unable to pick up the BBC World Service on our radio – we confronted El Jocoso without guides and in a thunderstorm. Even my mother, normally so placid with her three great boys, was in a bad mood. There had been shelling in Casa Tampica and she had left her hair dye in the Holton Hotel.

'Onward, Christian soldiers!' boomed my father, as he hammered in his first piton.

It was on the 8th of August that father suffered his fall. The three of us were scaling an almost vertical face. I was bored. I had just discovered boredom, and it was magic to me. To my left hand was a small ledge and on it, rather surprisingly, a tortoise appeared.

Pitching my voice to a tone of mild puzzlement, I called, 'What's a rattlesnake doing up here?'

My father looked round, startled. He slipped on the naked rock. The fifi hook attached to his étrier slipped. He reached too violently to grasp it, a tape snapped on the étrier, and he was gone. He slid fifty feet down a chimney, and became wedged there. When we called, he replied, although he must soon have lost consciousness.

Alec and I had been climbing on his right-hand side. We had to pick our way down and scale a different shoulder of cliff before we were able to lower ourselves to where father lay. By then it was late afternoon.

Shadows began to fill the valleys below us. The sun swung round towards the west and the Pacific Ocean. Once we heard the sound of firing, but the crackle of guns came up to us tinny and diminished. In the mountains, humanity becomes an abstraction. Night approaches fast in those mountains. Alec and I realized that we would only endanger our lives by trying to extract father from where he lay and make a night climb with him. We slept on a narrow ledge, clinging to each other. Once in the uneasy hours of dark, I heard my father singing to himself. 'From Greenland's icy mountains . . .' He sounded drunk.

It was after noon on the following day before we got a rope round father and managed to haul him slowly out of the chimney.

He was badly injured.

'Just a scratch,' he said, before passing out again.

His left leg was broken, together with several bones in both feet. The flesh had been scraped from his stomach, chest and face. His right hand was smashed and that shoulder dislocated. There was massive bruising, and he had lost a lot of blood in the night.

'That was all rather spectacular,' he said, as we sat him up and got him to sip some rum.

We had a six-mile descent, down El Jocoso to the little camp by a stream where mother waited with the mules. Alec and I lowered and carried father by turns. We were well aware of him stifling cries of pain, but there was nothing for it but to proceed. Darkness overtook us again. We camped uncomfortably, one on either side of father, to keep him warm. Although we had little to eat, the water held out, and we bathed father's wounds, which were beginning to look nasty. The flies were a problem.

The three of us reached the camp by the stream on the following afternoon. Mother wept to see father's state, and proposed that we set out for Chiguana, the nearest town where we might expect to find a hospital, immediately.

Unfortunately, as chance would have it, a few villagers had passed the camp on the previous day; finding they were friendly, my mother traded one of our two mules for a gallon of hair dye. We had only one mule left, an unfriendly beast called Estrelita.

On to the back of Estrelita father was loaded, and we started off, leaving much of our kit behind. Alec and I were exhausted. Happily, the way was mainly downhill to Chiguana, not far from the frontier with Argentina.

The night was filled with my father's delirium. He called persistently for his old schoolmaster to beat him. We decided in the morning that Alec should press on ahead and try to find a doctor in town, while I came on with mother and the recalcitrant mule.

What a journey that was! Father appeared to be sinking, day by day. In order to avoid a stretch of forest, in which mother thought she had heard firing, we crossed an expanse of igneous rock, red, potholed and uneven. The potholes, rarely bigger than Estrelita's hoof, were filled with little brackish puddles in which minute things swam – mosquito larvae.

In one of these potholes, Estrelita's front right hoof became trapped. She bucked and reared in fury in her efforts to get free. We had to calm her and untie my father, laying him down tenderly while we tried to extricate the mule.

'I'll light a fire under her,' I suggested.

But we were afraid she might then escape. Mother poured hair dye round the hoof; even that did not act sufficiently as lubricant to set the poor beast free. Eventually, after dosing father with more rum, mother and I sank down exhausted to sleep, leaving the animal to kick and struggle throughout the night.

When I woke, the mule was still stuck. My first thought was for father. I went to him. In his delirium, he had drunk several potholes dry, and was dead.

The heat on the rock flow became intense only an hour or two after sunrise. Mother and I decided that in the interests of hygiene we could not take father's body into Chiguana, but must bury him where he lay.

I set to work with the pick. The rock splintered and flew, alarming the wretched mule, whose leg was now badly inflamed. After two hours work, I had managed only to hack out a shallow hole hardly large enough to bury a tortoise. Father had been burden enough when alive; dead, he was nothing but a nuisance.

While I was still labouring away, my mother screamed in a rich contralto. I looked up. She was staring at a party of five men, heavily armed, who had appeared from behind a rock pile and now stood, several metres away, pointing machine guns at us.

'Are you any good with a pick?' I called.

Evidently they had no English. They wore camouflage uniform and, from the looks of them, had been living long in the jungle. Perhaps that accounted for their nervousness. They would not venture into the open where we stood, but shouted their demands at us.

'What can they want?' mother asked me. When I had no answer, she addressed them directly, stressing each word for their convenience.

'Who are you? Can't you go away? We have a dead person here. He died of the plague.'

Gun barrels waved at us, but the men stood their ground. One of them, a handsome man scarcely more than an adolescent, shouted something in a high voice. It sounded vaguely political, chiefly because it went on for some while.

'I think he said they are the Chiguana Revolutionary Liberation Army,' I told mother. 'We'd better be civil. Offer them your hair dye.'

The man was shouting and gesticulating. Now his meaning was clear. They wanted Estrelita. I understood something of his heavily accented Spanish. He said, 'Bring the moke over here and we will not shoot you.'

Picking up a stick, I whacked Estrelita on her rump. She kicked out but still could not move. The more I whacked, the more she kicked, the more the members of the Revolutionary Liberation Army shouted and raged. They clearly believed I was trying to trick them.

The leader let off a few rounds which went bellowing over our heads.

My mother lost patience. 'Come and get the bloody animal yourself, if you want it,' she yelled.

The revolutionaries charged. Possibly they were accepting my mother's offer; more likely they, like her, lost patience.

Mother turned and ran. I threw myself flat beside the corpse. The mule uttered its insane bray and broke free of its prison at last. Forgetting us, the revolutionaries ran in pursuit, firing sporadic shots as they went. They disappeared over the rocks, often falling.

'We'd better get on to Chiguana,' mother said, coming up to me, panting. 'That donkey was carrying all our papers, by the way . . .'

'What do we do with Dad? We can't leave him here.'

She looked up at the sky, where vultures were gathering.

'Can't we?' she said.

Alec met us in the cobbled streets of Chiguana with an English-speaking doctor. I practically collapsed in his arms.

The doctor was efficient and kind. His surgery was well equipped. In his care I remained delirious. I had contracted dysentery, of a type known locally as 'cordillera killer'.

The doctor's house was on the main square of Chiguana, with three steps up to his door: 'to deter the crippled and the halt,' he told me, genially.

I lay for several days in a small wooden room, convinced for some reason that I was on an ocean-going ship. My father made irregular appearances, singing hymns lustily as he climbed a mizzen-mast like a mountain.

Filth and ugly matter poured from my body. A little

square woman – to be identified when sanity returned as the doctor's wife – came to change my bedding and cleanse me regularly.

I sat up weakly one morning, and the ship's cabin had transmuted itself into a little square room in an isolated town in South America. Where had the illusion of the ship come from? Where had it gone?

The doctor's name was Santos. He was of medium height and middle age, rather a square man, to match his wife, with square capable fingers at the end of square brown hands. His face was open and honest and smiled readily, the generous mouth turning upward into a handlebar moustache.

'You're back on land again, my lad. You've been raving about galleons and sea creatures.'

'I did believe I was at sea, sir.'

'You gave me orders from the poop deck. The only poop was in your bed.'

'I'm sorry for that.'

He smiled. 'I'm used to humanity's mess. It's my stock-in-trade.'

Dr Santos told me that my mother would pay his bill. She and Alec were staying with a 'grand friend' of the doctor's, a Senor Porua, who lived nearby.

I was strong enough next morning to go and look out of the front window. A market was in progress. A stall selling apricots, peaches and melons stood outside the doctor's house. There were earthenware pots for sale, and men rode through the crowd on horseback. The scene was more reminiscent of the nineteenth century than the twenty-first.

When I remarked on this to the doctor's wife, she explained that the town was under virtual siege, cut off from the central government. The airport had been seized by one revolutionary force and the communication centre by an opposing one. Both forces shelled the town periodically. Chiguana had virtually no contact with the outside world.

My small room adjoined the doctor's surgery. I could hear him bullying his patients in a good-natured way.

'Of course you're ill. Look at the way you live. Your house is a pigsty. Cease to neglect your wife and she may not neglect your home. You eat too much. You smoke too much. You drink too much. You go to the whores of the Calle Minotauro. You have guinea pigs in your bed.'

That night I dreamed I was on a ship again, and Alec was captain. But when I awoke I was sane.

I washed myself and walked out the back of the house. The ground was steep, and soon gave way to the cemetery. Among the graves were small tombs like English beach-huts which, in the Catholic way, sheltered the remains of whole families, their likenesses memorialized in framed photos on the carved stones.

Remember my age and make allowance for it. I was just an English schoolboy. I remarked on what to me was exotic to the doctor over a hasty breakfast of coffee, bread and cheese.

'What's odd?' he asked, smoothing his moustache with a linen napkin. 'A surgery, like a chapel, should be near the cemetery. I cure no one. For all my medicaments, the peasants all wind up there, under slabs, sooner or later.'

'Does not that make you melancholy, sir?'

'For all these people's piety and prayers, they finish up out there, in decay. Worms get them all in the end. Do you think that knowledge makes the priests a whit less jolly?'

I saw he liked simply to converse. I was astonished. I had never met such a characteristic before. That was part of my inexperience.

After the surgery closed, he loved to drink wine and talk. To my ears, much of the talk was about death, a subject which made me nervous. I said something to that effect, in a churlish way – manners are something else we have not learnt at that age.

'I've nothing against death,' said the doctor, ignoring my tone and answering in good humour. 'If we didn't all turn into disgusting lumps of decaying meat, men would be even more arrogant than they are. Civilization is the art of concealing the corpse in us. The Church conspires towards the same end. There's too much pomp in funerals. We need a better way of disposing of bodies – something less ostentatious.'

This remark, which struck me as silly and offensive at the time, was to be recalled later. Reminded of my defunct parent, I said, 'Father believed in the Resurrection.'

The doctor laughed. 'My grand friend Porua has visited Italy more than once. He enjoys all this Renaissance art, full of noble statesmen, florid gestures, and people being resurrected. Yet what are people under their fine robes? Just matter – matter in decay.'

I noticed he himself dressed well.

'Sir, my position in the world is precarious enough. I don't wish to know what it is to be mortal, thanks. I intend to live forever.' Despite the boast, I spoke rather miserably.

'What you want is a woman, young feller-me-lad. I'll get you one when you're fully recovered. You have a sound prick on you, as I've observed. I'll find it a billet in a few days.'

At the mention of its name, the member referred to leaped up in hope. I was recovering.

Next evening, I was drinking his wine. Perhaps it made me too outspoken. Night had fallen over Chiguana and, as the doctor's wife had predicted, the Lower Bolivian Liberation Force had driven through the town, firing randomly and inspiring fear in all.

'Well, it's not so bad,' said Santos. 'Only one old woman killed, and she with a frightful goitre and her husband long ago disappeared in the hills. We've known worse. There's a treat on Saturday. I'm going to take you to the Bioskop to see a great old film from ancient days. Charlie Chaplin, in *Modern Times*.'

'That's ages old,' I said, contemptuously. 'Sentimental rubbish.'

He jumped up, spilling his wine. 'What, you dare say that, you impudent young fraud? You dare call *Modern Times* rubbish?'

I was alarmed, but stood my ground. 'I just don't like Chaplin.'

'Then what an unfeeling little brute you are, to be sure. The comedy, the poverty, the pathos, the loneliness, the hope – all beautifully in balance . . . If you don't enjoy that then you have no feeling for your fellow men.'

'He's not half as funny as Buster Keaton.'

'You dare say that in my house! Chaplin grasped the whole complexity of the human heart, its goodness, its beastliness – and you dare call that rubbish! Jesus!'

He grasped my collar. I struck out feebly in self-defence and hit him across the chest, which increased his rage. Next moment, I found myself frog-marched out to his front door. He kicked it open and flung me down the three steps into the street.

It was my sixteenth birthday.

Alec and my mother had taken shelter under the wing of Santos' 'grand friend', Porua de Madariaga.

Porua's house was large, rambling, and decaying. At the time, I took this decay merely as a sign of the times; I was comfortable with decay. I liked my room, reached by an open staircase, at one end of the mansion. It looked out over a garden so long overgrown it was returning to jungle. Porua's vineyards, long the source of the fortune of the de Madariaga family, were in the hands of one or other of the revolutionary parties.

While my mother attempted to sort out our family finances – no easy matter with the capital, La Paz, virtually divorced from all communication – I took on a job of work for Porua.

In his great house, almost bereft of servants and filled with damps, glooms, and moulds, Porua lived like a soldier under siege. He was a tall man, heavy in build, his hollow voice making him sound empty, like an old wooden drum.

Yet his great blue jowls appeared sufficient fortification against this world; while so immense was his dignity that it was some while before I realized he spent his nights in the arms of my recently widowed mother.

She, poor woman, had at last found a grown-up man, and showed her pleasure by fawning on Porua. Callowly, I was disgusted by all this; I avoided my mother and threw myself into the job of telling lies for *La Clava*.

Porua had three cars. They mouldered outside the *casa*, a-thirst for the gasoline which no longer arrived in Chiguana. He rode to work every morning on a fine stallion. I followed on foot to the offices of his newspaper.

With most other lines of communication knocked out by the civil war, Porua's *La Clava* played an important role in informing that isolated community. Not only had the various guerrilla movements cut all land means of communication; the staff of the paper, including the reporters, had left, to join one side or another in the hills. Some would say this made him the ideal publisher of a newspaper.

So I respected him, and was glad to work long hours in his stuffy little offices, learning better Spanish and the workings of a paper: learning also something about Porua, whom I studied with almost servile interest. This was my first real relationship with a grown man beyond the charmed circle of father, uncles, cousins, in which Alex and I had previously moved.

The coldness of his character shocked me. While he would spare a fly buzzing against his window pane, he was never better than harshly civil to anyone he considered his inferior. He was unsparing of anybody who worked for him. Only to his great black horse, which he rode about the town, did he show affection. I failed to see how tolerant he was of me, with my callow questioning of everything: I flinched under the coldness of his eye, yet did not perceive his isolation.

We sometimes worked almost till midnight, with a sub-editor, to get out the next edition of the paper. I could hear gunfire in the hills on occasions when I walked home. In response to some implied criticism I made of his treatment of the sub-editor, Porua regarded me in a sneering silence and then said, 'Why should I have regard for my fellows? Consider the stories we print in our columns. Are they not bulletins on the nastiness of mankind? Murders, theft, rape, calumnies, graft – our daily bread. Not one grown man, aristocrat or peasant, is worthy of respect when you really know him. Women are little better, only weaker in carrying out their ill intentions. Dogs shit in the street, children in their trousers. Only the horse has nobility.'

I was secretly thrilled by such misanthropy, arguing that such views were in conflict with his profession of Christianity, for Porua was a regular churchgoer.

He gave a short laugh, as hollow as his voice.

'You've much to learn. Christ was a fool to die for men. That's my opinion. What improvement did he make in the world? The sight of him hanging on the Cross – are we really supposed to worship that, defeat and death? Christ's preachings have merely made us more aware of the darkness surrounding us. I have a scorn of him.'

He made a curt gesture.

'My visits to the Church are to set an example to the brute population of Chiguana. They need a fear of heavenly retribution to keep them in order. Sometimes I also enjoy the music and the wailing. I am not entirely averse to the compositions of Monteverdi.'

He left the room abruptly, with the air of a man who has revealed too much of himself. I returned to the clutch of reports on my desk.

My father's nature had been sunny. To father, every man had been 'a good chap'. The darkest villain was 'a rather jolly fellow' in father's book. I remembered a banker friend of my parents who was on trial for having raped his twelve-year-old niece; father had tut-tutted and said, 'I suppose he could not hlep himself.' This lack of judgement, of the judgemental impulse, was revealed in Chiguana as weakness.

It was a part of becoming adult that I grew aware of the great invisible universe of personality which controls us as surely as do physical laws. This dawning knowledge made me aware of my isolation. I needed the woman Santos had promised me to share experience with. My state was an unhappy one compared with the other members of my family: my mother had become attached to the grim Porua, and Alec had formed a liaison with Nuria.

Nuria was the daughter of the de Madariaga family. She had an older brother, but he was studying architecture in Italy. Their mother had died when they were little more than infants and, I gathered, it was from that moment that Porua's misanthropy had set in.

Nuria's was a solemn beauty. She was not lively as are many girls of eighteen. She was studious, read much, and liked to talk about the cosmos. Her face was pale, her eyes grey, and therefore quite startling, her mouth prettily shaped, indenting at the corners in a permanent half-smile. Oh, I often studied that face covertly! She wore her dark hair in plaits about her head. She had a penchant for long grey velvet dresses which marked her, in my youthful estimation, as foreign and sophisticated.

'I mean to go to Italy one day, as my brother has done,' she told me, when I discovered her on a stone bench in the garden, reading a book. 'That is why I read Dante now. Do you read Dante?'

'No. Never. At least, I don't think so.'

'I am teaching your brother.'

Alec had never before shown any interest in Dante – or in women. He and I, together with that great boy, my father, had spent our lives in a world of eternal boyhood, being good chaps and climbing or sailing. Now father had gone, and here was Nuria, with a strong physical presence, as challenging in her way as her father.

The poisonous philosophies of both Soares and Porua were banished by the sight of the latter's daughter in her grey dress, red book in hand.

My relations with my mother were also marked by coolness. She resented my dislike of her relationship with Porua. Once, when I told her a lie about what I was doing, in order to evade hostile questioning, she said, severely, 'You're growing too like your father.' I thought about that for an hour before deciding to ignore her, as father always did.

As I rarely watched TV or read newspapers, my knowledge was scanty. There had been a story about secret arms deals with a Middle Eastern country involving the suicide of a French diplomat, but I recalled no names or figures.

'Make them up,' Porua said. 'We have to enlighten our readers. They are so insensitive to matters of veracity that accuracy is no virtue.'

So I made up my stories. There was the fictitious crisis involving tourists dying of food poisoning in Portugal, and another concerning a foreign minister who vanished without trace in Budapest, and there was the Chilean dope smuggler arrested in Miami who was found to have sixteen wives.

These reports had at least a grounding in real events, or my memory of them. But I soon had to rely more and more on my imagination. So the news became more and more sensational. Porua made no complaint. Nor did our readers.

One day we carried a headline **SECRET OF IMMORTALITY DISCOVERED**. It was the story of a German scientist working on seaweed in South Korea who had found how to elude death. A small queue formed in the dusty street outside our office doors to ask for the scientist's address. Then Porua gave his short laugh and said, 'Why should those pigs wish to live a day longer?'

One evening after night had fallen, I returned alone to the Porua mansion. Lightning flickered noiselessly in the western sky. I had been drinking in a bar with the sub-editor, who had become a friend. The town lay dead, exhausted after the day's heat. Some eternal quality in the atmosphere seized me and I stood silent, listening to dogs barking distantly in the hills.

A figure moved on a balcony above my head. It emerged from Nuria's room. The man came down the steps and began to cross the courtyard. I saw it was Alec, walking slowly as if in a daze, his right hand held up to his nose and mouth, his eyes downcast.

He saw me, apparently without surprise, and spoke tonelessly. 'This night I am in heaven.'

There was no pause in his stride. He did not look directly at me. He simply walked on towards his own quarters.

How my heart sank at his words. I understood their meaning and was full of jealousy. Next day, *La Clava* carried the bloodthirsty story of how the king of one of the United Arab Emirates had murdered his brother for love of a gorgeous American woman named Maria Nuria Nussberg.

As far as I can tell, Alec never went with a woman again, or had dealings with women. It was as if that one experience had been so charged with meaning it had forever changed something in his being.

It was a blow to Alec – I too had my regrets – when mother got papers and money through from La Paz. Suddenly we were preparing to return to the real world; mother, advised by Porua, was bargaining for mules in the market. I was reluctant to leave, being in the midst of fabricating a sensational case in which a Soviet spy ring had been discovered in Israel and an old ex-Nazi had admitted that he had helped liaise in secret South African military strikes against the colony on Mars. A pretty grey-eyed woman was being held, pending inquiries.

When bidding farewell to Porua, I tried to extract from him some word of praise for my activities on behalf of his paper.

'You are no better than our readers,' he said, fixing me with a look it took me years to forget. 'You found an opportunity to lie and seized on it avidly. You took pride in your lies. Do you consider that warrants praise?'

We made our way past the strongholds of the revolutionary armies to Antofagasta on the coast. At the sight of the Pacific Ocean, Alec was overwhelmed. Tears burst from his eyes when we were leaving South American soil and stepping aboard the cargo ship that would deliver us in Panama. The tears fell like rainbows on the deck, and he would not speak.

Within a year, Alec, with his share of father's money, had bought himself this small island of Uskair, off Barra in the Outer Hebrides. Perhaps he had already formed a notion of sailing alone round the world.

I lost touch with him. When I had finished with university, I qualified as an ecologist. In no time, I was established in the small world of the university as lecturer.

Someone once said to me, 'Nature creates women, but society has to make its own men.' I still think of Porua de Madariaga as a real man.

Alec became a real man. Somehow my father and I remained in boyhood, not developing, turning into big hairy ageing boys. So we were popular, and courted popularity, because we happened to be the sort of person society preferred, neotenic, forever in the larval stage.

I married a big hairy freckled jolly girl called Ruth. We have three children, all girls. Ruth is Chairperson of the local Consumers' Association.

Once, I met my mother in Kensington High Street. I was going to walk by, but she grasped my sleeve.

'Why do you hate me?' she asked. 'You and Alec?' She does not get on well with Ruth. She was looking much older.

Alec never married. Instead, he sailed alone round the world.

He was twenty-five when he began the voyage. In his thirty-two-foot ketch, *Nuria,* he set out from the small harbour under the shoulder of his Hebridean island. He was gone from sight of man for eight months. He slipped away one dawn. Five islanders, the total population of Uskair, not counting his dogs, waved him on his way. It was father's 'confronting the Unknown' again.

Although we took little heed of his departure, Ruth and I watched Alec being interviewed on TV when he returned.

'I was fortunate in my choice of boat, and my equipment gave me little trouble. All the electronic tackle performed without hitch. You just need to want to sail on forever . . . No, not for the notoriety, for the experience, for one's own sake. I reckoned that I needed to chance everything on a – well, it's a bit like roulette, when you feel an inexplicable urge to stake everything on one number . . . Yes, of course I was scared occasionally. It doesn't matter. Some of those waves at the bottom of the world – I mean you can tell by the look of them they have come from the beginnings of time and will roll right over you and go on rolling forever. Afterwards . . . I suppose I have told myself I must be a lunatic. But after all, other men have done it. Captain Slocum did it at the end of the nineteenth century.'

He looked modest when he said all this. It was the irritating Alec I remembered as a boy, perched dangerously twig-high in a tree.

'The best thing about it? You escape the twenty-first century. The southern ocean is absolutely apart from man – I mean in time as well as space. The seas are high and grand and you're in the rushing air all day, surrounded by stars at night, and the whole universe might be yours. You share it with dolphins and whales and albatrosses and the lonely satellite orbiting overhead. Oh, when you're down there, everything is worth it, everything . . .

'Sure, yes, it's good to come home. One of the most moving things of the whole voyage was when I saw Uskair loom out of the mist. In all the previous months, I had rarely seen land, never wanted to. But there was my island, Uskair. And as I changed tack, the harbour came into view round the headland, with the hill rising behind it, where pines grow in a sheltered spot, and then I could make out the white walls of my house through the binoculars. I was sure my dogs would be waiting for me. That was a great moment.

'No, I shall never do it again. Not twice. That would be tempting providence . . .'

With his manly modesty, my brother became something of a hero. He came to my university, lectured, and met Ruth and the girls. He seemed uncomfortable with us. Later, after mother died, we heard he was looking for a sponsor and planning another solitary voyage.

It was on that second voyage he encountered the Odonata.

Alec's autobiographical book, *Far From Land*, was published before he sailed. In view of what was to come, one passage is particularly striking:

'In the Southern Ocean, in that great reverberating blue-green world I shared with nature, I became intensely aware of the way in which men and women have trapped themselves within cities. Cities recreate in concrete the restrictions humanity has imposed on its spirit. The land had been left behind. The world chokes with people, living and dead. On Mars, the colonists are repeating the errors of Earth. We pollute our globe on an increasingly massive scale because something has died in us.

'Our civilization has become a cage in which we choose to imprison ourselves. In that great clean ceaseless world towards the Antarctic, all this became clear to me. I saw then that we shall die, wish ourselves into extinction, unless we find a new course. I would have been content then to die myself, rather than take my body back eventually to encumber the continent with yet another corpse.'

In *Nuria II*, Alec sailed back to that distinct world of high oceans. He was again his own master. I suppose few of us have imagination enough to project ourselves into his place. I am convinced that a special kind of solitary mind is required to endure such a voyage.

He was on latitude fifty-six, somewhere to the south of Heard Island, when he sighted wreckage on the water ahead. Something like a fin protruded from the water. Alec took it at first for a whale. Nearer, he thought it might be the tailplane of an aircraft, possibly Australian. A figure clung to it.

The wreckage was sinking gradually. The *Nuria II* made slow headway. The figure waved. Alec waved back.

Evidently the wreckage was becoming unstable. The figure suddenly jumped into the water. As it did so, Alec saw that it appeared deformed. He said later that the body was curiously broad, rather like a turtle's. There the resemblance to a turtle ended, for, after one or two splashes, the figure disappeared below the waves.

When Alec reached the spot, the wreckage lay waterlogged below the surface, sinking slowly deeper. He saw lettering on it he could not make out, although he had the presence of mind to record the scene on a video. Of the figure there was no sign. Drifting nearby, however, was a sort of transparent inflatable dinghy, low in the water, resembling a cocoon. Alec pulled it in with a boathook, and got it on deck with some difficulty.

Peering through the transparent cover, he saw what appeared to be bundles of bandages. He believed it was a kind of first-aid package from a life-raft which had failed to inflate. After tying it to the mizzen mast, he did not investigate further.

This indifference on Alec's part has been the subject of comment. My belief is that my brother wanted no intrusion from the outer world. It disturbed his peace of mind. His wish was to be alone in the deserts of ocean, as others crave the solitude of deserts of sand.

He had taught himself to sleep in brief snatches. He thought he heard noises in the night but did not bother to look. At dawn, he found that the transparent covering had split and thirty white insects had emerged on deck, each the size of a rabbit.

His impulse was to kick the creatures into the sea. Their very oddity deterred him from doing so. To discover a new species would be a wonderful thing. He continued with his tour of inspection, in which every knot, cleat, and screw came in for daily scrutiny.

With the sun shining on them, the insects became more active, and climbed the mainmast. My brother observed them, and captured them on video. Their bodies are carried on ten multi-segmented legs. Their heads have a horizontal split which gives the appearance of a visor. Within the split, vari-coloured eyes can be seen. The creatures might pass for terrestrial were it not for the thick twisted cable-like sensors which connect head and tail and run on either side of the body, lending a machine-like appearance.

Clustered at the top of the mast, the insects became immobile. Alec lost interest. The wind was freshening and he took in the mizzen-sail. When he next looked, great winged things were circling his boat. The backs of the insects were splitting, and new forms emerging from the husks – the adult forms we know as Odonata. The larval stages remained clinging to the mast, to blow away in the next gale.

The adults are beautiful and metallic. Shimmering moiré tints in fugitive pink, blue, and green suffuse their wings, while their bodies appear clad in abalone and mother of pearl. Their wingspan exceeds that of an albatross. Although they metamorphose like terrestrial insects, they have a lung-bladder which sucks in air or extracts oxygen from liquid. Along their flanks are arrays of proprioceptors which in part act like external arteries. These Odonata may never have been on Earth before, but they circled the *Nuria II* in an assured way and then set off northwards towards Australia with leisurely beats of their wings.

Glistening wing colours could still be seen after the insects themselves had faded into the blue.

Alec monitored a variety of radio signals, but rarely responded himself. However, he did consider this event important enough to send a report to an Australian station on Lord Howe Island.

Nothing more was seen of the Odonata for a couple of years. In that time, they adapted to the new environment, established themselves, and bred. In saying this, I subscribe to the generally held view that the creatures are of extraterrestrial origin. The notion that they were mutated terrestrial insects does not bear inspection. We may never be certain, but it seems most likely that the Odonata were part of a cargo in a trans-stellar vessel which crashed on Earth by accident. If it had not been for my brother, the Odonata would have drowned, just as the turtle-shaped biped drowned.

After two years, Odonata sightings in Australia began to mount, to be met by incredulity from the rest of the world. Next, sightings were reported in the Philippines and Singapore and Malaysia. The first living specimen was caught in Mosman, a suburb of Sydney, where it was perched under a hedge, devouring the carcass of a dead dog.

At this early stage in the Odonata's existence on Earth, such incidents led people to believe that Odonata killed dogs, other animals, and even humans. Scare stories abounded. In consequence, the creatures were exterminated whenever possible.

Still they spread. In the following year, they were sighted in India, spreading rapidly north. They were sighted in China, where those who attempted to eat them reported them to be tasteless or unpleasant. Within eighteen months, the Odonata appeared in Africa, southern Europe and in South America. At this time, serious attempts were made to eradicate 'the new plague', as a phrase of the period went. The attempts failed, and soon the whole world was confronting the unknown.

Photographs of Odonata were to be seen everywhere.

They were regarded as both beautiful and terrifying. Already, their arrival stirred fresh religious beliefs. In some quarters, they were regarded as being sent by god to destroy man.

A more scientific approach to the problem was forthcoming. As clouds of the invaders reached Texas, a UN fact-finding commission reported that the Odonata (it now became their official name) lived for only seven months in their adult winged phase. In that time, they fed exclusively on carrion; specimens kept in captivity refused to sample any living thing.

Almost concurrently, a report came from Bombay that the Odonata had been observed all over India, feeding on the corpses of Parsis. The burial customs of the Parsi sect involve dead bodies being exposed on a grating at the top of a Tower of Silence. All that is mortal of the body, except the skeleton, is devoured by vultures and the ubiquitous kitehawks of India, after which the bones of the departed fall through the grating into the tower below. Word even came out of Tibet that the Odonata had been assisting at sky-burials, where corpses are left in sacred mountainous places for the attention of scavenger birds.

Before the Odonata invasion, the morbidly repressed cultures of Europe and the United States were unable to face death, or to discuss the subject with the same openness of the inhabitants of India and the East. But the ever-mounting numbers of their dead were, in fact, a subject for concern. Millions of people had a horror both of burial and of cremation. Europe, in particular, was filling with old graveyards. The immense graveyard in Queens, New York, was famed as a particularly depressing city of the dead.

Almost spontaneously, people began to dispose of corpses via the Odonata. Some say the idea originated in Greece or Turkey as a tourist stunt. Others speak of a Spanish grandee who offered up the corpse of his lovely young wife in this way, hoping in his grief that her elements might be dispersed about the air. Yet others say that the poor countries of Africa put out their corpses to be devoured – by creatures regarded with superstitious awe – as the least burdensome method of disposal. Yet others accused bankrupt nations of eastern Europe of adopting 'Odonata funerals' as a way in which the state could economize on electricity and wood.

All these developments certainly happened within a few months of each other. Once fear of the glittering new flying things was lost, they became worshipped. They were clean creatures which did not excrete during their lifetime. They did not ruin crops or attack living things. They would not enter buildings. When they died, their carcasses were not corrupt, and contained useful minerals in small but quantifiable amounts. In the air, they introduced an element of beauty and grace.

It was inevitable that new religions should develop round them. As the Odonata became generally revered, so the tall towers grew up round the world's cities. Cities vied with each other to build more beautiful towers. None was built higher than six hundred metres, for the Odonata were low fliers. To the top of Odonatist towers the dead of all nations were taken, to be exposed to the four winds – and to the Odonata. As the habits of death changed, so did the habits of life.

Since then, a curious peace has descended on the world. No major wars have been waged, and few minor ones. Just as the dead might be said to take readily to flight, so the living found their spirits lifted. An unsuspected shadow had faded and gone.

Alec died suddenly in his sleep one night. His hair was white, as my daughters reported when they went to view the body before it was given to the Odonata.

Now he is known as The Man Who Changed the World, and there are statues to him everywhere. No one remembers he had a younger brother. But Ruth and I have inherited Uskair, and that's worth something.

PHILLIP MANN

An Old Fashioned Story

Not having the tool kit to hand and being of an impatient nature, Jody improvised by using the blunt end of a nail file to prise up the large toenail on Elizabeth's left foot. Revealed was the small copper screw which controlled the energy circuit. Two turns with the nail file and the screw lifted. Immediately Elizabeth's brown tanned body lost its appearance of robust health.

She slumped. Breasts became pouches. Skin became rubbery. The eyes lost their sparkle and turned upwards, becoming like boiled egg-whites. With an audible hiss the abdomen became concave and the firm thigh muscles turned to lard.

Jody looked at his handiwork with some alarm. He had never before gone so far as to deactivate Elizabeth's energy circuit. The transformation from nubile young woman to this flaccid thing of foam and plastic was almost too much for him. For a moment he thought seriously of calling in a specialist, but then he rallied. 'No,' he reasoned, 'the manual says that repairs and modifications can be made by the careful amateur, and that's me.' He looked at the body lying on the kitchen table and noticed that since the stomach had sunk, a fine hairline seam had become evident running from under the jaw right down to the crotch. He also noticed a foetid smell: a difficult smell to define, something of babies and something of machine oil. There was also a slight seepage coming from nose and vagina, and Jody wondered if he should have read more carefully the section in the manual entitled,

'Pre-closedown procedures'. He crossed to the sink and collected a full roll of kitchen tissues which he began to tuck round the body.

And at that moment the doorbell rang. This was followed quickly by the opening of the front door and a voice calling, 'Yoo hoo. It's only me.' Jody recognized the voice of Hildegarde, the girl who lived next door and who had been his friend and playmate since childhood.

'I'm back here,' called Jody. 'In the kitchen. I'm trying to mend Elizabeth.' He heard the crisp tap tap of Hildegarde's shoes and guessed that she had come to show him the new outfit she had bought during her visit to the city.

He was right. Hildegarde arrived and paused in the doorway, one hand up under her hair at the back of her head creating a French effect and the other hand on her hips. The dress was Empire style with high bodice and ankle length hem. It was made of yellow and green silk with blue lace round the neck and arms. On her feet were high-heeled boots with gold trim. 'Est ce que tu aimes my dress?' asked Hildegarde with an affected accent.

'Yes, very nice,' said Jody. 'Now come and help me with this. You can hold the manual while I do the manipulating.'

Hildegarde pulled a face at his obvious lack of interest and dropped her pose and entered the kitchen. 'What's wrong with her?' she asked.

'I don't know,' said Jody patiently. 'That's what I'm trying to find out.'

'Well, did she suddenly just stop moving and start to smoulder or something? My Joseph did that once. We'd forgotten to keep him topped up. He just stood there and started to fume. Then Dad came in and carried him out to the garage and filled his sack and whatnots with oil and that syntho-extract you can get at the chemists, and he was right as rain.'

'Hmm,' said Jody, his forehead wrinkling. 'I wish it were that simple, but I check her every week and there's never been a problem. Besides, she's got a daily vomit and douche cycle installed and if there were a fluid balance problem I'd know about it soon enough. Hell, the bed'd become a river. She's very clean."

'What happened then?'

'It was this morning, about half past ten. I was feeling a bit . . . you know. And no one was home. So then suddenly Elizabeth stops and lifts up her head and then she butted me right here.' Jody pointed to his forehead. There was a bump, covered by his blond fringe. Hildegarde reached out and touched the bump gently with the tips of her fingers. 'That's going to be sore,' she said. 'The skin's all cracked.'

'It is sore,' said Jody. 'Well, I switched her off for a while, for about an hour . . . thought I'd let her cool down. And when I switched her back on she was just like normal. But then later on we were out by the pool talking and she suddenly threw her glass into the pool and then tried to throw me in. I hit the safety switch and closed her down. And then I thought I'd try and mend her myself.'

'What do you think's wrong with her?'

'Just roguing a bit, I think. I've decided to strip her down, give her a tune-up and change her personality card. That ought to do the trick. And if it doesn't – '

'Harry knows a lot about Synthos,' said Hildegarde. 'Why not call him in? Remember he made those Siamese twins one time and that – ' Harry was the boy who lived two doors down the road. He could do everything well and he and Jody had been natural enemies from the day they learned to race their trikes.

'If I want Harry's help,' said Jody, 'I'll ask for it. For the moment I want to do this myself. More interesting that way. All right?' Hildegarde nodded. 'So, you hold the manual where I can see it and I'll open her up.'

Hildegarde took the manual and stood at the end of the table near the supine Elizabeth's head. She held the pages open away from her.

Jody bent to his work. 'Now let's see. It says here, "Release the top seal by gentle pressure on the larynx and then insert finger and slide downwards to open pectoral, stomach and bowel areas." Right. Here goes.' He pressed gently on Elizabeth's larynx and the mouth opened and then the entire throat flap. He slipped his finger inside the flap and slid it downwards and the skin opened easily. It slit laterally too at the diaphragm and flopped back. The inside of the skin was dark like fish skin and oily. Revealed within were a complicated array of plastic wheels and bands as well as micro-circuitry and inflatable pockets. The skeletal structure was of shiny stainless steel with ball joints and leaf-spring joints and feather-sensor couplings.

'Fan-tastic,' said Jody. 'Hell, it makes you wonder what *we're* like inside, doesn't it?'

Hildegarde's attention was on the pelvis. Here there was a modular arrangement of compressors, flexible bands and micro switches and all were mounted on a stainless steel girdle. 'What's that?' she asked, pointing to a small pocket of stretched fabric. Jody consulted the chart in the manual.

'That's the vaginal sack.'

'My Joseph's got one of those too. I saw it when dad was servicing him one day. Hey, what model is this?'

Jody consulted the front pages of the manual. 'Model number and inspection warranty will be found on the skull close to the right ear under the wig flap.'

Hildegarde took hold of Elizabeth's hair, which was now lifeless and lank like seaweed, and peeled it back from the skull. It came away easily like a teapot cosy to reveal neatly stencilled details. 'Model: Ovida Mark 2.4. Fem. Spec. 37. Card 4. Elizabeth the Entertainer. Available in coral, tan and ebony. Swim protected. Throw and jump fortified. Parts compatible with Ovida 1.5 – 2.4. (All sexes.) Note: this model has both vacuum and pneumatic functions. Inspected by Taurus and Virgo Electronics Inc. Brooklyn. Wgtn.'

'My Joseph's an Ovida 2.4 too. Hey let me look.'

Hildegarde came round the table and studied Elizabeth's pelvic arrangements in detail. She pointed to a series of bright bevelled studs mounted on a flexible plastic plate and connected to a small hydraulic piston. 'You see those,' she said. 'That's where the penis attachment fits. Isn't that clever?'

Jody looked at Hildegarde. 'Penis attachment?' he said. 'You mean they just clip on? I mean, I never thought . . .'

Hildegarde looked at him scornfully. 'Well, it's a bit more complicated than that but still pretty simple all the same. I've got two of them actually.' Then suddenly she blushed. 'They're quite different . . . well, the same but different. Similar. What about Elizabeth?'

'Never thought much about it,' said Jody. 'I just accepted the way she is.'

'Really?' said Hildegarde, and Jody could not tell whether she believed him or not.

'Yes, really. I didn't even know the models were unisex. I mean my Elizabeth doesn't look anything like your Joseph.'

'True. They're not even like brother and sister.'

'There must be something on their card that alters the physiognomy as well.'

'Must be. Come on let's find the card cache,' said Hildegarde with enthusiasm. 'This is fun.'

Jody grunted and consulted the manual which he now had to prop up on the side of the table since Hildegarde wanted to be actively involved in the investigation. 'Now let's see. "Personality Card. Destruction of . . . Duplication of . . . Mail-ordering . . . " Here we are. Replacement . . . page 15.' He thumbed through the pages. '"The personality card cache is located above the stomach pouch and to the right of the sternum auxiliary power pack. Note that all directions are from the Syntho's POV. The rib-hinge release screw is beneath the left clavicle. Care must be taken to release the six shock-adjusters and isolate the cache from the power pack before removing it from the twin flanges of Synaptic Bridge 3. See Illus. 88."'

'Sounds simple,' said Hildegarde. 'Remember how we used to play doctors and nurses? Well this is a lot better.'

The sternum and ribs were a single flexible unit. Jody found the rib-hinge release screw and turned it once. Immediately a servo-extension arm about the size of a pencil straightened and pushed, whereupon the entire rib cage and sternum pivoted upwards. The cache could now be clearly seen. It was about the size of a matchbox and made of a black plastic. It was tucked between two iridescent plastic extensions which resembled the spread wings of a butterfly. Together these wings constituted Synaptic Bridge 3. Bedded within them were thousands of micro paths which joined the cache to the furthest extensions of the body. 'Wow,' breathed Hildegarde. 'That's beautiful. You'd better be careful.'

At this point Jody decided that it would be a good idea to get the special Ovida Syntho tool kit from his bedroom. 'Don't you touch anything while I'm gone,' he said to Hildegarde. For her part she put her tongue out at him and said, 'Will you bring me a lemonade when you come back?'

When he returned with his tool box and the lemonade, he found Hildegarde with her arm deep in Elizabeth and her hair tangled in some of the white plastic cogwheels. He set his tool box down beside Elizabeth's head and placed the glass on top of it. Then he released Hildegarde by snipping off some of her hair. Finally he rotated some of the cogs with his thumb and managed to pull most of the hair free. But in turning the cogs a few strands of the hair managed to snake down deeper into the pulleys and drums of the spine. 'I told you not to touch,' he said. 'Now look what's happened.'

'Sorry. But I discovered how they do the breasts,' she replied. 'It's very ingenious. I got excited and that was when my hair tumbled loose. Do you want to see?'

'What?'

'How they do the breasts.'

'Oh. All right.'

Hildegarde reached inside Elizabeth again, feeling down the right side of her body to the place where the hips swelled. 'It's down here. There's a funny pump thing. Watch.' She pumped her hand vigorously for a few moments and Elizabeth's right breast began to swell and the nipple stood up. 'There's another pump on the other side for the other breast. Now I'll release it.' There was a soft bubbling sound and the breast and nipple subsided. 'Look. Can you see? There's a tuck in it so that part of the breast can fold inside. That's what you do if you want a male like my Joseph. You close the seal like this and *voilà*, no breast.'

'What about the nipple? You don't see men with nipples like that.'

'It unclips. When it's deflated like now there's no pressure to hold the nipple on and it just unclips. There. See.' She took the nipple between finger and thumb and squeezed and twisted. The nipple came free. 'Easy.'

'Let me look at that,' said Jody and he reached across and as he did so he bumped the glass of lemonade which tipped and fell emptying part of its contents on to his tool box and part into the open cadaver of Elizabeth. 'Now look what you've made me do,' he said. 'I wish I'd never opened her up.'

Hildegarde placed the nipple in his hand. 'Here, you look at this while I mop up the mess. Where's your squeegee?'

Five minutes later the mess was cleared and Jody could return to working on the card cache. Carefully he removed the shock adjusters and set them neatly in a tea cup brought from the cupboard. Then he started to disconnect the leads of the auxiliary power pack. They were stiff and he had to use more force than he wanted. Two leads came away cleanly but the third would not budge. In attempting to limber it free Jody accidentally closed a circuit in the power pack and for a few seconds power was fed to the spread body. Wheels turned, the legs lifted, the mouth bit, juices were pumped, the fingers beat on the table like castanets and the spine arched. Then a safety breaker cut in and the body slumped once more. But the damage was done. One of the spinal cogs had sprung loose under pressure and flipped right out of the body and rolled across the floor. A thick white rubber pulley-band had jumped its tracks in the pelvic girdle and disappeared down the right leg. Two small switches had smouldered briefly and burnt the soft foam rubber which made the hips swell. A spray of warm lubricant had spurted from the lower abdomen and left a spotty trail across Hildegarde's hand, arm and dress. She screamed and jumped back and then ran out of the kitchen and away. The front door slammed behind her. There may have been other damage done to Elizabeth but Jody could not tell.

But at least the third lead from the auxiliary power pack was disengaged and all Jody now had to do was to separate the card cache from Synaptic Bridge 3. This was accomplished without any trouble.

Jody unscrewed the top from the card cache and looked inside. He saw a square of white plastic lodged between two plates of black plastic. The white plastic showed a tab above the plates and was obviously the personality card. Using his long nosed pliers Jody gripped the plastic card and extracted it slowly. It came free with a click. Written on the card was the simple message 'Ovida Fem. spec. Card 4.' He set this to one side.

Located in the special tool box was a small file box which contained three alternative personality cards. These were supplied gratis with all Ovida Synthos by way of advertising. For the dedicated collector, thousands of other specialized types were available ranging from robust nineteenth-century working girls complete with wooden clogs to houri dancers of old Persia. These were also available in many personality shades from sunny and gentle to downright sado-masochistic. But such were very expensive and the cards were frequently custom-made to suit the particular requirements of the purchaser.

All Jody had at his disposal were four standard occupational types, all of which were basically useful and kind. Elizabeth the Entertainer had been his most complex card.

Jody studied the other cards.

Card 1. Norma the Nurse. Brisk and competent but with a tender manner. This card can be augmented to allow Norma to care for babies or the terminally ill. Note: Norma is not a doctor. For full medical functions consult Proctor the Doctor and Phyllis the Physician. Ovida International take no responsibility . . . etc.

Card 2. Myra the Muse. Myra is an advanced word processor and the ideal help-mate for the aspirant writer. She is introverted in manner but with a strong underlying sensuality. Apart from a compendious knowledge of literature, Myra also possesses optional verse functions and a rhyme memory of over 100,000 words.

Card 3. Carol the Cleaner/Cook. Thoughtful and confidential. The perfect companion for the lonely housewife who dreads the hours of boredom between breakfast and dinner. Carol has news and scandal circuits as well as an ability to cook over 200 meals. Note: Carol can be augmented with an anti-alcohol programme.

This was what was available and Jody didn't feel drawn to any of them. He was already missing the fun which Elizabeth the Entertainer had brought into his life. He read through the cards once again and finally selected Myra the Muse. Holding the card with his tweezers he slipped it into place in the cache.

The return journey of repair went without a hitch. First the auxiliary power leads made their connections smoothly. The shock adjusters fitted into place and the whole unit snuggled securely between the twin wings of the synaptic centre.

As Jody was lowering the rib cage and locking it into place, Hildegard returned. She had changed into a pair of bulky white overalls which had masses of pockets. With her was her male Syntho companion called Joseph. He was a serious-faced young man with red hair and freckles. His character was, as Hildegarde had often told Jody, sensible and studious with strong compassion circuits. He also had broad shoulders, narrow hips and the legs of a tennis player. Plus extras.

'How are you getting on?' asked Hildegarde.

'Oh, OK. Nearly finished.'

'Hear you had some problems,' said Joseph.

'Uh uh,' replied Jody without looking up, concentrating on his work. He had found the spinal cog that had jumped loose and by pushing and easing managed to limber it back into place. He next reached down inside the right leg and tried to find the band that had come loose. No luck.

'Ah well,' he said, 'this model has self-repair circuits.'

'Sure do,' said Joseph amiably and he cracked his knuckles.

'What card did you use for her?' asked Hildegarde. 'I brought some of mine over in case you wanted to *experiment*.' She pronounced this word with all kinds of innuendo and grinned wickedly. 'I brought Bruce the Builder and Randolph the Wrestler just in case. Thought they might be fun.'

'Oh thanks,' said Jody, 'but I've already put Myra's card in.

'Myra the Muse! Bor-ing,' said Hildegarde pulling a face. 'I've seen Dad use her.'

'No. Myra the Muse is a nice lady,' said Joseph.

Both Hildegarde and Jody stared at him. It was rare for a Syntho to offer an unsolicited opinion let alone a dissenting one.

'Well I need to study a bit,' said Jody, weakly, and he returned to his work, folding over the flaps of skin.

The body came together neatly. As the seams met they exuded an oil. This was a kind of protective insulation, for once the skin became charged the flaps would instantly bond. Jody replaced the energy fuse in the big toe of the left foot and screwed it into place and closed the toenail with a click. Immediately, and much to Jody's relief, the body began to firm and the seams disappeared. The breasts slowly shaped. Jody noticed that Myra's breasts were slightly smaller than Elizabeth's. He also noticed that he had neglected to replace the nipple. The jaw trembled. Fluid ran briefly from the nose and then Myra sniffed. The muscles in her arms and thighs came up to tone and flexed. It seemed to Jody that Myra's hips were wider than Elizabeth's and that her legs were slightly shorter and thicker. Not unattractive, he noted.

Fully formed, brown-skinned and vibrant, the body held its position in suspended animation. Jody reached up under the nape of the neck and found a micro switch and double clicked with his finger.

Immediately the body drew in breath. Myra's eyes turned in their orbits and then settled and focused. The mouth opened and closed a few times. There was a choking sound from the throat and then a pleasant contralto voice said, 'Myra sick. Please come quick.'

She sat up. Her head travelled through one hundred and eighty degrees, surveying the kitchen and those who were looking at her. She did not blink. 'My name is Myra. I live in a pen. Cry sorrow. Sorrow. My hair is gone.'

Jody picked up the wig and handed it to her. She took it carefully and set it on her head and adjusted it. A greater assurance came into her figure. She edged forwards on the table until her toes could touch the floor and then, using her hands, she eased herself upright and stood. 'I am Myra. I need clothes. Please dress me.' Her eyes settled on Jody. 'Please dress me, Jody. We have so much work to do. "Ars longa, vita brevis." "The lyf so short, the craft so long to lerne." Chaucer after Seneca after Hippocrates. Please give me your hand, Jody. Myra the Muse is sick.' Myra reached out her hand.

Jody reached out to meet her. But before they could join, before Myra could take one step, her right leg gave way and she crashed down on to her knees. 'Poor Myra's cold.' Then she writhed on to her back and began to scratch at her eyes.

Jody and Hildegarde started forwards but both were too slow. They felt themselves gripped from behind by strong fingers and hauled back. Joseph stepped swiftly between them. He came close to Myra and knelt down. He slipped his arms under her quivering body and lifted her up, and then turned and faced Jody. 'You should have consulted a specialist,' he said. 'You're just a boy.'

Then he turned and, carrying the still shaking Myra in his arms, exited from the kitchen. As he departed they heard the contralto of Myra murmuring, 'Howl. Howl. Howl.'

Jody rubbed his arm where the Syntho Joseph had gripped him. He could feel the bruise rising. Hildegarde scrambled to her feet and ran to the door. 'You come back here, Joseph,' she called. 'You come back here this moment. Do you hear?'

For answer the front door slammed.

Hildegarde turned to Jody in disbelief. 'Well, what do you think of that?' she said indignantly.

Jody shrugged. 'If I were you I'd get some of his circuits trashed,' he said. 'He could become dangerous. He's starting to rogue.' Jody nodded towards the phone. 'You can give the wardens a call now if you like. They'll soon round him up. They'll know what to do.'

'And what about Myra the Muse?'

'No worries,' said Jody, smiling suddenly. 'She was still under guarantee. I'll get a new one.'

WILLIAM KING

Visiting the Dead

The train rattled on through the dark carrying me towards the funeral. My skull ached with the pressure of unaccustomed gravity, my chest felt as if some small hard thing were trying to burst out of it, and the slightest movement caused a surge of nausea. What, from the comfort of high orbit, had seemed a trip of vital emotional importance was fast becoming a nightmare.

I looked at the vital signs monitor on the wrist of the Frame and, to my surprise, none of the readouts were red. The slight whir of the servo-motors caught the attention of the carriage's only other occupant; a slim dark-haired girl who had been studying me discreetly in the reflection of the blacked-out window. She turned to look at me; our glances met. Embarrassed, she felt compelled to speak.

'Well, Aunt Jane, what do you think of Earth after all this time?'

'It's strange, Deborah. I'm not sure I like all of it.' I attempted a gesture meant to emphasize my point but by the time the exo-skeleton shifted my arm, rotated my wrist and amplified my finger movement I had already spoken. The gesture and the heat took a lot out of me. I could feel gravity tug at me like the weight of my ninety-one years. I grimaced more in exasperation than pain.

'Oh, I'm sorry. This must be a hard time for you,' she said apologetically.

I looked at her closely. She had long hair, a snub nose, wide blue eyes and rosy cheeks. She leaned back, pushing herself into the hard leather of the coach, studying the ceiling as she adjusted her tee shirt. I tried unsuccessfully to see some trace of my dead brother in her. I nodded, feeling the wide, cushioned neck brace of the Frame biting where it had not been adjusted properly.

'Come far?' I asked, most banal question of many between travellers. She twisted her head to one side to look at me before she replied. I think she thought I was mocking her.

'Just from Glasgow. Mother asked me to meet you at the airport.' That courtesy must have cost her mother an effort. Sheena had never liked me.

'Been doing field study,' she continued. 'I don't know why they bothered to send me. It was just the same as the simulations.'

'Ah, but how would you have known that unless they had sent you? Surely it wasn't the same?'

She gestured empathically with her left hand. 'Oh yes it was, exactly the same. In every detail.'

I was impressed. Once, simulated experience had possessed a cartoon quality. Of course that was nearly thirty years ago, in the mid-twenties. Simulations were something I had given up when I moved to the Overtowns.

'How about touch and smell?' I asked. She gave me the sort of look you give a slow child.

'Of course,' she said. 'I forgot. Simulations are illegal in the Overtowns, aren't they? A decadent terrestrial vice.'

'We have more important things to do.'

'The starships? I saw a documentary on Gupta and Carmichael on the tube last night. Off to Barnards Star. Showed a lot of pictures of the ship. It looked really dull, just a big dumbbell. They set out ten years before I was born.'

'That would make her twenty-one. It's hard to tell these days; anti-agathics have come so far. Barnard probe left in '26.

'How old are you, if you don't mind me asking? You

have the same look as those two, sort of smooth and old.'

'Was born last century. 1967.'

'You don't look it.'

'Thank you. We have a good anti-ageing programme. Gene re-tooling, anti-agathics and so on. We need it for the starships.'

She didn't look too interested. I searched for another topic of conversation.

'It used to be so cold here in the winter,' I said. 'I can remember when it used to snow sometimes.'

She ran her hand through her hair and let out a long breath. 'No kidding,' she said. 'Before the greenhouse effect?'

'Before that and the sea rising. Before the central European desert. Rainfall was different.'

The by-products of centuries of industrialization had caused the build up of heat. I wondered if those previous generations had considered the consequences. Mine hadn't.

'I've been in the simulations of it,' she said. I was going to say that unless you had been there you couldn't know the difference but I remembered what she had said about the simulations. Maybe they really were that accurate.

We sat and talked all the way to the Portryan stop, exchanging information in the way only strangers on a train can. She told me to call her Debbie. At the stop a Grey Man inspected our tickets. I could not look him in the eye. I am not proud of my part in their creation.

The Castle was built by a returned explorer in the sixteenth century, a sprawling white pile covering many acres. It had a nasty annex built for the homeless in the housing crisis of '97, good air conditioning and, more importantly, facilities for the disabled.

Technically speaking a Frame is capable of taking stairs,

but not many people I know would risk it. Ramps and lifts are safer.

My room was standard. If the blankets had not been tartan and the wallpaper had not had a discreet bluebell pattern it could have been anywhere on Earth from Tokyo to Timbuktu.

I debated whether to call my brother's family but put it off. They knew I was in town, Deborah had gone ahead. I made the call I could not put off, the one to my doctor. I plugged the extension cable from the Frame into the phone. As I talked it would broadcast its information to orbit. I dialled the number.

Nancy Chan appeared. She looked pale and tense, not her usual jovial self. 'How is the suicide attempt coming along?' she asked.

There would be a three second delay throughout the conversation. It's a long way to the Trojan points. Even light can seem slow.

'Don't start that again, Nancy. I told you Brian was the last surviving member of my original family. I'll be damned if I miss his funeral.'

'You could have watched it by remote. Just because he's dead doesn't mean you have to try and join him. You know how bad the political situation is getting down there. Heimdal Station reports massive troop buildups in North Africa, Turkey and what used to be Soviet Georgia. Looks like the big one.'

The timelag suddenly seemed very long. My mouth felt dry. I shook my head.

'We've intercepted coded transmissions from Cairo, Tehran, Riyadh. All say the same thing. Troops been moving in from as far as Ethiopia and Pakistan. Looks like the hardliners have finally seized control in the United Islamic Republic.'

I remembered a tube broadcast I had watched in the arrival lounge at Heathrow, a satellite propaganda show straight from Tehran. A lean Arab had been explaining in Oxbridge tones why biological research had to stop in Federal Europe. He had shown some horror shots of experimentation on clones, said the creation of soulless automata was the work of the devil. Two Canadian tourists had laughed; a Grey Man had stopped sweeping and smiled, pleased by the laughter.

I shrugged. 'Surely it's not that bad.'

'It is. It'll be Jihad, holy war. A delegation has just returned to Tehran from The Hague. Euro-parliament refused to sign the Ethical Science Treaty.'

'I'm not surprised. Most of the European economy is based on Grey Men and other forms of vat labour. They won't give it up without a fight.'

'Well the Council is putting out a warning. Any Overtowner who isn't back up in one week may have to remain on Earth if war comes. Too dangerous to run a shuttle down through the interceptors and anti-missile satellites.'

'Thanks for telling me. I'll be seeing you, Nancy.'

'Yeah. Take care, Councillor.'

Nancy broke the connection. I decided to crawl from my Frame into the bed. It took a lot of effort. For a brief second I longed for the clear, soaring freedom of the Overtowns. It was a useless feeling so I pushed it aside.

I drifted off to sleep, feeling as if my chest was about to cave in.

Next morning I was awakened by the sound of a light rain tapping against the window. I lay in the warm bed, savouring my aches and debating my next move. I called the old family home and was greeted by Sheena. She informed me that the funeral would be at one p.m., then she cut the connection.

After breakfast I decided to go for a walk along the beach. The chance of seeing a place I had once loved seemed to outweigh the discomfort of travelling by Frame. Anyway I felt I was becoming acclimatized.

I clambered into the Frame and lumbered to the shore.

It was not as I remembered it. The old concrete seawall was gone, eaten away by the rising tides; the sea now flowed where the beach once had been. Part of the town was submerged. A bubble harbour nestled between the drowned remains of the two old piers. Warm rain pattered off my face and dripped down the carbon-fibre shell of the Frame. Palms swayed lightly in the breeze. Welcome back to Scotland, I thought. The shower slackened and died.

I studied the new harbour, superimposing my memories of the old. Where small fishing boats had docked, there were now pleasure hovercraft. A new hydrofoil sat where once great ferries had rested. Passengers disembarked while servile Grey Men carried their bags.

I walked along the new shorefront which once had been well above sea level, trying to ignore the tumbled houses and the fusty smell that came from them. Some kids on dwarf pachyderms raced exuberantly past along the remnants of roads where I remembered motorcars.

Nothing of the old days remained except the outline of the land. There were the two arms of the bay, reaching out to frame the distant sky, between them a sea the colour of stormclouds.

The slopes of the hills were bare of conifers, killed by acid rain at the end of last century. Imported palms had replaced them. On the hills were the mirror-bright condominiums where the population dream their lives away in Simulation.

The topography was the same but I knew that if I lived long enough even the shape of the earth would change, eaten by erosion and the hungry centuries.

'Aunt!' I heard a shout. It was Deborah. 'Folk at the hotel said they saw you come this way.'

She reined her pachyderm to a halt. I noticed the hairs bristling from its grey hide and its ugly stunted trunk. 'I wanted to talk to you about something.'

I nodded.

'I've never met anyone who has really been in space,'

she said. 'I may never get another chance if the news broadcasts are right.'

'War?'

'Might be. Border incident, some combatants opened fire on U.I.R. invaders. Turns out they were fifteen years old and unarmed. Tube just showed pictures.'

She seemed shocked and disorientated. I spoke as softly as I could.

'Those combatants wouldn't know any better. They would have been told to open fire on anyone crossing the border. They follow orders.'

'Tube says that the kids were probably boy soldiers from the Revolutionary Guard, sent to provoke an incident. It would say that, wouldn't it?'

'Might be right. There's been a lot of tension between the United Islamic Republic and Europe recently.'

Suddenly she pointed out to sea. I turned swiftly, almost overbalancing the Frame. I don't know what I expected – helicopter gunships maybe.

I saw them out in the deep water. A group of humanoids, leaping from the waves like dolphins, playing and throwing something large backwards and forwards. We watched them in silence until they sank beneath the surface and did not come back up.

'Swimmers,' said Deborah softly. 'When I was little we used to say that it was good luck to see one.'

'When I was little there were no Swimmers, not like those.' I looked back at her pachyderm, an efficient pollutionless mode of transport which fed on the palm leaves. The Swimmers were products of the same thing. Genetic engineering. My chosen career.

'Swimmers have a dome-city just outside the mouth of the loch. It's beautiful, but close up Swimmers don't look like us – more like seals.'

Another intelligent race, one I hadn't seen before except on the tube. I felt as if the world had grown strange and that I had stayed the same. Once I had designed combatants, combat replicants, for the Pentagon. It was hard to reconcile the image of the frolicking Swimmers with the biological war machines that stand guard along the European border, waiting for the Jihad.

The Swimmers farm the Atlantic algae fields that help counter the ecological imbalance caused by the destruction of the rain forests. Like the Grey Men they are servants of humanity, happy but not free, variations on a prototype I helped create.

We stopped at a café, sat drinking coffee inside a converted farmhouse. Grey Men waited on tables, smiled at customers, prepared food.

'Most of the old town is underwater now,' said Deborah. I took a sip of the coffee. It was hot and frothy. It took me back briefly to my teenage days, drinking cappucino and discussing all the burning issues.

'Fish probably swim in that old café,' I said. Deborah looked lost. 'A lot of the landmarks of my youth have gone.'

'We sometimes swim there using artificial gills. It's mostly just walls and the outlines of streets.'

Deborah was looking down into her cup. Some of the young ones I had seen earlier came in and sat down. They talked softly about the U.I.R. and what war might mean. There was tension in the air.

'What's it like up there in the Overtowns?' Deborah asked.

'Different. People are different. More purposeful. Have to be. Space is an unforgiving environment.'

'My mother says that they are all dreamers up there.'

I smiled. 'No, the dreamers are all down here. Most downsiders are settling into a sort of apathy. Work done by AI, robots, constructs. You name it, anything but humans. Most of the population seem to be hooked into the simulations.'

'What's wrong with that?'

'Nothing, just that nothing new is being done by people.'

'The big AI's are making far more discoveries than the Overtown scientists.'

'Your machines are doing the important stuff.'

'We made them. They look after us. Life's good.'

This was true. In the secular states wealth was everywhere. Even in the United Islamic Republic the standard of living was high for most of the population.

'Anyway as soon as the machines find anything out they let us know. We can experience anything we want through the simulations. I can visit truly alien worlds, meet truly alien minds created by an AI. It's a lot more interesting than the boring pictures the probeship sends back.'

'Yes, that's the problem. Those Downsiders who don't live in religious dictatorships are turning inwards, exploring fantasies instead of the real universe.'

'That's your problem if you're not happy with it.'

'Doesn't it worry you that your people may end up machine-dependent? That human evolution may have reached a dead end. Mankind needs challenges to grow. That's why we don't allow simulations or very smart AI's in the Overtowns.'

'Progress hasn't stopped here. We're just taking a different path. One you don't like. You sound like the Fundamentalists. No offence.'

It was an argument not worth continuing. Neither of us really understood the other. Deborah called for our bill. A Grey Man waiter brought it. He had happy, vacant eyes.

The funeral was a lonely affair. The cemetery was high on a hillside. It had escaped the drowning of the town. The church had not been so lucky. I could see its spire rising above the sunken streets.

There were very few at the service. Those who had come were all old. Formal religion wasn't popular among the young here.

The minister was a woman. Without the benefit of

anti-agathics she looked all of her seventy years. She conducted the whole service at the graveside. As her voice droned through the clichés of the eulogy my mind drifted to memories of Brian.

I tried to remember happy things but it was the horror of his last two years that haunted me.

The disease had eaten him away from within. It had taken the blurred lines of his face and pulled the thin bone structure out from below. The peculiar thing was that his face had re-acquired the lean angularity of his youth as death approached.

We had talked a lot over the tubelink as he lay in bed, discussed old times. We had gone over our old feud, decided it was silly. He had thought that I should have stayed behind, become a farmer. I had other plans. It had caused friction at the time.

Brian had felt that humankind should sort out its problems here on Earth before leaping into space. I couldn't wait that long. Of course Earth had sorted out its problems without help from either of us.

Cheap fusion, smart computers, genetic screening and the withering of the nation state had seen to that. The transition had not been painless. Food riots, holy wars and partial economic collapse had been landmarks along the way. There were new problems now but the old world was dead, drowned beneath the twin tides of resurgent fundamentalism and advancing technology. The conflict between the two had redrawn the map more than the rising of the sea.

We advanced. I took a cord with five others and we lowered the coffin into the grave. The smell of mud and freshly turned Earth was quite distinct. I dropped the cord. It fell away from my hand like the Earth below a rocketliner.

The minister said her final words. We dispersed from the grave towards the waiting cars. A lot of people with familiar-looking faces and cold expressions stared at me. We all shook hands.

'You'll be coming back to the house,' said Sheena.

'Do you think I should?'

'Oh, yes,' she replied. 'He'll want to see you.'

A small electric coach took us back to the farm. For a while the only sound was the keening whine of the motor as it laboured on the steep hill road. The countryside opened up to the wide open moor of the Ganlach. Great white windmills dominated the landscape. Giant propellers that looked as if they could have lifted a passenger airliner aloft quivered in the breeze.

At the close of the twentieth century this area had been a windfarm, selling power back to the national grid. Cheap fusion had done away with that idea. The towers still stood because no one had bothered to take them down. Polymer plastic has no value as scrap.

At the foot of one tower pink sheep, colour-coded for the insulin their milk carried, were watched by a Grey Man shepherd. I looked away.

'You don't like that do you?' said Sheena.

'No, I don't.' I could not keep the edge out of my voice. The vibration of the car was passing through the Frame and making my teeth rattle.

'They love it. It's what they were made for, menial work.'

'I know. That doesn't make it right.' The sad thing was that the Grey Men really did love it. We had engineered them well. They were perfect slaves.

'There's no need for you to look down your nose at us. It was you and people like you that created those constructs,' said Sheena.

'I know.' Too late to uncreate them now. The future had rushed at us headlong. We go forward or we go under had been our slogan. Had we been so wrong? Times change. The slaves were happy and would not be so if freed.

My sensibilities were products of the last century and the citizens of the new age did not conform to them. Whose fault was that?

The coach pulled into the farmyard and the natural stench of the place filled my nostrils. Suddenly I wanted to run but it was too late. I was on my way to a meeting with my dead brother.

The birds sang as I walked down to the stream. I knew I would find him there, lying on a rock, watching the fish. The grass crumpled under my feet and the copse of oaks was ahead, casting dappled shadows in the summer sun. I wore my nine-year-old body; my real one was in the Frame back at the farmhouse, wearing an induction helmet.

Deborah had been right. The simulation was perfect; the illusion pumped directly into the brain could not be distinguished from the real world.

He was just as I remembered him at thirteen, lanky and awkward with a thatch of blond hair and a smiling, rosy-cheeked face. No pain lines now.

'Hello,' he said and smiled. I didn't smile back. I kept my distance. The experience was too disturbing. There was an aspect of nightmare about it.

'You're dead,' I said. 'I thought you said you would never let them record you. What happened, did you get scared at the end?'

He nodded. 'Anything seemed better than death. It's for the kids too. They can visit me when they like.'

He picked up a stone and lobbed it into the water. I watched the ripples. A dragonfly hovered above them.

'Of course I won't look the same to them. I chose this setting for you. Do you like it?'

I shrugged. 'It's exactly as I remember it. So are you.'

He smiled slowly. 'Aye, it would be the same. The machine provides the big details out of my memories, the rest are filled in by your mind.'

'That means it's not accurate. It's blurred. My memories have probably altered details of the original.'

'What does it matter? How can you tell?'

I felt trapped. The echo of the question I had asked Deborah on the train rang in my ears.

'You're not Brian. You're just a computer program that thinks it's him, a sub-program in whatever is holding this illusion together.'

'No. You're wrong. I'm Brian. I remember every little detail of my life. I was recorded. They mapped my brain a bit at a time and transferred the results to a computer. I'm the same. I have the same emotions, the same reactions. I just live here now.'

'No you don't. You're just a simulation. You're perfect in every detail but you're no more him than a photograph would be.' I felt a coldness in the pit of my stomach, a growing sense of unreality and estrangement.

'I'm me,' he said. 'You have to believe that. All the emotions, the memories make me what I am. If I chose they could download me into a clone body and I would be back in your world. I would be the same person. The cell structure would be identical, my memories and personality would be the same. If that's not real what is?'

'What about your soul? Did they record that too?'

'Maybe. Anyway, I thought you were an agnostic?'

'I don't know. I'm confused.'

He seemed to become desperate. 'Souls? They were just the old way of explaining our personalities, our individuality. A superstition. All we ever were was software driving flesh. You know as well as I do that it can all be explained in terms of electrochemical reaction. Hell, you've built people. Biology and artificial intelligence research outdated the old religion.'

'Software souls driving meat machines? Maybe science is the new religion.'

'Look, we were brought up between two ages, the old explanations and the new. The last generation with a choice. The kids don't have the same problems with these concepts as us. They don't have the same fear of death either.'

'That's because they visit simulations where it seems the dead still live. The afterlife has invaded the real world.'

'Look, maybe they're right. Perhaps this is the only form

of immortality we will ever have. Don't you at least want to consider that?'

'No,' I almost screamed. 'I want to get out of here. How do I do it?'

'I'll get you out. You are wrong. I am me and I do care about you.'

I saw only genuine concern on his face. I nodded, embarrassed. I hugged him and he felt real. Then I was back in my body, tied into the Frame.

'I have to get back,' I said.

Deborah accompanied me to the station. All the way it looked as if she were trying to summon up the courage to say something. She carried my bag to the platform and we stood there. The silence grew. I looked at her expectantly. She stared at her feet, confused.

'You think he's gone forever, don't you? That's why you're sad.' I could see it came as a revelation to her.

I stared at her, trying to find the words. What could I say? My brother was gone, dead as the hope of heaven. To her it did not matter. She could visit him, visit the dead. Perhaps one day the dead would visit her. A sort of resurrection is possible.

The fundamentalists think it is a mockery of the work of God. I'm not sure I disagree with them. They say that the new science glorifies Satan. If Satan is the absence of God as darkness is the absence of light then they are correct.

The fear of nothingness is a terrible thing. Almost anything is preferable. It is this fear that fuels the Jihad, the fear that we are mortal and the universe doesn't care. God is supposed to care. They hate the Grey Men because the constructs remind them we are simply machines constructed from protoplasm. Do machines have souls?

I looked at Deborah and tried to find words. They did not come, so I stayed silent.

'You're not coming back, are you? Not ever.'

I nodded. 'If you ever want to come to the Overtowns, get in touch.'

She shook her head. Abruptly she stuck out a hand. I took it gently, afraid that the Frame might crush it. We shook hands. 'Saw it in a simulation,' she said sadly. 'Is that right?'

'Yes, perfect,' I said. She smiled. I boarded the train. She waved as it pulled out of the station. I tried to wave back but the clumsiness of the Frame and the smooth acceleration of the mag-lev kept me from doing so until she was out of sight.

Now war has come. The work of Satan is no longer to be tolerated by the believers. The godless and all their works are to be overthrown. This is the word from Tehran.

The armies of the righteous have swept through Spain and Greece but soon they will encounter the main strength of their enemy. Then they will die, finally and forever.

The believers see only the soft decadent face of their foe. They do not know what a terrible power they have roused, one that has sunk the lands and may raise the dead. The vats will spew forth a million combatants and nothing human can stand against them.

This struggle will determine the face of the new millennium. The believers think they shall win because they fight against Satan and for God. I believe the outcome will be different.

IAN R. MACLEOD

Well-Loved

Every city has a place like this. It lies at the back of everywhere else, where long streets lead nowhere both ways. It's mostly night here: there are rags of it left in the alleys even at midday. But it's where you have to earn and chance your living

Voices are circling the darkness, the lips and the hips, the words that bring the brakelights, the face to the windscreen, the open car door. You taste hunger and fear. You don't feel ready but you know you need to sell. No point waiting for that big limo, the clean and friendly face. They never take the trade here, and when they do they aren't real. They touch your skin as if it's shrinkwrap. You see the steel edge of pain slide behind their smile

Stepping to the kerb is like diving into a vat of something cool. You know the way you walk says *now* and *me*. The big leather handbag you lifted two days before bumps your side. For no reason, it feels like protection. You hear engine breath and see all the others, names you can place with needs like your own. But now they are nothing but meat, competition. There are streetlights but no stars, and looking up is like falling, like giving way. You wonder if you've taken too much, or if it's not enough. Next time, you tell yourself, everything will be fine, everything will be immaculate. And you focus on that and imagine that now is that time

A car slows. Your car. You don't doubt for an instant that this is the one. Smile at the window. Already, you're drawing yourself in, clicking on the robot, pulling away from thought. There's short talk of money, but you slide in beside him anyway and you're alone. He's got a hotel room. He wants the whole night. He says things about you, the way you look and smell, taking his hand off the wheel to touch as he drives

The city slides by like coloured rain. You can't stop staring at the child's toy at the bottom of the dash. A thing without much face apart from eyes and floppy little arms with half the fur chewed away. Could be a teddy, a rabbit, a fox. Well-loved, the phrase is. You can't stop staring

The hotel room, pink and baby blue. Trying not to look, you admire as though he made it himself. There's a Swap appliance in the corner. There always is. The rental company logo on the side. The power line goes to the same marbled socket as the teasmade. Maybe it's a choice, tea or Swap. But he fixed you a real drink from the paybar instead and it's vodka

The glass has a crack in it. Trying not to look, clicking on the robot. There's a plastic snowscene toy on the bedside cabinet. He picks it up and turns it in his hands as he sits easy on the bed. You wonder, although it breaks every rule, about his wife, his kids. He hitches up the knees of his suit trousers so as not to spoil the crease. His legs are quite brown in the gap above his sock. You comment admiringly on his tan with the right kind of smile clicked into place. You finish your drink and he gets you another, and you start to think that maybe this one is kind, this one understands. The whole luggage of hope spills out and you're dragging it around the room with your figure and your smile. And when you sense he's anxious to start you ask What's It To Be and you feel his doubt. There's even a moment when you hope he's not going to want to Swap

But

Let's Swap, he says. It comes out like it's a great, new idea. And that's how you take it: freshly minted for this baby pink and blue room, for this special occasion

He runs his Amex card through the slot on the Swap

appliance and you notice how his eyes and his hands are solid sure. There's an awkward wait until the credit beeps through, then you stand with your hands over the two Swap boxes like the contestants in Name That Tune. And you wonder if it's worth repeating that same old joke as he starts on it anyway. You both start to laugh, and you begin to get the buzz of the Swap

Then the slam of it

And you're in his body

The flood of being inside someone else

You're inside, looking out at your own face and you can feel how the dampness of his excited skin sticks against suit and shirt. His mouth tastes faintly of rancid walnuts and his big hands move lighter and easier than you'd imagined. You stare back at yourself. It's so much clearer than a mirror; you can see the faint smudge of mascara where you must have rubbed your eye. You decide your eyebrows are too thick and the pores too deep and wide. He smiles at you with your lips, out of your eyes. His hands are already exploring the newness of your body, running down and up. Then he pulls you close. And there's no hurry. But you start to do it anyway

When you come with his body into your own it's like the cold dive of stepping to the kerb. And you feel pity for men, just as you feel pity for women. You fall back on the sheets into the smell of his sweat and you gaze at your face across the pillow as the eyes drift shut and he sleeps inside your body for a while. It's hard to imagine the dreams that come to him in your brain, but your face looks sweetly blissful now, asleep, the way you never see it. You look even younger than you are. You think of your sister who died, your mother and the smell of cooking in the Sunday garden. You lean over so gently and kiss your lips with lips of stubble and the eyes blink open and he stares back at you. He stretches and growls and tries to look sexy in his borrowed woman's body as though what you see and feel matters

But

He gives up and lies restlessly still. The hotel is silent and each car on the dual carriageway outside is a separate noise, a separate identity. The eyes stare wide at the ceiling. You wonder what he wants but you're afraid to ask in the phlegmy growl of your borrowed voice

You're afraid to ask

But he says it anyway

He says it with your lips your voice your throat

He says Hit me

Now that it's out and the need is suddenly huge you realize that the sex before was just a veil to pull over it. You bunch his hands that felt so light before and feel them swing like lead. You can feel it. The power. He wants the taste of metal and salt. You straddle your breasts, jutting your suntanned knees against thin arms

You swing your fists down and you see your face go slack with the pleasure of it. There's an erection bobbing stupidly between your legs and you both come but coming isn't important. You hate yourself so much that it's hard to stop, even when he starts to kick and wriggle beneath you. You hate. You hate everything. You take it out on yourself. He fights you with thin, weak arms. The resistance is only moth wings and you can taste the power and the horror, the salt and the metal until something finally brims over and

You lie back, breathing. There's blood on your knuckles, blood on the bed board. He turns and curses you softly through split lips, saying You Don't Know When To Stop, You Stupid Bitch. And you stare at the lips and the puffing eye and wonder if this time there might be scars. And then, somehow, you both sleep

It's hard to remember the Swap back in the morning. There's just the hot pain of the shower and seeing the Amex card on the cabinet beside the snowscene toy and lifting the card by instinct as you shoulder your handbag. And suddenly you're back in his car and he's offering to drive you anywhere, just anywhere. The well-loved cuddly toy is still staring at you from the bottom of the dash. It's a shock when you look down at your own hands and when you try to say where you want to go your mouth feels as though it's filled with sharp stones

The car carries you off. The city is flat in the early light, like a black and white photo on a tin tray

His hands are easy on the wheel. He's a regular guy, talking about his family as he drives. He's even using what sound like their real names just to show that he's not afraid. His wife used to do Personnel and his eldest is called Tina. Tina's ten and dyslexic – the shit they had to take down at the school to convince them she wasn't just stupid. Haley's the other and she's only four. Tina's a fine kid, but Haley's the real looker, almost like that little kid in the *Poltergeist* movies who died. You know, cute. She'll get the boys crazy when she grows tits and an ass, might as well face it. A Dad has to admit his kids are gonna have a sex life

He nods down at the dash. That thing there you're looking at, he says, that cuddly toy, is Bib-Bob. Haley's pride and joy, and even now she's reached four Bib-Bob has to come everywhere. Jesus, she loves that toy, chews it till it's filthy and then screams murder when it goes in the wash

And you're dead right, he grins, this regular guy, Daddy's deep in the dog house for driving off this weekend for a conference with Bib-Bob still in the car

You pick the famous Bib-Bob up. And you smile a crooked smile with your crooked face. And Bib-Bob feels soft and light as something alive. But the man stops smiling as he drives and tells you to Put That Fucking Thing Down. And that's just what you pretend to do as you bend close to dash and slide Bib-Bob into your handbag, down there with the Amex card

He wants to drop you off close to where you need to be. Nothing's too much trouble. But you investigate your face again in the sun visor mirror and touch the puffiness and the scabs. Somehow that makes him angry. He stops the car anywhere and throws you out and drives off. But it doesn't matter. When you dust yourself down, hitch your bag and check where you are, you realize you're nearly there anyway

Ronno's dealing early. He handles the franchise for people like you, people who need some kind of ladder to climb out of the night. And you've got more than enough cash for the score. Ronno hands it over and doesn't ask about your face. He knows; he's seen it all before. Walking back to your big room in the old house that you used to share with Stephanie before Stephanie got busted, feeling the bruises tug at your arms, the score doesn't matter any more. It's often this way. Now that you've got it, tucked beside Bib-Bob in your bag and wrapped in tissue, it loses the pull

You pass a scrap of wasteland filled with sunlight and tall purple flowers and fairies of dandelion seeds drifting. You pause for a moment and there's a click of balance where everything but the light and the flowers is nowhere. It makes you wonder how it all happened. Did you start trading your body because you needed the score . . . or did you need the score because you were trading? But when you get back to the rotting house and up the stairs and across the loose beam and wodge some fresh newspaper into the broken panes you lie down on the stained mattress

And your fingers hurry with the paper

And it feels as good as ever. As good as you could ever imagine

As the loose haze fills out you take Bib-Bob from your bag and hold him to your aching face. Well-loved. He smells of fresh rain and childhood spit. He soothes your pain with soft and tiny arms, giving out some of the love that's been poured into him. And then you dream and Bib-Bob's big as the world and everything is nestled safe within him

It's already late afternoon when you awake. Bib-Bob soaks up the tears on the grubby cushion beside you, smiling with his little stitch mouth, sharing the secret of dreams you can't understand or even remember

There are voices downstairs. You check your face in the broken mirror and wash it in the stale water in the basin. You're starting to look like the Elephant Man. Not caring what they think, you stumble down to join the others. But no one says a word. They've all been there, on the wrong side of a Swap. You get inside a body that's filled with the wrong juice and you don't stand a chance. There are some smokes around and the atmosphere's good. Tony's on a special high, he's sold one of those odd pictures he does to a guy he met as a pickup. The guy's loaded and says he has talent. He wants him to move in, help with an exhibition. And Judi's Dad's written from Germany. The letter got here somehow, just like magic. And here it is. She holds the crumpled pages to her face and you think of the famous Bib-Bob upstairs in your room, just waiting to be loved

But the dark falls quickly. Before you know, the smokes have all gone and everyone's quiet and thinking about what's to come. There's only one way through the night, and that leads to the back of somewhere else, a street that goes nowhere both ways

You put on the robot clothes, and frown at your face and do what you can with what makeup you've got, which isn't a great deal. Everyone leaves alone and takes their own way to the place, through their own dreads and possibilities. There's no one to talk to now that everyone is just meat, the competition

The black air hurts like a toothache. You've got Bib-Bob in your bag and somehow just thinking about him makes you want to cry

But you keep your face as smooth and even as the puffiness allows and hang back in the shadows, letting the night kick into gear

The meat walks the kerb, cooing to the brakelights, the opening doors. You know there's no big limo, no clean and friendly face. The pickups are as much meat as you are, their skin is shrinkwrap, the blade slides behind their smile. So you step into the light and try to move your body like it's something fresh and real and the famous Bib-Bob's at your side in the bag you lifted three days before and Bib-Bob feels like some kind of protection. Already, you're longing for the score and you know the night won't end until you get it

The kerb is a cool dive. The streetlights spark and shine. Your face in the car windows as the brakelights whisper. You try to smile and pout but your skin feels dead. Your tongue searches your cheek and it's like puffy mushrooms. You see what they see reflected in the glass and the tyres scream the wet road as they pull away. You're the Elephant Man. In the makeup of a clown

Then one does slow and the face inside sees your face and smiles. He *knows* he *understands*. The brakelights grin, the car door opens. And you realize that he likes what he sees and he wants to do more, that he wants the taste of salt and metal. So you stumble back into the darkness and run down the street that leads both ways nowhere

There's a taxi. For Hire. The driver slows and says Jesus I Nearly Ran You Down but he can't see you in the dark and he takes you as if you're a normal fare. But when you climb out at the hotel the light catches your face and he screws his up in disgust like a paper bag. You throw the money at him and wonder where he gets all that righteous anger from, pimping lifts here in the city

There's music in the foyer like peach ice cream. Men buried in deep chairs, deep in drink and newspapers. You've pulled a scarf from under Bib-Bob in your bag and you've got it around your face like a Russian peasant

You take a risk and go straight to the desk. The clerk's got his nose buried in a computer screen and you move so quietly on your heels that he doesn't hear you. The carpet is soft as Bib-Bob. You scan the pigeonholes behind and find the room number from last night. He must be out; the key is on its hook. You know where he'll be, cruising for someone like you who isn't

You clear your throat and the clerk looks up without looking. And you ask for the key and he simply gives it you. You take the lift where the music pours loud and creamy. No one else gets in. You're glad it's just you and Bib-Bob, just you and him alone

Nothing about this is easy. If it wasn't for Bib-Bob at your side you'd turn and run. Walking the corridor is another cold dive and the key barely fits, like it's only just been made

The room. Looks bigger. The maid has wiped the blood off the headboard. The bed looks as if it's never been slept in, let alone

The Swap appliance. The lead to the marbled socket that also feeds the teasmade. It's tea or Swap and there's no competition. You take Bib-Bob out and the Amex card as well. Bib-Bob smells like Christmas and childhood. The Amex smells like the polished floor of a bank just after opening. You hug Bib-Bob tight. You gaze at him. He smiles back with his well-loved eyes, with his half-unstitched mouth. Bib-Bob soaks up all the world's tears and hurt. He's nothing but love

The Swap appliance. A little LCD you hadn't noticed before says Ready To Enter. You run the Amex through the slot and a credit bleep comes quickly. You kiss Bib-Bob's little face and you sit him on the Swap box facing you. He falls off it. You kiss him and sit him down again. And then you stand with your hand over the other box, like it's Name That Tune but you're the only contestant, unless you count Bib-Bob

And you wait for the buzz

And you smile at Bib-Bob

And you wait for the slam

And he comes back to his room a couple of hours later with someone else like you that he didn't even have to buy. But there's a body on the floor and the whole scene's blown. The thing is breathing and the eyes are wide but there's nothing inside. The pickup has hysterics. He slaps her around a bit to make her stop then he sends her away with enough money

He rings the Company. He's a Company man. They have shares in this hotel. And it's a good Company

And he's a good employee

And it could happen to anyone

So they take the body to a hospital, and the Company has shares in that too. They hook up the life supports for a while before they turn them off again. The thing is just lifeless junk. The sort that gets cleaned out of the gutter every day

And

Long before that, the conference has ended and he's back at home, parking in the twilight drive amid the Scots pines and the brown rooftops where swallows wheel. The lights are in the windows and children are in his arms. He's every hero. He's the voyager returning home from the quest. He's Ulysses. He's Frodo Baggins. He's Parsifal. And the kitchen smells of burnt toast and cinnamon. He kisses his wife as though she's freshly baked from the oven and What Do We Have Here In These Cases. Goodies for you and you and you. Tina and Haley clap and yell at jigsaws and snowscene balls and his wife preens You Shouldn't Have with a microdot bottle of exorbitant perfume. And lookee what we have here at the bottom of the case. The famous Bib-Bob himself

Haley's in tears with her arms out gimme-gimme tight to have the famous Bib-Bob even though she's getting a little old and had forgotten all about him whilst Daddy was away. There's snot on her upper lip and she wipes it away with Bib-Bob's ear. Then she swings him by the leg and does a Bib-Bob's-come-home war dance all around downstairs. She slams Bib-Bob on the dining room table and rattles him along the banister rails

Then Haley sits down in the warm laughter of the kitchen. She sniffs Bib-Bob, pressing him to her face and wondering why he smells of nothing more than old sheets. Wondering why he feels so loose and ugly. Bib-Bob used to be famous, great and wise. Bib-Bob used to stand astride the world. Bib-Bob's been away and Bib-Bob's come home. But nothing ever stays quite the same. Wrinkling her pretty nose, turning her eyes wide and bright to the swirling snowscene, she lets Bib-Bob fall to the floor

CHERRY WILDER

Looking Forward to the Harvest

All the way to the meeting my grandparents argued about what the Time Sense people might be called. I sat with my father on the front of the cart. He clucked to Ruby, our mare, and smiled at some of the talk but I could see that a lot of things that were said made him uneasy.

'Something with Temp,' said Nell. 'Not Temponaut.'

'Chroniast,' suggested Ralph. 'Chronist. Perichron.'

'Horrible! Mixture of Latin and Greek roots,' said Nell. 'What do we know about these people?'

'They must be classed as part of the Psi Wave,' said Ralph, 'people who claim to have developed strange powers after the crash.'

'They've never registered at a center,' said Nell, 'which means they've never been screened by those anal-erotic latterday bureaucrats who make *our* lives such a misery!'

'The autumn of our days,' said Ralph, 'as we totter down life's highway . . .'

'Damn right!' said Nell. 'We're long past the sere and yellow leaf, honey. We are deep in the winter of our discontent and spring will not be far behind this time.'

I hated it when they talked this way about being old and dying. My father said, privately, that they were a pair of tough old roosters and he had never known Nell to shed a tear, except once. Not in the hospital, not at the funeral, but days later he found her in our store room, weeping over her daughter's doctoral thesis and playing with a box of old broken toys. Anne Marie, my Mom, had died of a heart attack; she had been dead now for three years and five months.

'They claim to have an extra sense,' said Ralph patiently. 'A time sense. They imply that it is a mutation. What we need is a word for "time sense".'

My father cleared his throat.

'German,' he suggested. '*Zeitgefühl*.'

'Hey, not bad,' said Nell. 'Good thinking, Don. Zeit-Gefühl or Time Feeling, referred to as Zee Gee and the people themselves as Zee Gees.'

'Zee Jesus,' sighed Ralph. 'They sound like a defunct pop group. And remember that German speakers would call them Tzed Gays.'

The two old folks found this pretty funny for some reason.

I asked: 'Nell, what's a pop group?'

'Well, what do you think it might be, Linnit?'

She was always after me to think laterally and to play around with words the way they did.

'Pop might have to do with fathers. A slang name for a father-oriented commune like the Patriarchs of the New Jerusalem.'

'Not bad but you aren't even close. What might pop be short for?'

So it went on until I half-guessed, by way of Pop Art, which was pretty *un*popular on the center, what the expression meant; a pop group was a rock band, more or less. A group of pre-crash, commercial, youth-oriented music makers. We had a number of music makers at Hopewell Center. Guitars and guitar players were so plentiful they hardly counted but we also had fiddlers, piano players for the pianos, which were our cultural heritage, along with clarinets, flutes, tubas, zithers, saxophones . . . it was wonderful the condition these things were in. Better condition, sometimes, than the people who could still play them and who instructed other music makers. The music they made was mixed, partly classical, a lot of folk, and a lot that was based on that no-good commercial, youth-oriented rock. A friend of mine, Cholly, had made himself a bongo drum from a sauerkraut bucket and a piece of old inner tube; I played the recorder. There was no way to describe the music we made.

I loved to hear about rock bands/pop groups and everything to do with pre-crash youth. I urged Nell and Ralph to go on about pop groups they remembered, their dress, hairstyles, lifestyles, although it was enough to raise the hackles on my Dad's neck. This was consumerist nostalgia of the worst kind. He protested at last . . . you'll turn the kid's head . . . and Nell said she wished she had a beefsteak for every time he'd said that. I knew what a beefsteak was, of course, and had even seen my grandparents eating meat. It was one of the disgusting things they did which had to be borne with forbearance for the sake of their wisdom. They were a couple of old pre-crash Carnies . . . like the tuba-players and the cellists . . . who had come through into the New Age. They must be permitted to give us the benefit of their experience without contaminating us too much.

Mid-morning we crossed from the third westbound overland route on to an old piece of freeway; I had never been so far west from Hopewell Center before. One of our sign boards gave information about the old freeway and the two towns that it had connected.

'Wait!' said my grandmother. 'There used to be something along this way. Don, you don't mean to tell me these Time Sense people are living in a Bergstrom House?'

'Strange-shaped place on the side of a hill,' said my father. 'Has a collector wall.'

'Surely that must be Lewis's own house,' said Ralph. 'His demonstration model. Didn't you visit . . .'

'Yes!'

My grandmother was upset.

'Don,' she said, 'I visited that house twenty-five years ago at the invitation of the architect Lewis Bergstrom. I signed a visitors' book.'

My father shook his head.

'There's no one left from that time,' he said. 'These are entirely new people. They specialise in crop-reading. They stand in a field and recommend crops for the following season.'

'Is that why we're going to see them?' asked Ralph.

'They request family groups . . . people of three generations,' said my father.

I could tell he was stalling. Finally as we turned off the old freeway into a grassy lane he said:

'The Planting Committee asked me to check them out, if you must know. And they asked me to take Nell and Ralph along because they are two cunning old coyotes who can spot a fraud at ninety feet. Are you satisfied?'

'No,' said Nell, 'but I do believe you, Don. Let us pause and consider. They claim to have a time sense which enables them to go to or observe the past and the future . . .'

'If this . . . er . . . faculty is a mutation,' said Ralph, 'chances are that it came from the crash and therefore the mutants must be under twenty.'

'Just so,' said my father. 'Two young boys, seventeen or eighteen, a little older than Linnit.'

'Family name?' asked Ralph.

'Morgan.'

'Did we ever know anyone called Morgan back there?' asked Nell.

'Rings a bell,' said Ralph. 'I'll think about it.'

We came in sight of the house. It was built of wood and grey stone and it grew out of the hill in tall angular clumps like crystals. I understood, vaguely, the kind of house it was, although I had never seen anything like it except in art books. It scared me the way all pre-crash buildings did in varying degrees. I imagined myself creeping about in a big white wooden house built for an American movie family, going up the carpeted stairs. I imagined myself in the ruins of the tall cities, looking up, up, and screaming . . .

'Beautiful!' sighed Ralph. 'Bergstrom's Folly.'

'Yep,' said my grandmother, still uneasy. 'I don't want

to alarm you, Don, but that house is pure dynamite. Lewis built in all kinds of high-tech tricks . . .'

Ralph twirled his thumbs happily.

'Oh, I always say we've a lot to thank dynamite for, Nellie dear . . .'

'Twenty-five years,' said my father. 'The house hasn't too much kick left in it these days, I guess.'

'The pair of you can go jump in the lake,' said Nell. 'One old fella teasing me and one young fella breathing sweet reason. I don't know which is worse.'

I could not take my eyes off the House Beautiful that was full of high-tech tricks. If I was game to go inside maybe I would find a room that showed non-stop videos of heavy-metal bands, blasting away all round the walls at the touch of a button. And in the other rooms there would be holograms of pre-crash life: automobiles, jumbo jets, violence, sexual promiscuity, pollution, junk food, drug highs, late late movies, dancing, the Metropolitan Opera in New York, false gods, false prophets, neon lights, Coca-Cola, and the State of California. My true birthright of which I had been robbed: the twentieth century.

My father reined in beside a tree. There was a letter box and a name neatly painted on a board: G. Morgan, Advisory Services.

'Oh sure,' said Ralph. 'You remember, Nell. There was the dentist, Dave Morgan. Gave us dental advice. He even came out to the Ranch a couple of times.'

'So he did,' said my grandmother.

She ran a hand over her bushy head of white hair in a gesture I knew well. It meant sorrow and resignation: so it goes. Most of the people she and Ralph and my Mom had known had gone down in the crash. They did not speak of their personal experiences. When I was eight my Dad, who came from a founding family at Hopewell . . . one that went green long before the crash . . . confided to me that Nell and Ralph had a high-tech background. I worried in case they had worked in a reactor and helped nuke their friends but my mother, Anne Marie, said no, one day soon things would loosen up at the Center and I would be proud of my grandparents. The day had not come but what the hell, I was fairly proud of them anyway.

'Don't look so sad, little Linnit,' said Nell. 'We have to set up a parameter or two for these tests.'

Far away at the end of the green driveway, overgrown except for two wheel ruts, a boy in a red shirt began to walk slowly towards us.

'We must remember two things,' said Nell. 'First, these people may indeed possess unusual powers, whether it's telepathy, a sensitivity to agricultural conditions or even a deep empathy that enables them to convince others. Second, it is in their interest to cheat a little, to blind us with science.'

'Nell, anyone who tries to blind you with science is in for a shock,' said my father.

'Why, thank you, Don!'

'The boy will ask Linnit to step down,' said Ralph, 'so he can show her around.'

'Just answer his questions, honey,' said my grandmother, 'and remember what he asked. On no account let out that Old Nell was at this place before. Got it?'

'Sure.'

We all stared at the boy as he approached and he took it very calmly. He was good-looking, with tanned even features and thick gold-brown hair falling over his forehead. He was older than he seemed at first; he had looked more of a kid coming down the drive because he was short, no more than five four, five five.

'Mister Don Green?' he asked. 'Of the Hopewell Center? I'm Gavin Morgan.'

'Hello there, Gavin!' said my Dad. 'I'd like to introduce Nell and Ralph Mann, my wife's parents, and this is my daughter Linnit.'

There was a lot of hello there, pleased to meet you. The Morgan boy petted Ruby and gave her a piece of carrot from his pocket. He rode on the step as we came slowly into the shadow of that fantastic house. There were rock gardens, paved ramps and several outbuildings of the same grey stone. Just when I thought he would never ask . . . and thereby score a point against my grandfather . . . Gavin Morgan caught my eye and said:

'You like to step down, Linnit, and see our baby ducks?'

'I don't mind,' I said.

I was one of those Hopewell Center girls, candid, clear-eyed, capable. Neither a meek handmaiden of the Patriarchs in a long skirt and a headscarf nor a bareback rider from the Free Amazons, down south. I did my hair in a long pony-tail, wore blue linen trousers, and a shirt of knitted cotton.

I wasn't a known rebel or non-conformist on the Center but my attitude was not all it might have been. The Hopewell Counsellors knew that they did not possess my heart and mind. Home influences. Anne Marie, then Nell and Ralph. I thought of this as I stepped down from the cart and smiled at Gavin Morgan and followed him to the barnyard of the Bergstrom house. I was passing for a true-green Hopewell gal. I was deceiving him. Maybe he and his family were trying to deceive all the New Age Communities this side of the mountains with their time sense.

He questioned me very smoothly and in a nice way. He was truly friendly, he didn't flirt, he didn't patronize. By the time we had seen the six ducklings swimming in the pond he knew that my mother was dead, that my Dad was a member of the Planting Committee, that Hopewell had twice the acreage of any other commune, that the main crop was Indian corn.

We got on to what-we-liked-to-do. My hobbies were music, reading, painting and collage; the Center was very strong on Uses of Leisure Time. Yes, I liked to dance and was in the Youth Chain Group for the summer festival. So what did *he* like to do?

'Like to do?' he echoed. 'I like to be alive!'

Then, as if this was some admission, he said that he farmed here, around the house.

'We travel a lot doing the readings,' he said.

In the entrance to the stone barn there was a wooden caravan, dark green, with a chimney.

'Play chess plenty in winter,' said Gavin. 'Summers we go prospecting.'

'That's interesting. For gold?'

'For uncontaminated objects that we can bring to market,' he said.

We looked at a couple of pigs and a walnut tree. Gavin slipped away into the shadowy barn to see if he had shut the feed bin. When he came back his eyes were sparkling, he was full of the devil.

'Linnit Green!' he said. 'Just the name for a Hopewell girl. You like to dance that summer chain dance, Linnit?'

We had touched on this before. He was sharp and mischievous, his eyes were lighter brown and he had a long scar on his right forearm.

'Okay,' I said. 'Where's your brother Gavin? Off on another time track?'

He laughed aloud and said:

'Come on, Gav! She rumbled us!'

'She rumbled *you*,' said Gavin, coming out of the barn. 'This is my brother Owen.'

They stood side by side so I could admire the likeness.

'We were born on the same day and we had the same father and mother,' said Owen, 'but we're not twins. How come?'

'I know that one too,' I said. 'You have another brother hiding in the barn. Triplets.'

'That's right,' said Gavin seriously. 'Our brother Arthur died at birth.'

'I'm sorry,' I said. 'Look, could you take me into the house?'

'You're scared of it, right?' said Owen. 'Big towering house after those pressed-wood boxes and fake log cabins.'

'Where have *you* lived, anyway?' I counter-attacked. 'There are worse places than Hopewell.'

'Sure,' said Gavin.

They had this trick of reacting one after the other; it reinforced their moods. When they smiled it was as if the whole world was smiling. Now they frowned, the light went out of their faces.

'We were two years in a mute-camp, back east,' said Owen.

'Before Gwen, our sister, got us out,' said Gavin.

I knew this must have been very bad. I wanted to comfort them but all I could do was look at the ground and say again:

'I'm sorry.'

'Come on,' said Gavin, 'we'll see the house.'

'We have a right to live here,' said Owen slyly. 'In fact we're about the only persons who could . . .'

We took a low ramp, marched in through a door that didn't look like a door and we were in the kitchen. It was a very strange place. The inside colouring was all brown, purple-brown, tan and green from the indoor plants. There was a work center with a huge built-in range, two wall ovens, staring like dead eyes, and a three door refrigerator freezer. All this stuff was like the insides of a stranded space ship, indestructible but non-functioning. A place had been cleared under a copper hood for an ordinary wood stove. Steps went up to a gallery; the room had no proper ceiling. You could look up, up at redwood panelling and thick window walls of tinted glass. In the middle of the kitchen was a black marble-topped table; my father and my grandparents were drinking tea with Gwen Morgan.

She was taller than her brothers and a good ten years older. She was very good-looking with splendid bones, perfect teeth, bright blue eyes and a fat braid of tawny hair. But Gwen Morgan didn't look like the Harvest Queen, she looked worn, leathery and hard. Her hands were rougher than mine. She had lived as a refugee and dragged her brothers out of a mute-camp. I believed it. She wore a beautiful robe of pale gold 'purity silk'. The New Jerusalem has a corner on mulberry trees in our part of the world. It looked as though crop-reading was accepted by the Patriarchs and well rewarded.

'Well, I declare,' said my grandmother as we trooped in. 'I can't tell Gavin from his brother.'

Owen paid his respects to the visitors. Ralph said politely:

'So that's our proposition, Ms Morgan. You wouldn't mind giving us a little demonstration of the boys' powers?'

'Most clients,' said Gwen softly, 'have faith.'

'Do you mean,' asked Nell just as softly, 'that the phenomenon *depends* on faith of some kind?'

'No!' put in Gavin firmly. 'We can look forward and backward, Ma'am.'

'Do you have a standard demonstration?' asked my father.

'Nope,' said Owen. 'Just a guarantee. No success, no reward.'

'We receive our settlement in almost every session,' said Gwen. 'If there's the slightest doubt we don't proceed. We're completely frank. Where a damaged crop is observed we say so. That is the method.'

'It is self-fulfilling,' said Nell. 'You claim to see in the future that the field was not planted, then advise the farmers not to plant.'

'Not quite,' said Gwen. 'We never advise the holders to do anything. The observer reports on several fields at several points of time, past and future.'

'Have you ever observed any *unexpected* developments?' asked my father.

The boys looked at each other and at Gwen who gave them the high sign.

'One time,' said Owen, 'it was observed that a strange animal walked through a stand of corn, causing damage.'

'It was pretty unbelievable,' said Gavin, 'but there it was.'

'We didn't want anyone to harm the . . . er . . . animal

when it happened along,' said Owen, 'so we didn't name it. We reported animal damage, forty per cent of the western quadrant of the field.'

'The holders insisted,' said Gwen, 'and we took the unusual step of leaving the animal's description with a trustee.'

Ralph began to chuckle.

'I seem to remember hearing . . .'

'Sure enough,' said Owen, 'a guy turned up with one of these critters. Luckily it was far too valuable to be put down. They paid the owner to cart it away at once.'

'What happened to the field?' asked my father.

'It got trampled,' said Gavin. 'The circus proprietor had *two* elephants. When her mate was carted off the female tried to follow.'

'And trampled the western quadrant of the field just as you predicted,' sighed my grandmother.

'We don't *predict* the future,' said Gavin, 'we see what's going on at a future time.'

'You use exactly the same faculty to see into the future and into the past?'

'Yes,' said Gwen, 'exactly the same.'

'Okay,' said Nell, 'what's the range of your observation in either direction?'

'About fifty years,' said Owen flatly.

'How do you reckon the passing of time?' asked Ralph. 'Can you pin-point a certain day?'

'It depends,' said Gwen. 'I've documented all this, believe me. For crop-reading purposes we use existing landmarks, deciduous trees and certain devices of our own.'

'It would be difficult to test a reading of the future,' said Nell.

'Oh, I don't know,' said Ralph. 'What if the lads here stood on the drive and reported on the next visitors?'

'Are you expecting anybody?' asked Nell.

'Not definitely,' said Gwen. 'Today or tomorrow there should be callers from Brightwater and from Jerusalem.'

'And someone could drop in at any time,' said Gavin. 'We go out to private readings.'

'Like hunting for lost things,' said Owen. 'Seeing where somebody put the hammer or the keys.'

It was not only that tools were valuable – all the adults set a great store by them. To lose a hacksaw blade or the best knife was a sign of ill-fortune. Even at Hopewell we turned the place upside down looking for lost things.

'I have the ghost of an idea,' said Ralph. 'Let me think about it.'

Everyone took a breather; the boys gave me cookies and lemonade. My grandmother accepted another one of Gwen's walnut brownies. They were sizing each other up.

'May I see the house?' I asked.

'Thought we would show Linnit the front hall,' said Owen.

'Now that is where we came in, right?' said Nell. 'That impressive entrance hall with the hologram of the architect, what was his name?'

'Bergstrom,' said my father, with a despairing movement of his eyebrows which meant 'Don't overdo it, Nell!'

'Of course,' said Nell. 'Now I noticed that big old visitors' book resting on that futuristic contraption . . .'

'Come, Nellie dear,' said Ralph, 'no need to be afraid of an old non-functioning gizmo like *that*!'

I was beginning to have gooseflesh. These two old devils were kidding around about some artifact that might scare *me* plenty.

'If you're all agreeable,' said Nell, 'we might set up a little test dealing with the past.'

'We've done some observation in this house,' said Gavin. 'We saw Bergstrom meeting some people in the dining room. Gwen said they were . . . you know . . . film stars.'

For the first time I realized that the Morgan boys had missed out on a lot of things. It stood to reason. No one gave a damn about Uses of Leisure Time in the mute-camps. Could they even *read*? Would they consider an uncontaminated book a good thing to bring to market?

'I will need the visitors' book,' said Nell.

She waited for a second and said:

'*Linnit* must bring me the book.'

The point was not lost on them: no cheating. Gwen handed Owen a bunch of keys.

'Bring Linnit through the front door,' she said. 'We'll be in the dining room.'

Gavin and Owen led me out and around to the main ramp. We stood and looked at the world. It was early spring after a hard winter. The trees were coming in bright yellow-green all through the valleys: we saw every sort of willow, some birch, the early apples coming into blossom.

'Too late for this year,' said Gavin, 'if your Old Man decided to give us a try.'

'Please don't cheat,' I said. 'If this is some kind of swindle please quit, right now.'

'We don't need to cheat!' snapped Owen.

'How do you do it then?' I yelled. 'What *is* all this crazy talk? Do you go into a trance? Do you read minds?'

'Hush,' said Gavin. 'We *see* . . .'

He put an arm round my shoulders.

'Come in the house.'

Owen stepped up to the mighty redwood doors and went to work with the keys. He opened a small door set into the right-hand leaf. As we stepped inside he said:

'Pretty neat, eh? We never open the main doors.'

'Neat,' I said through clenched teeth.

The hall was awe-inspiring, much worse than the kitchen. There was a staircase surrounded by organ pipes or stalactites of stone. There was a great loftiness: everything swept upward, only the light poured down in golden shafts. I saw the hologram of Lewis Bergstrom and it didn't cheer me one bit. It was the size of a wall in our house on the Center and it showed a hawk-faced individual in black trousers, a white shirt and a black cloak lined with iridescent azure blue, like butterfly wings. He stood nobly poised wih a roll of blueprints in his hand before his own house.

'Take it easy,' said Gavin, 'here's the visitor's book.'

I turned away from Bergstrom and saw a huge shadowy figure taking a step in my direction. He had been taking this one step when the wind changed and he stayed that way. I should have been afraid but I wasn't. He was no more scary in this frozen attitude than a statue of King Tut. He was a robot, seven foot tall and very traditional. He had lumpy rounded contours of anodized metal, or was it plastic? He had domed lights and buttons and dials; he wore a benign expression on his non-human face.

'Poor guy,' I said. 'His eyes need dusting.'

'We don't even know his real name,' said Gavin sadly. 'We call him Zack.'

The visitors' book was balanced on Zack's upturned hands. It was 24 inches by 18, bound in dark red leather tooled in gold, and it had heavy cream paper. There were photographs and even newspaper clippings inside as well as signatures. I lifted it carefully so that the inserts wouldn't scatter but something did fall on to the carpet. Owen picked it up and we saw that it was a four-leafed clover that had been pressed between the pages. It seemed such a simple human thing to do in this monumental house . . . save a four-leafed-clover. I looked back at Bergstrom and wondered if I had been wrong about him. Was he more of a magpie than a hawk?

The boys led me down panelled corridors for about a quarter of a mile and we came to the dining room. It was positively cosy: the table might have seated eight, unextended. There was a ceiling and a soft golden carpet. On a sunny terrace through the glass wall there were stone chessmen on the red and grey tiles. The set was not complete. I saw three grey stones doing duty for white pawns and a billet of firewood labelled Black Rook.

My grandmother was ready to receive the visitors' book; she leafed through it. Gwen Morgan sat at the other end of the table doing embroidery in a round frame. Out on the terrace Ralph and my Dad leaned on the rail and pointed out into the springtime fields. We went out and joined them. The terrace was high up on the eastern wall of the house: you could see as far as New Jerusalem.

'There,' said Ralph. 'See the two schooners.'

They were greyish humps on the road, moving slowly: the Patriarchs used covered wagons. Ralph murmured something to my Dad then straightened up.

'I think we have something . . .' he said.

He led the way indoors.

'Nellie,' he said. 'I think we have a simple test situation approaching.'

My Dad explained about the wagons in the distance.

'So one of the wagons might be coming to this house,' said Nell. 'Right?'

'Right,' said Gwen warily.

'We *know* about when it will arrive in the afternoon,' said Gavin.

'But not who is driving the wagon,' said Ralph.

Nell clapped her hands.

'Fine!' she said. 'There's the selection process.'

All the Morgans began to smile too and at last I got the message. Only the men of the Waggoner clan regularly went out of New Jerusalem and their routes were chosen by lot. It had something to do with avoiding impure contacts.

'So what do you think?' asked Ralph looking out from under his jutting brow at the two boys.

'Pretty close in,' said Gavin to his brother.

'No, no,' said Owen, 'the light is fine. With this weather . . .'

'You may choose one of my brothers to stand on the drive and make the observation,' said Gwen.

'Alone?' asked Nell.

'It's the condition on which we insist,' said Gwen. '*No one*, I repeat, *no one* in the immediate vicinity of the observer. Have you been to a crop reading?'

'Yes,' said my father. 'One of the boys stands alone in the field.'

'What does the second boy do?' asked Ralph.

'Sits in the caravan,' said Gavin.

'Mugging up almanacs and long-range weather forecasts,' grinned Owen. 'Maybe sending thought messages or reading minds . . .'

'*You* brought up these subjects,' said my grandmother, 'and we'll be on the look-out for any evidence of these . . . er . . . skills.'

'There won't be much to see,' warned Owen.

There wasn't. We all trailed down to the kitchen again. Owen went out to the drive to a point where we could all just see him through the trees. He stood there. Once he seemed to be shading his eyes with his hands. We went back to the dining room and he came back in. He sat with my father at the kitchen table, wrote down what he had seen on a sheet of paper from Nell's notebook with one of Nell's ballpoint pens. She had looted four gross of these give-away pens from the Gold Star Novelty Company of Pasadena, long ago, and had used up two hundred and three so far. She never used them to trade.

My father sealed Owen's paper up unread in an unused envelope provided by Gwen. It had Lewis Bergstrom's name and address embossed on the front. Then they came upstairs again and my father showed Nell the envelope. He had signed his name across the back flap. He put it in his shirt pocket and buttoned the pocket.

Owen was not smiling.

'I give my word not to tell Gwen or Gavin what I saw,' he said. 'I know this test will have a good result.'

'Is it exhausting, this feat of yours?' asked Nell.

'Not especially,' said Owen. 'It takes concentration.'

'I've been studying the visitors' book and I have the material for another test. Look here, Ralph . . .'

The two old people bent over the book, nodding and laughing.

'Are you familiar with this book, Ms Morgan?' asked my grandmother.

'I looked through it when we first arrived,' said Gwen. 'I saw a few famous names. Those people are dead and the age they lived in has been discredited. For me it was a sad book.'

Ralph said cautiously to Nell:

'If you're really prepared to . . .'

'Nothing venture, nothing win,' she said. 'Linnit, bring this picture to Ms Morgan.'

It was the picture of a statue clipped from a glossy magazine.

'This bronze figure,' said Ralph, 'is it somewhere in the house?'

Gwen only needed to glance at the picture.

'Yes,' she said, 'yes, it's in the lower study. Just through here.'

I was completely disorientated inside the house. When I stepped out of a room I had no idea of the way I had come or the way back. Now we all went to the lower study. My grandmother kept hold of the visitors' book; the boys came in last.

The study was well-aired but unused; the books had gone; the room was rather dark because a steel shutter was half drawn on the balcony.

'We've had trouble with the shutters,' said Gwen. 'Rooms on this side of the house can't be used because of those drawn shutters.'

There was a massive desk and a wall decoration of thick glass and leaf shapes. The bronze statue was beside the balcony doors; it was nearly four feet high, a stylized female figure.

'If someone could read out what is on the brass plate?' asked Nell.

My father knelt down.

'"In what ethereal dances, By what eternal streams." For my wife Imogen Bergstrom.'

Nell gave a sigh.

'Lewis Bergstrom made the statue and had it cast in his workshop,' she said. 'I have information here about a ceremony . . . a dedication it is called . . . that was held in this room on a summer's day around twenty-five years ago. Could this information be verified?'

The Morgans drew together and so did the Green/Mann family. Gwen sat at the desk; my grandmother took a leather chair by the fireplace.

'What would convince you, Ms Mann?' asked Gwen.

'An on-the-spot report,' said Nell.

'You talk about "seeing",' said Ralph. 'Does that mean there is no sound? A silent movie?'

'It's almost impossible for you to believe in what we do,' said Owen, 'so why don't we just leave it as hocus-pocus that sometimes works, like water-divining?'

'We leave it like that *if* you make a convincing report,' said Nell grimly.

'Don't forget Owen's reading on the drive!' said Gavin.

'I'm not forgetting it,' said Nell.

'We could have two reports,' said Ralph. 'One from Gavin, one from Owen. Take all the time you need.'

The Morgans put their handsome heads together for a moment. I felt miserable and afraid. I was embarrassed by Nell and Ralph. I was afraid the boys would fail or be caught cheating. I was afraid of the Bergstrom house and at the same time I hated to invade the world of its former inhabitants. I had a bad attack of 'there are things we are not meant to know'.

Owen came forward and said:

'Gavin will go first. I'll stay with Mr Don Green while my brother makes his observation.'

'Fine,' said my father, cocking an eye at Nell.

Ralph walked all round the spacious brown room then we trooped out. We left Gavin standing by the desk, arms folded, smiling. The study had a strange-shaped key, a thick bolt of steel with heavy wards, which Gwen moved to the outside of the door. When we went back to the dining room my father took Owen out on the terrace. Soon they were playing chess.

My grandmother pointed out later that the precautions taken were primitive, you could drive a horse and cart through them. There was still an awful lot of distrustful coming and going. After half an hour by Nell's illegally accurate eternity watch Ralph let Gavin out of the study and led him down to the kitchen where he was permitted to make notes while the observation was fresh in his mind. My father let Owen into the study soon afterwards. When Gwen decided to start making lunch my grandmother said:

'I wonder if we could use your bathroom? Come, Linnit!'

Gwen led us past the study then around and along. The bathroom was on the other side of the corridor.

'I think we can find our own way back,' said Nell.

Gwen's face was cold and expressionless.

I could have spent time examining that bathroom but Nell told me to hurry. At the door she said:

'This is cheating but it's in the interests of science.'

She took my hand and nipped across into another corridor. We went through rooms that might have been bedrooms. The steel shutters were drawn so that the rooms were dark but my grandmother knew the way after twenty-five years. I wondered if she had the whole crazy Bergstrom house in her head like a map or a chip diagram. We were in a smaller room with a long walk-in closet.

'Lewis was always a little paranoid,' she said. 'Poor Imogen hated this kind of set-up.'

She slid open the closet and I was glad to see that it was empty except for a few black leather coat-hangers. In one place there was a set of shelves; she felt under the middle shelf and cursed. She took a screwdriver from the pocket of her jacket and went to work under the shelf.

'Pull!' she said, drawing back. 'Pull on the shelf!'

We pulled and the whole shelf wall opened without a sound. Nell put a finger to her lips and one by one we squeezed into something too small even to be called a cupboard. There was barely room for the two of us on a low padded bench. We sat and stared at a piece of pale amber glass with dark swirling patterns. It took a moment for me to work out what these patterns were: metal leaf shapes. We were looking into the study through the inset wall decoration; it was a one-way viewing window.

There was still nothing to see. A boy among the trees, a boy in an empty room. Owen Morgan had his back to us, he was quite close to our hiding place. I could hardly believe that he wouldn't look us in the eye when he turned round. The room looked more alive through the amber-coloured glass. I thought of the scene that Owen was trying to see – Lewis Bergstrom whipping around in his cape with the butterfly lining, along with a bunch of film stars and my grandmother, twenty-five years younger, in some kind of high-tech white overall.

Owen walked slowly to the corner of the desk and turned around. He gave us a grandstand view. What I saw was intolerably strange, it was beyond everything; it was a close encounter with a mutant of the New Age. It began as a glow on his forehead and around his eyes. First his eyes began to flicker, to shift and vibrate in their sockets, then the flimmering motion spread to his whole face. It was too fast for the eye to follow. I expected him to disappear, to flicker out of existence, out of one time into another. Instead he turned aside and looked at another part of the room.

I found that my grandmother and I were clutching hands tightly. I hardly remember getting out of the viewing room. We tip-toed back the way we had come like two zombies. We staggered back into the bathroom without a word. I took a drink of water, Nell wrung out a washcloth and pressed it to her forehead.

'Cheats never prosper!' she said.

'Gwen will come looking for us!'

'We've been gone twelve minutes,' said Nell. 'Are you all right?'

She pinched my cheeks to get some colour in them. As we walked past the study door we saw that Gwen had taken the key.

'Linnit,' whispered Nell sternly, 'we must get a grip on ourselves!'

'They can do it!' I whispered back. 'You saw how Owen . . .'

'The experiment,' she said out loud, 'is still continuing.'

Gavin made his report first while Owen sat alone in the kitchen. My grandmother seemed to have a good grip on herself but I was so quiet and strained that my Dad noticed. I said I would be all right after lunch; they gave me an apple. Gavin was very self-assured and natural. He stood at the end of the table and looked over his notes.

'The statue made a good landmark,' he said, 'and I tried to fasten on it. I was thrown for a while by the fact that it was covered by a green cloth. There was a day very close to the ceremony when a dark, Spanish-looking woman . . . might have been the housekeeper . . . stripped off the cloth and gave the statue a polish. Then, at night, Bergstrom came into the study, got down a book and made a note at the desk. He took off the cloth too and stood admiring the statue.

'I kept looking and I think I got the time Ms Mann wanted. There were seven people in the room. Bergstrom didn't look much like his portrait of course, he was short, for one thing, shorter than me, and grey-haired. Then there was a beautiful woman with red hair. She wore a long skirt. She came in through the balcony door with a smooth-looking guy in a black sweater. They stood side by side turned towards Bergstrom who was standing beside the draped statue. There were a couple of spectators standing before the fireplace: a young girl and another older woman. The Spanish woman was there holding something on a tray that flickered and sparkled, maybe a set of glasses that caught the light. There was a guy taking photographs, only he was hard to see because he had a light on a stand. Anyway, Bergstrom uncovered the statue and as he backed away through the room the good-looking couple began to dance. It was part of the ceremony. They danced together, you know, holding each other. Then they stood still. The housekeeper dropped the tray and began to cry.'

There was a long silence. My grandmother shook her head in wonder and said:

'Remarkable. I wonder what Owen can add to this?'

'Without the music,' said Ralph. 'What *was* the music anyway?'

'How should I know?' said Nell bitterly. 'One of Imogen's great successes. A tango. Could we hear Owen in the study?'

'Are you convinced?' asked Gwen.

'Yes, yes,' said Nell. 'That was a convincing report. I guess if someone could see but not hear that little ceremony we might very well come up with something like that. Please let me complete the experiment.'

Everyone was pleased when she said this. Gwen smiled and flung open the door to the corridor and called downstairs for Owen. Ralph had one of his rare bursts of old man's energy. He began to hum a tune and said 'Take it, Linnit!' The tune was 'La Paloma'. My Dad took it up too, we sang and clapped our hands. Ralph took hold of Nell, who laughed, and they were off, dancing the tango all the way along the corridor and into the study.

'That's it,' said Gavin in my ear. 'That's the dance!'

Owen came in.

'I think that's the dance!' he said. 'The one those things were dancing!'

When order had been restored he made his report.

'We take turns scanning for detail,' he said. 'Gavin gave the broad outline. It was a weird scene and I couldn't understand what was going on. I used the statue as a marker of course. I watched for Lewis Bergstrom. He was producing some kind of home movie. There was this woman by the fireplace and a girl with her. They looked very embarrassed. Then there was a dark woman who came in last carrying something on a tray. This is strange but I swear it was a cake with tiny lighted candles on it. Would that be right? She stood there holding the cake and Bergstrom uncovered the statue. Two figures came in from the balcony: the dancers. They were dolls or robots like old Zack in the front hall. The crazy thing was that the male dancer was a copy of Lewis Bergstrom. The female had dark red hair and wore Spanish dress. They danced that tango dance, dipping down and turning and crossing their legs. Bergstrom was filming all this, he went behind a lamp on a stand. The lady with the cake stood watching the dancers with a terrible expression. At last she dropped the tray and covered her face with her hands.'

'Even better,' said Nell. 'Some of the detail is most telling.'

Gavin hung his head, not satisfied with his performance.

'Cake!' he grumbled. 'Robot dancers. And of course Bergstrom was the photographer.'

'Indoor is tricky,' said Owen. 'Light and shade. Moving subjects.'

I couldn't stand it any longer.

'Nell,' I said, 'maybe this is an embarrassing question but *what was going on*? Doesn't anyone care what those people were doing all those years ago?'

The Morgan boys, side by side, looked at me in surprise. I felt queasy when I saw their faces, shining with success, and I imagined a tremor in their brown eyes.

'We *saw* what they did,' said Gavin.

'Linnit shows a human interest,' said Ralph.

Gwen Morgan said quickly:

'Of course we'd be interested to see the original material. Who signed the visitors' book that day?'

'Good question,' said Nell. 'It touches on the problem of interpretation. How many signatures would you expect?'

The boys went into a huddle.

'Two,' said Gavin. 'The woman by the fireplace and the young girl who was with her.'

My father, who had brought along the visitors' book, clutched it to his chest and cried out:

'Nell, you terrible woman, *you have gone too far*!'

He put the book on the desk, unopened, and took me roughly by the arm.

'Linnit, we're leaving!'

'No!' ordered Nell. 'We'll see this right through, Don!'

She opened the book at the place she had marked. The Morgans had drawn together watching this performance by the Green/Mann family, complete with sound effects.

'I didn't play quite fair,' said Nell, 'and neither did Lewis Bergstrom. That inscription on the statue might suggest that it was a memorial to his wife. In fact it was a memorial to her talent.'

'She wasn't dead?' asked Gavin.

'Far from it,' said Nell. 'Imogen Bergstrom retired from her own Hispanic Dance Company after an injury to her hip. She was the dark woman who brought in the birthday cake for her husband.'

'Birthday cake?' asked Owen.

'You really didn't know that a cake with little candles . . .' I said.

'They never had one,' said Gwen. 'Come to that *I* never had one. In our family we never ate a grain of sugar because of our teeth.'

'Good God!' said Ralph. 'Nellie . . .'

But Nell was still explaining the scene.

'It was the cruellest thing,' she said. 'Lewis couldn't understand Imogen's reaction. He had acquired . . . illegally . . . two android dancers. One was a copy of herself, the other of Imogen, both looking young and beautiful. A big surprise for all those present.'

'You didn't recognize anyone that you saw at that time?' asked Ralph. 'Owen?'

'No,' said Owen. 'I'm not well up on the sort of people

who might have visited the Bergstroms. There was something. Outside influence, I guess. The young girl looked to me a lot like Linnit.'

My father uttered a groan.

'Linnit, baby,' he said, 'I didn't expect . . .'

So I understood and I came into some place outside of time where the wish to know and to understand went beyond sadness. I stepped past him and looked at the visitors' book. There were two signatures on the page.

Cornelia Todd Gormann

Anne Marie Gormann

I knew the handwriting of my grandmother and even my mother's handwriting hadn't changed so much as she grew older. Someone else . . . Bergstrom? . . . had written a note on the facing page. *Cornelia Todd; Ralph Gormann, Nobel Prize for Cybernetic Research, 2025.* I looked up and saw my grandmother's face, full of sorrow.

'Come,' she said.

I took her hand and we walked together to the fireplace where she had been standing with her daughter Anne Marie, on a summer's day twenty-five years ago.

'It was embarrassing for the spectators,' she said, 'and not only because Lewis was flaunting these custom-built dancers before his poor wife who would never dance another step. Ralph and I were engaged in cybernetic research, including the creation of androids . . . humanoid robots. The problem was how such beings could be accepted by society. There was a great difference between the robot major-domo that we mocked up for Lewis's fine house and a creature that looked fully human, possessed high intelligence *and* superhuman skills. Lewis Bergstrom saw nothing wrong in using androids as toys but we surely did. The crash came before the problem was solved.'

The Morgan boys came and stared at us both very keenly.

'Yes,' said Gavin. 'It could be.'

'You were here,' said Owen, 'but Linnit . . .'

'That was my mother, Anne Marie,' I said. 'We had a strong likeness.'

'You made Zack?' said Gavin. 'You and Mr Mann?'

'Gormann,' said Nell. 'He was an adapted transporter made to look like everyone's idea of a robot butler. He was called Robert. Made at the Todd Gormann Research Ranch. Used to be a name to conjure with.'

'Isn't that pretty high-tech for Hopewell Center?' asked Owen.

'They know who we are,' said Ralph. 'The New Age must compromise in order to survive.'

There was a loud sob. Gwen Morgan was looking at the visitors' book and she was dissolved in tears. She turned to Ralph.

'Doc? Doc Gormann?'

She took a faltering step towards my grandmother.

'Ms Todd, Ms Todd, it is Gwinnie, Gwinnie Morgan . . . I came to the Ranch with my father. Do you remember? David Morgan, the dentist!'

'Gwinnie?' said Nell. 'That little kid . . . Oh my dear . . .'

So she began to cry too. They fell into each other's arms and Ralph went and embraced the pair of them. That left my father and me and the two boys blinking, grinning, blowing our noses. There was not a dry eye in the house. I thought of future observers watching the scene . . . why are all these people laughing and crying? The coincidence was not as great as all that. David Morgan had been a dentist with a fancy practice in Los Angeles, including Nobel Prize winners and architects and the stars of the Hispanic Dance Company.

There was a settlement with the Morgan family and a lot of reminiscence. About the great escape, for instance, where David Morgan flew his wife and daughter out in his private plane, not long after the crash. We ate lunch with stuffed zucchini, wild rice, olives, six sorts of cheese, pickled walnuts and honey cakes. They even had a ham in the store cupboard, which made the day for Nell and Ralph.

We set out for home at four o'clock. No other visitors had showed up; the shadows were lengthening on the drive. Owen said:

'Remember the first test, Ms Gormann.'

'I'm remembering,' said Nell. 'You reckon this is a good time for us to observe your driveway?'

'Should be!' he said.

The boys waved; they waved at *me*, with identical smiles.

We went the whole length of the drive and observed nothing more than the trees and the grass. An old crow walked across the path. We turned out of the driveway and saw the covered wagon from New Jerusalem. It was just getting ready to turn in and the driver was wrestling with the horses. My Dad took Ruby and our rig off the path.

The Waggoner was dressed like any other patriarch: greyish linsey-woolsey trousers, a collarless cotton shirt, a knitted sleeveless vest of black wool and a black straw hat. Beside the driver was a young boy about ten years old dressed exactly the same. As the wagon righted itself and drew level I heard my grandmother curse under her breath. I felt a physical shock as if I had been punched in the midriff. The driver was a woman in man's clothes: she was a Proxy.

The Patriarchs of the New Jerusalem had never had enough people willing to serve the Lord in the New Age. Only men could vote of course and conduct business, as laid down in the Law. They had plenty of Law in New Jerusalem and their lawyers had created a legal fiction. A woman could become a Proxy for her younger male kin, or in certain cases, the head of a household of women. There were a lot of rules laid down for a Proxy in dress and behaviour. Other communes in the valleys below the mountains took it as a joke, an eccentricity of the Patriarchs: Now I saw that it was as cruel and stupid a piece of patriarchal behaviour as anything they did.

The woman was over fifty; we knew that because she wore a false fringe of beard hitched to her ears. She had a long, pale face and the saddest expression I ever saw on a human being. Her eyes were very dark, almost black, and they were full of grief and misery. The boy was angry and ashamed, looking first at the woman, then at us, jutting his jaw. The two sorrel horses fretted and stamped in their traces.

Male patriarchs spoke only to other men, on the outside, unless it was an emergency. Handmaidens of the New Jerusalem, if they ever got close enough to outsiders, spoke only to women. My grandmother said:

'We are from Hopewell Center. My name is Cornelia Mann. Good day to you.'

The woman almost touched her forehead and her lips in the women's greeting, then she remembered and nodded to us like a male patriarch.

'Praise God!' she said in a loud unsteady voice. 'I am Deborah Waggoner, proxy for my grandson Nahum here.'

'You need any help, Ma'am?' asked my father.

'Thank you kindly,' said the woman, looking sideways at him. 'I guess I am getting the hang of it.'

The boy, Nahum, suddenly began punching the woman on her arm and shoulder.

'You broke the law!' he shouted. 'You ain't fit!'

The woman did nothing, she sat rigid. We all stared at the boy and what we felt showed in our faces. The kid blushed brick-red. The woman said quietly:

'Get in the wagon, Nahum.'

He scrambled over the back of the seat and we heard him bawling and hitting at the sides of the cotton cover.

'Deborah was a judge in Israel,' said my grandmother unexpectedly. 'Ms Waggoner, I don't suppose you'd consider giving up this masquerade and taking asylum at Hopewell with little Nahum, there?'

This wasn't as crazy as it sounded. Only last year a widow and her family had taken asylum from the New Jerusalem in the Hopewell Center, after a string of misfortunes with the Law of the Patriarchs.

The woman turned towards us and took a firm grip on the reins.

'My daughter-in-law,' she said, 'my son's wife, Leah, was brought to bed of twin daughters last week. Same day that my son Ezra was taken in a three wagon pile-up at the saw mill. I must stand proxy.'

She concentrated on getting the reins right and the horses lined up for the driveway. Just before she told them to go she said:

'Take a blessing, Sister Cornelia.'

She stood up and shouted to the horses and they obeyed her. We saw the wagon go swaying down the green aisle to the Bergstrom house. My father already had Owen's envelope out of his shirt pocket; he whistled softly and passed around the clumsily printed paper. Owen had written: 'One of the Waggoners must be dead. An old woman is driving a wagon dressed as a Proxy. It could be Ezra's wagon from the sorrel team.'

My grandmother made a short angry prediction of her own at that moment and it is coming true. The New Jerusalem is having trouble with its proxies. Those poor legal fictions have taken to raising their voices, cropping their hair, drinking ale and forming a Work Guild. Proxies make good riflemen and archers. The Patriarchs have sown the wind and they will reap the whirlwind.

We drove on home from late afternoon to early evening. I kept dozing off, propped against my dad, on the front of the cart. I was in shock; too much had happened. I fell into a dream about a chain of dancers who were all strange beings. When I woke Nell was saying:

'A great deal to consider . . .'

'Still have doubts?' asked my father.

'We can't rule out prior knowledge of a number of things,' said Ralph. 'I had the feeling they might not be telling all they knew.'

'Neither were we,' sighed Nell.

We never did tell. I don't believe that my grandmother has told another soul about what we observed in the Bergstrom house that day; she hasn't even told Ralph. When she found that the Morgans were the children of an old friend and colleague Nell decided that certain things weren't meant to be known. She and Ralph plainly enjoy their visits to the Morgans and not only because of ham and roast duck.

As for me, I'm not sure that 'enjoy' is the right word. I've been back to the house, twice, at Christmas time; it doesn't scare me any more. The boys and I go wandering through all its cold upper floors dusting off the monitors. We are a great team: dripping tallow on the carpets, singing and dancing and kissing and kidding around, bringing life back into the beautiful dead rooms. Owen and Gavin can turn their heads aside and *see* what has been, but I can guess, I can interpret, I have a touch more imagination.

We think of Lewis Bergstrom, who designed and built houses for a new age that never happened. He died, Nell says, in Europe at an exhibition, just before the crash. No one knows what became of Imogen, his wife, but the boys say she was the one who cleared out the house. Had to leave a lot of the heavy stuff behind including the bronze statue, a memorial to her talent.

So the house stood there, impregnable as a fortress, until the Morgans came. They were the only people who could live there because they were the only people who could get into the house. Bergstrom had an emergency set of keys concealed on the outside of the building. The boys looked back patiently until they found out the hiding place. I believe this story. I have decided to give Gavin and Owen the benefit of the doubt, permanently. But not for the same reason as my grandmother.

No one in the valleys is very logical when it comes to mutants. A psychic gift is fine but how about a gift that is accompanied by frightening physical changes? How would you like it if your daughter took up with a mute . . . or with two mutes? My father is a sensible man but the Morgans were always a little too way-out for him. He never went back to the Bergstrom house. I rehearse all kinds of speeches, I try to please him. In the end all I can do is hope that he will understand. Once I had a crazy dream about having twin girl babies like poor Leah Waggoner. There they were, lying in their cradles, and one kept disappearing, flimmering right out of sight.

The Morgans read the crops last year and they'll be back in the spring. I will be eighteen years old. I have looked into the future and I know exactly what is going to happen. Owen and Gavin will turn up in their green caravan, looking good, bringing me the past and the future. They'll ask me to go with them and I'll go. In the flicker of an eye.

KIM NEWMAN

Twitch Technicolor

Playing the buttons was all well and good, but Monte thought sometimes you had to get your hands in the colour. He had Bela Lugosi frame-frozen in mid-snarl, stretched black and white over the video easel, wooden stake jutting. Patiently, he combined film overlays in his plastette. Red was the key here. People like red best of all, and there would have to be a lot of it in the *Dracula* remix. It was integral to the property; perhaps a major factor in its lingering appeal. Finally satisfied, he inserted the plastette into the assessor, and sat back while the machine digitally encoded the precise shade that had struck him as proper. When it was done, the assessor pinged like an antique oven, and Monte plucked the now-primed squirtstylo from its lightwell.

He squeezed a blob of red onto the tip of his forefinger, and examined it. It was fine. Then he dabbed the electronic image/analog with the stylo, dribbling red between the reproduction lines. The monochrome filled in, and the gore gushed from the dead actor's starched shirtfront. The film looked better already. It was the personal touch that distinguished the Monte Video product from the competition's all-machine 'enhanced' remix jobs. He plugged the stylo, and noticed phantom rinds of red under his nails. His hand looked as though it belonged to a murderer. He shook his fingers, and the red vanished in a static crackle. He adjusted the easel to give him a screenview, and assessed his handiwork. He keyed ADVANCE, and the film slow-forwarded a few frames. Lugosi completed his snarl, his hand clawed at the stake, blood flowed freely. The red grew, a blob in the centre of the image. It was fine. Monte keyed SAVE, and the colour took. The vampire's glowing eyes and skullhead cuff-links lit up, the exact red of the blood on his chest and about his mouth.

Michaelis Monte could remember the beginnings of the remix business, the ineffectually 'colorized' films of the '80s. He had been among the first to test the potential of image/analog encoding, the process that enabled a skilled remix man to have an original moving picture reduced by the assessor to a particle chain of information bits and then rebuilt again in accordance with his own vision. With his own technologies, he had stolen the march on the majors, resisted many an attempted corporate rape, won all the Dickie awards going, and marked out Ayatollah's share of the marketplace. Monte Video's *Dracula* was already a q-seller on advance orders. Securing the rights from the schizoid corporate descendants of Bram Stoker, Universal Studios, Hammer Films, the BBC and about twenty others who had dipped their claws into the property had been a lengthy and costly battle. With such an important acquisition. Monte might in any case have taken the time to handle the remix himself. Thanks to the Troubles, he was being forced to do the hands-on work personally. He was still the *primo uno* in the business.

Trevor, Ruby Gee, Consodine, and now Tarnaverro. All remaindered. Someone had it in for his remix men, or was trying for a stranglehold on Monte Video.

He keyed PROCEED, and the assessor took over, absorbing Monte's decisions, replacing the drab greys of the original with dayglo colours. He liked to think that Monte Video's *Dracula* was the movie Tod Browning would have turned out in 1930 if he had been free from the censorship requirements of the day and had access to unlimited technical resources. Browning had been forced to have Van Helsing stake Dracula off-screen, with only a tame groan to mark the villain's death, but now the anti-climax could be fixed. Lugosi floundered through the vaulted crypt, eyes aflame like an electric Antichrist, pushing aside curtains of butterfly-wing/stained glass cobweb, recoiling from a succession of violently violet neon crucifixes. Then the vampire was down, and Peter Cushing was on top of him, hammering furiously, driving in deeper the killing stake.

Actually, Edward Van Sloan had played Van Helsing to Lugosi's Count Dracula, but since nobody remembered him any more, Monte had decided to mix in Cushing's definitive performance from the 1958 version. In fact, aside from Lugosi and Dwight Frye as the fly-eating Renfield, he had recast the whole film: James Dean as Jonathan Harker, Marilyn Monroe as the victim-cum-vampirette Lucy, and Meryl Streep as the heroine, Mina. He'd even stirred in Humphrey Bogart as the comic cockney asylum attendant. There weren't enough David Manners or Helen Chandler fans to make a dent in the marketplace, and Monte was always in favour of anything that added to the commercial afterlife of a property. His instincts had made him a rich man; rich enough to afford an unparalleled fine art collection – 3-D religious postcards, popster necrophiliabilia, Woolworth's clown prints. Michaelis Monte was well-known as a man of influential tastes.

Onscreen, Dracula putrefied spectacularly, maggots bursting from his eyesockets. An entirely apt Jimi Hendrix guitar burst accompanied his deathscreams. Monte upped the zynth. More noise, more music, more scream. He infilled with more red. The last of Dracula should be a bloody pool on the lining of his opera cape, red on red. 'Fuck you, Count,' said Peter Cushing, 'and the bat you rode in on.' It was well said, and Monte's vocals people had taken a lot of care to perfect the actor's clipped voice pattern. Hendrix segued Tchaikowsky, winding up the film with the snatch of *Swan Lake* that had been heard in the Transylvanian prologue, and the end titles strobe-flashed as Cushing led Dean and Streep out of the crypt into the rainbow-bright sunrise that lettered out 'THE END' in the sky, and subliminally flashed an expensive ad for Coca-Drugs.

The message pore in the top right of the easel spiralled open. Monte saw an inset of his own doorstep, from the p.o.v. of the monitor-eyed stone eagle perched atop the lintel. Sally Rhodes stood on his WELCOME mat, drenchcoat belted tight, hat-brim pulled low over her domino breather. She looked the eagle in the eye and gave a tight smile. Monte pulled over the nearest slab, and ran the routine checks. The image in the pore proved true; a first-generation, unscrambled mimesis (he supposed that he only had himself to blame for the fact that you couldn't routinely trust anything you saw on television any more). The household recognized her heat pattern, cross-checked the clearance of the Sally Rhodes Agency with the latest listings, and gave him manual control over the door. He palm-printed an okay, and the pore closed as Sally Rhodes was admitted into his hallway.

Monte had scheduled this meeting for late evening in an attempt to avoid embarrassment. He had, of course, been keeping the state police updated on his Troubles, as he was obliged by Law to do, but it was no secret that Monte Video was financially able to afford access to private sector policing. The Sally Rhodes Agency was known for its discretion, and Monte found that quality worth a hefty annual premium. He was even willing to overlook Sally Rhodes' tactless jibes about his business and taste in *objets d'art*. In a market rife with piracy, Monte Video rarely suffered from bootlegging, and the last large-scale operation to try infringing its copyrights had been permanently retired thanks to Sally Rhodes.

Monte met her in his gallery. The paintings were asleep, but the room was a-whisper with their steady breathing. Sally Rhodes was admiring his shagpile Rothko. 'There is some interesting work being done with sub-sentient jellies and acrylics at the moment, don't you think?' he ventured. The poised young woman turned and held up a hand in mock horror, waving it as if to ward off Dracula with a crucifix. He missed the point.

'That shirt,' she gasped. 'It's . . . it's . . .'

'It's called a paisley pattern,' he told her. 'The lemon yellow and eggshell blue combination is my own idea.'

'You didn't have to tell me, Miki. My grandmother told me about the 1960s. They must have been hell to live through.'

'I wouldn't know. I was very small at the time.'

'And now you're very big?'

'Quite.' He adjusted his chrome and lucite love beads. 'Are you in a position to make a report?'

'Only a preliminary. I note that you've lodged provisional declarations of war against Agfa-Daiei and Disney-McDonald's. You know what kind of commitment that will entail?'

'What choice have I got? Someone's been singeing my remix men. With Tarnaverro gone, there's a severe crimp in my output. It has to be an alliance among the competition. They want me scuppered before Frankfurt.'

'Perhaps,' said Sally Rhodes. She peeled off her domino, and sniffed with distaste the herbal-scented air. 'Do you have a roomscreen handy? I've got a tape to run for you.'

He accessed the downstairs suite, which came complete with a full editing slab, and a glasswall display of Monte Video's topselling remix jobs: *Citizen Kane, Battleship Potemkin, Psycho, Faster Pussycat! Kill! KILL!, King Kong, High Noon, Double Indemnity, The Best of Sergeant Bilko, The Elvis Autopsy Video, The Seventh Seal, The Breakdancin' Nun*. Monte thumbsigned the slab, and a framed poster for the Bob Dylan/Sylvester Stallone/Glenda Jackson/Madonna *Women in Love* remix rose into its ceiling slot, revealing a milkwhite wallscreen. It was the only colourless thing in the house.

Sally Rhodes unscrambled the sequence lock on her briefcase, and produced a video cassette. It was a Monte Video

Own Brand product. 'This is from Tarnaverro's office,' she said. 'I've established that it was what he was working on when he was killed.'

'Then it should be *Captain Blood*?'

'1935, Michael Curtiz, with Errol Flynn and Olivia de Havilland. Warner Brothers. Right?'

'Your pardon?' he double-taked. 'Oh, forgive me, I always forget you're a, what are they called?, film *buff*.' He spat the word with distaste, recalling the petitions that used to flood into his slab.

'Let's pass over that, shall we?' she said, shuffling fiche notes. 'You've kept up on your autopsies, I trust?'

'Yes.'

'But let me remind you. Tarnaverro was attacked by someone with a long, sharp, heavy blade. A carving knife, a machete, or a sword. He was almost literally hacked to pieces.'

'Yes. That's why I suspect those Agfa-Daiei bastards. The multi-nats like to throw in a scare when they open hostilities.' In his struggle to swallow Thorn-Futura-McAlpine before the combine swallowed him, Monte had authorized as bad or far worse. 'And you know what the axis are like.'

Being market leader was a precarious position. Since the Troubles started, with Trevor, Monte Video had lost over 20% of its employees to the marketplace. Even disemployment was better than being an unmourned casualty in a corporate skirmish.

'It may not be that simple, Monte. Have you ever thought to match the methods of assassination used against your people with the properties they were working on?'

Monte was startled. 'No. Why should I?'

Sally Rhodes held up her fiche. 'Trevor was the first. Two months ago. He was blown to bits by some kind of frag charge. He was remixing *Battleground*. Ruby Gee was expertly kicked and trampled to death. Her current assignment, *The Gold Diggers of 1933*. Consodine had his throat ripped out by some kind of animal. Remember the werewolf jokes in the newsies? His last property was *Lassie Come Home*. Do you see it?'

He wanted it keyed out for him.

Sally Rhodes slid *Captain Blood* into the VCR maw, and began to play the buttons. As always when you slot a cassette at random, the sex scene faded on. 'This is the sequence Tarnaverro was remixing when they got him. We had to clean the blood and guts off the tape. The assessor was clogged.'

Onscreen, Errol Flynn was extensively sodomizing the cabin boy. It had seemed wasteful not to feature the star's most legendary endowment in the film, and all the historical research proved that buggery would have been a way of life on the all-male pirate ships of the seventeenth century. Besides, they had wanted to work up a role for the teenage David Bowie. There was a little ghosting, and Tarnaverro's green notation blips came and went in the corner of the image, but otherwise it was fine. It was an effective addition. Sally Rhodes was distracted, not looking at the action, but waiting for something else to appear. 'Look, here it is, here's where it happens – ' she framerfroze ' – look at this line.' There was a thick band of different quality colour, crossing the screen like a ripple. She ADVANCED frame by frame, demonstrating the glitch's progression. It was a diagonal wipe from left to right. Inside the band, the colours were different: a little like the pastel shades of three-strip Technicolor, not very realistic and far too thin for Monte's taste. When the band had passed, all colour had gone. Bowie's face faded into Olivia de Havilland's, and, a cut later, Errol Flynn had his clothes on. There was a ruckus outside the cabin, and Flynn was bounding, cutlass in hand, to the door.

'So this is where Tarnaverro broke off. This is the original version.'

'Not quite,' said Sally Rhodes, tapping a finger to the screen, initiating PAUSE. A horde of pirate extras cowered in tableau as Captain Blood laid into them. They were typical Warner Bros. swashbuckler extras: scarred, scurvy sea-dogs with earrings, three or four knives apiece, striped headscarves, leather boots, stupid expressions. But in the middle was a balding pirate with Coko-doke bottle glasses, and a twopiece whaleskin suit. It was Tarnaverro. The woman took her finger from the screen, and action resumed. In a long shot, Flynn threw off two huge attackers. Tarnaverro was in the mêlée, turning to run. His glasses fell off, and were kicked over the side by a sneering Basil Rathbone. The remix man made a dash for safety, and tripped over De Havilland's skirts. Flynn smiled, impossibly beautiful in the smoke of battle, and ran the interloper cleanly through. He heaved the body off his cutlass, and Tarnaverro fell into the sword-waving throng. The pirates hacked at him merrily. He even got his own close-up, still twitching, eyeballs free-floating, a coil of rope grey under his head. Then, he was out of the film – another dead extra – and Flynn was facing up to Rathbone, jeering at the villain's frenchified ringlets.

Monte was appalled.

'Elaborate, isn't it?'

He had to agree. 'It would take expert remixing to . . . to do *that*. But it's pointless . . .'

The film went on. Monte waved down the sound, but the black and white figures still danced on the wall. He had to think.

'Mr Monte, do you know a Caspasian Kleinzack?'

'Of course. He's a remix man. With Agfa-Daiei. I've been trying to get to him. With the Troubles, we'll need to net a few top defectors to keep up our output. He's not up to my standards, or Tarnaverro's, but he's a professional jobber. Is A-D involved in this?'

'Unlikely. I mention Kleinzack because he's dead too. The newsies haven't got it yet, but he's definitely a casualty. I think A-D have had others, and there's been a total security clampdown at McDisneyworld. Someone doesn't like remix men, Miki. Kleinzack was shot. He was working on *My Darling Clementine*. Do you know the property?'

'1946, John Ford, with Henry Fonda as Wyatt Earp and

Victor Mature as Doc Holliday. 20th Century-Fox. You're not the only one who can remember things. A-D screwed me out of the rights in a nasty negotiation last year.'

She smiled. 'That's the one. A-D buy their policing from the Salvation Army. That's fundamentalism for you. I've got a few friends in The Sal, and I was leaked some fiche. According to them, Kleinzack was deleted with something exotic, a Buntline special. Ever heard of it? No reason you should. It was a white elephant showpiece of the Wild West, with an eleven-inch barrel. Wyatt Earp had one. Do you see the pattern? The Sal aren't saying any more, but it's my guess that if you were to screen Kleinzack's *Clementine*, you'd see a technicolor twitch, and it would wind up with a lab-coated Kraut remix man blundering into the crossfire at the OK Corral and getting his globes shot out.'

Later, after Sally Rhodes had gone, Michaelis Monte had a few stiff drugs. He was rattled, no doubt about it. In previous corporation wars, the higher echelons had been off-limits. You can't negotiate a peace with a frazzled corpse. But this new thing, this campaign of terror, didn't appear to be a particular respecter of the ethics of monetarist diplomacy. He found Sally Rhodes' conclusion unutterably creepy: 'someone, some*thing*, doesn't like what you do, Miki, and is taking extreme measures to shut you, and everyone else in your line, down.'

He was safe in his household. The defences were on, the grounds were secure. There were no human agents in the system to turn traitor, and the governing AI had had its loyalties freshly upgraded. Killflies were loose in the corridors of his retreat – he knew his employees referred to it behind his back as The House on Haunted Hill – and were coded to administer lethal injections to any moving thing that didn't match Monte's displacement configurations. He was as protected as a man could be.

He sat on the psychedelic bubble couch, and looked at his tiger-striped echt-Mondrian. The painting stirred in its sleep. He let the pleasant warmth of a soother seep through his body, calming him. As he watched, the painting's breathing grew ragged. It died, colours fading to grey, jelly congealing behind glass. It had happened before. A fault in the heating. There was nothing to worry about, the soother in his bloodstream told him. Deep in his brain, an unsoothed fragment of his consciousness screamed.

He floated back to his easel room. As he passed the sensors, his body heat registered. Overhead banks of lights lit up, then shut off when he had moved on. There was darkness in front and darkness behind, but he was always in the light. Safe, in white light.

Behind him, black eyes shone in the darkness.

Monte heard the swish, and turned. he couldn't see, but he had a strong afterimage. A tall man, with a heavy cloak.

He had to be alone. A 3-D wallplan proved it. He showed up as an orange pinpoint, winking in a corridor. There were no other warm bodies in the house.

He arrived in the easel room just too late. The twitch was disappearing off the lower right corner of the screen. A black and white picture remained. Monte stood over the easel, and watched as the camera tracked around an empty crypt. Lids fell off coffins, and creepy-crawlies – giant spiders, rats, an armadillo – scuttled in corners. Dracula's sad-eyed wives waited, infinitely patient, in long white shifts for their Master's return.

In his system, the soother reached the zenith of its effect. The tranquillising bulk of the pill had dissolved, putting a potentially dangerous dosage into him, and the emetic core spread in his gut. If he wanted to drug any more, he would have to empty his stomach. He wasn't soothed right now. Fear played his buttons, icy fingertips keyed his vertebrae. He would have to empty his stomach.

His bathroom was mirrored and luxurious, richly carpeted and hung with turquoise and scarlet silks. The design was copied from a Cecil B. DeMille spectacular of the 1920s he had rejected as too outmoded to be worth even a thorough remix. Jewel-encrusted gold taps shone against lime green, veined marble sunken taps. This was the focus, far more than his austere bedroom, of his fantasies and fulfilments.

Monte bent double over a puce and ginger toilet bowl, fashioned like a triton's horn, and vomited tidily. He slammed down the oyster-shaped lid and sat on it. The emetic had a calming side-effect. He felt bad, but was instantly better. He got up and walked to the sink – a mustard replica of the font in Salisbury Cathedral – and washed his face.

Behind him, a door silently opened.

Monte peered minutely at his face in the mirror. It was possible to be flabby and haggard at the same time. He bared his teeth. They were filmed yellow. Then, the thing took him. He saw the hand that gripped his jaw and felt the one in his hair, but neither showed in the mirror. He was held fast by emptiness. Arms like metal bands gripped him. Angling his eyes down, he could see the dark sleeve of a dinner jacket and the black folds of a cloak; but in the mirror (onscreen?) he was struggling only with himself. His paisley collar was yanked away from his neck. Cold lips clamped to his throat, ice-chip teeth sank in . . .

The turquoise and scarlet faded first, turned dead and grey. Then, his shirt calmed down and resolved itself into a dingy, indeterminate smear. His vision slowly bled, the technicolor twitch passing from left to right before his eyes . . .

He felt himself emptying out. Feebly, he raised a hand to push away the unseen face pressed to his throat. He had no more feeling. His hand flapped, chilly and wet, in his field of vision.

The last things he saw were his fingers, stained forever with the black of his own blood.

IAN LEE

Once Upon a Time in the Park

Once upon a time in the Park there used to be quite a lot of equestrianism. And almost every day there was natation in the serpentine lake. On the paths and even on the grass itself there was perambulation of both a directed and an undirected kind. And bicyclists of different ages and levels of fitness were allowed to pedal to work along the road by the lake. On a handful of summer days, after noon and ices at the lakeside pagoda café, there was a display of human heliotropism. More often, there was scope for pluviometry. It was all very constitutional.

Athleticism was tolerated in its place, alongside a little ornithology or urban archaeology. Joggers who were guests at nearby hotels puffed and panted away the excesses of the night before or the night to come. There were team joggers too, running for rugby practices or, in the case of the posse of squaddies from the Royal barracks, sometimes even for punishment. The fattest and most unfit amongst them would pant red-faced and sweaty at a great distance behind the leaders. Tubby tubs of blubber rub-a-dubbing along. It was all very British.

On occasion I used to see Prince and Princess Malcolm out for a morning ride, he looking more and more like George V with each passing season, she remote like a snow-capped Alpine summit atop an eighteen-hand chestnut mare. They were always accompanied by some anonymous bodyguard and sometimes by a lesser royal; for instance, Lady Antonia Doesntmatter, daughter of Princess Margot, or the Duke of Hargood or Avon or one of those other ones who tries to do an ordinary job in the City. Squadrons of cavalry too, some mornings. And on less auspicious days, I would see commoner mortals walking the face of the Earth. Lord Harrington, for instance, or Norman St John Paul Stevens or Sir Roy Geldhough out for a jog before a tough morning's creativity. I know how he must have been feeling. There was a wonderful absence of vehicles, save the odd Panda or a grocery delivery to the café or the restaurant.

When I used to cycle through the Park myself, I found all this uniquely reassuring. Everyone knew his place, you see. There was the illusion of democracy and freedom as the compartments were somehow orchestrated into a picturesque heterogeneity that carried no threat of republicanism.

For Ron, the chargehand gardener, however, the essence of the Park had always been to serve the King through the medium of horticulture. Although the public was allowed in, they were always there on sufferance: they could pass through, they could even stay awhile for a picnic or other recreation but visitors they would remain. They were not encouraged to stay overnight. When horticulture was extended to include the new techniques of bioengineering, this was seen by Roy as a cause for rejoicing, as the scope for service was thereby increased. The area of the Park given over to 'projects' could be increased and the public's access could be more tightly controlled. The notion grew within Ron that the real purpose of the Park could be pursued with increased efficiency and thoroughness and that extraneous activities of the Park could be reduced, curtailed, limited and finally eradicated.

At that time, when I was still a free agent, most things in the Park were still natural. The greatest exception was the deckchairs. These, in their bioengineered form, so closely mimicked the look of their natural prototypes that at twenty paces one could not tell the difference. They grazed upon the sloping sward. But whereas one might once have taken such a description as metaphorical, even poetic, it was now no more than a slightly quaint description of reality. Indeed, they moved so very slowly, nibbled so minutely and collected payment with such delicacy and tact as would surely convert any but the most hardened naturetarian to the benefits of bio-improvement. The natural geese, on the other hand, still messed up the road with excrement of tourist bread and cheese. Ron had not yet perfected the Goose-guano beetle he was working on to clear up after them.

But Ron was not looking to introduce change precipitately. As a gardener, he took his cue from the pace of the natural world. While by no means a haystalk-chewer, he did nevertheless maintain a strong sense of the need for change to be evolutionary and for the strategic plan of the Park's development to include the timescales not only of the marigold and daffodil, but also those of the rhododendron, the camellia, the flowering cherry and the oak. And though he found to his satisfaction that he was extremely adept in all the new bioengineering techniques, he was not tempted to introduce too many new species too fast or to micromanage the lifestyles of all the plants and creatures in his charge.

Ron particularly loved his rose garden. The rose beds were set in an area of lawn fenced off behind low railings at the eastern end of the Park. They were meticulously tended and packed with such an exquisitely balanced stock that from June to September they presented a picture of loveliness that would bring gasps of wonder and delight from all who looked upon them. In the early evening the sweet perfume of La Reine Victoria and the Duke of Windsor (for sentimental reasons Ron favoured the heavily fragrant old roses and floribundas with distinguished names) would hang so sweetly in the air that even the surliest jogger or transiting alcoholic would slow his pace to drink in the beneficent aroma.

Looking back, I can fix the turning point of both my life and Ron's to the very second. The carriages from the Palace were making their fortnightly exercise along the main road through the Park and for once the Lord Chamberlain of the Household had decided to accompany them in order to take the air. It was a fine morning after heavy overnight rain and there was a slight breeze from the east. On passing the rose garden the Lord Chamberlain became aware of the heavenly aroma and called for his carriage to halt. The black horses stood stock still, plumes of breath visible in the cool morning air, the black shiny carriage with the Royal coat of arms standing behind them like a hearse.

As it happened, Ron was walking almost exactly opposite the carriage as it stopped and the whole following scene took place as neatly as though choreographed for a formula TV drama. The Lord Chamberlain addressed Ron directly, seeking to know who was responsible for the roses. Having discovered that the answer was standing before him, he immediately ordered that six dozen of the choicest and most scented blooms should be delivered to the Palace that very morning.

At that same moment I was cycling along, minding my own business (more or less) but had allowed my attention to become distracted by the sight of the Lord Chamberlain, who was tall, distinguished and wearing a black morning coat, in conversation with Ron, who was round-shouldered, shifty and had his overalls held up with a tie.

Some days in the Park, when the tarmac is wet and the sun is still low in the morning sky, the glare from the road is so intense that one cannot see where one is going at all. On this particular day, thus distracted and blinded from all normal sensory contact and control, and at the very moment the Lord Chamberlain was ordering the six dozen roses for His Majesty, I crashed into a Panificio Siciliano bakery lorry, which was intent on delivery to the lakeside restaurant and coming along on the wrong side of the road. I was killed outright.

The postillion of the Royal landau, unfortunately, was listening to a personal stereo and remained unaware of my plight, which was beyond the scope of his peripheral vision. The Lord Chamberlain's senses were fully occupied with the roses and Ron's were fully occupied with the Lord Chamberlain. The bakery driver, who had a part-time job in the Paddington mafia and didn't want to get involved with the police, made an extraordinarily rapid assessment of this situation and then scooped up my body and my bicycle and threw it into the back of his lorry along with the big brown paper sacks of French sticks. An hour later, unobserved, he left my remains in some rhododendron bushes behind a statue dedicated to the cavalry of the Empire, which is where Ron found me late that afternoon.

One thing you have to admire about Ron is his far-sightedness. He had already, within hours, realized that a special relationship with the Lord Chamberlain of the Household and a contract to supply roses could well be the opportunity of a lifetime. Somehow Ron knew that, like the inexorable burgeoning of a wigwam of sweet peas, this opportunity would grow and grow but would need food and attention if it was to survive. He knew that his empire was going to expand and that he would need more resources of all practical kinds. When he came across my body, still fresh, and the discarded bicycle, still oiled, he knew that an evening's work in the laboratory could produce something very useful at almost no cost.

I was never heard of again. Work thought I was ill, home thought I was just staying late at the office or had gone on somewhere for a drink or someone's leaving or birthday party. By the time I was reported missing – late the next morning – there was no evidence of where I had gone at all.

For many weeks life in the Park showed no discernible change. As I went round with Ron about his business, helping him carry manure for the roses, I became more familiar with the range of life within the Park. Ron would talk to me about it; he knew that he had restored some sentience to my creaking frame, though to this day I cannot be sure whether he knew how much. He spoke as though he were speaking to himself and it was thus that I became aware of his deepest fears and longings. I also, of course, without volition and therefore without guilt, became his accomplice.

The mornings remained quiet, even stately, and very British, the riders, swimmers, walkers, tramps, soldiers and occasional celebrities acknowledging each other's presence with the barest nods of recognition, each wrapped in his or her own private communion with nature. Later in the day, the swarms of tourists would invade, running, littering, sprawling and trampling without thought beyond immediate gratification of base desires. The stench of decayed meat began to float from the franchised hot-dog and burger cabins. Ron would become more and more irritable as the day went on, as this scum formed on the surface of his beloved Park, as the deckchairs were abused, as people who were really no better than common peasants would use the rides for sand fights or even open defecation.

By the early evening on a warm summer day the scene by the serpentine lake would metamorphose again from the morning's Britishness into a Byzantine phantasmagoria. Half close your eyes and you could imagine yourself on the corniche at Abu Dhabi. Swarthy faces and flashing eyes and wrists patrolled the lakeside drag. There were sheikhs and princes (at least Ron said they were) and lofty Bedu, leavened with darker faces and crinkly hair from Zanzibar or the smaller, wirier shopkeeper class from Gujerat via Dubai. Ron had learned the distinctions of caste like a true phylum/species-trained horticulturalist. Away to the west and north-east the jewellery and perfume counters of Selfridges and Harrods lay in ruins. Back here men in white shoes and bracelets, neck chains and open-necked shirts would parade with the nonchalance of the very rich. Behind them, wrapped dolls waddled in black, faces beaked. Other dolls adopted a different style, brightly coloured in silks and taffeta that fluoresced in the early evening sun. Perfume clouds trailed behind them like a fog.

On benches by the side of the road sat cabals of older men, their walking sticks propped beside them as they watched life unfold. The waves of young people would lap along the shore, linking arms, unlinking arms, turning in twos and threes, forming and unforming in smaller and longer lines like some vast slow Levantine parody of a chorus line. Small children in designer dungarees weaved in and out of the throng on brand new roller skates or bicycles. They would obstruct the innocent passers-by with the insolent contempt of the true believer for the infidel. The tables turned indeed. But for them the wheel was a toy, whereas for me it is now a way of life.

I've been wheeling through the Park for so long now and been having so many different thoughts about its features that I've come close to thinking I can adopt the identity of any of the normal features of the Park itself. Ask me to be a Canada goose and in the flap of a feather there I am on the end of that enormous wobbling V gliding through the heavens. Ask me to be a boathouse and I can stand at the water's edge decaying gracefully unnoticed. But deep down I know that these are only the idle fantasies of a creature who has been bioengineered once back from the dead and become morosely fascinated with both the potential of the techniques but also their terrible limitations.

Though a genius in many ways, Ron did not have a fully developed or balanced imagination. When he discovered my body and wrecked bicycle, he was preoccupied with thoughts of his new role as purveyor of blooms to the Royal Household and was thinking about all the extra fetching and carrying he was going to have to do. What he did therefore was turn these fortuitous remains into a self-propelling and partially self-loading wheelbarrow with some simple digging and raking capability. It is not really what I had planned for myself and I have not yet managed to convince myself that it is a noble calling.

But a wheelbarrow is what I now am.

Anyway, as I said, for some weeks in the Park nothing discernible changed. But gradually the Palace's requirements for flowers started to grow and in addition to roses they started to ask for irises, gloxinias, carnations, chrysanthemums, sweet peas, tiger lilies and many other varieties. Day by day, imperceptibly at first but then with an ineluctable momentum, Ron's pace of activity started to increase. He began to tell me how things were getting too much for him, though try as he might he didn't have it in him to complain. For Ron's devotion to the monarchy was as total as his craving for perfection in gardening and his suspicion of outsiders of any kind. The thought that he had now achieved a position of prominent service to the Royal Household filled him with an overwhelming pride and dedication that was close to fanaticism. There was no question of not responding to the challenge and Ron could not let the grass grow under his feet.

He could see that the requirements were set on an upward path and he could see that a plan was necessary. Ron's plan, arrived at in long conversations with himself as he and I ferried horse manure from the gathering points along the rides to the original famous rose garden, had three parts.

First, there was a need to increase manpower and productivity. Second, it would be necessary to expand the area devoted to production and consequently reduce and control the depredations of the so-called public. Third, he would have to find ways to bump up the yield from the earth itself.

Ron was not the only gardener, of course, but he was

the chargehand and, I think, the only one still fully human. The other gardeners, once naturals too (though some of them perhaps not in the present generation), were now adapted into shadowy creeping figures, underlings who rooted for weeds in the undergrowth like vermin. They rarely came out into full sunlight except perhaps in the very early morning when there was still a fresh dew to lick from the grass. Ron would tease the school-leavers amongst them good-humouredly. 'Mind where you're licking that grass, young Davey!' he would call. 'That's where the dogwalkers let them do it!' Then he would wink at any curious passer-by and say, 'It isn't really' and give a throaty chuckle.

As the first part of the plan, Ron made a bid to the Park authorities for more school-leavers and made arrangements in the laboratory to optimize their adaptation in favour of horticulture and play down the other park-keeper functions such as litter-collection and being friendly to the tourists. In fact, park-keeping was quite a popular option. Fashion was moving against the electronic adaptation which school-leavers who went into offices were forced to undergo; electronics were regarded as rather passé and being turned into a personal computer had come to be seen as nothing better than a rather macabre joke. On the other hand there was an upsurge of interest in the natural sector, including farming, reserve management and park-keeping. Guard-dog and horse characteristics were probably the most popular but there was no great difficulty over some of the more agricultural or artisanal adaptations either. The bulk of Ron's workforce ended up somewhere between an old-fashioned navvy and a dog. It was hard to place them exactly on the social scale but somewhere close to the level of the pig/roadsweepers or the goat/office cleaners wouldn't be far wrong, I suppose. Most of them were quite happy.

Once he had the extra manpower Ron set about extending the cultivated area. He had noticed one or two of the more ill-bred tourists picking flowers from beds that were only protected by low ornamental railings, so some of the new recruits were set to building high interwoven wood fences. Elsewhere, Ron planted thick pyracantha hedges on a plan which, within three or four years, was to reduce the open area of the Park to a quarter of its former extent. To protect the pyracantha in the meantime high wire screens were erected and the public were directed into an ever smaller sector by the lake's edge.

But always the bagladies, the messengers and the dogwalkers were trying to encroach. 'I can deal with the ordinary public,' Ron was fond of saying to me, as we trundled some fresh load of fenceposts to the latest enclosure, 'but some of these bloody weirdo groups are no better than terrorists.' The bagladies were a strange bunch. Displaced from their traditional habitat on the Embankment by new development and hounded from the streets of the city by the new breeds of dog-police, they had started to try to colonize the outer fringes of the Park. They were naturals themselves, of course, and in their unadapted state, ironically enough, were singularly ill-equipped to deal with the more natural conditions in the Park as it was. As the Park under Ron's supervision became more intensively organized, however, so it became a more attractive habitat to the bagladies. And when he (we) branched out into vegetables, the pressure of the bagladies' advance became a major preoccupation.

The messengers and the dogwalkers were a different problem, though both equally anarchic in their way. The messengers were young men and women who had been grafted into bicycles and whose job it was to make deliveries across the city. The Park lay on one of their main routes and they did not take kindly to some of the new restrictions being imposed by Ron. The dogwalkers were local residents, many of them influential: magistrates, justices of the peace, church wardens. They, too, objected to the infringement of their freedom to wander in the Park. But deep down even they felt the sovereign mystery of ancient hereditary power and, trembling, shrank from the thought of choking the Royal nourishment.

The fences sometimes got pulled down nonetheless and sometimes tracks would be found in the new beds, or signs of paws having dug in search of bones. A few times the bagladies came at night and broke through into the greenhouses where it was warm and there was straw. Once a couple of them were found dead after eating something that might have looked like a tomato but was really only the halfway stage in an experiment of Ron's. But what's a baglady more or less in this city nowadays, said Ron. If they didn't die peacefully in here from eating a mutant tomato then they'd be out there getting mown down by the motorcycle delivery gangs or being forcibly rehabilitated by the caring constables.

The police called round for a chat, ostensibly just to pass the time of day. They seemed more interested in the state of Ron's nursery than they ever had before. Sergeant Bulstrode listened to Ron describing his plans for the future and his explanation of how the fatal tomato came to be in the greenhouse rather than a safe laboratory. Having considered the matter, the officer decided that, in the circumstances, there was insufficient evidence of foul play to warrant pursuing an investigation, especially as one of the certain consequences would be disruption of the supply of vegetables and flowers to the Royal Household. He didn't have the bottle.

As he was leaving, however, the worthy sergeant flexed his nostrils at the door of Ron's workshop (I was standing just outside) and said, almost as some sort of self-exculpatory joke:

'I think I smell a rat.'

Ron looked startled for a moment and then looked down at a pile of dead *ratti norvegici* that had been rounded up from the margins of the lake that morning by a special sniffer squad of his own bioengineered spaniel/parkhands.

'Ah yes,' said Ron, winking slyly at me. 'We can't have vermin eating the Royal vegetables, can we?'

As the weeks went by, Ron became noticeably shiftier, sure evidence that he was working to his plan. As I said, the third part of the plan was to make the earth itself more fructiferous. I first noticed how he had become disappointed with his geraniums and had fretted for days over what he was going to do about them. 'They really need bringing on a bit,' he would say, half to himself, half to me, as he stood over the beds, letting a handful of soil trickle through his fingers like sand. He'd tried a whole lot of different remedies and all the bioengineering tricks suggested by the Expert System but still they didn't really grow the way he liked to see them grow. He'd begun by getting the parkhands to start a premium compost heap, consisting entirely of natural organic vegetable matter. Then he had us all out on shit patrols. 'Goose and dog, and try and get us a little bit of mallard, will you?' he'd say. 'Them geraniums love a little bit of mallard in between their toes.'

I suppose it was a natural progression from bread to compost to goose guano and then on to dead animals. Ron would have said it was the natural order of things, a question of hierarchy. His first move into the sentient field was a cull of the moorhen population on the lake. 'Too many of them,' he said imperiously, hitching up his overall trousers, then looking over his shoulder with a little duck of the head like a guilty schoolboy. 'No one's interested in bloody moorhens anyway.' Tragic perhaps, but one could hardly deny that he was right.

But it didn't stop there. Before we knew where we were he was on to the mallard, then the tufted duck, then the pochard, then the Canada geese, then the great-crested grebe, then the mute swans and finally the black. Ron had a finely developed sense of hierarchy indeed. If a cormorant or three were to happen by for a few days away from the coast, they would be lucky to escape the netting parties. He even took a heron one morning, which put a spring in his step for the rest of that day.

Ron had branched out into vegetables in a big way and he was doing really well. He had a contract with the palace that was little short of phenomenal. They were really doing some entertaining down there these days, what with all the grandchildren and the parties. The Gay Prince was living up to his sobriquet in both the common and the archaic senses of the word. In the summer there were garden parties practically every day, leading to cucumber consumption on a scale unmatched anywhere in the Western world. And Ron, shifty old Ron, still given to shrugging and looking over his shoulder as though the crops were after him, had got an enormous piece of the action. One might even suspect that his simple devotion to the service of the monarchy could not help becoming tainted with simple greed.

Most of the Park was now under cultivation. The bagladies had been pushed back and there was high barbed wire to keep the dogwalkers out from where they weren't wanted. More security guards had been 'developed' by crossing some of the old ones with stray policemen or soldiers, especially some of the tubbiest stragglers from the morning runs. 'Don't really matter about the fat,' said Ron. 'Let's be honest; the sedentary type of guarding duty don't really require athletes, now do it?'

Toll charges on the lakeside road together with turnstiles at either end had succeeded in eliminating the messengers. Only the Arabs could still afford to stroll there at teatime, which they did, imagining themselves by the Gulf, the rowing boats as dhows, the shoreside market selling produce and trinkets like the souk in far-off Muscat, fragrant, dangerous and eternal. They seemed oblivious of what was actually going on around them.

The Royals still used what they could of the Park, of course. After all it was still their Park. The turnstiles were pulled aside in the mornings to allow them through with their bodyguards for their morning ride. They waved minimally at Ron and me as if they saw us and looked at amazement at the acres of crops we were now superintending. Sometimes a lofty nostril might be seen to curl at the sight of a lowly parkhand forking something mushy and corrupted into the soil; for the Royals came to the Park now not for exercise but as on some kind of pilgrimage. Though goodness was not obvious at all stages of the wondrous plants' production, they had experience of its emergence in the final culinary sacrament. They looked upon their land and went home uplifted and content.

The fact was that Ron's vegetables were coming to have near-legendary taste and quality, and the Royal Family was growing strong upon them. Regular visitors to the Palace were clamouring, often in a quite unseemly fashion, to be invited back, as they too felt their strength and wealth increasing in direct proportion to the number of dinners and lunches they had. Ron was hard-pressed to keep up with demand. He set up subsidiary market gardens in other Parks throughout the capital; but the Palace responded by taking over more buildings and starting to host more dinners. In a very few weeks a spiralling metaphorical waterspout of horticultural activity and consumption could be seen tottering heavily above the city. Instead of the boats and fish and seaweed of Biblical memory, this twister was devouring cartloads of artichokes, asparagus, aristocrats and cut flowers.

And as court society thrived, so did the creation of new peerages, viscountcies and dukedoms. This novice aristocracy found itself surrounded with the sort of people it could do business with and what's more in such agreeable circumstances and at such delectable boards. The King became insulated from his people as the richness and power of Ron's produce was absorbed into the bloodstream of his body politic like a drug.

But Ron, both figuratively and then literally, ended up getting carried away. First, there were simply one or two reports of dogs not coming back to their owners. The dogwalkers, relegated to the periphery of the Park, began, in response, to form vigilante groups and walk their dogs in groups for safety. Bull mastiffs, Alsatians, Dobermanns became the most popular breeds. Dark satanic rumours started circulating among the bagladies and they began to stay well clear of the Parks.

Then, one morning during a particularly hard gallop one of the Royal bodyguards was found unconscious after having become separated from his charges. His horse had disappeared. Fortunately Ron was at hand to explain that it had thrown its rider and had broken a leg and had had to be destroyed on the spot and he had just been trying to be helpful by disposing of the body. The bodyguard himself had concussion and wasn't able to provide an explanation of how he had come to be thrown in the first place. No one sought to question Ron's account of what happened because after all, didn't he have the big vegetable contract with the Palace? As far as I was concerned, the horse was the largest load I had wheeled and it was more than I would like to try again.

But Ron's inner zeal had begun to sprout and in the dark corners of his soul was beginning to grow strongly and head for the light. The leaves were falling and the tourists came and went. Not quite as many went as came but what the hell, said Ron (to me, when we were alone), who notices a little Japanese tourist more or less? Or an Arab. Or an African, don't get me wrong, or a Greek or a Yank, I'm no racist, or an Aussie. The hoteliers just think they've skipped without paying their bills and since they've been ripping them off anyway they don't bother to report anything. Their cousins and mothers and uncles and brothers in the desert or the outback just think they've gone native in the lucrative seductive West. More camels for us, they say, so why should we worry?

But when a minor Royal went missing the authorities no longer found it possible to turn a blind eye. Lady Helen Somethingorother, quite well down the chain, not even rating a personal bodyguard, was the first to go. But the police were in the next day, sniffing around, trying to interrogate any parkhands with the power of speech. And although Ron managed to keep them off the scent, they spent a few awkward weeks asking lots of questions without ever really digging up anything they could use.

Ron lay low for a while but one day the Lord Chamberlain raised an eyebrow as if to convey the message that the quality of the courgettes was in detectable decline. It was enough for Ron to feel that he was on a slippery slope towards treason and that he had once more to devote himself with new zeal to his primary objective – the service of the King. Soon a few other minor nobles ceased to respond to dinner invitations – Lord Harrington, the 3rd Duchess of Grantham, whose great-grandmother had once been Prime Minister, Viscount Savile OBE – and though there was never any evidence, nevertheless eventually the rumours reached the King.

Ron was summoned for an audience and the King asked all the right questions. Ron, in awe and wonder that he should actually be in his Sovereign's presence, found it hard to do more than shrug his shoulders and look shifty. But in the end his devotion reached down to release the catch on some deep trapdoor of honesty within him and Ron fell through. Yes, the success of his vegetables was due to the extra special quality of the compost he used and yes it did involve special organic matter all right higher organic material all right all right human organic matter yes noble human organic matter. Yes it had started with leaves and discarded sandwiches and had moved up the hierarchy through horse manure to dead pigeons to rats to dogs to horses yes and each time the fertilizer had moved up the evolutionary chain the flowers had become a little brighter and the vegetables had become a little more tasty and yes nutritious. But the need was there, your Majesty thrived; there is no higher honour than to serve your Majesty.

'Except, it seems, to be served *to* His Majesty,' remarked the King, almost under his breath, appalled and delighted by this example of loyalty and allegiance he beheld. Then louder, so that the court could hear, he said:

'You, Ron, have a heart and spirit finer than that of any noble in our Kingdom. We will be forever in your debt for the bounty you have heaped on us and our family. You realize, however, that natural laws have been broken and that amends must be made. We must consider what is to be done.'

The King paused for a long moment, his gaze steady on Ron's abject kneeling figure, then said:

'Leave us now.'

Ron rose with a new steadiness in his shoulders, not shrugging or looking behind him. He came back to the Park and winked in sombre mood as he gave us our instructions.

So it was that, after the digitalis from his favourite patch of foxgloves had been administered and after some of the inner circle of parkhands had minced and pelletized his body, I had the honour and the sorrow – in accordance with his last wish – of wheeling Ron's body to the rose garden where his great career had begun. I tipped his remains into shallow trenches – at roughly nine-inch intervals – and with my rake hand that had once been a bicycle-chain wheel I spread the rich earth over his final act of devotion.

RICHARD CALDER

Mosquito

Our rendezvous, the *Café Gung-Ho*: he, iridescent in the one shaft of light to breach its Happy Hour shade, and I, seeing that beauty for the first time, poised in the doorway, thinking Fatal, O so fatal. The bar was deserted, save Harry, a few girls (humans, no gynoids; Harry is a purist), and the radiant one, tall, blonde, and cobra-eyed. Breathless, I went to meet him. Dressed like a man, I tried to walk like a man. But I was restive; I wanted to flirt. My *alter ego*, imprisoned by day within this safe-house of masculinity, rattled the bars of her cage and sulked.

'Kuhn Harry, I sorry,' I said in my best Charlie Chan, 'Zipper not tell me you want. I come straight here.' We assumed our roles. I played the all-purpose oriental; Harry, the street-smart Brooklyn babe to whom, far from home, unsure of yourself, you could confess your appetites and trust your money.

'Yeah. Don't worry about it. Lord Chandos don't want to hear about Zipper.' Acquainted with my schoolgirl crushes, and seeing how I had abandoned myself to those bodice-ripping eyes, Harry concluded 'Let's talk business,' and ordered drinks. I made the *wai*; sat down; a Mekong appeared before me.

'Lord Chandos wants to take a girl back to London.' The boss paused for sales-pitch effect. 'A *dtook-gah-dtah*.' Of course. Why else was I here? Milord wanted a wind-up toy, a doll. I stole them; Harry fenced them. Our customer – despite the insistence of his beauty – was just another *farang* exhausted by human love; one whose lack of credit had led him east to seek the services of a rustler. But what beauty it was; a beauty from the land of ice and snow where, once, I had been happy.

'Dtook-gah-dtah?' I said. 'No problem. My speciality. What kind of girls you like, sir?'

'Bad girls,' he said, deadpan. 'And call me James.'

'Yes, Mr James. Cartier? Rolex? Tiffany? All fake, of course. All imitation. But very good quality. Very reasonable price.'

'Harry tells me half-a-million gets me Cartier.'

'You have good taste. Cartier doll very nice. Very *Déco*. Very bad. But doll have no rights, no civil status. You need passport or you never get her out of country.'

'Passport's my department,' said Harry. 'It'll need a visa, too. I do both for 200,000 baht.'

The Englishman sighed. 'I'm no longer a wealthy man, Harry.' Sweet *farang*, I could believe it. You seemed one of those ruined European aristocrats who, impoverished by debts, sought our cheap imitations of the toys to which they had become addicted but could no longer afford. Automata were the playthings of the rich; but here in sex-city (where the boys are so pretty), city of angels, dolls, and of night, we fake everything – TVs, software, designer jeans, life.

'In all the world,' I said, 'you cannot get better price. And anyone tell you Mr James, Thai lady-dolls are number one.'

'We're putting ourselves at considerable risk. Apart from the trouble of lifting a doll, the Eurobunnies – sorry, James – are down on us for copyright infringement. Someone out there has killed three doll-rustlers this month alone. It's hot: we don't do this for fun.' Our customer looked uncertain and Harry proceeded with the hard-sell. 'Mosquito's just amazing. He'll get you a Cartier doll, no sweat. He can pass through the pornocracies – Patphong, Nana, Cowboy, Suriwong – like a ghost through walls.'

'As you say,' said the stranger, inhaling languorously on his cigarette, *'amazing.'* He looked askance, ready to snare my reaction, adding, with studied disinterest, 'What's the secret?' Against my will, ravished, a sad, sad slave to lust, I smiled conspiratorially. Harry saw (he knows my little ways), and drummed his fingers on the table.

'Secret is 700,000 baht. Half of it up-front. Secret is no one knows outside this room. Secret is letting us do our job with no questions asked. Then you get your *dtook-gah-dtah* and everyone's happy.'

Milord swept back his golden hair. '700,000 baht,' he reflected. 'I'll have to think it over.' Harry's lips didn't move, but his face screamed Timewaster! The stranger pushed aside his glass and rose. 'I've some things to do. . . . Nice bar you have here.' Harry picked up a copy of the *Bangkok Post* and pretended to scan it.

'You know where to find me . . .'

'And good to meet you, Mosquito.' His right hand was gloved, concealing, perhaps, a prosthesis. Teasingly, he squeezed my arm. It was an intimation of fellowship, of understanding. 'Mosquito: why do they call you that?'

'Just a name,' I said, 'a silly name.'

And then he was gone.

When he had touched me, I had felt a pin-prick in my arm, like a discharge of static. I lifted my shirt-sleeve and recognized the tell-tale mark – like that of an insect-bite – left by an epidermic tracer.

'What's wrong?' said Harry.

'Mosquito bite Mosquito,' I said, scratching. Harry burrowed into his paper. A nasty, unidentified virus simply called *klong fever* was ravaging Bangkok. It was said to be transmitted by insect-bites, only affect males, and leave its victims impotent. But since no *farang* had been known to succumb, Harry had shown little concern.

The tracer could be removed with tweezers; but its itch, counterpointing that which I felt in my loins, made me reluctant to destroy it. I wanted him; and he, it seemed, wanted me. Did I ask myself why? No, my darlings. Mosquito has an extravagant heart. Closing my eyes, I beheld the blazing lines of Mr James dancing across my retina, like the afterimage of a fierce summer's day your aching eyes have forestalled on. I saw him, incandescent among dark, London streets, a lean man dressed in light, window-shopping for automata. His cold eyes appraise their wonderful, jewelled forms, as he walks down Piccadilly and into Bond Street. And there, in a Cartier showroom, he sees me, and falls hopelessly in love.

I heard Harry throw aside his paper; the scrape of his chair. 'Make hoochie-coochie with a customer again,' he said, 'and I'll break your arms.'

That's Harry.

That evening, back at my condo, I prepared for work. Seiko mechanettes (they of the regenerative maidenhead) had recently been decanted for bars in the Silom Road, and Harry wanted a report. On the heat-ruptured surface of my dresser I placed my creams, paints, and powders, my unguents and emollients; then, laying out my she-clothes, I sloughed off my daytime skin and became The Doll. My alias winked at me from the other side of the mirror. She has a delicate, child-like face, my sister, with vestiges of puppy-fat about the cheeks. Bobbed hair gives her an appearance of delinquency, as do the eyes, crescent and puckish, burning like black suns. The lips are set in a pout, communicating both desire and disdain. And the complexion – the faultless, lacquered flesh of the gynoid – proclaims her synthetic. Her sartorial ensemble? A leopard-print body-stocking and six-inch stilettos. The genitals, of course (always a problem), have to be secured with scotch-tape, giving the appearance of a distended *mons veneris*. I smiled, checking my fangs. Perfect.

I lay on the bed and browsed through some physical culture magazines while the radio murmured of love lost and found to the indifferent whup, whup, whup of the fan. The microscopic transmitter throbbed, caterwauling across the city to Milord. I pressed it to my lips. Instantly, the imperative of that evening's work was subverted by a premonition that he would call, not tomorrow, not next week, but tonight. And I preened myself, again and again, jittery as a girl preparing for her first date. My deceptions were unrivalled, if incomplete. Harry, who had paid for my implants and other, more radical, surgery, had insisted I retain a flow of testosterone in my veins. Only a man could imitate a doll. Women, it was said, were too real. For dolls are not women; they are man's dream of women. Made in man's image, they are an extension of his sex, female impersonators built to confirm his prejudices, sexual illusionists. I too was practised in sexual-sleight-of-hand, my womanhood as unreal and as pathologically exquisite as a doll's. So exquisite, it was almost grotesque.

The intercom buzzed. 'Someone to see you, Madame,' said Zip. 'A Mr – ' But Zip was given no time to complete the formalities. Instead of 'James' (my heart lurched, telling me it was so) came the announcement of electromagnetic crackle and bar-brawl sound effects. I rolled off the bed, nauseous with anticipation. The hallway stank of roasted bakelite. Mr James had been unnecessarily heavy-handed; Zip was a valet, not a security guard (though his cosmetic musculature and barrel-chest often led people to conclude otherwise). I breathed deeply, trying to remember my lines, quell my stage-fright, ignore the anxious clickety-clack of my high-heels on the teakwood parquetry. I made my entrance.

Milord stood over a broken coffee-table, silk jacket ripped, panama askew, his leather-gloved prosthesis smoking; and Zip, horizontal amid the debris, scorch-marks either side of his shaven head, looked up at him dead-eyed with a demeanour as hard and vulnerable as the Mapplethorpe portraits that lined my walls. Hands on hips, lips quivering like a spoilt, refractory child's, I cued-in: 'You want kill me too?' His eyes grazed my body like the featherlight tips of rapiers. It was a good body, I reassured myself; an expensive body; a body I always regretted having to camouflage by day. Exaggeratedly feminine, it was grafted onto a small-boned, somewhat adolescent infrastructure, like a piquant allegory of innocence burdened by desire. 'You very naughty, Mr James. Just look at poor Zipper!'

'Mosquito?' I curtsied in acknowledgment. 'Good God, I've seen lots of he-shes in Bangkok and some of *them* were fantastic . . . but you . . . Seems you might be worth all this trouble.'

'I think Trouble your middle name, Mr James.'

'Sorry about Man Friday.'

'Not organic. Not *modern* doll. Backed-up. Running in an hour.' He straightened his hat and fumbled in his pockets.

'Chocolates? Flowers?' I asked, mock-expectant.

'Seem to have lost my cigarettes.' I bent down, retrieving a silver cigarette case lying beneath a scree of broken glass. I helped myself.

'Light me.' Like a tiny, nervous dragon, a Dupont flickered and withdrew. 'Nice lighter.'

'Nice workmanship,' he said, screwing a monocle into his eye, and awarding me a detailed examination. 'Unreal.'

'Unreal as a doll. Unreal as love . . .'

'And cool. I'm impressed.'

'Tracer. Stung me in *Gung-Ho*. I know you come. I not stupid.'

'I don't believe you are, dear boy, or you would never have allowed me to find you.'

'Curiosity, Mr James.'

'Desperation, I'd guess. O, I know all about *you* Mosquito . . .' He turned his back to me, stepping over Zipper and walking to the window, to stare down at the night-transfigured city thirty floors below. 'Aren't you tired of working for that American pimp? Is he the one who tells you not to speak and act like some second-rate Suzie Wong?'

I let fall a tear, not altogether crocodile, but prompted more by the exigencies of coquetry than by genuine sorrow or regret. It was wasted. He did not deign to look me in the face.

'Harry likes me to talk that way,' I said, throwing off my Third World guise. 'Says it reassures the clients. What *exactly* do you know about me James?'

'Everything, little Mosquito . . .' A blue-grey nimbus of spent nicotine was forming above his head, like the signature of a prosecuting angel. 'How would you describe your childhood?'

'Idyllic.' He laughed.

'Spoilt little rich boy. Your father a big name in sericulture. And your youth?'

'Gilded.'

'But O so soon tarnished! You studied at Cambridge, yes?'

'I was happy there . . .'

'I'm an Oxford man myself. Anyway, you took a postgrad in Comparative Literature. Your thesis: "The Second Decadence: Literature of the 1990s." Then you got into that scrape with Lord Dagenham's son. And he only fourteen. How *wicked*. Your father ordered you back to Thailand. Cut you off without a satang. Poor Mosquito, it's been downhill ever since . . .'

'How do you know all this? And why tell me?'

'Because I'm feeling philanthropic, dear boy. How much money do you get from the American?'

'Not enough to leave him. The apartment's his. He keeps nearly all the money from our jobs. Even Zipper's on loan. My father's made it impossible for me to get a decent job . . .'

'I wouldn't have you wasted on decency, Mosquito. The next job – it's going to be just you and me. And this time you'll take enough of the percentage to enable you to shake Harry off for good.'

'So much?'

'I need my doll, Mosquito. My Cartier doll. And I need

her tonight. Passport, visa – I have my own contacts for that. But I must have my doll before morning.'

'Do you need your doll so bad, James?'

'Name your price.' He about-faced; I held his reptilian stare. There had been other Englishmen. Some, quite pretty. None had offered me escape. But I had known that one would come who would be special, who I would recognize by his incomparable beauty, who would, at last, carry me off to his castle in the sky. My prince.

'I don't want money, James,' I said tremulously, 'I want to go back to the land of ice and snow. Take me with you, James. Take me to England.' In petulance, he swung open the plate-glass doors and stepped onto the veranda. The tropical night crashed into the room. I followed him outside.

'Dear boy, what sort of foolishness is this?'

'The first time I saw you . . .' I began; but he cut me short.

'Please – let's not make this complicated. Mosquito, you don't want to go to Europe.' He waved his hand over the roofs of Bangkok. 'Look out there. You think Europe can compete with this? The Old World is dead, Mosquito. Names: that's all she has. The names of her jewellers and goldsmiths, her clockmakers and couturiers. And now even they are being taken from her. Forget Europe, Mosquito. She has been plundered and raped. Nobody speaks of her any more.'

Below us, the city glistened like a well-oiled body, rippling under the stars. It offered forbidden technologies; flaunted stolen ideas. It mocked the impotent West. Europe had sickened, its economy in misrule. An empire of style, it had surrendered manufacturing to the Pacific Rim and the Americas, investing instead in the refinement of those luxury goods coveted by the Information Revolution's *arrivistes*: jewels and perfumes, elegancies of cloth and design, and, most perverse of fabulations, the *automata*. But with the passing of the *aube de millénium,* Europe's fashion-masters were confronted by a world increasingly fickle, increasingly Philistine. Japanese disinvestment prompted recession, and from the Atlantic to the Urals, the continent was eclipsed by foreign vulgarizations of its genius.

James was very still. I rested my head against his shoulder, and he let it stay. Like so many of his kind, he had come to ask the sweat-shops of Bangkok to provide consolation for his lost toys. Outside, tattooed upon towers of glass and jade, vast holograms of Buddha recalled the transitoriness of all things.

'I can do it, James.'

'I used to have a collection. Even as a child,' he said, in child-like reverie. 'Being without them these last few years . . .' And those cold, grey eyes softened. 'It's been hard,' he said, 'hard.' His flesh was hard. I felt its panel-beaten contours through the cool silk of his Italian suit; and on tip-toes, I sought his mouth. He arched an eyebrow, his face hectic with the effort, it seemed, to at once express irony, contempt, and desire. 'So little Mosquito wants to be my R and R?'

'I want – I want to be your doll.' I pulled his head down and found his lips. 'Please,' I said, 'I want to be part of your collection . . .'

'Cartier? Tonight?' he mumbled.

'Yes,' I answered, 'anything.' And not unreluctantly, he allowed me to kiss him.

In time I was sure I could make him love me.

A *tuk-tuk* sped me along the Sukumvit Road. Before leaving I'd thrown on a skirt – just long enough to conceal the bifurcation of my thighs – and put in my green, luminous contacts: trademark of a Cartier doll. (Cartier nanoengineers in Geneva had revived Jeanne Toussaint's panther-jewellery designs of the 1930s.)

I had arranged to meet James later at the *Honey Hotel*, where I would present him with my catch. Nana Plaza would be my hunting-ground.

At Soi Asoke I hailed a long-tailed boat, the *klongs*

having reclaimed much of the city, making it once more the Venice of the East. The taxi churned the dark waters of Sukumvit, scattering the reflected images of pagodas and shopping-malls that sat like peroxide lilies on a black pond stained white by the city's glare. The traffic thickened and before me rose Nana, a gigantic lily-pad, pale and bright, a night-bloom releasing its bouquet of sex into the smog-filled air. Above, an insect-sussuration: autogyros, caught like moths in searchlights panning the sky, were falling to earth in swarms, unloading cargoes of sweet-toothed breeders eager for Nana's delights. I paid my ferryman and alighted.

Nana was doll-city, very gynoidal, very het. It still possessed some of the shantytown ambience of sixty years ago, when it had soothed the nightmares of American GIs; but now, superimposed upon its skyline of poured concrete and twentieth-century slum, were undulating whip-lash curves and geometric lines copied from the European *art nouveau* and *art déco* renaissance of the *aube de millénium*. This stylistic heterogeneity was exemplified in the person of Nana's mammasan, Madame Kito. Kito, the daughter of a *farang* and a doll, belonged to that caste of half-humans we called *bijouterie*: hybrid jewels as distinguished from all-precious *joaillerie*. Ostracized by humans and automata alike, *bijouterie* lived as pariahs, envying and hating those whose holistic integrity so rebuked them. Whenever I came to Nana, Kito's lonely, jealous, violent heart called to mine.

I moved through a confluence of dolls. A few repros were at work – ball-jointed, porcelain-skinned 'antiques' who offered their brass, umbilical keys to passers-by – as well as a handful of aboriginals – non-reflective pieces of walking, talking AI, who, like Zipper, were from a time before nanotechnology replaced microelectronics. In one doorway, a matching pair of crystal torsos – Lalique? – displayed, like deep-sea, tropical fish, neural-networks of polychromatic liquids. (The opposite, of course, of most configurations. Dolls, like my favourite candies, are usually soft on the outside, hard within.) But enough of Nana's denizens approximated my own design for me to cruise the doll-saturated streets in anonymity.

Walking with a gynoid's sexual precision, I checked-off each bar name, seeking my prey. There was *House of Dolls, Tin Lizzie's, Columbine's, Club Puberty*, and an SM parlour, *Judy's*. Some crew-cut boys eating at a noodle-stall called out: 'Where you going, pretty sex-doll?' and 'Over here, clockwork *poo-ying*!' Ahead, the bar I sought signalled its wares via a sign featuring neon-green eyes, beneath which, in gothic script, flickered: *Willy Hofmannsthal's Doll Keller*. Willy was a Cartier *aficionado*.

In the acid noon of the *Keller*'s lightshow, amber-skinned dolls with incongruous, jade-green eyes, performed, in bamboo cages above my head, their generic dance, *The Lordosis*. Many of these girls – those who danced, those who waited upon customers – were state-of-the-art Cartier: *poo-ying mee-ow* (or, in European nomenclature, *felis femella*), the results of cross-specie genetic splicing. They sported whiskers, tails, and pointy ears, or else were leopard-spotted, or striped like tigresses. Compared to these kittens my reshaped lines were *passé*. But Willy's dolls seemed unconcerned. They were too busy lifting beer-glasses to the lips of their *farangs*, and prattling their babyish sub-tongue: their programmes – inspired by an aesthetic of cuteness – stage-managing their mimes of little-girl adoration. I found the number one girl and told her I had a message from Madame for Mr Willy. I was led upstairs.

He was an old man, sitting on the bare boards of a room naked but for a rice-paper screen. On his knees was a laptop. The green, spectral light of its VDU had him mesmerized. I coughed; his head turned with a rheumatic scrunch, and, while his watery eyes focused on my loveliness, the powder-blue visage of a cat peeped inquisitively from the folds of his dressing-gown. He stroked its head. 'Ah, Gudrun, one of your sisters has come to call. What can we do for you, Miss Cat?'

'Madame Kito want doll. She have friend come stay. Yakuza.' The pornocracies guarded their dolls well (when renting a doll, a *farang* was required to leave his passport with the bar as surety); but in the six months I had doll-rustled no one had called my bluff. I knew Willy would be an easy sting.

'Kito, Kito. Always Kito,' he sighed. 'It isn't fair, is it, Gudrun?' The cat jumped from its silken enclave to bathe in the laptop's green effulgence. 'It all used to be so different. But home is so far, far away . . . Do you remember what it was like, Gudrun? This doll here – competent workmanship – but a quasi-human structure like the rest. Unredeemed carbon! Now I remember *real* Cartier dolls: *joaillerie* whose insides gleamed with jewels and ivory, platinum and gold. But Thai protein engineers have no skill with ribosomes or RNA. No skill with catalytic antibodies. They just shuffle the genome, or what little they know about it, then pin it all together with polymers and steel. They do not understand the alchemy of the flesh! In Europe, Gudrun, we build atom by atom, nanocomputers controlling molecular tools to make gears, motors, levers, little molecular-sized components that have the same kind of structure as metals and stones, ceramics and resins, each one programmed to replicate itself, to take its place in the divine clockwork . . .'

His spine had become upright, and his body spasmed, as if galvanized by an unseen puppet-master. Long, skeletal fingers tapped the keyboard, and as from a magic-lamp, a hologram materialized above us, glowing like ectoplasm in the darkened room. It was a cut-away diagram of a gynoid, its flesh stripped away to reveal its brazen ingenuities. Slowly, it began to revolve. 'Tabitha. My *kleinkunst*. In whose arms do you lie now? O Gudrun, she was so very beautiful. Look! What architecture! What supernatural clockwork! Peerless somatics, faultless autonomics. The sacrum, the ilium, the acetabulum of crysoprase, mother-of-pearl, and vermeil. The bloodstones of the abdominal aorta. She was an angel, Miss Cat, a living jewel. Genitalia?

O, no! Not like these imitations made today, just sex, sex, sex. She was an angel . . .' He passed a hand across his face. 'All the money, Gudrun, that our science gave us, spent on status symbols: arts and *objets* and toys. Now we *farangs* have forgotten how to make anything except toys, and nobody wants to buy them, Gudrun, nobody wants to buy.' The cat licked her paws, and the hologram continued to revolve, like a ride in a deserted fairground.

'Madame Kito . . .' I ventured.

'Yes, Miss Cat, I know, I know. A doll for Madame. Take one. They took my doll a long time ago. My Tabitha. My Tabs. They cannot harm me any more.'

Through the streets we walked, two cat-girls arm-in-arm, invisible amid the midnight crush of Nana. I had chosen one of Willy's more conservative models; *felis femella* is difficult to smuggle. I looked at my companion. Why did James want her? A biochip-and-steel, glycerine-hulled fake? Her scent was cheap. Her make-up overdone. How could her sexual obviousness, her sensationalism, console him for the loss of a genuine Cartier doll? Still the European sons came to Bangkok, their taste either hopelessly corrupted, or forfeit to an overweening desire to again possess a mechanical love, however *nonpareil*. Back in London, tiring of his new mistress, it would be I who Milord would turn to for consolation. And in me he would find a *real* doll.

Soon, a water-taxi was speeding us through the night's swelter and towards the *Honey*, where Milord awaited delivery of his *dtook-gah-dtah*.

'Cute,' he said, after he had had her perform a variety of party-pieces and tricks, 'but not a *spiritual* toy. Not like . . .'

'Like a real doll?'

'Sleep,' he told her; and she stretched out on the bed and closed her eyes. The room, brothel-scaped in red and gold, was giddy with mirrors. A poster of one of the latest automaton starlets hung from a flocked wall, her flesh transposed to the glossy world of a photo-mechanical: a two-dimensional limbo as deathlessly precious as the world of a pressed flower. The poster, like the TV that covered half the ceiling, was interactive and ran *jeux vérités* software. Milord stroked his doll's overextended thighs, as smooth and glistening as yellow wax. 'She'll do. For my purposes.' The photo-mechanical was sniggering at me. I couldn't see the joke. The air-conditioning was broken, the room hot and airless, and I needed a drink.

'When do we leave, James?'

'Little Mosquito,' he said tenderly. His leather-sheathed hand reached out to offer a caress. I tilted my head, closed my eyes, and saw us, together, in the rain-shiny London streets. His copper-tipped index finger and thumb clasped my temples.

'Are you pleased with me?' London melted in a blue-white flash, and darkness, cold and impassioned, slapped me to the floor, tied me up, stood back to watch me twitch and convulse, then embraced me, like a repentant lover. When I came to, Milord was pouring himself a Scotch from the mini-bar, his smoking claw plucking ice from a thermos.

'Sorry about the ECT, dear boy, but I fear this really is the only way to "say goodbye". Don't try to get up. Your vertical hold's rather wonky.'

I knew I had lost. I would always lose. Because I'm not the real thing. Because I'm not even a poor fake. Because I'm just a fake of a fake. Not even *bijouterie*.

How I longed for genuineness . . .

The photo-mechanical, startled by the commotion, had stepped out-of-frame; now she peeped round the borders of her world, angry at having been disturbed from her little death.

I just wanted to be your doll, Mr James; just wanted to be part of your collection. But no time for self-pity. He loves me, he loves me not. So it goes. He was just like the rest, only prettier. Smile. Keep him talking. This psycho was manoeuvring for the *coup de grâce*. Delay.

'You were supposed to take me with you.' My lips were as numb as my arms and legs. 'You were supposed to be the one . . .'

'What a revolting idea.'

'Then let me go. There's no need for this. I won't tell.'

'O? And you seemed to have such a crush on me. Truly, I was flattered . . .'

'Mr James, I'm not worth it. I'm just a romantic fool. Why are you doing this?'

'Perhaps you think it's the money? You think I circumvented Harry because I'm a poor, penniless Europunk? It's true, money was a problem, once. My family had shares in Cartier. When the crash came, we were ruined. I had to sell everything, including, of course, my dolls. But now Cartier pays me very well. Very well indeed.'

'I don't understand.'

'Mosquito, you don't understand *anything*.' He sat astride me, a playground lout, the copper electrodes held tauntingly before my eyes, like creepie-crawlies he might at any moment put down my blouse. Reflected in his monocle I saw a green-eyed little fool, my sister, her red-lipped mouth agape in a comic-book cliché of 'pain and surprise,' incapable of further supplication. Milord was enjoying himself. He was a nasty boy.

'People seem to prefer the second-rate. Copies. Imitations. We thought at first President Kennedy would help. But all he did was pontificate about Protectionism and the need for Free Trade. As long as no one pirated American intellectual property, Washington didn't seem to care. Afraid of upsetting Tokyo and her allies. Then Brasilia vetoed us at the GATT. The world was flooded with dolls from Bangkok and Manila. Why couldn't you have stuck with your radios and TVs, your cameras and washing-machines? Why manufacture *automata*? It was all we had left. The only thing that made us special. You stole our copyrights, our names. Cartier, Givenchy,

Lalique, Fabergé, Coty – all the Houses from London to St Petersburg. And now we have nothing left. But that will change, Mosquito. I am, if you like, part of the vanguard of quality-control. A recruit to the guerrilla army of Taste. I buy dolls for the House of Cartier. Counterfeit dolls. And in Paris, Mosquito, they *change* them. Thai dolls aren't like their Western originals. Nanoengineers here use foetal tissue as a template. A *dtook-gah-dtah* is, in many respects, remarkably human. We have, after all, the evidence of *bijouterie*. Cartier Paris set out to bridge the hardware-wetware divide; to write a computer virus that could be transmitted from machine to man . . .'

'Klong fever?' I said, finding my tongue.

'Of course. It's an STD: computer-language translated into biology through enzymes man and machine both share. Every doll, after its programme has been infected, is shipped back to Thailand, a man-hungry pathogen. But none of you will suspect: dolls are supposed to be disease-free. And the real beauty of all this, Mosquito, is that the virus is an ethnic weapon. Only orientals are affected. It's prejudiced against certain *kinks* in your DNA: the gene, for instance, that gives you those pretty, slitty eyes!' He forked his fingers and made to gouge me. I flinched; he relaxed his threat. 'The virus only commandeers cells displaying those idiosyncracies that characterize your poor, overconfident race. Then the pogrom begins. It replicates, targets the hypothalamus, and creates a hormonal imbalance, causing impotence in the male. In, say, three generations, your gene-pool won't fill a Petri dish.'

'Revenge. Is that all you want?' Mr James was a considerable disappointment. 'I thought you had more Imagination. More Fascination.'

'I want,' he said, wiping a hand across my mouth and smearing my cheek with lipstick, 'to see your industry suffer. I want an end to cheap imports. I want a world I know only as a memory to return, a world of grace and style, of beautiful *automata* . . .' The black, leather-sheathed hand descended.

'This is all too impromptu, Mr James.'

'The others – they were just petty thieves. They didn't have your class. It's a pity you have to share their fate . . .'

And it was then that those same elements of irony, contempt and desire that I had earlier seen at war in his face, reappeared to continue their struggle. He bent down to kiss me. Not merely the will to survive, not merely the bitterness of a jilted heart, but lust, thick and muddy, prompted me to draw back my lips and bite deep, deep, my cruel dental work injecting customized protozoans, my mouth filling with blood and his scream.

He jerked backward, as if shot by a high-powered rifle, and fell trembling and shivering by my side. Already, he had passed from a mild sweat to chronic dehydration. His mad, beautiful eyes – delirious with the last stages of malarial fever – regarded me with puzzlement. 'That, darling,' I said, 'is why they call me Mosquito.' With a great effort I managed to sit up so that I was able to cradle his head in my arms. His blood was thickening, turning his brain into a stew. He was so beautiful. One of the most beautiful men I had known. A fatal beauty. 'Didn't you even like me,' I said, 'a little?'

I left the hotel with his panama over my eyes, and with my mouth still filled with the saline taste of blood, still echoing with his scream. His voluminous clothes undermined any attempt at inconspicuousness. But the concierge had seen a doll enter, a man leave. After they had found the body, they would ponder on how a Cartier doll had come to murder her client; they would open her up, look for faults, scratch their heads, destroy her; they would forget about the ill-dressed man.

In the small hours, above the *Gung-Ho* in Harry's private rooms, I changed into some spare he-clothes and sprawled out on the sofa while the boss quizzed me about those new Seiko dolls I was supposed to have checked out. I lied fantastically. I was in no mood to talk of mad *farang* scientists and their poisonous girls.

'That Englishman,' he said, after we had finished a bottle of Mekong. 'Hear from him again?'

'No.' I flushed; but the shadows hid me. It was not shame, of course, but embarrassment. I had been such an idiot.

'Good. Why is it always Englishmen with you, Mosquito?'

'Because . . .' But I was so tired. Tired of this ridiculous body, this extravagant heart. A fly droned lazily in the torpid confine of the lounge; moonlight was seeping through the blinds. I remembered another moon-lit world, the land of ice and snow where, once, I had been happy. Even in the last days of empire, it was a land of masques and bergomasques, of enchantment, of moonlight calm, sad and beautiful. Life then was a long *fête galante*, a fairy-tale. I had wanted to be part of that marvellous world, that land of satisfied desire, part of its genuineness. More than a woman, I had wanted to be *joaillerie*. They were not like their eastern sisters, but elegant courtesans with the most ethereal of manners, the beloved mistresses of lords, the trusted confidantes of ladies.

I sometimes think I shall never return.

'I'm through with Englishmen,' I said. It was dollworld, not they, that I had been enamoured of. Ah, I am a fake of fakes, an impostor; my life, a banal porno-flick, a cheap *jeu vérité*. But sometimes, half-awake, half-asleep, I dream that I have put off this unwieldy flesh; that, more than a woman, I have become a doll. A real doll, beloved of princes and kings.

'My funny Valentine,' laughed Harry, 'we'll have another customer tomorrow. Another Englishman, perhaps. Go. Go home. Go home to Zipper. Go on, before I break your arms. Go home to bed.' And I did.

But the dream, unreal as love, persists.

DAVID BRIN

Piecework

It annoyed Io's best friend to give birth to a four-kilo cylinder of tightly wound, medium grade, placental solvent filters.

For five long months Perseph had kept to a diet free of sugar, sniff, or tobac – well, almost free. The final ten weeks she'd spent waddling around in the bedouin drapery fashion decreed for pieceworkers this year. And all that for maybe two thousand Euro-dollars worth of industrial sieves little better than a *fabricow* might produce!

Perseph was really ticked.

Outwardly, Io made all the right sympathetic sounds, though actually she had little use for her friend's anger. It had been Perseph's choice to hire her womb to a freelance codder of dubious pedigree, without even vetting him through an agent.

'They're all sperm crazy,' Io had warned months earlier, as the two of them sat together on her narrow con-apt balcony, watching a twilight-flattened sun squeeze berryjuice colour into stained horizon clouds. Nearer, a warm mist sublimed from the boggy reed beds of the Mersey estuary, a haze presently fanned into tattered wisps by homebound flocks of noisy sea birds.

'There's no profit in placental jobbing, and no hope for advancement,' Io told Perseph that evening. 'Me, I'll stick to egg work.'

'But egg jobs cost you to get started,' Perseph complained. 'And a failure can ruin you with non-delivery charges. *Then* where's your investment?'

As if Perseph knew what the word meant! Like most

pieceworkers, the tall brunette never saved a penny out of her delivery fees, blowing it all on the move-party circuit until it was time to return to her dole cheques and her next surropregnancy. No wonder Perseph stayed with placental-fab. Some people just had no ambition.

Io vividly recalled that evening, several months ago, when the two of them watched silent marsh fog diffuse raggedly over the muddy river banks into Ellesmere Port's cattle yards, softening the complacent lowing of the animals, if not their pungent aroma.

Twenty-four hours a day, lorries pulled out from the milking sheds and parturition barns, carrying bulk loads of gene-designed oils, polymers and industrial membranes. The mass production of specially bred fabricows dwarfed the output of smalltime contractors like Perseph or Io. Rumour had it ICI housed their pampered creatures here on the south bank to intimidate the pieceworkers living in derelict marinas and towering co-op houseboats nearby.

If so, the cattleyards had an effect on Io opposite to that intended. They boosted her morale, reminding her that there were still some things neither animals nor machines could do as well as a human craftswoman. No fabricow would ever produce wares as fine as hers!

That evening, months ago, Io's friend had only just begun her latest surropreg and still yearned passionately for the chemical pleasures now denied by her guild rules. Of course, soon Perseph would be substituting a mellow high from her own hormonal flow. Meanwhile, though, she made pretty miserable company.

'No way, Io. I don't think I could hold out long enough to do egg work. It takes so long, I'd go crazy for a party.'

'But Pers, look what Technique Zaire's paying for a prime cockatrice, these days. Or a shipbrain – '

'A shipbrain! Hah! How would a piece like me ever get seeded with a shipbrain? If *I* ever signed up for eggwork they'd knock me up with . . . with a traffic cop!' Perseph laughed, a sound Io felt had grown more bitter of late.

Io shook her head. 'All I know is I don't want to have

to scrimp for another ten years. Two more successful carries and I'll have paid for tuition and a licence, and have enough left over for nestworks. Anyway, eggcraft leaves me needing less retroconversion.'

'Hmm,' her friend had said, dubiously. 'Meanwhile you live like a tweenie, saving all your bonuses, cashing in all your hobby and travel 'lotments. I swear, Io, sometimes some of us think you – ' Perseph bit her lip. 'Well, you just don't party enough.'

'I've got no time for move-parties, Pers. You know that. There's college . . .' Instantly Io knew it had been a mistake to mention it. 'College' had such a posh sound to it, even if she were just attending evening classes.

'Argh,' Perseph had twisted away in disgust, a motion that set her visibly gritting her teeth. She grunted, covering her already tender abdomen. 'Io, you make me tired just thinking about it. Some ambitions just aren't worth the effort.'

That conversation had distilled the difference in their views, and from that day forth they had simply avoided the subject.

But now Io recalled the occasion with eidetic detail as she walked alongside a slowly crawling recovery couch, brushing her friend's sweat-damp hair while postpartum enzymes dripped into Perseph's veins, gradually displacing her cheeks' chalky pallor with a healthy colour one could hardly tell from natural. Over one armrest, a glowing monitor measured Perseph's recovery from the strains of labour, pacing the slow forward progress of her couch to the strengthening of her vital signs. Pieceworkers in the sperm trade hardly ever got visitors on delivery day. What would be the point? So these moving couches weren't equipped with sidecars, only tiny, spring-mounted jump stools. Io preferred to walk, eyes ever alert for the maintenance carts and cleaner beasts scurrying about on pre-assigned courses. Normally, she'd simply have called after Perseph got home. But Io had been in the neighbourhood, so she dropped by to surprise her friend.

Now she was starting to wish she hadn't. Though Io knew her reaction was old-fashioned, these wholesale decanting centres tended to give her nausea.

She brushed Perseph's black ringlets while rows of other recovery couches periodically emerged from unloading bays like new vans off assembly lines, each conveying a tired, limp, freshly emptied pieceworker. Occasionally, as the doors opened, cries spilled into the vast recovery hall – from the panicky ululations of an ill-trained first-timer all the way to the rhythmic karate-shouts of a skilled veteran – the melodies of modern industrial labour.

No, Io vowed within her thoughts. I'll stick to egg work.

The brush caught on a knot of Perseph's hair. The woman cursed, 'Wrigglers!'

'Sorry, Pers, I – '

'No, damnit, look at that! I knew it!' She bit her thumb at a shimmering holoribbon traversing the vaulted ceiling, carrying late quotes from the Bio-Bourse.

'Meconium! I knew I should've delivered three days ago. Look what's happened to solvent-filter prices since then! But no, I just *had* to try to put on those last few grammes.'

Disgusted, Perseph shifted on the bed, causing a large lump to jiggle beneath the sheets, like a hunchback dwarf under a tent propped by her shrouded legs. 'Hey! Watch what you're doing down there!' Perseph slapped the squirming bulge.

Snuffled grunts, a phlegmatic fart, were her only answer.

'Damn, cheap model cleaners,' she muttered. 'I'd do better without them.'

Embarrassed, Io looked around. But none of the other recovering workers riding nearby trollies seemed to notice. Some slept complacently. A few spoke on hush phones, only their expressions hinting whether they were talking to agents or loved ones. Others watched soaps on tiny armrest TV sets while tailored enzymes dripped into their arms, cutting the time the Company had to maintain this service on overhead. The couch amenities were required under the Piecework Labour Act. There, at least, the guild had actually done some good.

A few of the ladies on nearby carts looked high already, probably on smuggled-in drugs, taking advantage of their very last moments free of surropreg discipline.

'Look Pers, I'm glad I caught you coming out. But my lunch break's almost over, and I need a protein fix before going back to work.'

'Work?' Perseph had a dark glitter in her eye. 'Have you got a *job* now, too?'

'Uh, yeah.' Io instantly regretted the slip. 'It's – it's only quarter time, Pers. One of my teachers noticed my reading level was up to . . . well, I've been filing records at a psycher's office. It's no big deal . . .'

'College *and* a job. Crapadoodle.' Perseph shrugged. 'All right, go and squeeze in lunch.' She jabbed idly towards Io's abdomen. 'Can't let the little toaster starve, can we?'

Perseph punched a button activating the Soap Channel on her armrest TV – no doubt to annoy Io, who quickly averted her eyes from the seductive flickering images. Io avoided *all* addictions.

'Um, yeah. I'll – I'll come and see you after you're back on your feet.' But Perseph had already focused on the detergent drama. 'Ymmm,' her friend said.

Stepping away, Io had to move nimbly to dodge a careening service cart. By instinct her hands moved protectively over her swelling body. She felt motion within, responding to her increasing heart-rate – almost as if the thing inside her were actually alive.

Her tender left breast throbbed.

'Green shit!' Perseph's voice really carried this time, drawing looks from all sides. 'That does it!'

The sheet flew back. With both hands, the dark-haired pieceworker dislodged a small furry creature from between her thighs. 'Get out! Women have sealed their own capillaries for hundreds of years without pissface little lickers like you. Beat it!'

A plaintive cry. Service uncompleted. Meal unfinished. The artificial beast dodged Perseph's kicking feet and crouched at the end of the chaise, mewing for a handler to come and take it from this unappreciative woman.

Io turned quickly and hurried away.

The usual crowd loitered by the exit, eyeing each weary pieceworker as she emerged blinking into the sunlight.

Pedicabbies offered rides home on government vouchers. Codders passed out their cards and offered to show off their licence tattoos. The inevitable scraggly pair of Madrid-Catholic protesters walked their wellworn tracks, placards drooping disconsolately.

The codders were the worst. Of course you had to have codders to run the sperm trade. Placental filter makers like Perseph could never afford to have their own genetic programming done. Even a bundle of high quality platinum-sieves only paid off in five figures, and a woman was limited by law to twenty-five surropregs over a lifetime. So it was men who underwent the expensive treatments to have their reproductive cells modified, amortizing the cost against the commissions they received from each pieceworker who carried their wares.

The codders who haunted the exits of decanting centres were generally of a pretty low order – either desperate to grab their percentages on the spot, before their tired clients could blow their fees, or so hard up for customers they'd hawk their patterns to women coming straight off decanting.

The idea made Io feel queasy. Imagine even thinking about another knockup within two hours of labour!

And yet, she saw several pieceworkers of her acquaintance emerge from the recovery bay and stroll gingerly over to the crowd of strutting males – all dressed in bright, tight-fitting tanktops, their multicoloured leggings converging on codpieces tied with laced bows. The codders treated their prospective clients with exaggerated courtliness, offering folding stools, drinks, and sprays of flowers to any fem willing to sit and hear about their exciting, latest-model designs.

And they say romance is dead, Io thought ironically.

'Hey Io, milady. You are the fair one, aren't you?'

Hair processed flat, parted down the middle in the latest style, his leggings were yellow and bright pink, and the padded codpiece a polka-dot combination of the two. He was lacing up one side, as if he had just finished showing off his licence to a client.

'Um. Hello, Colin,' she nodded. The codder was part of Perseph's party circle and so, by convention, a friend of Io's as well. Though there were many types of friends.

'You're here furly early, no Io?' He eyed her surropreg garb, barely yet filled out with the fruits of her own production.

'I came down to see Perseph.' She nodded towards the recovery bay. Colin's eyes widened.

'Fave babe! Thank you, Io. I'll station this ever-welcome selfsame to whip out my card just as she re-enters the hurly world.'

'Just make sure that's all you whip out, Colin. There's ladies present.'

Colin guffawed. As Io intended, he took her remark as a sarcastic, off-colour jibe – unit coin in the strange protocol of jest-bonding. He couldn't know that on another level Io had meant every word, literally.

'So when's your time to give over and do your work the natchway, Io?'

'By natural, I assume you mean by grunt and shove? Letting a codder like you take ten percent of my fees and all the credit? No thanks, Colin. Egg work may be harder, but it's between me and the designers – '

'Between you and cold glass and rubber, you mean!' Colin's stiff grin said this was still repartee, but his voice was chill. 'Do you actually like it *like* that? Are you *sure* your profile reads hetero correctly, Io? None of us boys see it that way.'

Io felt a wave of anger. Who had told this cretin about her profile? Had Perseph? Was it possible to trust *nobody*?

Colin loomed over her, showing teeth. 'You know, Io, sometimes we get an idea you think you're better than the rest of us. Just because you stayed in tweenie-school, and prefer popping off toasters instead of honest filters, like your friends. That doesn't make you a watch-fobber. You were born down here, babe. Grunt and shove is how *you* got started.'

Io's gut churned. In her Immature Interactions class she had begun learning how to parse exchanges like this – the way Colin was trying to intimidate her with words, body stance, and vague, intimated threats of friendship-withdrawal. Funny how one took this sort of behaviour for granted, until the day somebody finally gave you a model. Showed you that it was a *process*, like any other in the world. Then it all seemed to pop into focus, and suddenly looked so very silly and primitive.

Ah, theory was fine. But practical applications weren't in her curriculum until next term, and that wouldn't help Io now. She didn't know how to disarm this fellow's aggression, not without leaving him angry.

Oh, what the hell. Io decided she really didn't care what this tissue-stuffer thought of her, anyway.

'Read my lips, Colin.' Io leaned forward and mouthed words in street talk.

'Wrigglers . . . count zero; joppy turning floppy.'

Colin rocked back, paling visibly as his hands began a zigzag motion to avert bad luck. Too late, he caught himself. 'Heh. Ha-ha, Io.' He grinned, blinking away sudden perspiration as he glanced to see if anyone else had noticed. 'Very funny.'

He wouldn't forgive her soon for making him show his superstition openly like that. Io winked. 'Didn't mean it, Colin. Keep 'em high, boy. Both the count and the jopper.'

She turned and left before he could reply, making off through the rank of pedicabs, past the limp, resigned pickets, across the bus lanes and out into the streets of Liverpool proper.

The crowds were as she'd always known them, teeming, bustling. All her life, Io had been awash in a sea of people. It was the way of the world, and would be until the population control measures finally took effect.

At least this century frowned on ostentatious class distinction, and coloured synthetic fabrics were cheap. So nobody dressed shabby unless they wanted to. It took a sharp eye to pick out the types – the dole-fed majority, who spent their days seeking distraction at state-subsidized entertainments – then those with service jobs and some status – and finally the elite, the proud ones, the ones with real work to do.

Mostly the difference could be found in the eyes. Workers had a *look* . . . as if they *belonged* in the world, and weren't just marking time. Every time she noticed that look, Io felt more determined than ever to stay in college. To fight for not just any certificate, but the very highest. Nothing less would do for the survival of her soul.

A sudden wet touch behind her right knee sent panic flashes up her spine. She whirled, heart pounding, her right hand at her breast. Io looked down and sighed.

Bright brown eyes briefly looked into hers. A wet nose snuffled. Its fur was shaded in the blue and yellow bee-striping of official authority . . . the colours of a traffic cop.

The doglike creature, programmed with perfect knowledge of the vehicle code, dismissed Io with a snort and moved on. Traffic cops never forgot a face or odour, never forgave an infraction until the fine was paid. Watching it wander off through the crowd, Io found it hard to believe highly skilled pieceworkers once manufactured such creatures, back when they experimented, before a final model was certified to reproduce itself.

Still sniffling, hunting violators, the traffic cop turned and disappeared into the crowd.

Io rested her back against a cool display window as people surged by. She looked down the street, seeking distraction as her heart-rate slowly settled again.

Apparently it was rubbish day here. Open-lidded green bins showed that the first set of lorries had already been by. But the red, yellow and silver dustbins still stood tightly sealed on the kerbs awaiting pickup. Not far away Io saw a Recycle-Authority policeman ticketing a local merchant for failing to sort all the non-ferric metals out of his organic mulch. As the dispirited proprietor looked on he got no sympathy from the passersby. Certainly not from Io.

At last, calm again, she felt able to plot a route through the crowds towards a place where she could sit down to a palatable meal.

At least there's less rationing than there used to be, she thought, though they say it can come back, anytime.

Io wasn't really hungry, but that didn't matter. She ate more for the thing within her than for herself, anyway.

The 'toaster', Perseph and Colin had called it.

'I don't do home appliances,' she said, under her breath.

Still, the street slang struck Io with its wry aptness. Again, the product throbbed within her.

Yeah. Time to go feed her toaster.

. . . By the year 2000 overpopulation had brought on three ominous consequences. The first of these had been foreseen by thoughtful people long before . . . that the needs of over six billion human beings simply exceeded the carrying capacity of the planet. Topsoil, mineral ores, fresh water, and the genetic pool of natural species, were among the non-renewable resources rapidly being depleted. Alternative, sustainable practices had to be found, and quickly.

A second effect of overpopulation, however, went almost unnoticed until quite late, and that was the matter of creative unemployment.

Most of the interim solutions enabling society to feed and house the billions arose out of productive technologies controlled by a small, elite labour force. The rest of humanity was utterly dependent, unable to make any noticeable difference. Some countries masked this by providing 'jobs' in a 'service economy', but in the long run serious alienation grew out of the frustrated human need to do work, work that is appreciated, work that is of real value to society.

Then there was the third great problem – that of misapplication of education. For while mammoth literacy campaigns had elevated the general level of culture, a great many people spent years learning to do things that actually required little, if any real facility. Meanwhile, the most delicate, most demanding job in history was being performed almost universally by unskilled labour . . .

Io closed the book when twinges in her left breast surged again – prolactin-powered hot flushes that were made worse by a basic lateral imbalance.

The clash was fundamental. On one side an organ had been modified by premier industrial technicians and was now setting up to execute complex designer chemistry. At the same time, however, out from under her other arm protruded its conservative twin. Responding to pregnancy hormones, that breast was happily creating archaic precursors to next-to-useless fluids, fucking with her brain, making her imagine impossible things.

Though she tried to hide her discomfort, Io's agent noticed as he performed her weekly checkup.

'I warned you against leaving one tit in natch-state,' Joey reminded her while taking colour readings and sonograms of each gland. 'Here I get you a bid to produce a really choice secondary product, Mobil's latest lubricant for high-torque tools, and you insist on only setting up at half capacity! You know what that does to your rep, Io? It *advertises* that you aren't serious about going fulltime pro. What am I going to do with you, hm?'

Io put her textbook aside. 'You'll let me do it my way, Joey. That's what you're going to do. Anyway, I'll be producing with my left breast, also.'

'Producing what? Colostrum and homosap milk? What'll we do with that stuff, make cheese? Have you seen the latest futures? With the birthrate down again, they're a glut on the market!'

'They won't be when I deliver,' she assured him. 'Trust me.'

Nearby, the General Diagnostics surropreg monitor buzzed smugly, a reassuring, complacent sound where it would have blared for bad news. Pushing back a wisp of thinning blonde hair, Io's agent tore free a printout of her checkup results, while still muttering irritably. 'Trust me, she says! What are you doing, Io, reciting my lines? I'm the one that's supposed to say "trust me". You? You're supposed to say, "Oh, Joey, I don't know what I'd ever do without you".'

'That's what I like about you, Joey. You're even more old-fashioned than I am.'

As if to confirm it, and apparently unaware of the irony, Joey put on archaic eye-spectacles to scan the test results. 'You call it old-fashioned to retire on me, just when we've got that body of yours tuned to real premium capacity? Whatever happened to the work ethic?'

'I *want* to work,' Io affirmed as she craned to read the chart for herself. Nowadays she knew what the data meant, probably as well as Joey did. 'I just want to move up to a more demanding job.'

As she'd expected, everything was nominal. Io took care of her body. She picked up her blouse. 'So can I button up, now? Or are you getting turned on by preggirls, these days?'

'Sarcastic too. Just for that, I won't tell you what I think you're carrying. You can find out on delivery day. Get dressed and get out of here, Io.'

One of Io's classes had recently covered status bluffing, so she knew better than to let herself be drawn in by Joey's bait. Obviously he had no more idea what Technique Zaire had planted in her womb than she did. 'You probably let them hire me to make a traffic cop,' she sallied, reaching for her book and jacket.

'Smartass. Just be on time for your next checkup. And stay out of trouble. And if your left tit makes you think any more weird thoughts, just remind yourself that toasters don't suckle; neither do traffic cops. And human milk fetches less than three pence a gramme.'

'Five,' she said as she turned the antique door knob. 'You'll see, Joey. Five pence a gramme, or I go back to knitting.'

'Hah. That'll be the day.'

But Io knew the price had to go up. It was just one reason for leaving her left mammary gland alone, no matter what unlikely illusions its archaic secretions sent churning through her head.

Some of her courses were clearly relevant to her chosen future profession. In other cases, however, the applicability seemed much less clear. For instance, Io had to fight off ennui as her Industrial Reproduction lecturer droned on and on, covering stuff Io had learned way back during her apprenticeship in the egg trade.

'. . . Until the nineteen-eighties,' the elderly woman academic said at the front of the hall, 'some still imagined that cloning human beings would be as simple as cloning, say, frogs. In theory, all you had to do was replace the 23 chromosomes in the nucleus of a woman's ovum with a complete set of 46 from, say, one of her skin cells. Implant this "autofertilized egg" and nine months later you get a baby genetically identical to the donor. Voilà.

'Then we found out just how different mammals really are from frogs. For it seems that, during conception, human sperm does more than just deliver 23 chromosomes to match the mother's contribution. It actually *preconditions* certain of those genes to leap into action during the critical moments after fertilization. These genes are only activated if delivered in a sperm. Similarly, other genes only express working enzymes if they originated in an egg . . .'

A sudden throbbing from Io's bracelet told her of a message coming in. Normally, she would store it for later. But with Professor Jackone going on repetitiously about ancient history, she felt safe to take a look. Carefully tuning down the brightness of her old communicator, so as not to disturb the students around her, she pressed the Read button and aimed the tiny holographic image onto her lap.

HAMPSTEAD TRAVEL AGENCY SPECIALIZES IN TOURS SPESHALLY SET UP FOR PIECEWORKERS. <MORE>

The glowing letters were not an advertisement. Obviously, they were part of a message from Perseph. And Io knew it amounted to something of an ultimatum.

Io pressed the button again; another row of letters replaced the first.

TRIP ALL SET UP FOR YOUR TERM BREAK, SO COLLEGE NO EXCUSE. NOR YOUR 'JOB'. YOU CAN'T CASH MORE VOUCHERS, SO COME ON! <MORE>

Perseph was right, of course. The term would be over soon, and her own piecework delivery wasn't due for another six weeks or so. Also, the law limited how many travel vouchers one could exchange for cash, so her most recent one would go to waste if she didn't use it.

Of course, Io's abdominal distension was already greater than most placental freelancers like Perseph ever reached, so walking long distances was out of the question. But Perseph had covered that excuse, also.

I really could do with a trip, Io told herself.

And yet, the idea left her uneasy. Her friendship with Perseph had begun in the back alleys of Liverpool when they were only girls, taking turns guarding each other's ration books, teaming up killing rats for bounty money. Nevertheless, their drift apart had really been foreordained from the beginning.

Once, she had hoped to draw her best friend into sharing her own enthusiasms – her ambitions for higher things. But such wistful attempts had only served to anger

Perseph. She inevitably misunderstood, assuming Io was putting on airs.

For her part, Perseph seemed as anxious in her own way to salvage something between them. That meant getting Io involved in the activities of her guildmates and her born social class.

Well, Io thought. If she can't or won't join me, I can still join her. At least this time.

Suddenly, the lights in the lecture hall dimmed as Professor Jackone began showing slides. Io hurriedly tuned down the brightness of her wrist projector.

'. . . as you can see,' the lecturer enunciated as a holographic image took shape at the front of the auditorium. 'If we try to clone a mouse *without* any sperm-preconditioned genes, what we get is a queerly warped embryo, one which dies quite soon in the womb because the *placenta* never gets started.

'Alternatively, when an egg is prepared using *only* genes taken from sperm nuclei, something radically different happens.' The image in the tank shifted again. This time, there was no embryo at all, only a tangled, exaggerated mass of folded fibres easily recognizable to anyone familiar with the modern filter trade.

'. . . so while both the mother's and father's genes are equal in the final makeup of any infant mammal, at the beginning it is genes from the mother's egg which controls how the embryo starts development, while genes from the sperm take charge of setting up the placenta, that organ lacking in fish or reptiles, whose complex organic filtration chemistry nourishes the mammalian foetus to term. . . .'

The same old stuff . . . Io pressed again to read the rest of Perseph's message.

COME, IO. JUST FOR THE FIRST WEEK. THAT'S ALL. YOU NEED THIS. PERS KNOWS WHAT YOU NEED. <END>

The letters seemed to blur for a moment, and Io knew no flaw in her aged watchcom was at fault. She wiped her eyes while the professor's voice reverberated on all sides.

'At first this news, while astonishing, was of little interest outside the halls of science. Certain fanatical feminists were disappointed to learn that men weren't quite as non-essential as they'd hoped, but to most of the rest of humanity it seemed just another interesting fact of nature.

'Scarcely anyone guessed the long-range importance of this discovery, or its potential industrial applications. . . .'

Io touched the face of her watch. In rapid Morse pulses she silently tapped out Perseph's private access number, and a reply to her friend's offer.

OKAY, I'LL COME. AT LEAST PARTWAY. AND THANKS, PERS. I THINK I REALLY DO NEED A BREAK. YOU'RE A TRUE FRIEND. – IO.

True to its reputation, the travel agency set them up with a tour which required no walking at all. It was a party train bound over the Arctic, from Oslo via upper Norway and across the great faery bridges spanning from the Faeroes to Iceland to Greenland to Labrador. It was a December journey into the heart of winter, a trek across a desert as romantic and empty as anything to be found any more on the surface of overcrowded Earth.

Twin superconducting rails, hanging parallel two hundred metres above the frozen waves of tundra, looked like beaded strings of drawn dew that began in nothingness behind them and speared ahead to a parallax union in the pure blackness ahead. Only the rhythmically reappearing pylons – lonely, slender stalks planted kilometres apart – reminded the passengers that there was any link at all with the death-grey ground.

Io, to be frank, preferred sunshine. But when Perseph showed her the tickets Io had forced a smile and an outward show of enthusiasm. After all, she could debark at Iceland or Greenland and still have enough vouchers left for a week in the Canaries.

Anyway, someone had once told her that aesthetic appreciation, while not exactly required for the certificate she sought, couldn't really hurt an applicant. So it was that Io found herself spending hours in the train's observation dome, watching and slowly learning to admire the daunting desolation.

Overhead, the aurorae shaped everchanging draperies of shimmering blue and yellow gauze, or – if one preferred – rippling currents of diffuse oxygen atoms, ionized by the sun's electric wind, sheeting along lines of magnetic force.

Now and again those gaudy curtains would part unpredictably and reveal a slowly wheeling tableau of bitter-bright constellations, familiar, and yet filled with eerie portent in this chilly, alien setting.

The caribou herds had long ago departed south for the season, along with the more mundane breed of tourist. During wintertime completely different tribes of itinerants moved in to share these rails with the freight-heavy transports. For instance, those relying – like Perseph and Io – on state travel allotments to exercise their citizen's privilege to see the world – on off-peak hours.

And then there were others, folk whose manners told in ways more subtle than clothing or fashion that they were employed, that they had real jobs, that they had chosen this strange journey not for budgetary reasons but out of a taste for moody expanses, or perhaps a cherishing of the night.

By unstated courtesy, the parties kept the raucous stuff to the other cars, though the observation dome was a favourite trysting spot for lovers. At times the closeness of such intertwined pairs made Io feel wistful and poignantly alone.

Unfortunately, such feelings weren't alleviated by Perseph's incessant attempts to match her up. Finally, one evening in the bistro car, Io's companion snapped at her irritably.

'Sometimes you just confuse the bloody hell out of me, Io! What does it take to turn you on, eh? We showed each other our charts. Yours was straight hetero, and

I kept that in mind. I've introduced you to your type of guy.'

My type? But Io bit back her initial response. Perseph's facial expression was friable. Exasperated. Irises and flesh tones both showed clear signs of a hashtite high well past its peak and entering depressive phase. Perseph's once straight antenna-braids were drooping now as hairspray slowly gave way under assault from perspiration and a party running at desultory medium-broil.

'But you saw my profile also includes things like high selectivity and strong bonding, Pers. I can't help being made that way. I sometimes envy you your chart, the freedom your personality gives you to come and go as you like. Tease, squeeze, thank you please. But I've got no choice, Pers. I've got to hold out till the time's right for me.'

'Hold out for Mr Watch Fob Job, you mean,' Perseph said bitingly.

'For when I've got a job of my own, Pers. And for the sort of man who'll respect that in me. A codder would never understand what it is I'm after. You know that.'

A tick manifested at the corner of Perseph's left eye. 'And what's wrong with codders?' she asked. 'Some of my best friends are codders!'

Io looked around nervously. The party crowd at nearby tables were watching an act on stage at the front of the car, performing an amiably vulgar dance to the tempo of the gently thrumming rails. Once, Io would have found the show, the tight, acrid atmosphere, the frenetic party odours, attractively distracting. But no more. Artificial highs had begun to pall on her years ago.

Smoke and garish lights made black sinkholes of the window behind Io's shoulder, and yet she envied the quiet beyond those perspex panes.

'Hey.' Io forced a grin, trying to cut through the bad mood. 'Don't get me wrong, Pers. Codders are fine. It's just I can't ever get to know one for ten minutes before he offers to strip down and show me his specialty.'

For an instant Perseph's eyes were as deep and untelling as the nightview behind Io. Then she seemed to come to a decision. Her laughter would have made a good dissertation topic in one of Io's classes.

'Yeah, they're like that, aren't they? Even when I'm halfway in the middle of a surropreg, waddling around like a Blackpool publican, half the codders I know are always trying to talk me into trying out their wares in advance. I keep telling the ones I introduce to you that you're in the egg trade, and not interested in their merchandise. But I suppose habit's hard to break.'

'Hey, now.' Io laughed. 'I'd like to think they weren't coming on to me just because they thought of me as a fallow belly to plant. Ever occur to you they might've found me appealing?'

'You? You skinny-arm charity case? With that out-of-date yellow hair?'

Io feigned an insulted look.

Now Perseph's laughter was heartier. 'Gotcha! First you're offended when they come on to you. Then you'd be hurt if they didn't, right?'

'No, I just wish they'd . . .'

'I'll tell you this though, Io. I *like* codders. Some of them have gone far into debt to finance their conversions. The Freelance trade would be impossible without them. We'd have to take as many risks as you and your egg – '

'Pers, I never said – '

'And something else, Io. They put a lot more *enthusiasm* into their work than Joey and his hoity-toity ovum designers do. Ever thought there could be pleasure involved in this business, Io? No, I didn't think so. But I tell you it's a hell of a lot more natural with codders than with Joey's lot and all their tubes and wires . . .'

Perseph had that gleam in her eye again, a seething sexual energy. She was talking herself into it. Io knew it would culminate quite soon in her friend grabbing the nearest tumescent codpiece, without even asking to see the owner's prospectus, let alone his tattoo.

'Pers, are you remembering to take your pills? You don't want to get knocked at a *party*, for the love of – '

'You mind your own damn business!' Perseph stood up and her chair fell over. 'I don't give you advice on your blasted eggs. Don't *you* tell me where I ought to shop for seed!'

All at once Io knew. This wasn't the first time for Perseph. That unsatisfactory load of commercial grade solvent filters she'd delivered some months back – she hadn't taken the job through a city agent, or even negotiated the superpreg herself. She'd gone and let some random codder inseminate her – probably just somebody who pleased her sexually – as if that said anything at all about the quality of his wares!

Mixing business and pleasure, letting your professional standards lapse, these were the beginning of the end for a craftswoman, especially a pieceworker. Io had an instant fey vision of Perseph in a few years – too far gone to win decent contracts, physically too shabby to draw a codder into making a deposit on spec. She'd wind up taking bulk grade semen and producing goods no better than a fabricow's. Finally, she'd lose her guild standing, and it would be the dole for her, fulltime.

The dole would kill Perseph. Without the focus of work, *some* kind of work, the lure of drugs and soaps would soon take her out of the world.

It was only a narrow precognitive instant, but at that moment Io's eyes locked with the other woman's in momentary complete communion. Io's cheeks felt aflame with how, in that moment, she involuntarily betrayed her friend, not only by seeing, but by *showing* on her face that she had seen. From Io, Perseph had not received the lies that were a comrade's duty to tell, but a severe mirror, laying bare a fate she already knew, deep inside.

'I – I've got to make a phone call.' Perseph started to turn, unsteadily.

'Pers, I'm sor – '

'Oh, go abort a hydrocephalic traffic cop!' Perseph snarled. She whirled, knocking over their drinks, and made her way unevenly among the tables, leaving Io alone in the middle of a crowded room suddenly too filled with truth.

. . . it can be hard for a modern citizen to realize just how inefficient our ancestors were, even in the bustling industrial centres of the fabulous Twentieth. But what enabled the people of those times to build the first globe-spanning culture, to tame nature, to educate the masses and begin the conquest of space, was a system that depended essentially upon profligate waste.

For instance, a single gramme of gold – vital for modern electronics – could be acquired only by tearing out of the Earth, pulverizing, and washing several tons *of ore. Beyond the now obvious environmental effects, this also required prodigious use of energy, which was already growing scarce even by the turn of the century.*

From high-tech consumer goods to simple breakfast cereals, far more resources had to be put into each item the consumer bought than ever came out as product. With seven billion people to feed – and clothe and educate and entertain – there was only one option, to switch to renewable processes that used resources more efficiently. The alternative was to face a culling such as had not been seen since the Black Death.

Biotechnology offered a way.

Today, gene-tailored microbes refine gold and other vital elements directly from sea water. Organic solvents, once unbelievably dumped into sensitive watersheds by shortsighted businessmen, are now recycled through filters grown specially for the purpose by pampered, well-fed fabricows. And these same animals' modified milk glands produce lubricants to replace long-vanished petroleum oil in our vehicles. In this way we make use of efficient fabrication methods evolved over billions of years by Nature herself.

As for products at the very cutting edge of technology, whose quality standards exceed what can be accomplished with animals, these are today put into production by a labour force dedicated to high craftsmanship. And yet, these jobs are not restricted, as in the past, to the skilled or the privileged. Rather, they are attainable even on a part time basis by men and women of good health from any social . . .

. . . from ARE YOU INTERESTED IN BIOFAB? London, 2043.

She met him in the Reykjavik airport lounge.

His manner was courteous, his stance and bearing unselfconsciously athletic.

The clothes he wore showed tasteful reticence, not the bright excess that overcompensating dole clients so often mistook for fashion.

And, although he was obviously Eastern European in origin, he had the good grace not to wear leather here in the west, where sensibilities now rejected products made from the death of animals.

For a while they talked about the books she had been studying, while awaiting her flight. But soon they were in one of those exciting, open-topic conversations which touch lightly on the fascination of the world itself. Io made no effort to suppress the sudden feelings coursing through her. The methods of emotional control she had learned in college were still too new, too abstract to her. And anyway, who wanted to damp down anything as pleasant as hope?

In his rich, cosmopolitan accent, Wiktor offered to buy her dinner. There was plenty of time, and no hint that he wanted or expected anything in return but her companionship. She accepted demurely, then hurriedly added a smile, lest he take her shyness for reluctance.

As she had secretly hoped, he passed his credit card across the face of the robot *maitre'd* at the first-class dining room, and took her arm as a pink ribbon of light guided them through a maze of candlelit tables to a window setting overlooking the lights of the city.

He also made mistakes . . . smelling the wine cork instead of feeling it, for instance. Obviously he had dined in class before, but neither was he so accustomed to this lifestyle as to be blasé or patronizing.

Io only knew about wine corks from having read an obscure magazine in Joey's waiting room. It actually pleased her that Wiktor showed such minor lapses, an almost imperceptible trace of latent, slight awkwardness. She had no ambition to stake a place in the circles of the rich and renowned. But his nodding acquaintance with the finer things spoke of the relaxed eclecticism, the comfortable worldliness of a professional . . . a man with a real job. Someone who *did* something.

Would she, in three years time, be able to walk into a place such as this without feeling heart palpitations? Would she wear such a relaxed smile? Or order from a menu with such confidence?

Would she meet the sort of men who made the world move and grow better with their skill? Perhaps one who cared about the same craft as she was studying so long and hard for now?

Naturally, the subject of his actual profession never came up on this, an initial encounter. Her present trade was obvious from her attire, and from her tumescence, but they never mentioned it. He spoke instead about the Aurorae, visible even from here, so near the urban lights. A hint indicated that he might once have seen them from *above* – from space – but he did not follow up on that, nor did Io pursue it.

It was perfectly all right to speak of Earthly travels however, since all classes were encouraged in tourism. The superconducting rails made it cheaper than many other entertainments people might have demanded, and social planners considered it helpful. Tourists waged few wars.

Io felt ashamed of how little she had seen, how little she had to tell. But Wiktor made up for her lack. He had been to Merseyside many times, for instance – both Liverpool and Ellesmere Port – and he spoke with fondness of the Lake District, her own favourite place in all the world.

Against her usual habit when in production, Io allowed herself a single glass of wine. Of course she had memorized the tolerance tables long ago, and knew no harm would come to . . . to her toaster.

Sudden memory of that colourful euphemism triggered a nervous giggle. But then it also caused her to think of Perseph, and that made her suddenly sad. Their parting had been cool. Io had no idea what the future would bring, but the note of finality between them made her vision film as she thought about it.

Gyrating emotions. Damn. An occupational hazard. But what a time to have an attack of surropreg blues!

'I – I don't know what's got over me,' she said as she wiped her eyes. 'Would you excuse me while I – ' she gestured in the direction of the lavatories. His smile was bemused, understanding. 'Of course,' he said. 'I will order you that especial dessert I mentioned earlier. And,' his grin broadened. 'A glass of fruit juice.'

'Thanks. That might be best.' She laughed, and departed with a smile.

He didn't even try to pressure me into having another glass of wine, she mused as she negotiated her abdomen towards the ladies' room. Many men would have taken it as a challenge to try to get her drunk, even knowing she would be leaving within the hour. It was a rite of machismo she'd never understood, however many times it was explained to her. Wiktor, though, seemed a gentleman.

A low wall topped by a decorative hedge separated the dining room proper from the gilt wallpapered passage to the toilets. On her way out again, Io paused to check her composure. She wanted to maintain a friendly openness that would invite him to ask her watchcom number. After all, he said he passed through Liverpool on occasion. Perhaps he might call.

Io took a momentary guilty peek through the shrubbery, feeling like a little girl spying covertly on an older boy, the object of a delicious secret desire. A waiter had just turned away from their table. Walking towards her, he occulted her view for a moment. Then Wiktor could be seen moving a freshly filled glass of orange liquid to her setting, beside a place containing something reddish and gold – the promised dessert.

His quick glance in her direction almost made her duck down. His facial expression puzzled Io, briefly as he fussed with his jacket pocket. For an instant he looked relieved. Then Wiktor turned to his left – her right – and seemed to nod to somebody seated among the dim booths and shadowed dining cubbies.

Had he recognized someone he knew? Hardly surprising, considering the circles he kept.

Composing her features, Io emerged from behind the wall and smiled as she approached the table. *He is old-fashioned,* she thought as he rose to hold her chair for her. 'What's this?' She dabbed her fork at the creamy eruption on her plate.

'A surprise. You'll like it.'

A forkful hesitated near her nose. 'It smells spicy.'

'It is.' He smiled. 'That's why I ordered you something to drink. But I'm sure you'll love it.' With that he winked, and took a portion from his own serving into his mouth. The goggle-eyed pantomime of pleasure which followed made Io laugh.

The dessert was delicious. It also made her eyes water. 'Well!' She coughed. 'I certainly won't have any trouble with my sinuses during the flight!'

'It always makes me thirsty,' he said, taking a sip of wine. Watching his eyes, she reached for the brimming glass of orange juice.

Would she have suspected anything if she had not continued taking classes? Had she never studied the hard-won wisdom of a century's research, she probably would never have known about those subtle cues given off by child and man, in eye and face and voice, that betray the inner unease.

But then, Io's knowledge was still abstract. So maybe it was instinct – unreliable but desperately useful when it strikes – which made her notice the intense way Wiktor watched her hand.

She put the glass down before it was more than an inch high. His gaze immediately flicked to her face. 'Is something wrong?' he asked.

Please. No. She prayed.

'No, nothing's wrong.' She lifted another forkful of the pungent sweet. 'I was just savouring the taste.'

He seemed to notice the speculation in her eyes, and averted his gaze. That was a mistake. Now he *avoided* looking at the juice glass.

The second spicy taste added power to the first. Io's throat burned, her nostrils felt singed. Still she kept her hand on the table, and concentrated on remembering her lessons.

Speaking with a measured voice, she said, 'Actually, I think I will have another glass of wine, after all.'

Rapid impressions she read almost instantly – brief panic-contraction in the pupils . . . a faint, barely noticeable flush wave, crossing his cheeks at an unsatisfactory angle . . . that involuntary frown, quickly compressed into a slightly asymmetrical smile with the practice of an accomplished poseur . . .

An experienced liar, then. But not a trained one.

The man Io would someday marry would not lie. But he would have taken schooling in what lying *does*. How it is seen, detected, known.

This man, for all his money and worldliness, had never been to school.

'More wine? In your condition?' He laughed teasingly. A little patronizingly. 'Now, Io. Don't try to prove how tough you are. Be a good girl and drink your vitamins.'

My vitamins? Io thought. She reached for the glass.

Here are my vitamins, you son of a fabricow.

'Jism!' he cried, leaping to his feet as she spilled the drink across the tablecloth.

Two confirmations in one action. An innocent man would not have shouted so over only a silly puddle.

Nor would a real professional use a curseword specific to a certain type of freelance artist.

'You bitch, how did you kn – ' He stepped forward, and so came within Io's seated reach. With one hand she grabbed the loose folds of his stylish cotton trousers. With the other she stabbed down hard with her dessert fork. There was a loud tearing of fabric. Shouting for strength she had never used before outside the decanting room, Io yanked.

The resulting tableau held for a long moment. Staring patrons. Aghast waiters. Io, panting with upraised fork, ready to strike again, this time at a loathsome sight.

Under the torn trousers, hanging like a broken flag, lay Wiktor's codpiece, the emblem of his calling. His tattooed licence told of a costly modification – placental platinum extraction filters of the very latest design.

No wonder Wiktor knew his way around style. Just one of the altered wrigglers he produced in millions could set a pieceworker on course towards her best bonus ever. And for him a healthy commission.

'Why?' she whspered.

Motion resumed. Hurried footsteps approached behind her.

'Officers!' Wiktor pronounced loudly, for all to hear. 'I want to press charges against this madwoman, for assault with intent to injure me!'

Hands pressed upon her shoulders. The fork was ungently pried from her fingers. Io shook her hair back and looked him in the eyes, defiantly.

'Shall we take the tablecloth along to the police station, then?' She gestured toward the orange stain.

A quick blinking of the eyes, a bobbing of the Adam's apple as he suddenly swallowed. 'Wait!' Wiktor said as the guards began pulling her away. His sour expression was her bitter reward. 'I – I have changed my mind. I will forget the incident . . . so long as she boards her flight and gets the hell out of here.'

Oh, I'm sure, she thought, watching him squirm. Men

who would poison women – such men had personalities based on contempt for others. Probably until this very moment he had never even considered what might happen if he were caught. Now it was just dawning on him, too late.

'Who?' Io asked, simply, demanding a price.

As if it were costing him his gall bladder, he spat the word. 'Perseph.'

Io knew from the look in his eyes that she would have no need for revenge on her former friend. Far from the type of man he had tried to appear to be, this was a cowardly, predatory creature, the sort who preyed exclusively on those weaker than himself. Io felt certain he would never come near her again. *Perseph,* though – perhaps watching even now from some shadowy corner of the room – had real cause to worry about Wiktor.

'*What* was it?'

Sweat beaded on his lip and brow. There was an implicit arrangement here, truth in exchange for escape. But in fulfilling his part first, Wiktor knew he was giving himself over fully into her hands.

'Para – Parapyridine 4,' he whispered rapidly, trying to make the words for her alone.

Io felt suddenly dizzy. The hand that had touched the juice glass trembled as if defiled. The substance named would not have affected her own health in the slightest. But it would have ruined the product she carried, and made her own eggs utterly useless for anything in the future. She'd be lucky to be able to make solvent filters if she had taken any of that stuff.

'*Why?*' She repeated her first question.

His face was now utterly resigned. 'You were getting too damned high-almighty. Wanted to climb out and leave your friends, your guild. We . . . they . . . thought it would do you good to be brought down a peg.

'It was for – for your own good . . .' he finished lamely. His handsome confidence was now so completely gone that Io felt stunned that she had ever been fooled at all.

'Excuse me, Madam, is this fellow admitting to having done you some harm?'

Io turned, noticing the blonde Icelandic policeman for the first time. Obviously, he had followed bits of their low, clipped exchange, picking up on hints with obvious skill. His eyes flicked from her surropreg garments to Wiktor's tattoo, to the stained tablecloth, narrowing with dawning suspicion.

He spoke English as educated Icelanders do, better than the English. 'Perhaps you'd like to file charges of your own, Madam?' he asked.

For an instant, Io stared at the policeman's face in sudden revelation. There she saw compassion and more . . . a *confidence* completely unrelated to arrogance . . . a serenity that only came of skill and the sure knowledge of one's own usefulness. Face to face with the real thing, Io wondered how she had ever been fooled by Wiktor's sham.

Inexperience and wishful thinking, I suppose. She would have to talk this over with her teachers.

'No,' Io said softly. 'I will not press charges. But would you please walk with me to my boarding gate? I think I could use a hand.'

Her last word to Viktor was to thank him over her shoulder for dinner. The evenness of her tone must have been more unnerving than anything else she might have said. She left him standing there, pale and exposed.

The officer's gentle strong grip on her arm helped Io walk head high. Somewhere in the restaurant's gloom, she knew she was being watched by one more person – someone lacking the guts to show herself. Io didn't bother searching the shadows for those familiar eyes. She would never see them again.

. . . Earlier we have seen excerpts by writers extolling the benefits of an industrial order based on efficient biological assembly processes. And there is no doubt that these techniques are in large measure responsible for the relative comfort of today's

nine billion human beings, not least the fact that they have not starved.

The mysticism of the Madrid Catholics, their religious revulsion towards even completely voluntary use of human reproductive systems for industry, is not shared by many others these days. Rather, the right of the poor to use their bodies' talents for their own benefit is enshrined in law, so long as volunteers are qualified and restrict themselves to licensed, non-human embryonic material.

Nevertheless some dissenting voices have spoken critically of this system from more rational grounds – scientific, biological, economic and cultural. Some fear that our fundamental attitude towards life itself is changing, subtly but profoundly, as each day passes. And these changes are taking place without adequate thought to the possible long-range consequences. These are doubts that must, in all fairness, be taken seriously. . . .

– from A SURVEY OF MODERN PROBLEMS, New York, 2049.

. . . The time may come when these peculiarly severe licensing laws may be relaxed. But for now, the intrinsic value of this particular product to society – by far the most valuable item produced by any society – has convinced lawmakers and voters alike that one particular career calls for schooling, qualification, and respect above any and all others . . .

– from THE CERTIFICATION ACT, 2039.

Another penalty of egg work was the lengthy, all too realistic process of labour. Io took the doctors' word for it that it was still a bit easier than the 'real thing'. But that was small comfort.

Not that difficulty or exertion held any great fears for her. Io knew what she was doing.

Still, Joey held her hand through the agony of transition. And afterwards he wiped the perspiration from her brow. It was all just part of the agency's service, he told her. Just one more reason why so few of his clients ever left him.

Io knew better, of course. Joey actually cared, bless him.

'Did I remember to curse you for getting me into this?' she asked after the worst was over.

'Nope. You forgot.' Joey smiled. 'You missed your chance. The tradition is that nothing said during transition can be held against you. Maybe next time.'

'I told you, Joey, there isn't going to be a – '

'Hush. We'll speak of it later. Now, you concentrate. The worst may be over, but you still have hard pushing ahead.'

'Okay, Joey.'

Tremors. Foreshadowings. Io focused on her breathing and was ready when the next contractions came.

'Good, good,' the industrial midwife told her. A technician in the service of Technique Zaire, she commanded her team with crisp precision. 'Now please to be ready for a last effort.'

'Ah.' Io replied in a sharp exhalation. 'Ah!' Then she lost track of time. Lost track of consciousness. Moment by moment she did as she was told by those whose job it was to help her. Several times she cried out in the ways she had been taught, conserving her strength for the final moment.

When it came, it was almost anticlimactic. Passage, release, evacuation. A parting of that familiar connection.

Emptiness.

The scurrying techs had no attention to spare for her. Even Joey rushed forward, eager to see. When he returned, his eyes beamed. 'I – I thought it would be a shipbrain, Io, but I was wrong. It's a *starbrain*!'

'S – starbrain?'

'Yes! It's a fine, big, healthy starbrain. The only biomanufactured product licensed to use true human genes! The only one capable of sentience!'

Io's lower lip trembled. Tears welled in her eyes. She began to sob. Joey, mistaking her tears for joy, kept on exulting, obliviously.

'Jeez, Io, it will *think*. It'll pilot starships. Why, they're even talking about a bill to give starbrains *citizenship*, for heaven's sake! Do you know what they're *paying* for a healthy . . .'

Joey's voice droned on, a low ululation of misplaced enthusiasm. Io shut it out. She flung an arm over her eyes so she could not see when they came forward with a swaddled something to show her.

They did not know. They could not know how she felt.

Her breasts throbbed as they attached machines for her first milking, to release the straining pressure. To begin harvesting secondary product from the right. Tertiary from the left.

Tertiary product. Colostrum and homo milk, at five pence a gramme.

Her left breast sent unwanted signals to her brain.

'Io, I've just been told they're so happy with you they want to renew . . .'

'Oh, Joey,' she cried. 'Go away, please!' Io's head rocked. 'Just go away.'

And so they left her then, to listen to the rhythms, to the machines, to the beating of her heart, to the singing in her veins.

It has to be worth it, she thought. She prayed. *It has to be!*

To: Ms Iolanthe Livingstone
93 Marina Drive
Ellesmere Port, Merseyside

From: British Division
Department of Certification
and Accreditation

Dear Ms Livingstone:

It is our great pleasure to inform you that your test scores, your record of experience, and the recommendations of your instructors have, in totality, persuaded the Board that you are indeed qualified for the certification you requested. By your assiduous efforts you have acquired skills of great importance to humanity. Skills which may lead, at last, to a generation of people no longer plagued by the age-old evils of cruelty and fear and neurosis and unfulfilled potential – evils which so nearly destroyed our world, and hard beset us still to this day.

Towards that brighter future, you and your professional enthusiasm will surely add new strength and purpose.

Therefore, from this date forward, you are hereby licensed to engage in the most demanding and important occupation of them all.

Congratulations. We are certain you will be a very fine (mother/~~father~~).

For the sake of the children . . .

IAN MCDONALD

Listen

Brother Innocence is out in his boat, riding the waters, riding the waves of the sea. With rod, and line, and skill, and stillness, he is hunting the fish that swim the cold waters about the island at the end of the world. All is shiver, all is shimmer, all is stillness. Brother Innocence waits. Brother Innocence listens. He can sense the big fish down there in the cold waters. The hook waits, the line, the gaff. Still. Close. *Come fish come.*

Then he hears the sound. The sound of a flyer coming across the waters at the end of the world. Brother Innocence listens to it beating on the sky. Hunting is forgotten. The big fish swims away. Safe today. Oars touch the water and carry the currach over the waves to the shore. He watches the flyer approach. It is one of the new kind: a shapeshifter. So, they are allowed to make machines that can change shape again. As it comes across the water he watches how its form changes: wings retract into rounded stumps, propellers swivel upward and elongate into rotors. The flyer is new to Brother Innocence, but the yin-yang World Health markings on its side are familiar. So; it happens again. Another survivor to watch and ward and accompany into the grey shadowlands.

The aircraft touches down at the end of the beach near the big rocks like grey, beached whales. A boy scrambles out onto the sand. He takes shelter among the whale rocks as the flyer shakes itself free of the island at the end of the world. From his rocks the boy watches until sight and sound of the aircraft are gone. Then he sits down on the grey whale rocks with his head in his hands.

Brother Innocence makes no move towards the boy. He waits. He listens. Listens in the way that only a very few can listen, a listening that has set him apart from all other people and sent him to his island at the end of the world. As yet, he can hear nothing. He will. Later.

This boy, this survivor, this one-in-ten-thousand, what is he like? Scruffy. Frayed jeans gone green with age. Torn Fair Isle pullover. Bare feet. They always send them to him with bare feet. They will have told him nothing. Brother Innocence despises them for that. For all their shapeshifting flyers and proud emblems, they are cowards. Brother Innocence runs his currach up onto the beach. Still he does not go to the boy. But he feels the resonance in his mind. It is a quicksilver thing, an echo, a mirror image shaped like a mind, no sooner grasped than gone like the quicksilver porpoises which dive through the cold waters of world's end. It is almost not there at all, but it is a beginning. Brother Innocence climbs the stony path to his home, a scatter of turf-roofed oratories and meditatoriums. Deep within his noontime devotions, the first scatterings of impressions come bursting into his contemplations like rowdy gulls: *lonely beneath the shoulders of cold grey whale rocks: whisper of wind in the needles of pines: sea like steel and silver, mirror of the cold in the bone: alone, alone*. He is ready then.

Under a sky the colour of plovers' eggs, Brother Innocence makes his fire. He builds it carefully, ringing it with stones, sheltering it from the wind until the flames die down into coals crusted with white ash. He cleans and guts a sea-bass. He slides the fish onto a holly-wood spit and broils it over the embers. He closes his eyes. He sees: *himself. Old man huddled by a tiny fire glow under the enormous sky of world's end.*

'You like fish?' says Brother Innocence without looking up from his fire.

'I hate fish,' says the boy. He sounds surprised.

'Pity,' says Brother Innocence, still without looking. He

brushes wind-blown sand from his fish with a gull feather. 'You're goin' to be kind of hungry here.'

'I'm hungry now,' says the boy.

'I don't doubt it.'

'Have you anything else than fish?'

'Some cheese. Some yoghurt. Vegetables, eggs, back at home,' says Brother Innocence.

'I hate cheese, I can't stand yoghurt, I loathe vegetables and eggs make me puke,' says the boy. But he comes anyway.

That night there is a storm. The first of the great storms of autumn. It comes without warning. All of a sudden it is hurling itself on the island at the end of the world as if it would tear it loose and cast it into the sea. But this drystone bothy has seen many autumn gales and in the warmth of a fire of turf and pineknots there is comfort, and security, and, in a sense, fellowship.

'You don't say very much,' says the boy. His name is Daniel.

'Silence suits me well,' says Brother Innocence. 'It is a gift to me, silence.'

'What do you mean?' Daniel lies on sheep skins by the fire, chin propped on knuckles. He has heard enough of the voice of the storm. It is human voices he wants to hear, human stories. But Brother Innocence will not oblige. His task is to listen, not to tell. As Brother Innocence is content with his silence, Daniel finally rolls into sleep. The storm shakes the island at the end of the world, and Daniel dreams. Still in his chair, Brother Innocence listens to the dream.

The dream is of a great plain of wheat. In the middle of the great plain is a small town. In that town are mothers and fathers and preachers and teachers and gas station attendants and policepersons and firepersons and storepersons and lawpersons and the farmers who grow the yellow wheat. Nothing ever happens in this town, which is just how people who live in towns like this like it. Until one night the dry winds of summer blow a spore of the Shining Plague from the dead cities of the western seaboard across the mountains and valleys and plains of wheat, and come the morning one third of the people who wanted their own town always to be just the way it was are dead, huddles of shining black crystal.

In the dream there is a meeting of all the town elders. Behind locked council chamber doors they reach a terrible decision. Even before the black flyers of World Health come out of the sky, the people choose to quarantine themselves. Strictly. Absolutely. Not a soul in. Not a soul out. We do not need your soldiers and your guns, thank you, say the town elders. We can look after ourselves. We will seal the plague up in our small town on the great plains and those who live will live and those who die will die. So the flyers return to the sky and when they come back again the scientists in the silver isolation suits find two thousand mounds of black crystal in the streets.

A whole town has died.

All save one. The World Health teams find him tied to his bed with torn handkerchiefs. He is emaciated, dehydrated, bloodied where he has torn at his ties. But he is alive. He has survived. He is the one-in-ten-thousand.

With the morning the storm clears. New light fills the morning edge of the world, red sun rising above ragged black squall clouds low along the horizon. It lights Brother Innocence wandering down the tideline. He is troubled by what he has seen in Daniel's dreams and memories. The great dying going on there, down below the horizon, disturbs him. Gulls hover and dip above his lowered head. His prying, poking stick goes seeking out the treasures of the storm line. Nothing to be found. Someone has combed this beach before him. Far down the sand, a black silhouette kneels.

Panic stricken, Brother closes his eyes, summons the sharing of selves. Has he found them? Has he been there?

Relief. The boy has not trespassed beyond the black rocks to the point. Then what has he found? *Music! Listen! Hands busy building. Sounds have their architectures; the shell contains the song of the sea, the stone the song of the earth, the tree, the white gulls' feather, the song of the wind.*

What is this he is building?

Patterns of shells thrust end-down into the sand, a baffling maze of interconnected spirals major and minor. At the centre of each spiral is a pillar of dribbled sand surmounted by pieces of jetsam from the storm's edge. A rattle of black crows' feathers. A pair of desiccated crab-claws. A salt-bleached bone. A plastic bottle scabbed with gritty oil. A piece of ship's timber, painted blue, named 'Amelia'. A pebble of sand-scoured bottle glass, green and opaque as the sea itself. Brother Innocence steps into this mandala of shells and sea-wrack.

'No!' cries the boy. Cry flat, sharp as the crack of a beaching whale. 'You have to do it this way. Follow the spirals.' Bemused, Brother Innocence enters the maze of spirals within spirals about spirals and the spirals spiral him round; winding him inward to the central sanctum where Daniel squats, waiting, fingers resting on the cold sea-rippled sand.

'Heard it in the night,' he explains. 'At first I wasn't sure it was there at all, I kept losing it in the storm but the more I listened the more I could hear and the more I could hear the more I had to know what it was, where it was coming from. So I waited until the storm had passed and I went out and I felt it calling me, along the beach, to this place where it all seemed to come together, to focus, to turn into something else.'

Spiral-led, Brother Innocence joins Daniel at the focus of the maze.

'Listen,' says Daniel, 'do you hear it?'

'Hear what?' says Brother Innocence.

'The music,' says Daniel.

But Brother Innocence hears only the sound of the wind in the dune grass.

Again Daniel says, 'Listen.'

But Brother Innocence hears only the cry of the gulls and the barking of the seals out at sea.

A third time Daniel says, 'Listen.'

And Brother Innocence listens with all the disciplines of a contemplative. With all the sensitivity of his talent. *Windwhisper sandslither seaslumber, wind in the feathers wind in the bones wind in the pinecones wind humming across the streamlines of a sea-ground glass lens.* And he hears it. It is all those things. It is none of them. It is a chord. A harmony, a song shaped from wind and wuthering which transcends all material origins. It is unspeakably beautiful. It is unspeakably terrible. And it is gone.

Brother Innocence stands shaken at the focus of Daniel's maze. Then, smashing shells, stamping pinecones glass pebbles crow feathers bird bones into the sand, he kicks the listening place to pieces.

'You don't come near this place again, you hear?' he shouts at Daniel. 'I don't want you comin' down this end of the beach again.'

Too high. Too far. Too soon. Above all: too close. Brother Innocence fears for his ward. Brother Innocence fears for himself. He *heard*.

By evening the high tide has smoothed away the shells and the spirals. Daniel does not go down that end of the beach again. But it is not the end of the listening places. There are other places he finds where natural elements are focused into something preternatural. Places of stone and wood and spirit. Cairns and arches and circles of piled stones on a bald hill top which focus the light into the shadows of some other place where strange geometric entities spin, half-glimpsed, less comprehended. A secret wooded glen where mobiles of leaves and sticks and berries bend gravity until, impossibly, the trees seem to be both crashing down all around and tearing free from the earth to leap into the sky. Torn fishing nets and glass floats and empty bottles arranged over the backs of the grey whale rocks which somehow draws the seals and the porpoises and the hovering sea-birds to wait and worship. *Tabernacles,* Daniel calls them, child of Bible-believers. Brother Innocence marvels. For the first time he allows himself to hope. None of the others could ever bring the things inside their minds out into the real world. Perhaps Daniel is the one, the true survivor. And then the fears come: what if he is not?

The hopes and the fears drive Brother Innocence to do something he has only done once before. In the night, when Daniel is asleep, he opens the wings of his mind to listen with his brethren. It is not a thing any of his kind do lightly. To turn listening mind to listening mind is like turning two mirrors to face each other. Reflections of reflections of reflections. A man may be lost in the infinite regress of reflections of his own mind. But Brother Innocence is old and wise. Enclosed in the stone sanctuary of his oratory, he opens his mind to enclose a whole world. In the darkness, lights burn, the soul-glow of others like himself.

Touch . . .

The dancing dapple of leaves in a clearing lost in the great forest where the young man lives with his ward.

The wind in the yellow grass as the old, bent woman leaves her earthen house dug into the plains to fetch water for her dying ward.

The narrow band of blue that is all the universe the man who lives in the deep, shadowy canyon can bear.

The cold breath of the glaciers high above the mountains where the young woman has built her lodge.

With each one he shares his hopes and fears and the things that he has seen and heard and asks, 'Is he the one, is he?' Then, as the kaleidoscope of mutually reflecting sense impressions threatens to engulf him, comes the reply. 'Wait. Wait. Wait.' Brother Innocence touches mind after mind after mind and from each he receives the same reply: 'Wait. Wait. Wait.' Last of all Brother Innocence touches the light that glows all alone in the great white desert. He feels the sting of the sun upon the shoulders of the woman on top of the red stone pillar. They know each other of old, from the days in the Unit when she, seizing upon a small irritation of speech, gave him his name: Brother In-A-Sense. They share souls. She reads his heart. Then, in answer, she shares with him her hopes, her fears. They take the form of a vision; of the end times after Brother In-A-Sense and those like him are gone.

Fifty of them. Fifty are all there are. Some have crossed a continent to come to this meeting in a desert place. None have come empty handed. All have brought some thing, some object which in some fashion symbolizes the people they have come to venerate. Under a vicious sun, they arrange their objects and found things and weave them in and out of the natural things of this high mesa in a pattern subtle and intricate. It is not a task completed easily or quickly. It is dark by the time the final stone is slotted into its place. But as that stone completes the pattern, the mesa rings with power. Streamers of light flow along the subtle, intricate channels of the grand design. Woven within the web of light, they speak. Their language is only partly verbal, there are dimensions of mood and posture and scent and place beyond normal comprehension. But Brother Innocence, sharer of souls, understands.

One by one, they speak.

'Ephemeral generation,' they say, and Brother Innocence has images of butterflies, mayflies, red desert poppies. *'Bridge between two evolutions, leading nowhere,'* says another, in visions of desert arches, rainbows after the spring storms. *'You knew you could only be the intermediate step,'* says another, and a fourth continues, *'Yet, sterile, childless, doomed to obsolescence, you loved us, guided us faithfully.' 'And for that, we thank you,'* says yet another.

'And for that, we grieve for you,' they all say, all these survivors, these inheritors, and the wind chases the words away.

Then Brother Innocence asks his question: – Is he the one, is he? – *Someday, there must be one.*

– Why? Can't a plague just be a plague?

– *Because that condemns the whole race to death. Because it denies hope. In ourselves. In our future.*

Again: – Do you think he is the one?

– *I hope so.*

She believes in human evolution, human improvability. Brother Innocence believes only in humans. That is why he fears. And hopes. But he is not alone in his hope, and that is good. It is time, he thinks, to tell the truth. Gently. Hard truths must be told gently. He begins with his own story. He waits for a storm night, of wind and rain and a darkness so huge it seems to swallow the island at the end of the world whole, a night for voices, and stories. And this is the story he tells; the story of the man who heard too much.

For thirty-three years the man who heard too much lived in one of the great cities of the western sea-board in those glad days before the plague turned those bright cities into mortuaries. In his thirty-three years he had gained an education, a job selling advertising and a woman who he knew would make him happy for the rest of his life. And he was no more, or less, extraordinary than any other man of thirty-three years. Until one afternoon, one Saturday afternoon, while recuperating from a bout of shopping in a quiet coffee shop in a corner of a big mall, he quite suddenly leaped to his feet clutching at his head and screaming for them to stop stop go away; reeling, stumbling, knocking over tables, chairs, shopping trolleys, spilling pots of hot coffee over babies in buggies, all the time screaming stop stop stop Oh God Oh God shut up shut up! until he fell to his knees beating his fists on the floortiles with all the Saturday afternoon shoppers steering their trolleys around him not quite not staring or asking whazzamadderwiddim? whazzrrong? Geezdrunk*bum*. But what none of the Saturday afternoon mallcrawlers could ever know, not even the dear woman who would have made him happy for the rest of his life, was that God or Karma or Destiny or WhatEver had opened each one of his senses to the lives of each one of the three thousand shoppers in Todos Santos mall that Saturday afternoon and that he was drowning in the ocean of their experiences: thoughts, feelings, emotions, sensations, fears, hopes, everything they touched tasted smelled heard saw; breaking over him like a drown-wave of roaring voices.

– *Silence. Silence!* He begged to be struck blind, deaf, insensible. *Silence. Please.*

But in the hospital where they put him there was no silence.

And there was no silence in the special facility where the men from the newly-founded World Health took him to study what they called his 'phenomenon'.

And there was no silence in the special unit with the others who exhibited this 'phenomenon'. It was worse there, for he felt not just those twenty other minds, but the reflections of twenty times twenty times twenty. Some went mad, but some held on. And some learned mastery.

Not until the helicopter which marooned him on the shore of the island at the end of the world was a blink of dust in the sky, did he know silence and peace.

'You're an empath,' says Daniel. Resinous pine-knots flare; flameshadows caper on white-washed stone walls.

'That's one name for us. World Health would much rather you referred to me as a Very Low Frequency Electromagnetic Field Receiver, which is more accurate and less mystical but is one heck of a mouthful. In a sense, we're all awash with these very long-wavelength electromagnetic radiations; you know about frequency and wavelength and all that? Seems our brain generates it just by thinking. What's special about us empaths is that we are, in a sense, like radio receivers, we pick up the radiation your brain gives off like dowsers pick up electromagnetic wobbles in the ground to find water. Human radios. Dowsers of the soul, in a sense.'

And that is one question answered. The gentlest. Two more remain. First: what is the plague? That is a crueller question. Second: Why am I here? That is the cruellest question of all.

Everything in its time. Brother Innocence listens and waits. He is very good at that. Then, on a dirty day of grey wet clouds and dismal drizzle, he asks and answers the first of the questions. Man and boy are cleaning out the goatshed when he says, without preamble:

'It's a man-made thing. You probably know that already. But it's not a living thing. That might surprise you, but it's true. The plague isn't an organism. It's an artifact. A machine, you might say. The Third Industrial Revolution, originally. I didn't know there'd been a Second Industrial Revolution between the First and the Third, but anyway, here it was, the revolution of nanotechnology. That's the manufacture of machines the size of living cells which, like cells, can create specialized copies of themselves to perform different functions. They can reproduce like living cells, if there's raw material for them to build from, and they all link together, like the cells in the human body, into a complete machine. You take one spore too tiny to be seen and from it you can grow automobiles, aircraft, televisions, all in a matter of minutes. What's more, you can program your nanomachines to rebuild what they've already made. If you don't like your automobile, you can change it into a refrigerator, or into a microlight. Shapeshifters, you might say. That flyer that brought you in is a nanomachine. It's only now, thirty years on, that we're finally getting the Third Industrial Revolution. For all the good it'll do us. But the first nanomachine, back then, had to be the nanocomputer which could later program all the others to make them do what they were meant to do.

'A company called Mach NanoTek patented the prototype nanocomputer; it was a spore designed to build computers modelled on the way the human brain works; that is, not doing one thing at a time, like the old computers did, but doing all kinds of different things at once, like you walking and talking and chewing gum and bouncing a ball and listening to the radio at the same time. And all this at the superspeeds of modern computers. Some pup, was the Mark One Nanocomputer.' Brother Innocence forks goat-muck onto the rain-soaked cobbles of the yard. 'Well, you know what happened. The prototype escaped. I've heard some folk say it was deliberately released, and they've even invented some madman they think did it. I don't know, I don't think anyone would be that crazy or that evil. Anyway, it's loose. Within two years of its escape from Mach NanoTek, it had spread in inactive spore form to every part of the world. And then, people started to die. One or two at first, then whole townsful.' *Huddled crystal carapaces in windswept streets.* 'World Health tried to contain it by quarantine; it was a good try but all it did was slow it up a little. You see, it's latent in eighty percent of the Earth's population, and all it takes is one active case to trigger a whole infected population into activity as well as infect the previously uninfected.'

'Forty-eight percent of infected cases go active,' says Daniel.

'That's right. In a sense, it's its very success as a piece of engineering that makes it so deadly. It was designed to mimic the human brain, and in the central nervous system of its hosts, it finds the perfect model. So when it goes active, it starts to deposit silicon crystals throughout the victim's C.N.S. It leaches minerals and trace elements from the host's body to supply raw materials. Eating earth is a common symptom in the latter stages, but usually the victim dies before the process of siliconization has got that far.'

'Usually,' says Daniel the survivor.

'Usually,' says Brother Innocence.

But in the long nights when the winter constellations hang close in the sky, Brother Innocence walks the landscapes of Daniel's dreams. These are alien places: the parasite in Daniel's brain is twisting his mind. The song of the atoms. The secret life of rocks. The sacrament of water. The mystery of light. And the Tabernacles, with their spirits of tree and stone and wind and sea made incarnate, are tools to understand these mysteries. Night after night Daniel wrestles with angels in the dome of his skull and Brother Innocence watches. And waits. Understanding too huge for a single mind to contain. The alien within. Twelve times before, Brother Innocence has seen his wards come to this point of confrontation with the alien inside them.

It is the dawn of the winter solstice. And Brother Innocence wakes suddenly, shatteringly, from the light sleep of old men. Impressions of cold, clean footprints along a tide-washed shore. Clouds. Wind. Stars. A sea calling. Daniel, gone. (*Bed sheets still warmly creased.*) Gone? Where? No. Not there. Not there. Old bones protest, old feet cold as stones, heavy as stones, as the old man runs down the beach. The moon is low. The horizon is limned in grey. Perhaps, perhaps, he has not gone there . . .

He should have told him. He should not have waited to be gentle. But he could not bear to feel Daniel's hurt. An old man's remorse as he runs, panting, aching, along a cold beach.

The small ravine among the black rocks is filled with shadows. Shadows and gleaming black crystals. Nothing lives in that small ravine any more. Only crystals. Where there was once grass: clumps of crystal. Where there had once been a wind-scoured tree: crystal branches, crystal trunk. Ferns, spirals of crystal. Flowers, heathers, whin bushes, even the lichen scabbing the rocks: crystal. Brother Innocence climbs down into the defile. Crystals snap and fall to powder beneath his feet. In a valley of shadows Daniel is a solid darkness in the shelter of the big rock. At his feet, the graves. Twelve graves. The names on the crude pitch-pine head-boards are almost obliterated by the mass of clambering crystals.

'That's why I'm here, is it?' he says. 'To end up like that.'

'No,' says Brother Innocence. 'It's not like that, Daniel.'

'Don't lie!' shouts Daniel. 'Do not lie to me, old man!'

'I've never lied to you,' says Brother Innocence. 'But at least know all there is to know before you judge me. So, I didn't tell you everything about the plague. I'm sorry. I was a coward. We empaths tend to be cowards; we can't bear to feel the pain we cause in others. I wanted to be gentle, but it wouldn't let me. I'm sorry. So, the truth. The truth is, it isn't a plague at all. It's a symbiont. So, you're asking, a symbiont that kills its partner? World Health believe that, successfully linked together in symbiosis, infected humans are an evolutionary step towards the humanity of the future, in a sense, a symbiosis of man and machine. The reasoning goes like this; as humanity reaches out into the cosmos, into realms of experience and understanding infinitely greater than any ever imagined before, so his consciousness, his awareness, in a sense, must be made capable of accommodating what we find out there. The theory is that out of the fusion of human and nanomachine, neuron and viron, comes new perceptions, new understandings, new ways of processing information; an altogether new consciousness.

'Personally, I don't agree with that: I've lived on this island thirty years and I've seen the plague spread from my old homeland to obliterate half of humanity. I'm old and old men have a natural inclination towards cynicism. There are other empaths who believe wholeheartedly in man's improvability; me, I'll believe in the new humanity when I see the new humanity.'

'So do you think I'm one of these new humans?'

'You baffle me, I'm afraid. You make an old cynical man hope. You see things no one else has ever seen, hear things no one else has ever heard.'

'It's like a pressure in my head, all these thoughts, building up and up and up until I feel I'm going to explode. I have to let them out, I have to try and make sense out of them; that's why I built the Tabernacles, to try and make sense out of what I was feeling.'

'And you bring them out of the invisible world into the visible. Your thoughts, your feelings, made visible, not just here,' the old man touches his heart, 'but here,' and he touches his eyes, his ears, his lips.

Then it is as if Daniel remembers there are twelve graves at his feet.

'And what about them? Were they the new humans too?'

'They were survivors. Like you. I watched them as I have watched you. I watched them struggle with this new consciousness. I watched them fail. And in here,' he touches his heart again, 'I felt them burn and die. That was what World Health sent me here to do. To go with them, to go with you, as far into death as any man may and still return. And to bring back what I find there to help those who come after.'

'After me? Is that what you mean? Was I brought here to die?'

'We hope. There must be a first.'

'Must there?'

The sun is up now. The light only emphasizes the raw cold.

'I hate you,' Daniel says.

Brother Innocence nods. Out in the cold waters, seals are calling to each other.

The conclusion is close now. Brother Innocence can sense it. Shapes vast as moving continents are wheeling in Daniel's thoughts. He struggles to comprehend. He fails. Struggles again. Fails. Brother Innocence no longer dares to enter his oratory to contemplate. His meditations and disciplines of the spirit are haunted by desolation. Foolish old man to have hoped. Cruel old man to have held out that spark of hope to Daniel. Desolation. Cold. Too high. Too far. Too soon. As it always was. Barefoot in the frost, Daniel calls upon his Tabernacles for revelation. Nothing.

The Final Tabernacle; that is Daniel's name for it. Three days without sleep, without rest, without pause even for food or water: in its hunger for symbiosis the viron parasite drives Daniel to frenzied hyperactivity. Pots pans pillows; boots bread brushes, plastic chicken-feed sacks; cups, cheese, cutlery. Brother Innocence is a man who has renounced possessions but what few are necessary to maintain life on the island at the end of the world are taken by Daniel and melded into his Final Tabernacle. Brother Innocence watches in amazement the careful juxtapositions and balancings, the suspendings and pivotings, the creation of complex chains of connectivity between objects with no possible earthly connection, mapped out with lengths of green baler twine: the thing's final connection to the strange, sourceless power that slowly turns the wheels and cogs and carousels and elevators; slowly at first, but gathering speed, faster, faster, until the unlikely contraption sings with movement and life.

It is a thing of sunlight, Brother Innocence realizes, waking with the dawn, sleeping through the night. And when the pale winter rays are full, it is a delicate dragonfly of hummings and whirrings, of complex orbit and gyrations, enfolding Daniel within its spinnings and wheelings. Hours, days, he sits crosslegged amid the flying pots and pans and whirling carousels of shoes and plants, moving from his meditations only to tune a spindle here, turn a potted plant *so* there, tighten a thread, crank a ratchet. Still he does not eat, does not sleep. He drinks what dew settles on his lips. Like his Tabernacle, he must be a thing of sunlight. Brother Innocence's comprehension is only fleeting; he does not dare look into Daniel's mind too long for fear that what he sees there will burn him up. But one thing he grasps from the mental fire is that in their very mundanity, their very banality, the plates and shoes and shovels and rooftiles of the Final Tabernacle are a lens through which Daniel will magnify his consciousness to encompass his revelation of a new universe.

'Daniel, are you coming in now?'

'Daniel, something to eat?'

'Daniel, drink this soup, it's good, go on, try it.'

'Daniel, at least put this quilt around you.'

Useless. Too far. Too high. Too soon. Much, much too soon.

'I don't want to lose him!' cries Brother Innocence to the sky and the sea and the stones. 'Don't do this! I can't see any more, I've seen too much already.' But all Brother Innocence can do is wait. And listen. As he always has. And when it comes, it makes sure that he sees it coming. All that day the boy's mind has been filled with dark, circling raven shapes that Brother Innocence fears to name, much less touch. When it comes, it comes by night. The cry wakes Brother Innocence from his old man's sleep. He has been expecting it. He dresses quickly, warmly, and goes into the yard.

His heart flutters in fear.

The Final Tabernacle . . . is insane. Berserk. Spinning out of control. Faster faster faster wheels spin cranks pump pistons heave, faster, faster, creaking shivering shuddering.

It is not a think of sunlight any more. It has found another source of power, Daniel himself. Trapped within scything, slashing wheels, Daniel is being drained even as Brother Innocence watches. He calls the boy's name, two, five, ten times. But Daniel has been taken by the symbiont. Lost. He does not even know what his Final Tabernacle is doing to him. Black crystals glint at the tips of his fingers, in the folds of his eyes.

'Daniel!' He cannot reach the boy. Not this way. But there is another way. Brother Innocence breathes deep, closes his eyes. Opens himself to receive. This time there are no Unit-taught disciplines. This time there are no barriers, no restraints. Brother Innocence casts himself into the storm of emotion and is swept away.

He begins in darkness. A nothing, a gno-thing, a gno-on, the fundamental unit of consciousness, tinier than the tiniest unit of length, shorter than the briefest tick of time. Growing. Developing. Expanding. Rising up out of darkness into the trinities of quarks in all their strangeness and charm: growing: now he has left behind the domain of quarkal physics to stalk the quantum jungle of particles real and particles virtual, particles temporal and particles spiritual. Before him loom the probabilistic wheels within wheels within wheels of the atom; growing faster, he shatters its contemplative orbits as he passes into the realm of molecules and elements, where the rules are simpler and stricter than the grand incoherencies of quantum theory. Growing, expanding: his glowing gno-on of consciousness spirals along chains of molecules to the complex compounds and the wilderlands of organic chemicals on the border of life. Faster now, faster still: the pilgrimage from prion to virus to bacteria to cell is but the blinking of an eye. In a dazzling rush he expands to fill his own body . . . And leaves it behind.

Outward: the two lives are reduced to dots on their stark stone island at the edge of the world, that island to a dot in the dark ocean, that ocean to a gob of spit in the face of planet Earth; that Earth to an eyeball, a marble, its moon a round white skull one moment, a grit of white mica the next: abandoned, forgotten. Outward, outward: he swells to encompass the entire solar system . . . And beyond. The lonely clouds of waiting comets. And the stars; close, familiar stars, their solar systems, their planets, rush in upon the fringes of his consciousness, faster faster they crowd upon him until Earth's local group is a scattering of pearls lost in the dark. He reaches out into that darkness and for what seems an eternity he travels through formless clouds of stars. Then, brilliantly, terrifyingly, he breaks free and the great wheel of the galaxy turns within him. And still outward; leaping into the greater void between galaxies. Earth's galaxy and her clan sisters are engulfed, and the federation of kindred clans that constitute the superclusters: a thousand superclusters, the mega-cluster, a thousand megaclusters . . . With the speed of the imagination, Brother Innocence approaches the edge of existence. Within him, motes of sand and starshine, a universe turns. Before him, the void. With a roar, Daniel hurls his mind towards that void where Brother Innocence dares not go. In the instant Daniel's consciousness topples over the edge, Brother Innocence breaks the empathic link.

Darkness.

The Final Tabernacle has spun itself to destruction. And in spinning Daniel's consciousness to the edge of understanding, it has sucked him dry as a bone. Grey flesh, pale, withered, cold as stone in the dawning light.

Darkness.

Brother Innocence feels for life. A beat of pulse. A spirit of breath. A glow of sentience.

Darkness . . . Wait.

A spark. Dim. Cold. A life-ember. Ebbing. Fading towards extinction. But alive. Extinction: survival. For thirty years Brother Innocence has waited and listened. Now the choices are his.

'I won't let them have you,' he says. He reaches into himself to a secret place. He has always known this secret place was there, but he has always been afraid to touch it. It is not a place of receiving. It is a place of giving. He reaches out with it to take the life-ember. Life energy, his energy, his life, goes out of himself like a great wind to fan the spark into flame. He empties himself; gives and gives and gives until he can no longer stand upright, until the blood roars in his ears like the sea. And still he gives. And gives. And gives.

It is not enough. The life-ember flickers, flares. But the darkness around it is too strong and cold. And Brother Innocence is old and weary and has nothing more to give.

– Help me, he prays. Help me!

The prayer goes out across the world. In the forest clearing and earthen huts and shadowfilled canyons and mountain valleys and desert mesas and the lonely places where the empaths have fled to listen, and wait, they look up from their labours. They listen. They see. Everything else is forgotten. Each of them reaches down to that same secret part of themselves they have always been afraid to touch, and they reach out to Brother Innocence on his island at the edge of the world.

The old man gasps, shudders as a thousand lives are channelled through his one. The power drags him to his feet, sends him stumbling through the scattered debris of the Final Tabernacle. He cradles Daniel's head in his fingers and feels the darkness, the dark needles of crystal. He cries aloud as the power goes out of him. It is an agony. It is a joy. Such strength might snuff out the smouldering life glow if it were not tempered by Brother Innocence. He feels for a heartbeat . . . Yes! Breath flutters in the lungs: Yes! Blood swells and surges through the arteries: Yes! Yes! In the mind a great light shines, a light so pure, so holy that Brother Innocence cannot approach it. Cell and crystal, neuron and viron, human and nanomachine, are one, fused, symbiosed, and they burn with light.

'Brother Innocence . . .' The voice is a ravaged whisper. 'I know . . . I am . . .'

'Yes, son,' says Brother Innocence. 'Yes.'

Soon they will come, thinks Brother Innocence as he looks out at the horizon where the low winter clouds gather in yellow and blue. Soon the men from World Health will come in their shapeshifting flyer. He does not want them to come. There is so much he has to learn, so many questions he has to ask. Has to ask . . . Daniel's mind is closed to him now, impenetrable behind the burning light.

'I don't know if I can explain it to you properly,' Daniel tells him. 'It's like the old problem of trying to explain colour to a man born blind. I still have just these five senses, but it's as though they can see into other dimensions that were closed to them before. It's as if I can see everything clearly for the first time, that I can see everything, all at once, complete, entire . . .' He loses it again, because, for all his listening gifts, Brother Innocence is the man born blind. Daniel loves to take his five new senses out along the goat paths that cross the island at the end of the world, to hone and sharpen them on the familiar before turning them on the unfamiliar world of the Shining Plague. Together, he and Brother Innocence come to a deserted Tabernacle, a place of razor-shell windchimes suspended from driftwood timbers thrust into the earth. 'Remember, I used to have to make these things to see and hear and feel? Not any more. It's everywhere now, the music, the vision. I don't think I can explain it to you any better than that.' He sets the windchimes tinkling but all they make is noise. The song is ended, the vision faded, the music and light have gone within, where Brother Innocence can no longer sense them.

Walking along the beach with the evening gulls flocking above their heads, Daniel says, 'In a sense, that final expansion of consciousness was the rite of passage. I was made one with the universe, everything, from the darkness within to the darkness without, I touched it all, understood it all. And I would have stayed there forever, I think, if I had not been called back into real life again. That was where all the others failed, the darkness swallowed them, there was no one to give them the strength to draw back from the edge. Can you understand any of this?'

'In a sense,' says Brother Innocence. Together they walk on, down the beach, to the crystal valley and the twelve graves there.

And then, out in Brother Innocence's currach, hunting the fish that swim in the cold waters about the island at the end of the world, they hear a sound. The sound of aircraft engines coming across the cold waters.

'You didn't have to tell them,' says Daniel.

'I'm afraid I did,' says Brother Innocence.

'Shall I get rid of them? I can if you don't want me to go.'

'You can do that?'

'Easy as blinking.'

'Better not,' says Brother Innocence. Daniel smiles and dips his hand into the cold water.

'I suppose I'd better go with them,' he says. 'There's a lot I have to do.' Brother Innocence smiles and bends to the oars and together they come in to the shore, riding the cold water, riding the waves of the sea.

KAREN JOY FOWLER

Game Night at the Fox and Goose

The reader will discover that my reputation, wherever I have lived, is endorsed as that of a true and pure woman.
– Laura D. Fair

Alison called all over the city trying to find a restaurant that served blowfish, but there wasn't one. She settled for Chinese. She would court an MSG attack. And if none came, then she'd been craving red bean sauce anyway. On the way to the restaurant, Alison chose not to wear her seatbelt.

Alison had been abandoned by her lover who was so quick about it, she hadn't even known she was pregnant yet. She couldn't ever tell him now. She sat pitifully alone, near the kitchen at a table for four. *You've really screwed this time,* her fortune cookie told her. *Give up.* And in small print – *Chin's Oriental Palace.*

The door from the kitchen swung open, so the air around her was hot for a moment, then cold when the door closed. Alison drank her tea and looked at the tea leaves in the bottom of her cup. They were easy to read. *He doesn't love you,* they said. She tipped them out onto the napkin and tried to rearrange them. *You fool.* She covered the message with the one remaining wonton, left the cookie for the kitchen god, and decided to walk all by herself in the dark, three blocks up Hillside Drive, past two alleyways, to have a drink at the Fox and Goose. No one stopped her.

Alison had forgotten it was Monday night. Sometimes

there was music in the Fox and Goose. Sometimes you could sit in a corner by yourself listening to someone with an acoustical guitar singing 'Killing Me Softly'. On Monday nights the television was on and the bar was rather crowded. Mostly men. Alison swung one leg over the only empty bar stool and slid forward. The bar was made of wood, very upscale.

'What can I get the pretty lady?' the bartender asked without taking his eyes off the television screen. He wore glasses, low on his nose.

Alison was not a pretty lady and didn't feel like pretending she was. 'I've been used and discarded,' she told the bartender. 'And I'm pregnant. I'd like a glass of wine.'

'You really shouldn't drink if you're pregnant,' the man sitting to Alison's left said.

'Two more downs and they're already in field goal range again.' The bartender set the wine in front of Alison. He was shaking his head. 'Pregnant women aren't supposed to drink much,' he warned her.

'How?' the man on her left asked.

'How do you think?' said Alison.

'Face-mask,' said the bartender.

'Turn it up.'

Alison heard the amplified *thwock* of two football helmets hitting together. 'Good coverage,' the bartender said.

'No protection,' said the man on Alison's right.

Alison turned to look at him. He was dressed in a blue sweater with the sleeves pushed up. He had dark eyes and was drinking a dark beer. 'I asked him to wear a condom,' she said quietly. 'I even brought one. He couldn't.'

'He *couldn't*?'

'I really don't want to discuss it.' Alison sipped her wine. It had the flat, bitter taste of House White. She realized the bartender hadn't asked her what she wanted. But then, if he had, House White was what she would have requested. 'It just doesn't seem fair.' She spoke over her glass, unsure that anyone was listening, not really caring if they weren't. 'All I did was fall in love. All I did was believe someone who said he loved me. *He* was the liar. But nothing happens to him.'

'Unfair is the way things are,' the man on her right told her. Three months ago Alison would have been trying to decide if she were attracted to him. Not that she would necessarily have wanted to do anything about it. It was just a question she'd always asked herself, dealing with men, interested in the answer, interested in those times when the answer changed abruptly, one way or another. But it was no longer an issue. Alison was a dead woman these days. Alison was attracted to no one.

Two men at the end of the bar began to clap suddenly. 'He hasn't missed from thirty-six yards yet this season,' the bartender said.

Alison watched the kick-off and the run-back. Nothing. No room at all. 'Men handle this stuff so much better than women. You don't know what heartbreak is,' she said confrontationally. No one responded. She backed off anyway. 'Well, that's how it looks.' She drank and watched an advertisement for trucks. A man bought his wife the truck she'd always wanted. Alison was afraid she might cry. 'What would you do,' she asked the man on her right, 'if you were me?'

'Drink, I guess. Unless I was pregnant.'

'Watch the game,' said the man on her left.

'Focus on your work,' said the bartender.

'Join the foreign legion.' The voice came from behind Alison. She swivelled around to locate it. At a table near a shuttered window a very tall woman sat by herself. Her face was shadowed by an Indiana Jones type hat, but the candle on the table lit up the area below her neck. She was wearing a black tee-shirt with a picture on it that Alison couldn't make out. She spoke again. 'Make new friends. See distant places.' She gestured for Alison to join her. 'Save two galaxies from the destruction of the alien armada.'

Alison stood up on the little ledge which ran beneath the bar, reached over the counter and took an olive, sucking the pimento out first, then eating the rest. She picked up her drink, stepped down and walked over to the woman's table. Elvis. That was Elvis's face on the tee-shirt right between the woman's breasts. *Are you lonesome tonight?* the tee-shirt asked. 'That sounds good.' She sat down across from the woman. She could see her face better now; her skin was pale and a bit rough. Her hair was long, straight and brown. 'I'd rather time travel, though. Back just two months. Maybe three months. Practically walking distance.'

'You could get rid of the baby.'

'Yes,' said Alison. 'I could.'

The woman's glass sat on the table in front of her. She had finished whatever she had been drinking; the maraschino cherry was all that remained. The woman picked it up and ate it, dropping the stem onto the napkin under her glass. 'Maybe he'll come back to you. You trusted him. You must have seen something decent in him.'

Alison's throat closed over so that she couldn't talk. She picked up her drink, but she couldn't swallow either. She set it down again, shaking her head. Some of the wine splashed over the lip and onto her hand.

'He's already married,' the woman said.

Alison nodded, wiping her hand on her pant leg. 'God.' She searched in her pockets for a kleenex. The woman handed her the napkin from beneath the empty glass. Alison wiped her nose with it and the cherry stem fell out. She did not dare look up. She kept her eyes focused on the napkin in her hand which she folded into four small squares. 'When I was growing up,' she said, 'I lived on a block with lots of boys. Sometimes I'd come home and my knees were all scraped up because I'd fallen or I'd taken a ball in the face or I'd gotten kicked or punched and I'd be crying and my mother would always say the same thing. "You play with the big boys and you're going to get hurt," she'd say. Exasperated.' Alison unfolded the napkin, folded it diagonally instead. Her voice shrank. 'I've been so stupid.'

'The universe is shaped by the struggle between two great forces,' the woman told her.

It was not really responsive. It was not particularly supportive. Alison felt just a little bit angry at this woman who now knew so much about her. 'Good and evil?' Alison asked, slightly nastily. She wouldn't meet the woman's eyes. 'The Elvis and the anti-Elvis?'

'Male and female. Minute by minute, the balance tips one way or the other. Not just here. In every universe. There are places,' the woman leaned forward, 'where men are not allowed to gather and drink. Places where football is absolutely illegal.'

'England?' Alison suggested and then didn't want to hear the woman's answer. 'I like football,' she added quickly. 'I like games with rules. You can be stupid playing football and it can cost you the game, but there are penalties for fouls, too. I like games with rules.'

'You're playing one now, aren't you?' the woman said. 'You haven't hurt this man even though you could. Even though he's hurt you. He's not playing by the rules. So why are you?'

'It doesn't have anything to do with rules,' Alison said. 'It only has to do with me, with the kind of person I think I am. Which is not the kind of person he is.' She thought for a moment. 'It doesn't mean I wouldn't like to see him get hurt,' she added. 'Something karmic. Justice.'

'"We must storm and hold Cape Turk before we talk of social justice."' The woman folded her arms under her breasts and leaned back in her chair. 'Did Sylvia Townsend Warner say that?'

'Not to me.'

Alison heard more clapping at the bar behind her. She looked over her shoulder. The man in the blue sweater slapped his hand on the wood bar. 'Good call. Excellent call. They won't get another play in before the half.'

'Where I come from she did.' Alison turned back to the woman. 'And she was talking about women. No one gets justice just by deserving it. No one ever has.'

Alison finished off her wine. 'No.' She wondered if she should go home now. She knew when she got there that the apartment would be unbearably lonely and that the phone wouldn't ring and that she would need immediately to be somewhere else. No activity in the world could be more awful than listening to a phone not ring. But she didn't really want to stay here and have a conversation which was, at worst, too strange and, at best, too late. Women usually supported you more when they talked to you. They didn't usually make you defensive or act as if they had something to teach you, the way this woman did. And anyhow, justice was a little peripheral now, wasn't it? What good would it really do her? What would it change?

She might have gone back and joined the men at the bar during the half. They were talking quietly among themselves. They were ordering fresh drinks and eating beernuts. But she didn't want to risk seeing cheerleaders. She didn't want to risk the ads with the party dog and all his women, even though she'd read in a magazine that the dog was a bitch. Anywhere she went, there she'd be. Just like she was. Heartbroken.

The woman was watching her closely. Alison could feel this though the woman's face remained shadowed and she couldn't quite bring herself to look back at her directly. She looked at Elvis instead and the way his eyes wavered through her lens of candlelight and tears. *Lonesome tonight?*

'You really have it bad, don't you?' the woman said. Her tone was sympathetic. Alison softened again. She decided to tell this perceptive woman everything. How much she'd loved him. How she'd never loved anyone else. How she felt it every time she took a *breath* and had for weeks now.

'I don't think I'll ever feel better,' she said. 'No matter what I do.'

'I hear it takes a year to recover from a serious loss. Unless you find someone else.'

A year. Alison could be a mother by then. How would she find someone else, pregnant like she was or with a small child? Could she spend a year hurting like this? Would she have a choice?

'Have you ever heard of Laura D. Fair?' the woman asked.

Alison shook her head. She picked up her empty wine glass and tipped it to see if any drops remained. None did. She set it back down and picked up the napkin, wiping her eyes. She wasn't crying. She just wasn't exactly not crying.

'Mrs Fair killed her lover,' the woman told her. Alison looked at her own fingernails. One of them had a ragged end. She bit it off shorter while she listened. 'He was a lawyer. A.P. Crittenden. She shot him on the ferry to Oakland in November of 1870 in front of his whole family because she saw him kiss his wife. He'd promised to leave her and marry Mrs Fair instead and then he didn't, of course. She pleaded a transient insanity known at that time as *emotional* insanity. She said she was incapable of killing Mr Crittenden who had been the only friend she had in the world.' Alison examined her nail. She had only succeeded in making it more ragged. She bit it again, too close to the skin this time. It hurt and she put it back in her mouth. 'Mrs Fair said she had no memory of the murder, which many people, not all of them related to the deceased, witnessed. She was the first woman sentenced to hang in California.'

Loud clapping and catcalls at the bar. The third quarter had started with a run-back all the way to the fifty-yard line. Alison heard it. She did not turn around, but she took her finger out of her mouth and picked up the napkin. She folded it again. Four small squares. 'Rules are rules,' Alison said.

'But then she didn't hang. Certain objections were made on behalf of the defence and sustained and a new trial was held. This time she was acquitted. By now she was the most famous and the most hated woman in the country.'

Alison unfolded the napkin and tried to smooth out the creases with the side of her palm. 'I never heard of her.'

'Laura D. Fair was not some little innocent.' The woman's hat brim dipped decisively. 'Mrs Fair had been married four times and each had been a profitable venture. One of her husbands killed himself. She was not pretty, but she was passionate. She was not smart, but she was clever. And she saw, in her celebrity, a new way to make money. She announced a new career as a public speaker. She travelled the country with her lectures. And what was her message? She told women to murder the men who seduced and betrayed them.'

'I never heard of her,' said Alison.

'Mrs Fair was a compelling speaker. She'd had some acting and elocution experience. Her performance in court showed training. On the stage she was even better. "The act will strike a terror to the hearts of sensualists and libertines."' The woman stabbed dramatically at her own breast with her fist, hitting Elvis right in the eye. Behind her hand, Elvis winked at Alison in the candlelight. 'Mrs Fair said that women throughout the world would glory in the revenge exacted by American womanhood. Overdue. Long overdue. Thousands of women heard her. Men, too, and not all of them entirely unsympathetic. Fanny Hyde and Kate Stoddart were released in Brooklyn. Stoddart never even stood trial. But then there was a backlash. The martyred Marys were hanged in Philadelphia. And then . . .' the woman's voice dropped suddenly in volume and gained in intensity. Alison looked up at her quickly. The woman was staring back. Alison looked away. 'And then a group of women hunted down and dispatched Charles S. Smith in an alley near his home. Mr Smith was a married man and his victim, Edith Wilson, was pregnant, an invalid, and eleven years old. But this time the women wore sheets and could not be identified. Edith Wilson was perhaps the only female in Otsego County, New York who could not have taken part.'

Alison folded her napkin along the diagonal.

'So no one could be tried. It was an inspiring and purging operation. It was copied in many little towns across the country. God knows, the women had access to sheets.'

Alison laughed, but the woman was not expecting it, had not paused to allow for laughter. 'And then Annie Oakley shot Frank Butler in a challenge match in Cincinnati.'

'Excuse me,' said Alison. 'I didn't quite hear you,' but she really had and the woman continued anyway without pausing or repeating.

'She said it was an accident, but she was too good a shot. They hanged her for it. And then Grover Cleveland was killed by twelve sheeted women on the White House Lawn. At tea time,' the woman said.

'Wait a minute.' Alison stopped her. 'Grover Cleveland served out two terms. Non-consecutively. I'm sure.'

The woman leaned into the candle-light, resting her chin on a bridge she made of her hands. 'You're right, of course,' she said. 'That's what happened here. But in another universe where the feminine force was just a little stronger in 1872, Grover Cleveland died in office. With a scone in his mouth and a child in New York.'

'All right,' said Alison accommodatingly. Accommodation was one of Alison's strengths. 'But what difference does that make to us?'

'I could take you there.' The woman pushed her hat back so that Alison could have seen her eyes if she wanted to. 'The universe right next door. Practically walking distance.'

The candle flame was casting shadows which reached and withdrew and reached at Alison over the table. In the unsteady light, the woman's face flickered like a silent film star's. Then she pulled back in her chair and sank into the darkness beyond the candle. The ball was on the ten-yard line and the bar was quiet. 'I knew you were going to say that,' Alison said finally. 'How did I know you were going to say that? Who would say that?'

'Some lunatic?' the woman suggested.

'Yes.'

'Don't you want to hear about it anyway? About my universe?' The woman smiled at her. An unperturbed smile. Nice even teeth. And a kind of confidence that was rare among the women Alison knew. Alison had noticed it immediately without realizing she was noticing. The way the woman sat back in her chair and didn't pick at herself. Didn't play with her hair. Didn't look at her hands. The way she lectured Alison.

'All right,' Alison said. She put the napkin down and fit her hands together, forcing herself to sit as still. 'But first tell me about Laura Fair. *My* Laura Fair.'

'Up until 1872 the two histories are identical,' the woman said. 'Mrs Fair married four times and shot her lover and was convicted and the conviction was overturned. She just never lectured. She planned to. She was scheduled to speak at Platt's Hotel in San Francisco on November 21, 1872, but a mob of some two thousand men gathered outside the Hotel and another two thousand surrounded the apartment building she lived in. She asked for police protection, but it was refused and she was too frightened to leave her home. Even staying where she was proved dangerous. A few men tried to force their way inside. She spent a terrifying night and never attempted to lecture again. She died in poverty and obscurity.

'Fanny Hyde and Kate Stoddart were released anyway. I can't find out what happened to the Marys. Edith Wilson was condemned by respectable people everywhere and cast out of her family.'

'The eleven-year-old child?' Alison asked.

'In *your* universe,' the woman reminded her. 'Not in

mine. You don't know much of your own history, do you? Name a great American woman.'

The men at the bar were in an uproar. Alison turned to look. 'Interception,' the man in the blue sweater shouted to her exultantly. 'Did you see it?'

'Name a great American woman,' Alison called back to him.

'Goddamn interception with goal to go,' he said. 'Eleanor Roosevelt?'

'Marilyn Monroe,' said a man at the end of the bar.

'The senator from California?' the woman asked. 'Now that's a good choice.'

Alison laughed again. 'Funny,' she said, turning back to the woman. 'Very good.'

'We have football, too,' the woman told her. 'Invented in 1873. Outlawed in 1950. No one ever got paid to play it.'

'And you have Elvis.'

'No, we don't. Not like yours. Of course not. I got this here.'

'Interception,' the man in the blue sweater said. He was standing beside Alison, shaking his head with the wonder of it. 'Let me buy you ladies a drink.' Alison opened her mouth and he waved his hand. 'Something non-alcoholic for you,' he said. 'Please. I really want to.'

'Ginger-ale, then,' she agreed. 'No ice.'

'Nothing for me,' said the woman. They watched the man walk back to the bar and then, when he was far enough away not to hear, she leaned towards Alison. 'You like men, don't you?'

'Yes,' said Alison. 'I always have. Are they different where you come from? Have they learned to be honest and careful with women since you kill them when they're not?' Alison's voice was sharper than she intended, so she softened the effect with a sadder question. 'Is it better there?'

'Better for whom?' The woman did not take her eyes off Alison. 'Where I come from the men and women hardly speak to each other. First of all, they don't speak the same language. They don't here either, but you don't recognize that as clearly. Where I come from there's men's English and there's women's English.'

'Say something in men's English.'

'"I love you." Shall I translate?'

'No,' said Alison. 'I know the translation for that one.' The heaviness closed over her heart again. Not that it had ever gone away. Nothing made Alison feel better, but many things made her feel worse. The bartender brought her ginger ale. With ice. Alison was angry suddenly, that she couldn't even get a drink with no ice. She looked for the man in the blue sweater, raised the glass at him and rattled it. Of course he was too far away to hear even if he was listening and there was no reason to believe he was.

'Two minute warning,' he called back. 'I'll be with you in two minutes.'

Men were always promising to be with you soon. Men could never be with you now. Alison had only cared about this once and she never would again. 'Football has the longest two minutes in the world,' she told the woman. 'So don't hold your breath. What else is different where you come from?' She sipped at her ginger-ale. She'd been grinding her teeth recently; stress, the dentist said, and so the cold liquid made her mouth hurt.

'Everything is different. Didn't you ask for no ice? Don't drink that,' the woman said. She called to the bartender. 'She didn't want ice. You gave her ice.'

'Sorry.' The bartender brought another bottle and another glass. 'Nobody told me no ice.'

'Thank you,' Alison said. He took the other glass away. Alison thought he was annoyed. The woman didn't seem to notice.

'Imagine your world without a hundred years of adulterers,' she said. 'The level of technology is considerably depressed. Lots of books never written, because the authors didn't live. Lots of men who didn't get to be president. Lots of passing. Although it's illegal. Men dressing as women. Women dressing as men. And the dress is more sexually differentiated. Codpieces are fashionable again. But you don't have to believe me,' the woman said. 'Come and see for yourself. I can take you there in a minute. What would it cost you to just come and see? What do you have here that you'd be losing?'

The woman gave her time to think. Alison sat and drank her ginger-ale and repeated to herself the things her lover had said the last time she had seen him. She remembered them all, some of them surprisingly careless, some of them surprisingly cruel, all of them surprising. She repeated them again, one by one, like a rosary. The man who had left was not the man she had loved. The man she had loved would never have said such things to her. The man she had loved did not exist. She had made him up. Or he had. 'Why would you want me to go?' Alison asked.

'The universe is shaped by the struggle between two great forces. Sometimes a small thing can tip the balance. One more woman. Who knows?' The woman tilted her hat back with her hand. 'Save a galaxy. Make new friends. Or stay here where your heart is. Broken.'

'Can I come back if I don't like it?'

'Yes. Do you like it here?'

She drank her ginger-ale and then set the glass down, still half-full. She glanced at the man in the blue sweater, then past him to the bartender. She let herself feel just for a moment what it might be like to know that she could finish this drink and then go home to the one person in the world who loved her.

Never in this world. 'I'm going out for a minute. Two minutes,' she called to the bartender. One minute to get there. One minute to get back. 'Don't take my drink.'

She stood and the other woman stood, too, even taller than Alison had thought. 'I'll follow you. Which way?' Alison asked.

'It's not hard,' the woman said. 'In fact, I'll follow you.

Go to the back. Find the door which says "Women" and go on through it. I'm just going to pay for my drink and then I'll be right along.'

Vixens, was what the door actually said, across the way from the one marked *Ganders.* Alison paused and then pushed through. She felt more than a little silly, standing in the small bathroom which apparently fronted two universes. One toilet, one sink, one mirror. Two universes. She went into the stall and closed the door. Before she had finished she heard the outer door open and shut again. 'I'll be right out,' she said. The toilet paper was small and unusually rough. The toilet wouldn't flush. It embarrassed her. She tried three times before giving up.

The bathroom was larger than it had been, less clean, and a row of urinals lined one wall. The woman stood at the sink, looking into the mirror, which was smaller. 'Are you ready?' she asked and removed her breasts from behind Elvis, tossing them into a wire waste basket. She turned. 'Ready or not.'

'No,' said Alison, seeing the face under the hat clearly for the first time. 'Please, no.' She began to cry again, looking up at his face, looking down at his chest. *Are you lonesome tonight?*

'You lied to me,' she said dully.

'I never lied,' he answered. 'Think back. You just translated wrong. Because you're that kind of woman. We don't have women like you here now. And anyway, what does it matter whose side you play on? All that matters is that no one wins. Aren't I right? Aren't I?' He tipped his hat to her.

IAN WATSON

The Eye of the Ayatollah

Three years earlier Ali lost his right eye and part of his face during one of the battles against Iraq. Which battle? Where? He didn't know. His cloaked, hood-clad mother had joyfully seen him off en route to paradise on the back of a fume-coughing truck packed with trainee revolutionary guards, all of about his own age, which was sixteen. Blood from Mother's finger adorned his forehead; she had cut herself deep with a kitchen knife.

What did Mother look like? Almond eyes, broad nose, big creamy cheeks, generous lips. The only time Ali ever saw more of her body was briefly when he was born, an incident which he neither understood at the time nor subsequently remembered. Her blood on his forehead was sacramental.

The truck drove all day and all night through dust – towards, latterly, the dawning thud and *crump* of heavy artillery. The recruits chanted and sang themselves hoarse and prayed for death, the door to paradise.

Arriving at a shattered moonscape masked by smoke, Ali and his companions were issued with hand grenades and sent out across a mine field in the direction of the thunder. Ahead, a torrent of boulders could have been tumbling from the sky – as though here he stepped close to the very heartbeat of God, the compassionate, the merciful. The land-mine which blew his neighbour apart, arms and legs flying separately in the direction of heaven, tore off the side of Ali's face.

The next few weeks were nebulous for Ali. He himself existed inside a black, mute thunder-cloud occasionally riven by the red lightning of pain. Finally the crowded hospital released him, since he could walk and his mattress was needed; and hidden Mother welcomed half a martyr home. Neighbours admired Ali's scars and the remains of his empty eye socket.

Yet the war ended inconclusively.

Ali often visited the Fountain of Blood downtown to gape at the plumes of red-dyed water spurting as though from severed arteries. Part of a host half a million strong, he screamed for the death of the Satan-author, blasphemous apostate lurking in that Western devil-land.

Yet it wasn't the Satan-author who died; it was the Ayatollah, father of truth, beloved of God, the merciful, the compassionate.

Grief racked Ali, grief wrenched a million hearts, five million. Ali burrowed like a mole through the dense conglomerate of one of the hugest crowds in history, millions of pebbles of flesh cemented by the sand of rageful sorrow – through into the Beshte Zahar Cemetery. No, not so much cemented as surging, *churning* like the ballast and cement and liquid in some giant, horizontal concrete-mixer. Fainting, shrieking, reaching, clawing, crazed with bitter woe: a million locusts, and only one leaf to feed at – the coffin, soon to arrive. He fought his way into the inner square built of freight containers. Thousands of mourners were beating their heads with their fists in unison. Mystics were harvesting bowls of earth from the bottom of the grave, and passing these out – the crowd ate the precious soil.

A helicopter landed. Moments later, a tumult of young men hauled the shrouded body from its coffin. Hands tore the shroud to pieces, each scrap a precious relic. 'Ya Ali, Ya Hussein,' cried ten thousand voices. The thin white legs of the holy man jutted aloft like bare sticks, as his corpse slumped.

Ali, clawing, was in the forefront but his defective vision foxed him. As he fought his way to the rear through the tide of bodies he puzzled at what his right hand clutched, something resembling a slippery ping-pong ball. Panting, he paused long enough to glance. His palm cupped a glazed, naked eye. With a tail of optic nerve: a kind of plump, ocular tadpole.

Had a miracle happened? Had a piece of the shroud transmuted itself into Ali's own lost eye, now restored to him? Was he not himself named in honour of the martyr Ali, who founded the true school of Islam?

At last his brain caught up with what his fingers and their nails had done: he, Ali the half-faced, had torn out one of the Ayatollah's eyes.

Behind him, shots rang out. The helicopter landed once more . . .

Later, Ali heard how the corpse eventually entered its hole in the ground, to be covered by flagstones heaved hand over hand, and how a dozen of the cargo containers were piled across the grave. No one would or could say what state the body had been in finally.

The eye sat on a shelf by Ali's bed, staring unblinkingly at him. (For, lacking eyelids, how could an eye blink?) Its gaze appeared to track him about the little room, the pupil stretching into a squint to follow him.

Ali prayed. He thought about preservatives. He wondered what best to do. How could he possibly plunge that holy eye into alcohol even of the medicinal variety? So he visited a pharmacy to ask advice about – so he said – pickling a dead frog; he returned with a jar of formalin. Once afloat in that solution of formaldehyde, the eyeball definitely swung from side to side keeping an eye on him.

On *him*, on mere Ali the half-face? Oh no. Simply alert, awaiting, on the look-out. Ali prayed. Ali dreamed. A vision visited him. The holy man had been a hawk. What was that hawk's eye hunting for? Why, it was surveying all of the Earth, searching for the hiding place of the Satan-author.

*

Events deployed as the will of God decreed. Truly dreams were troubled in Tehran during those days. Angels guided Ali to the office of Dr Omar Hafiz, doyen of the country's ballistic missile programme, who for his part had dreamt originally –

– of exploding a nuclear weapon on Tel Aviv to free the Palestinians. Those high-explosive birds aimed at Baghdad were a side-show. Alas, lack of a warhead derailed the project. So next, Dr Hafiz dreamed of a reconnaissance satellite to spy on Iraqi army positions; but peace had been declared. Lately Hafiz dreamt of using the prototype rocket to put a communications satellite into orbit to criss-cross the whole face of the Earth: the *Voice of God*, broadcasting the truth . . .

An angel had also visited Dr Hafiz.

'We *can* fly your hawk,' he assured Ali. 'The cold of space will preserve the eye from corruption. It will look down on Europe, America, Africa. That Satan-author may have hidden anywhere. He may have bought plastic surgery. The eye will find him. With its miraculous perception it will recognize him. He is what it seeks; for fifty years, if need be.'

'And I, the half-face,' said Ali, 'need to be on hand when our hawk finds its prey, do I not? For the eye was given into my hand, was it not?'

Events unfolded like a fragrant rose from a bud. Surgeons renovated Ali's face, rebuilt his orbital bone, gave him a glass eye. Tutors nurtured his smattering of English and French into something resembling fluency. Commandos offered him the sort of weapons training he'd sorely lacked when he rode to war. His forged passport identified him as a naturalized Australian.

Soon his country launched its first Earth satellite named the *Eye of the Ayatollah*, and announced to the world (as well as to the Satan-author, wherever he was) that the orbiting instrument package did indeed contain exactly that. Benighted infidels outside the harbour of Islam laughed – uneasily. Corrupted souls within the harbour of Islam glanced askance at the night sky.

No one beyond the inner hierarchy knew the whole truth about Ali. Whenever Ali shut his left eye, he looked down through his artificial eye upon the countries of the Earth from space. For his glass eye was more than a bauble. Through it, miraculously, the youth could see whatever the holy man's searching eye could see through the zoom-lenses of the satellite; as had been promised in the vision confided to Dr Hafiz . . .

In the cold void above the topmost air, the *Eye of the Ayatollah* orbited for a year, two years, five years . . . Disguised as a dinkum Aussie immigrant on holiday, Ali wandered the world as frugally as he could, financed by an American Express gold card. Universally acceptable; he still regretted the expedient.

The orbiting eye seemed to twitch as it was passing over Pakistan, and there went Ali; a solar flare must have been responsible. Again, over Nicaragua, it spasmed; thus Ali went to that strife-torn land. Perhaps a cosmic ray had hit the eye.

He found himself in Sweden, in Ireland, in America, England, France. Always keeping watch. From his hiding place the Satan-author published another book, redoubling Ali's fervour.

Seven years passed. The eye watched. Ali watched.

At long last the eye throbbed. It was gazing down upon an island off the south-west coast of Scotland; upon a tiny isle that nestled against a bay of its parent island like a new-born baby whale beside its leviathan of a mother. The eye passed over, but not before imprinting Ali vividly.

He flew to London, collected a gun and grenades from a certain embassy, and caught a train to Glasgow.

He would need to wait there for some weeks till the satellite would be poised to pass over the same part of Scotland again. Buying maps and guides, he soon learned that the name of the mother island was Arran, and of the islet: Holy Island, a title which set his teeth on edge.

As the time approached, Ali took a bus to the coast then a ferry to Arran. Renting a modest car, he reconnoitred this pinnacled island of granite bens and fells, glens of bracken and frisky streams rushing amidst great boulders, mounds of moraine, dark conifers, and wild red deer – suddenly giving way in the south to rolling heathery hills, calm pastures, sandy beaches with a few palm trees.

Ali checked in to a hotel in the small sea-side town of Lamlash opposite Holy Island. He had brought a hammer, and was pretending to be an enthusiastic amateur geologist. Binoculars too; he was an eager bird-watcher.

How that islet dominated the shore. Its two-mile stretch of jagged cliffs and rugged moorland sheltered wild goats, long-legged diminutive Soay sheep, shaggy Highland cattle; and birds, birds. Holy Island was a nature reserve, a field study centre. From its southernmost tip a lighthouse beaconed across the Firth of Clyde.

Unholy island, thought Ali.

Apparently a Christian saint called Molaise lived on the isle in the time of the prophet Mohammed, bless his name. The saint's cell could still be visited; Vikings had defaced it with runic inscriptions. The Satan-author also skulked in a kind of cell. Did he think he could walk free in safety upon those moors amongst the goats? The bars of his cell were the eye-beams of an authentic holy man, whose organ of vision lived on.

But first the instrument package enshrining that organ of vision must re-enter the atmosphere and parachute down to Earth; for such had been Dr Hafiz's design. Thus the hawk would pounce.

Studying his maps, Ali chose a glen leading to a ben. He telephoned a cover number in Australia, to alert Tehran. Next evening, the important part of the *Eye of the Ayatollah* descended and soft-landed in the bonnie upland heather.

*

The following morning, Ali took the ferry over to Holy Island in company with half a dozen ornithologists. The sea was choppy, the breeze was brisk, so spindrift soon coated the lens-studded box that held the eye, which Ali wore around his neck like some gold-plated camera. Already that camera-which-wasn't had attracted a few curious glances. Was Ali some aviphile oil sheikh travelling incognito who couldn't forsake at least one token of ostentation?

'Ah,' he told himself, 'I'm but the humblest servant.'

Fortunately the crossing did not coincide with a time for prayer; however he found that his vision was fogging. Ducking down out of sight behind some cargo he opened the golden box and cradled the holy eyeball naked in his palm once more. The soft ball seemed to burn icily as though still frozen. Inspired, the Half-Face popped his glass prosthetic from its rebuilt orbit and replaced it with the Ayatollah's own.

His vision swam. He saw two scenes at once: the hellishly gaunt, approaching cliffs licked by sea-spume, and what he could only interpret as a glimpse of paradise, the slope of a verdant valley where fountains of milk gushed, spilling down in streams, where all manner of jewels glittered – a landscape girt with a dance of scintillating pastel auroras like diaphanous rose-and-pink veils of maidens, though minus the maidens. Ahead was a curiously imprecise promise of ecstasies without substance, as if he was seeing this terrain in some warmer Eden of the past, courtesy of an angel.

Some such subconscious, submerged vista must always have lurked in his inner gaze, as a cynosure, a focus. In this mystical moment he appeared to remember the lost object of all his buried desires. The whole island swelled with the light of joyful creation, the conjuring of mischievous beauty. Honey flowed like lava from one hilltop.

He shut the eye that was his own; and through that other, holy eye he saw only the sternness of cliffs again, their stark uncertainty. Gulls screamed battlecries. The sun was an ulcer of yellow pus, its afterimage a ball of blood. The impact of waves faintly echoed that torrent of boulders he had heard on a previous occasion at the battlefront.

'Why, Satan-author,' Ali said to himself in surprise, 'you are in hell already.'

When he closed his holy right eye to regard the scenery with his left eye, heavenly auras sparkled again, interference patterns between two modes of vision, awakening deeply hidden memories of a time when he had perceived the world freshly with wonder, long ago; of a time when he had been born and had to create a universe around himself.

'In hell indeed,' he added, 'unless your eyes see otherwise.'

After he left the ferry to mount the island, he hiked with either his right eye open or his left, the holy eye mapping out barren geometries of rock and sky and grass, the other eye teasing the tastebuds of his soul with that shimmer of scanty pastel veils behind which raw beauty beckoned.

He stepped out, he halted, he stepped out. The holy eye led him along a stony track towards what had once been a crofter's cottage and was now a sprawling homestead with mirror-glass windows surrounded by a high wire fence, supposedly to deter goats. The only guards these days were gulls.

The Satan-author sat at a desk. Haggard, yes. A nervous twitch in one eye; almost totally bald. Yet as he looked at this intruder who pointed a pistol as though out of habit, the author smiled.

'So it has come at last.'

That damnable smile, of sanity still sustained!

Ali shut his holy eye. Seen through his left eye, a nimbus surrounded the author's head. Ali reverted to his right eye, tightening his grip on the gun as he scanned the despicable face. A moment later he looked with his left eye too, and his vision swam again dizzyingly, so he closed the left eye.

'You look like a human traffic light,' remarked the author as though choosing wry last words for posterity, fit for some future dictionary of quotations.

Ali's holy attention was caught by a paper-knife used to open the author's voluminous, redirected correspondence, all his envelopes full of cheques paying him lavishly for his blasphemy in the currencies of Satan, dollars, pounds, francs, marks.

Now Ali's left eye also noted the knife with the sharp point. A roseate halo stained the blade with diluted blood. The handle was iridescent mother-of-pearl. Ali remembered the battle against Iraq and suddenly felt cheated. Strange desire surged within him.

'Which,' he asked, as if this was a riddle, 'which is my real eye? My true eye?'

Perhaps amazed at the idiosyncrasy of human nature, the author stared at this man who opened one eye then the other turn by turn, squinting at him. Was he really being offered a choice as though in a fairy tale? A choice between life and death – or only a choice between types of death?

He hesitated, then spoke at random. 'The left eye.'

'An angel guides your words.' Ali snatched up the knife, opened both eyes at once, and pointed the steel tip at the holy one.

The author tensed, imagining that he had chosen wrongly – perhaps could never have chosen correctly! – but Ali skewered the eye of the Ayatollah, drew it forth dripping humours, and stabbed the knife and its jelly burden down upon the desk.

'This,' said Ali, 'is the eye that sees hell.'

A weight of years-long possession drained away from Ali's heart; and for the first time since he could recall, his own left eye leaked tears.

NEIL FERGUSON

One-Way to Wap Wap

Julia Raxell, Professor of Human Psychology at the Sherman Fairchild Center for the Life Sciences, Harlem, was called away from an important Briefing Session in the Oval Office to take a call from her attorney, Marcus Senior of the law firm Marcus and Marcus. It was an awkward moment. Her specialist expertise was about to be required. The Professor had been invited to attend the Briefing in her capacity as adviser to Secretary of State Serge Ashkanasi, to whom she was on loan from the Institute. When she was not on loan she was the Secretary's current preferred sleeping partner.

'It's for you, Julia,' the President said.

With his famous wry grin he held the handset for her to take, generously overlooking the clear breach in etiquette.

Julia – her canary yellow silk blouse open at the neck – flushed. Receiving a private outside call was plain unprofessional. Fortunately, the Briefing had not quite gotten under way. Navy Secretary Rikov and State Security Chief Greg Gregori had yet to arrive. Taking advantage of the lull before the brainstorm, the President returned to the window. With his back to the room, he continued to watch the snowflakes fall onto the lawn below. No doubt he was wondering whether anyone had remembered to straw-mulch the roses this year, recalling what had happened last year, when nobody had.

Secretary Ashkanasi, similarly, was reclining an elbow against the big white carrara marble fireplace inside which a simulated log-fire flickered fairly convincingly. He was in conversation with General Phibbs on matters of current State Department and Pentagon Policy: Y'know, we must get together for another round one of these days, General. Sure, Serge. Whyn't you name the day! You think you can afford it? If you're so confident, let's make it a thousand a hole this time? Well – the General shook his head – I dunno. It's an expensive way to find out how bad your game is. I'll tell you right now, you want to save the dough, free of charge. The two men joshed and chuckled. The General played golf no different to how he chaired the Pentagon Foreign Strategy Committee, with a straight back. He didn't know how to bend and he hit hard. Every hole was a target to be taken out, an enemy position on an aerial reconnaissance map.

The purpose of their conversation – both men tacitly recognized – was to provide a buzz to cover the awkward position in which their colleague, Julia Raxell, had unexpectedly found herself: talking private business into the President's telephone. In the circumstances it was the gentlemanly thing to do. Julia, meanwhile, held the handset to her ear in silence. She glanced in Ashkanasi's direction.

'It's Marcus Senior. My attorney . . .' she said. 'Can you believe it? Wants me to give him instructions . . . *now*!'

In the silence that followed the President continued to watch the snow-flakes. Everyone in the room knew that Julia's annulment hearing was coming up next week. This was a tough time for her. It was something they had all been through, including the President. Ashkanasi nodded. He held up three fingers behind the President's back, meaning that was all she had. Three minutes. Not a second more.

As Julia opened the door to leave the room Navy Secretary Vic Rikov dashed into her from the other side of it. He was still wearing his uniform greatcoat on which there were dark smudges alongside the gold-lace where the snow-flakes had blotted into the blue nap of the fabric.

With his dashing white peaked cap under his arm, snow on his shoes, he might have just stepped down from the bridge of a Baltic frigate. He was holding a plastic cup of coffee in one hand and he had difficulty in juggling the cup and the cap whilst at the same time holding open the door for the ash-blonde thirty-three-year-old female member of the team to pass through. She took the call in the communications annex contiguous to the Oval Office.

'Kay, Professor Raxell,' the House security operator informed her. 'Go 'head now.'

Julia let old Marcus Senior have it. 'Now listen here Marcus, I'm in the middle of a meeting – with the President of the United States. You heard of him, right? What the hell you think you're doing, calling me up in the middle of my work like this . . .'

At his empty desk in his empty trading premises, Julia Raxell's almost-but-not-quite-yet ex-husband let his wife run on till she ran out of breath. The sound of her voice when she was sore only excruciated his feeling of vulnerability. He had never felt so vulnerable in his life. He had his back to the wall. The Raxell Communications Company, so called, was in the hands of the Public Auditor and the almost-but-not-quite-yet defunct office was stripped bare, packed up ready for auction – hardware, software, light-fittings, paper-clips – to the highest bidder, and you could bet that would not be IBM. This was probably the last occasion he would be making use of his own equipment. Probably the last occasion he would be able even to call it his own. Lonesome, he had programmed the company's latest unsold product, ANALING – a linguistics analysis facility capable of breaking down oral language production – speech – into its constituent parts: lexis, semantic functions, register, intonation. It was a useful package if you wanted to find out to what extent two parties were actually communicating with each other or, sliding into ambiguity and misunderstanding, whether they just thought they were. Husbands and wives, for example, hardly understood each other better than air traffic controllers and airline pilots. It perplexed John Raxell that he had been unable to persuade any individual or agency to see the usefulness of such a system – let alone purchase one. People *wanted* to misinterpret each other.

He watched Julia's tirade appear on the display unit in front of him almost as soon as the words came out. *'Listen here/ Marcus . . .'*

On the screen the analysis ghosted the transcript:

(function)	**IMPERATIVE**
(register)	**INFORMAL**
(use)	**SUBORDINATES & CHILDREN**
(intonation)	**RISE-FALL**
(acceptability)	**IMPOLITE ?**
(omission of honorific in greeting formula)	**INFORMAL: SOME MALE ACCEPTABILITY**
	FORMAL: *IMPOLITE*

'I'm in the *middle* / of a meeting with the President of the United States// You heard of *him*, right? . . .'

(function)	**INFORMATION ORIENTATION**
(statement false ?)	**HYPERBOLE**
(use)	**JOCULAR EFFECT**
(statement true ?)	**CONTEXT FALL-RISE INTONATION: *SARCASM***

John Raxell watched the shadowy reflection of himself overlaying the refractive surface of the VDU and the analysis of his wife's utterances. Since Julia was mistaken about the identity of the person whom she was speaking with, the computer found itself unable to gauge her register. The moment she paused for breath he spoke as softly as he had ever spoken to her in all their years together.

'Honey . . . ?/. . . '

(social function) VOCATIVE
(distinctive use) DOMESTIC INTIMACY
(acceptability) *UNCERTAIN*

There followed a pause which was measured on the screen in units of appropriacy from **INTERRUPTION** to **COMMUNICATION FAILURE**.

Finally, her voice falling and rising as if she were inside a darkened room, unsure who, if anyone, was inside it with her, Julia said: 'John/. . . ?' Raxell shut his eyes and hoped.

'. . . Is that you, John . . . ?'

'Sure it's me. Who did you think it was? Marcus Senior?'

'You bastard! Who do you think you are?'

'Your husband?'

'Not for long! Mind telling me how you got *in* here? You can't invade my privacy like this and expect . . .'

'Listen, Hon. So long's you need access to a main-frame I can reach you. You're going to have to get used to the idea. Like it or not, wherever you go in the world, you'll be talking to *me*. I'm in your baggage. So long's you want to interface with the world to which you are accustomed – travel, communicate, earn money, buy commodities, teach school – I'll be able to reach you.'

'But John, why – when we are no longer living together as man and wife – would you want to do that?'

Raxell groaned.

'Oh, Honey! You think it has anything to do with *me*? I can't help it if my computer has gotten used to your computer. Hardly surprising, when you consider how long they've been together, programmed to maintain two distinct but interdependent identities. Twelve years seven months, to be exact. That's a long time in the life of a computer. They speak the same language. They share each other's innermost secrets. OK, so *we're* not compatible anymore – but *they* still are. I can't help it if your passwords and codes are still integrated into the Read-Only Memory of my database, literally burnt into the microtechnology of its circuitry. It's going to take me a while to excise every reference to you, Hon. And that's *my* database. I can't wipe *yours*. I'm not in a position where I can do that. You'll have to do that yourself. Or find someone else who can do it for you.'

'Hold on a minute there, will you?' Julia said. 'You'll be telling me next they could have a baby!'

'No. They could never do that,' Raxell said. 'But *we* could have!'

Julia Raxell exhaled air through her mouth.

'It's too late in the day, John, for this conversation,' she said, not unkindly.

'Sure, Honey. I didn't call you up to put the bite on you. I just wanted to let you know I hand over the keys of RCC this afternoon. Marcus Senior'll have your half of the cheque for you, soon as the bank clears it.'

'John, I'm sorry/ . . . I never meant this to . . .'

(function) APOLOGY
(intonation) RISE-FALL: *APPROPRIATE*

'Forget it, Hon. / Business was bad, anyway. Anyway,/I hear you're going on a trip. Good luck where you're going.//Say,/where *are* you going?'

'I'm not permitted to tell you.'

(function) REFUSING PERMISSION
(register) FORMAL

'Unfortunately, Julia, you can't keep the information from me. See you at the hearing.'

Raxell hit the EXIT key.

As if it were that simple.

Out of respect for Julia, the President delayed opening the Briefing until she had slipped back into the room and taken her place at the oval table between Vic Rikov and

Greg Gregori in front of her Coca Cola Company beaker and presentation pack. She attempted an apology which everyone pretended they had not heard. They knew what she must be going through. Besides, although her position was the least senior among those present it was not, at this moment, the least crucial. All the President's training and experience had been inside corporate advertising organizations and, he claimed, he was unable to work on a project without the continuous throughput of the psychological consequences of any course of action. It was his professional instinct.

'Okay, Vic,' the President murmured.

Admiral Rikov, while melted snow rilled from the polished peak of his cap onto the polished cherrywood table, outlined the agenda. The President's party would rendezvous with the carrier USS *Iowa* at an unspecified point in the North Eastern Micronesian section of the Pacific – ETA 1900 hours local time tomorrow – and from there would proceed under cover of darkness to the secure base-camp established on the southernmost landmass of the double atoll of Bikini. The Adversaries – as Rikov quaintly called the representatives of the 3-CA – would probably be already installed on the northern landmass. The Summit would commence on the isthmus equidistant between the twin peaks of the atoll soon after the breakfast photocall the following day.

The President, his eyes shut, nodded.

This, Greg Gregori said, was a real great place to throw a summit, whoever had thought of it. For a start, Bikini was a long way from any other place and it would not be a difficult task keeping media terrorists out. 'Except the ones we are going to speak with, of course!' (Laughter.) 'On top of that, it falls close to the Japanese Theatre. The only major power not aligned to the Three-Continents Alliance,' he said. 'Just about the only people we can call our friends these days. By the way, who *had* thought of it?'

Ashkanasi shook his head.

'Don't look at me,' he said. 'I can't rob Julia of the credit this time!'

The assembled company fractionally rotated their chairs to face her, waiting on her to speak.

'I have to confess, Gentlemen,' she started with what she hoped was a self-deprecating smile, 'that the security suitability of this location was not uppermost in my mind when I floated this project. In fact . . .' She paused. 'It wasn't in my mind at all.'

Laughter.

'Bikini is no longer associated in the public's imagination with the site of the early nuclear tests carried out in the nineteen-fifties – although we can do some work on that – but, of course, with the female split bathing garment named for the French couturier who invented it around that time. These days it's the other way about: the shape of the atoll on the map immediately suggests the top half of a bikini, if not . . .'

With angled thumbs Julia's hands framed the relevant section of her own anatomy to illustrate her point.

'A pair of woman's breasts.'

The members of the President's Summit Strategy Advisory Group, studied the twin peaks on the front of Julia's open-necked canary yellow silk blouse no differently than if it had been a contoured briefing map.

'Our camp will,' Julia continued, 'be *here*. Their camp – *here*. And we meet – *here* . . .'

She had their attention, no doubt about that.

'The exploitation of this image will have a positive effect on the public's perception of the Summit, bringing together as it does – not too far below the level of consciousness – the two things most people are most concerned about: Sex and Death. Whatever happens – I mean, whatever the outcome of the Summit – we are not going to come out losers.'

'If I understand what you're saying, by surrounding it in an aura of sexuality we can take on the Soaps and beat 'em?' the President said, getting down to it. 'Right?'

Julia shrugged.

'I wouldn't want to overstate my case, Mr President. But, well . . . Yes. It will help our stand and have a knock-on effect in the public's imagination. The Administration can only benefit.'

'Our stand, I take it, hasn't changed any,' General Phibbs growled. As the Pentagon representative at the meeting it was his duty to safeguard the Coca Cola Company's slice of the international movie theme merchandise and distribution industry. Besides being one of the most effective weapons in his armoury, the Company was a major sponsor of the Initiative. '. . . Since the last round of talks?'

There was a general shaking of hands. Unanimity. No question. For economic, political, even historic reasons, an International Agreement to limit satellite video and TV access was not in the US interest. Never had been. Nossir. The Cultural Export Limitations Summit was a tiresome ritual, something every Administration had to live with. The trick was to get from it some spin-off advantage, to strike a posture that was more credible than the posture struck by the wishywashy confederacy of nation states – Muslim through Communist – that made up the Three-Continents Alliance, brought together, it looked like, by no more than their shared opposition to the US policy of upholding the individual's right to freedom of choice.

'Our *official* position hasn't changed none, either,' Ashkanasi reminded everyone. 'We sincerely expect the cultural terrorists of the 3-CA to accept a ceasefire in the electronics disinformation exchange, sure. But if they don't, we have no intention of censoring our programs according to their criteria until they quit stirring up trouble in US spheres of influence. We have the right to sell our products where we like, the same as they have to preserve their goddamn cultural identity. To that end we are going to present a reasonable package that they can't possibly accept. Make *them* appear intransigent. We shall be tying in a run of episodes of *The Conways* and the *Dez Dexley Show* for the same as their fucking folk dancing documentaries – Sorry, Julia – and get *them* to throw up their hands and walk away from table.'

The President nodded. His famous blue eyes, now open, twinkled. This was his territory. Boardroom deals. Packaging. Selling a product. Raking a competitor. At this game he was hard to beat.

'Mean everything you say,' he said, quoting himself as he rose to his feet – the Briefing Session was over. 'But don't ever say what you mean.'

Half-undressed in the belly of Airforce One, en route towards an aleatory pair of co-ordinates in the north-eastern section of the Micronesian Ocean, Julia Raxell had a nasty turn. It was 3.28 a.m., Pacific Time. Naked on the bed next to her, Serge Ashkanasi, his sperm inside her, was propped up on one elbow listening in silence to the communications handset he was holding to his ear, the cord of which was stretched across her semi-disrobed body.

After a moment Ashkanasi said: 'It's for you!'

He turned in the bed to look her in the eye. His face glowed white in the moonlight.

'Me . . . ? It can't be! Who is it?'

'The Sherman Fairchild Center for the Life Sciences.'

'But they're in Harlem. Manhattan!'

And the handset was connected to the internal communications system of Airforce One.

'Here! Speak to them yourself! They know all about your trip. Even where you are!'

Ashkanasi, with a perplexed sneer, handed her the phone.

'In my fucking cabin!'

Warily she put the piece to her ear.

'Honey . . . ?'

The President's airplane suddenly seemed to lose power and plunge towards the surface of the planet.

'Oh no! I don't believe this!'

'Hope I'm not butting in on anything,' her husband said. 'I mean, if you're in the middle of boffing Serge, I can easily call you back . . .'

Any second now the plane was going to hit the surface of the ocean.

Raxell lay in the semi-darkness of his hotel bedroom watching the President stepping on and off his personal airplane, waving to the TV cameras. It was a good picture, for which Raxell was grateful because he spent a lot of time in the room, recently, watching TV. He spent a lot of time there not watching it also – when he wasn't sleeping, dreaming, eating, going to the bathroom. In fact, the place was already beginning to feel like home. It already contained the apparent disorder in which he customarily kept his clothes and his computer hardware. The newspapers on the bed. The telephone under the newspapers. The easy meshing of communications systems. The half bottle of Old Times at hand. Comfortable – he might have been living out of the room for years – he sipped his iceless whiskey while he watched the Channel Eleven pictures of the twin peaks of an island in the middle of a blue ocean – Bikini, which he had never seen before. He couldn't hear what the news reporter had to tell him about the place, however, because the TV sound was set at zero and he was wearing an audio headrig set on max.

Alongside the TV, on a second screen, words moved: the Linguistic Analysis of the conversation he was listening to.

Inert among the newspapers, the terminal of Raxell's computer lay half inside the bed next to him, the matt white of its slim plastic frame half protruding from the sheets. The terminal, like the TV and the telephone, was on line to the less wieldy data storage and processing equipment which occupied the adjoining room, connecting him to the technology which connected him to his wife. It wasn't a bad arrangement although Raxell might have liked it better if they didn't have to occupy separate rooms.

Courtesy of the signal being emitted from the uterine device inside his wife's womb – allowing him, through her computer-dependency, to plant trojan horses inside all the computers she was dependent upon – Raxell listened to the President of the Republic conferring with the man whom his wife was currently making her womb available to.

'I don't know, Serge. They're not going to like *that* . . .'

'Fuck what they like! The US has a 49% stake in most of their production and distribution companies. If they don't like it, we threaten to withdraw our capital. Bring down some governments!'

'If we do that,' the President drawled, 'we going to kill the goose that lays the golden egg. We won't have a market to sell our products in. We'll, ah, how shall I put it? Go bust.'

'They need our know-how.'

'They already have our know-how.'

'They have *today*'s know-how! We have *tomorrow*'s! We got the brains and the economic system that can attract the brains. For as long as the brains sell themselves to who pays most, the brains will be working for us. The member states of the 3-CA are going to pay for our systems in cash. Most of it . . .' Ashkanasi chuckled. 'Borrowed from us.'

'What happens if we ever run out of cash,' the President said, 'to pay the brains?'

Raxell could hear Serge Ashkanasi consider the possibility. Like all the President's conversations, this one was being recorded and stored in the Congress Archive on Independence Avenue, Arlington, in case Congress ever needed to establish his knowledge of any matter. Or the President, for his part, his ignorance.

'We enter a post-capitalist mode of production period, I guess,' Ashkanasi said, deadpan.

Both men guffawed.

'Right! They're going to let us keep our equity in their companies just so long as they need the products those companies produce. It's a delicate ecological balance – between the US and the 3-CA. We need . . .'

'All I'm saying . . .'

'We need their debts and their tin-mines and a market in which to sell our leisureware as much as they need our cash, our tin cans and our consumer communications systems.'

'Fuck, all I'm saying is that we demand they reduce their tariffs on our software distribution! Free up their so-called cultural autonomy to some healthy competition!'

'I don't know, Serge. They're not going to like that.'

The President's party and the delegates of the 3-CA faced each other across the entrance to the old Navy laboratory next to the disused ball park – the laboratory that would soon serve as the Summit Treaty Room and the ball park almost as soon, judging from the two teams lined up behind the delegations, as a ball park.

On one of the two screens in his hotel room on 32nd Street, Raxell watched a looped video recording of the news shots of the US and foreign politicians entering the Treaty Room on Bikini atoll. There was no denying that for once the 3-CA had gotten it right. The new designer-label suits worn by the US personnel looked tired alongside the ironic period elegance of the foreigners. The President didn't look too bad but he was playing opposite an Eritrean Rita Hayworth, an Aztec Monty Clift, a Nordic dead ringer for Ingrid Bergman. The poor bastard didn't stand a chance. The representatives of the world's remaining ethnographic regions were obviously got up to look like Hollywood heroes in order to make a point. With the US cameras aimed at them, why throw away the opportunity? They could hardly appear on TV dressed in their own colourful national costumes and then complain that their native identities had been vandalized by US media technology. They were elegantly demonstrating the extent to which they had been culturally colonized.

Raxell had watched the loop – slowed up and at normal speed – almost thirty-seven times. He especially liked the bit where the Latin American Clark Gable showed Ashkanasi, in an appalling powder-blue three-piece and tie, how to open a bottle of vintage champagne – the graceful gangster communicating with the worthless cop who would no doubt eventually shoot him. He liked the bit where Mrs Raxell found herself standing alongside the President for the photo session group shot. She was wearing her dark glasses and pale cotton belted tunic dress, short but not too short. She looked very pretty. Sexy and competent. The President could have done a lot worse. Raxell had always liked that dress.

Brushing aside the newspapers, he fished out the terminal and had his computer request the land-line access number from the Archives in Arlington and, when the number came up, had the security system on the *USS Iowa* put through his call.

Unattaching one half of the headset, he lifted the telephone to his ear. He waited. In one ear he could hear the Bell telephone call-tone and, in the other, the telephone in the US airbase on Bikini atoll ringing in the room in which the President was hemming and hawing with his closest adviser.

In his right ear he heard Ashkanasi say: 'Are you expecting a call?'

'I don't believe so.'

In his left ear the call tone ceased.

'Hello, this is the President,' the President said into both of Raxell's ears.

'For the Secretary of State, Mr President,' he said.

'It's for you, Serge.'

The President must have covered the set with his hand.

'Who is it?' Ashkanasi said.

'He knows me,' Raxell said before the President had the

chance to relay Ashkanasi's request. 'We already spoke. Earlier in the night.'

'Says you know who he is . . .'

The President relayed the information without pausing to consider how the exchange had been transacted.

'*Raxell!*' Serge Ashkanasi bellowed into the telephone. 'I ever get hold of you, fuck, am I going to kill you?'

'Hear me out, Serge,' Raxell said. 'You're poking my wife, right? I'd like to propose a deal. You have her drop her annulment proceedings in the NY City District Court and I'll help you penetrate the 3-CA's security computer.'

There followed – both over the phone and over the headset – a lengthy silence. Lengthy enough to tell Raxell what he needed to know.

In the slow rake of the powerful self-focusing Army binoculars Julia Raxell regarded the ocean from the southernmost tip of the mutant geological formation – the left nipple as the pilot inside the hovering TV helicopter would see it. The ocean was bristling with communications antennae and air activity of the two rival fleets. Stood off on the eastern horizon, the grey US carriers faced the gaudy rainbow flotilla belonging to the members of the 3-CA.

She lowered the binoculars a few inches.

On the faded diamond of the abandoned US Navy (Marshall Islands) sports area the final plays of a semi-serious game of softball were being enacted between teams drawn from the home fleet and the visitors. According to the improvised scoreboard the Pittsburgh Tigers – semi-jocularly so called – from the Austrian ship *Der Rosenkavalier*, were drawn against the Cleveland Redskins of the *USS Texas*. The Reds were teeing off the Tigers, just as you might have expected, although it looked as if the Tigers were beginning to rally. From the anxious face of the 3-CA pitcher as he looked over his shoulder, hoping against hope for a strike-out on three and two with the bases loaded, she closed the span of her vision to the surface of the atoll itself. On the rising terrain between the baseball diamond and where she was standing a brindled form of lichenous shrub appeared to be struggling to gain purchase among the dust and rusty Coca Cola cans. Ants the size of lizards conveyed dew-water inside used rubber prophylactics. Hybrid forms of local fauna were rallying against the conditions which had obtained in their habitat since the war declared on it by an adversary higher up the evolutionary chain than themselves.

Behind the growl of the helicopter engine a roar went up from the crowd watching the ballgame. Either the 3-CA pitcher had gotten his strike-out or the US batter his homerun. It almost drowned out the tweet-tweet of the communications handset inside the breast pocket of Julia Raxell's tunic dress. Underneath the pocket her heart sank. She knew from the calltone frequency who was on line: Secretary of State Ashkanasi, the only person besides herself who possessed the day's oneoff confidential access number. It was the call she had been dreading. Perhaps it had been a mistake to enter into a sexual liaison with a man who was in a position to pull rank on her whenever he felt like it.

'Darling . . . ?' she purred into the handset.

There followed a short pause.

'Ah-mm . . . I'm sorry, Julia . . .'

She recognized the voice immediately. It wasn't Ashkanasi's.

'. . . I hope I didn't give you a shock,' the President continued as if nothing were amiss, a gentleman in whose presence a lady has inadvertently broken wind. 'But what I have to tell you has priority. Fact is, we're on alert here. Green, going on amber.'

'What . . . ?'

'We've been penetrated. Our security – shafted. Some nut has successfully hacked his way into the technology ring-fencing Bikini. Ours and Theirs.'

'Shit! That's impossible! . . . Oh, I'm sorry. I . . .'

'Don't worry, Julia. My own feelings precisely.'

The Professor of Human Psychology at the Sherman Fairchild Center for the Life Sciences, Harlem, fifth-sensed that there was more to come. Why was he telling her? She had nothing to do with security. That was Greg Gregori's department.

'How do you know?'

It always paid, she had found, when dealing with a person who was about to be diagnosed as psychotic, to challenge his epistemology first.

The President hesitated. 'How do we know what?'

'That they are in.'

'Simple. He told us details of our bargaining position we didn't tell anyone yet. What we have in the hole. We must presume that the hacker is in a position to pass this information over to our adversaries. Either we abandon the talks or consider . . .'

'But how do you know,' she interrupted deftly, 'that the hacker knows what the third party – in this case, the 3-CA – intend to do? It's the oldest trick in the book. The double bluff people subject to paranoid fantasies specialize in, from Iago to Hitler. Nearly everyone falls for it. I mean, did he tell you anything you didn't already know?'

'We didn't know some nut had a fucking bug up our ass,' Ashkanasi growled.

Julia was momentarily at a loss what to say. What register would be approriate in a situation like this?

'He knows,' the President continued, 'that we intend to do the opposite to what we will say we are going to do. That's good enough for me.'

'With respect . . .' It was her duty to tell him. 'Everyone in the world knows that.'

'I mean *exactly* what we intend to do. Things only Serge and I ever discussed. Not what you and Rikov think we are going to do.'

'How could the hacker know that? We use the one-off Turing system in all our communications. It hasn't been cracked since it was invented. Around 1943, I believe.'

'Right! How could he? Fact is, he didn't need to crack

anything. He has put together some wacky software that can tell what a person is thinking from what he says.'

'Or she,' Julia muttered.

'It can decipher *language*. It takes all the linguistic factors into account. The words. Grammar. Intonation. Stuff you don't even realize when you're speaking. It's a wonder anyone ever opens their mouth! So he didn't need to crack our Turing codes. He could work it out just from listening in on a conversation. Two people speaking over a telephone. On TV. Any public utterance.'

'Oh no . . . !'

The distant roar of the softball crowd broke over the ocean like an ocean dragging against a pebbled shore.

'. . . *Raxell!*'

She listened to the President nodding over the communications channel.

'Why no one thought of it before I don't understand.'

'I see.'

'I thought you would. Now you appreciate why we're on alert here.'

'Amber – going on red,' Ashkanasi said.

'You know, he tried everywhere to sell that system,' Julia said. 'He couldn't give it away. No one was interested. No one could see its application.'

At least that was one thing she could never be accused of. She had always believed in her husband's product. Language systems. It was her husband – author of the most comprehensive linguistics dictionary in the country – that she was not a hundred percent certain of. His obsession with colonizing her womb. Babies. Diapers. PTA.

'Don't worry about Raxell,' the President told her. 'We're buying the company that recently bought *his* company.'

'What?'

'He's joining the team. He's probably on his way.'

'Serge . . . ? What's going on?'

Ashkanasi said nothing.

'I'm real sorry it has to be like this, Julia,' the President said, sounding real sorry. 'We don't have a lot of choices. Raxell's holding the gun. We have to pay what he's asking.'

'Me!'

'I'm sorry?'

'What about *me*?'

'What about you?'

'Am I fired?'

Her tears fell silently onto the magnolia plastic handset.

'No way! If you still want your job, it's yours. Seems at this stage of the negotiations we need the services of a linguistician. Just as we needed those of a psychologist to set up the negotiations in the first place. Who knows, by the time we're through we'll need someone who can sell us a one way ticket to Wap Wap.'

'But . . . John and I are in the middle of divorce proceedings. You can't expect me to . . .'

'Plenty of time for you to cut out, if that's what you feel you need to do. We'll understand. On the other hand . . .'

'I stay. John and I don't appear at the District Court on Wednesday. We try and make a go of it.'

'That's up to you and Raxell.'

'Well, thank you, Mr President! For selling me back to my ex-husband!'

'On red,' Ashkanasi said.

'Serge says we're on red, Julia. We're running late. We have to go ahead. Look, I wanted to break this to you myself. I sincerely hope you'll decide to stay with us because I value your contribution to the negotiating team. But, of course, that's your decision.'

The line went dead.

Below, the ballpark was going wild. The Tigers had, miraculously, turned the game around. It was all over. Her affair. Her political career. Her role in formulating Government policy. Either she went back to wearing a white coat in Harlem, a medium-sized fish in a small pond, or she agreed to suck John Raxell's cock. Or maybe worse – have his baby. As the President had rightly said, it was her decision.

The downdraught of the descending Navy helicopter – the engine screaming – forced her to hold down the hem of her cotton dress with both hands in order to prevent it from flying up over her pants.

BARRINGTON J. BAYLEY

Light

I walk but do not walk upon the dusty highway, never taking a single step. I carry a pack upon my back, for I am a traveller. Ahead I can see the spire and roofs of a town, which I approach but never reach. By the roadway are fields where women and girls gather wheat into sheaves, bending and never straightening, never bringing any action to completion.

It is afternoon. The sun is hot and bright in the sky, and casts a dazzling yellow light which thickly covers the landscape. But even the yellow light does not move. There is another light, the light from outside, and that light is the only thing that moves, trapping us in one moment forever. While in the town are taverns I would visit, and people I would know.

Life calls. But the future is silent.

He hadn't much friendship to give, and when he did try to give some, it was usually rebuffed. And so John had become taciturn, knowing how likely he was to encounter frustration, and cultivating a withdrawn, uncompromising manner. There was only one person he could call a friend, and then it was a friendship that had never been put to the test – with Austin, a regular visitor who liked to discuss questions of a 'philosophical' character.

Otherwise his social contacts were desultory. There was his sister with whom he had continued to share the house since the death of their parents, but whom he quite strongly disliked, and there were his work colleagues at Cordville laboratories. He had often felt that his reticence and awkwardness there made a tolerated obstruction, as it were, in the smooth stream of interpersonal relations.

On the morning of 29th July, a Saturday, Austin called by as John was sitting in his study examining one of two paintings that had long hung there. It was the one over his desk, a reproduction of *The Organ Player* by Titian, and it was, possibly, his favourite work of art. A swarthy brigandish figure occupied the left side of the frame, seated at an ornate but compact organ, sly face dreamy with lust as he played, for he was leaning towards the naked female stretched smiling on the couch to the right. The voluptuousness of the scene was enchanting. The two were in a small but airy chamber, glassless arched windows opening on to the type of paradisical landscape beloved of renaissance artists, with winding roads, castle-topped knolls and fleecy white clouds. John never grew weary of studying it. He fancied he could feel on his skin the warm breeze entering the chamber. He revelled in the organ's baroque decoration, its pipes and stops, he admired the byzantine floridity of the player's raiment, all making a thrilling contrast with the glowing flesh tones of the woman, who after the renaissance manner was devoid of pubic hair.

His friend's arrival interrupted John's reverie, while not ending it completely. Austin took an easy chair. Slim, slightly seedy, he had a left eye that bulged noticeably more than the other. He noticed John's continuing attention to the picture, and it made him restless and excited. Finally he spoke.

'I can tell you something about pictures. They contain the secret of the universe.'

'Really?' John said, and pushing aside any chance he might have had to cut him off, Austin rushed on. 'I discovered it when I was visiting the National Art Gallery in London. I was looking at a big painting there, I don't know who the artist was, or rather I *do* know who the artist was, it was God. A woman was on her knees scrubbing the marble floor of a palace, and she had stopped, scrubbing brush in her hand, to look up at a picture on the wall. Suddenly I realized that I could project myself into the picture and become the cleaning woman. In just the same way she could project herself into the picture she was looking at. In that picture, there might well be another painting hanging on the wall, another world to go into, and so on through a stupendous number of transitions. Eventually, there might be a painting of me looking into the picture at the National Art Gallery. The cosmos is a circuit of perceptions. A circuit, moreover, that can be travelled. And do you know, that's exactly what I did!'

John had listened politely to the account. 'But one term in the series is unique,' he said. 'The one where you really were in the National Gallery.'

'No, they're all the same,' Austin insisted. 'Our world is a picture for someone else to look into.'

'Well,' John said slowly, 'there have always been two opposed positions in philosophy. One sees the world as perceptual at root, and matter as an appearance. That's your view. The other regards matter as the true reality, and perception as something that emerges from it. As a physicist I'm bound to say that no amount of thinking or imagining can cancel the real world.'

He hadn't been able to resist pursuing the point, but Austin's only answer was the complacent smile of one who knows better.

John knew he was prone to these flights of fancy, and had spent time in mental hospitals. The story of his very first schizophrenic episode was one it still delighted John to recall.

As Austin told the tale, he had been at sea at the time, serving in the Royal Navy, when he had developed the power to work magic. Up to then he had accomplished only small magic – turning ashtrays into bunches of flowers and feats of that sort. But, with the cold war at its height and the outlook for mankind looking bleak, he had decided upon a major thaumaturgical operation: to propel the world into heaven by the force of his will.

In order to carry this out a measure of peace and solitude seemed necessary, and a warship is a crowded place. Accordingly Austin had made off with the ship's launch. His plan had begun to go wrong with the ship below the horizon, when he had lost control of the boat's steering, which was of an unusual type. The launch had carried him helplessly round and round in a circle, and while this happened he had seen beautiful young maidens in flowing gowns go gliding across the surface of the ocean.

Austin made a gesture. 'I like that one best.'

He was pointing to John's second piece of art. It was hung where it caught the light from the window, and unlike the Titian it was an original. It certainly was striking; at any rate John had been sufficiently struck by it to pay fifty pounds to a small art shop. It bore no title plate; and he had never been able to decipher the name of the artist, which was an illegible blue scribble in the lower right corner. The impression it made was rather as though Pieter Brueghel the Elder's *The Harvester* had been painted by Van Gogh. A young man walked a dirt roadway between wheatfields. His back was nearly to the viewer; his face was unseen.

The painter had caught him in midstride. The pack he carried indicated that he had made a long journey on foot. By the roadside peasant women gathered into sheaves the wheat scythed by their menfolk further off.

Anticipation was in the air. In a short while the young man would arrive at the town whose rooftops were visible over the horizon, and the imagination was compelled to wonder what would befall him there. But even more fascinating was the Van Goghian aura that lay over the whole scene. The flaring yellow of wheat, of sun, somehow of the air itself, seemed to burst and glare out of the canvas. John had been reminded of another peculiar painter, the wealthy eccentric Claudaire, who had given his pictures magical luminosity by using paints made from ground gemstones, adding traces of various phosphors, and by this means achieving an end dreamed of by the makers of stained glass windows: pictures that seemed the produce of their own inner light.

This thought had led John to interest himself in the special alchemy that gemstones exerted on light. The deep intense glows, the prismatic fires, the watery dispersions, the dichroism whereby a gem displayed two distinct colours if viewed in different planes. The high refractive index of some stones particularly impressed him. Diamond, the best example, slowed light down to a mere 77,000 miles per second, hardly more than two-fifths of its velocity *in vacuo*. Even the humble rock crystal reduced its velocity of transition to 120,000 miles per second, lopping 66,000 mps off the *in vacuo* value. Then there was the phenomenon of birefringence as in ruby and sapphire, yielding two different speeds for light transmitted across different axes.

What did all this signify? John had begun to wonder if light in its purest form, coherent light, might have special artistic properties, an obvious and fruitful thought since his work at Cordville Laboratories lay in the field of lasers. So he had gone to his workplace and borrowed gas lasers in the three primary colours: red, green and blue. He had fixed them together in a frame and used them to produce a white compound beam which he had then widened through a magnifier. It was a surrealist parody of sunlight, hard and sharp, bereft of the softening influence of intermediate wavelengths, of higgledy-piggledy wave trains. And, lacking an original Claudaire, he had shone it on the one original painting he *did* possess, the *pastiche* Van Gogh.

The effect transcended anything the Frenchman could have achieved with his extraordinary gem-paints. The picture had leaped to life. For a moment it actually had seemed to move. Like his mentally disturbed friend, John had been able to imagine he looked into a real world of tangible depth and brightness.

He had found no opportunity to experiment on other oils, and although he had repeated the exposure several times thereafter, the initial flash of vivacity had never been repeated. Probably it had been psychological. Nevertheless the unnamed painting had never looked quite the same to him since. The young man on the roadway seemed poised in an eternally repeated moment; every time the picture caught his eye, John expected to see him move.

Voices from the back garden roused him. He suggested to Austin that they move there, afraid that his friend was about to launch into an idiosyncratic speech which there would be no halting. He led the way into the living room, and thence through French windows that opened on to the lawn.

His sister Gertrude, ten years older than himself and to his sensibilities an ugly woman, held court. On a garden table was tea and lemonade. Three others were there, two of them young girls of about eleven or twelve. For some reason not clear to John, Gertrude was one of those adults who young girls liked to visit. He recognized one of them; she seemed to be in the house constantly. She looked up and cheekily smiled at him. Shyly, he smiled back at her pretty, mischievous face.

The remaining member of the tea party was Gertrude's latest attempt at a male relationship. John had been told his name was Clarence, and he did not like him any more than he did Gertrude. About sixty years old, he was tall and smarmy; he followed the practice of combing slicked-down black hair across his balding pate. In John's eyes there was something almost mouldy about him. He was sure his interest in Gertrude was predatory, as with most of the obsequiously 'gallant' middle-aged swains she turned up with.

At the moment Clarence was telling 'the little girls' a 'charming story' about a teddy bear, to which they were listening with fidgety boredom. '. . . And that,' he finished, 'is why teddy bears love all good children!'

Pleased to catch the end of the tale, Austin took a vacant seat and turned to Clarence like a conman with his mark. 'Do you know why human beings are represented as anthropomorphized animals, in such a lot of fiction?' he asked him. 'It's rooted in human nature.' He then began an extemporized lecture, as usual without waiting for his listener's consent, and John moved away, knowing what was coming. Austin had a knack of trapping someone's attention, with remarks which at first sounded interesting and full of ideas, but after a couple of minutes his exposition became a bewildering monologue which ceased to make sense. With amusement he watched Clarence's face become a wooden mask as he failed to keep up with the roller coaster of Austin's thought. The gist of what Austin had to say was that before the world was created there were animal spirits, and that these now inhabited the human psyche. But it was expressed with infuriating circumlocution. After long practice John was more or less able to follow Austin's erratic reasoning, but few others could.

With a scornful glance at her brother, and ignoring Austin whose access to the house she had frequently complained of, Gertrude rose and went through the French windows. Surreptitiously John turned his attention to the eleven-year-olds. What was it that made young girls like to hang around other people's households? They weren't doing anything, just sitting there, content to be present. The one with the mischievous face – Angela was her name – sat with eyes downcast, smiling to herself as if at a secret thought.

He followed Gertrude, glad to have dumped Austin for a bit. She was seated at the dining table, her face frozen with resentment. She spoke, in bitter accusing tones.

'Do you have to bring that lunatic in when I'm entertaining?'

He shrugged. Gertrude had never married, and like him had lived in the same house all her life; her affairs with men had all been failures. She no longer worked, having opted to live off the modest inheritance left by their mother, and consequently her life consisted of a daily emptiness, fraught with a disappointment which even at her age she sought to remedy. She was a frosty-faced fifty-year-old woman in search of romantic love, with less and less promising material.

Still, John had to admit that her approach to life was more positive than his own. Recently she had even made a show of altruism, joining a team formed to put a brain-damaged child through a rigorous and time-consuming programme of exercises. The idea was that other areas of his brain could be brought into play. John too had been approached about joining the team, but he had refused. Disease and injury frightened and repelled him. He had once visited a hospital where he had seen a five-year-old boy dying of cancer, doped into permanent semi-consciousness. The spectacle of young life so utterly defeated had haunted him ever since. And even Gertrude had withdrawn from the team when her duties became onerous.

Austin's voice continued droning on in the garden. John retreated back into his study. He fell once more to gazing at the unnamed painting. Yes, it figured that Austin would like it. The great slashing yellows, the air of arrested reality, was redolent of schizophrenia. He imagined the lost name of the picture to be *The Traveller*, and he even identified himself with the walking figure who would never reach the town towards which he gazed with such hope. John likewise felt that life was a cheat, that its enjoyable part had never begun for him and never would begin. At forty years of age he had never had a girl friend and had never had a sexual experience, though he had spent hours at a time thinking and thinking and thinking about it. He had long ago given up on such a project, when he had realized that he was incapable of getting along with women.

Once he had written in his notebook: 'I am a mutated fruit-fly with too many legs.' He had read that the male of the Drosophila fruit-fly, favoured research tool of geneticists because it could so easily be made to mutate, had a mating dance which had to be performed to exactitude. The deformities of the mutants caused them to fumble the steps, at which the female would lose interest and fly off.

And the truth was that he found the prolonged mating dance of the human sexes undignified and repugnant. The grimacing signals by which men and women noticed one another, the corkscrew skills of flattery, dissembling and manipulation, the exploitative attention which turned, once gratification had been obtained, into disinterest and betrayal – everything that he had seen in plenitude in his sister and her odious companions.

Yet for all these rationalizations John was sometimes swallowed up in a gulf of loneliness. Paradoxically it only made him feel disgust for what human contact he did have, so that he ended up with an urge to seclude himself even more.

He took his eyes from the painting as Austin came in. He was smiling broadly, pleased with his one-way exchange. 'I caught a fish there,' he boasted. 'We are slowly educating them.'

'You are, at any rate, Austin.'

Enjoying the flow of his own words, his friend paced to and fro and produced another of his cosmogenic visions. It concerned a giant who had a son with whom he played chess. In the course of the game the father grew bigger and bigger while the son became smaller and smaller. That was how the world got divided up into macrocosm and microcosm, universe and atom.

Austin glanced at his watch. 'I'd better get back home. Marjorie wants me to cook dinner. Her mother is coming tonight.'

John walked with him up the front path to his car. As he did so he saw Gertrude driving off with Clarence. Lost in thought, he went back to the house. Absent-mindedly he sauntered into the living room.

Angela was there, seated on the couch reading a comic book she had brought with her. She was alone; the other girl had gone. The French windows had been closed and the gauze drapes drawn. She smiled up at him, uttering a breathless 'Hello.'

Unexpectedly John's heart jumped. Abruptly, with complete conviction, he knew why she kept visiting the house. She was the ring-leader: she would come with one or other of her friends, or failing that she would come by herself. The association with Gertrude was the lesser part of it. Her welcoming pleasure when he entered a room, her enthusiastic chattiness to him, all of which he had taken in his innocence only to be childish amiability, assumed its real meaning. His heart pounded at the thought of what was being offered. The blood roared in his eardrums, and a longing which, as it now appeared, had comprised his whole life, but which had been secret even from his own knowledge, flooded through his belly. From then on he seemed but a witness to someone else's actions. To imagine negative outcomes – her running from the house to blurt accusations, or reacting with fright and hysteria – almost deterred him, but instead he found himself sitting beside her on the couch and offering to read to her from her comic book.

Three days later John left work early and went and sat in the town park to think. The unreality of everything around him formed a distorting lens on his consciousness. An immense distance seemed to separate him from his surroundings. It was late afternoon, and the air was limpid. Chatter rose from children playing on swings and slides, mingling with the sounds of traffic and birdsong, but all these noises were merely absorbed into a vaster silence, dissolved into meaninglessness.

On a stretch of grass before him girls were practising with hoola-hoops. He found his gaze fixing on their jean-sheathed backsides as they gyrated round and round. He was, he supposed, a pervert, and that made him feel even more apart from the world, as if shut up in a box, as if no one should speak to him. He had gone all the way with her. That Saturday afternoon was a beacon in his mind. Yet it hardly seemed fair. At the age of forty he had had sexual intercourse for the first time in his life, and now those who had been sexually rampant since their mid-teens would universally condemn him.

Because something serious had happened. The silly girl had talked – not to her mother, of course, but to her best friend, the same who had departed and left her alone in the house with him. The friend had blabbed to *her* mother, who had gone rushing to Angela's mother. The police had been informed. By now knowledge of the incident was current in John's home district. So far his thinking was dazed, not knowing how to react. It was unlikely his work colleagues would have heard the story yet, but the suspicion that they might have had proved too much for him, and he had excused himself.

He got up, eventually, and walked home, feeling like an alien from another planet as he went through the streets. He paused when he reached the house and took a good look at it. Half-timbered and quite old, he could imagine it inside a picture frame. He thought of Austin's notion of the world as pictures within pictures. If only escape were that easy.

He got a shock when he went into his study. The two pictures were missing from the walls. Much of his paperwork was gone from his desk too. He called through the house for Gertrude, but got no response.

He found her in the back garden. She had lit a large bonfire, on which she was burning his clothes. The remnants of the Titian reproduction were disappearing in the flames along with his best suit, while in one hand she held the smaller painting, the original, ready to follow. Her body was hunched up with tension. Her face, white with mortification, spat words of hatred and indignation at him, but they were little more than a mutter, as though she barely had the strength to utter them.

'Filthy paedophile.'

He protested. 'What are you doing with my things?'

'Clearing them out. Nothing of yours is staying in this house. When you come out of prison – that's where you're going, you know – you needn't come back here.' She waved the painting in the air. 'The girl's been examined, did you know that? The police know everything you did to that poor child. Oh, it makes me feel *ill*. They should cut it off, that's what you deserve!'

John was at a loss to know how to meet her anger or distress. The day before, he had learned that Clarence had parted company with her, for what reason she had kept to herself. She sniffed, then sobbed. *'Oh!* Why do I have to endure this? How can I hold up my head?'

'It's my house too,' John mumbled.

'Then we'll sell it.' Her nascent tears vanished. She sneered and came closer, encroaching on him. 'Or why don't you kill yourself? That's all you're good for. Go on, why don't you?'

Her voice was cracked and vehement, like the voices of certain neurotic German women he had met. As she spoke, a dim film went reeling through John's psyche. It was of their life together, all the resentments, the jealousies, the quarrels. From out of a murk, as if forced up by pressure, came a flickering scene he did not remember recalling before, of her fiddling with his genitals when he would be well under the age of ten, giving him his first orgasm. Had that really happened?

He reached out an impotent hand as she flung *The*

Traveller into the fire. He made no attempt to retrieve it, only watched disconsolately. The flames were rising in the early evening air, pretty in their colours as they attacked the painting. The oil paints, put on with a palette knife in places, sputtered and writhed, and the canvas curved and curled as it was destroyed, so that in the moment before the young man on the highway was consumed John was deceived into seeing him move, and put down his leading foot. Then the fire was licking and crackling round the empty frame.

He trudged back into the house and sat on his swivel chair. Opening a drawer, he found his notebook, undiscovered by Gertrude.

In it, he wrote: 'The rocks on the surface of the moon have lain unmoving for billions of years. During that time, photons of light have crossed the universe in ceaseless flight. Two versions of eternity: which is the more desolate?'

The sound of a car caused him to put away the notebook. He looked quickly out of the window and saw with relief that it was Austin's. He went to the front door and let his friend into the study. Austin took his usual seat. He raised his eyebrows in surprise.

'Your pictures are gone!'

'Gertrude removed them.'

Austin nodded blankly. He seemed cheerful, as was the norm with him, and pensive, as was also typical. Presumably he hadn't heard what was happening yet. John had no idea how he would react when he did. He turned his swivel chair as his friend began to speak.

'I had a reason for coming to see you today,' Austin said serenely. 'I want to tell you about a strange dream I had last night. I dreamed the sun went nova. I was walking in the street with Jenny and the boys at the time. We knew it was going to happen: there'd been a two minute warning. But when it came it was very quick. The sun expanded in a flash, much too fast for anyone to see, practically instantaneous. In a split second everything was engulfed in a white-hot gas. Odd, isn't it, how the sun, the provider of life, should be the ultimate in destruction as well? The Earth simply vanished, consumed. There was only this white haze, very bright. I was aware of it, because I had survived the vaporization of my body. Once you were in it, the haze actually seemed quite cool, hot as it was. Nearby I could just see the face of our younger boy, Robert, like a faint image or memory. I don't think I was the only survivor by any means. It had happened so fast that nothing had had time to be destroyed. Everyone was still there, suspended in the white haze.'

'That's very interesting,' John said. He heard the sound of a second engine pulling up. He looked out of the window. A police car had parked outside the gate. From it emerged two men, one young and uniformed, in a flat police cap, who glanced anxiously towards the house, not liking what lay ahead. The other was plainclothes and older. His face was expressionless. He had done this many times before.

A panicky feeling assailed John. *My God,* he thought, *what am I going to tell them?*

I am a man in a painting. I walk but do not walk upon the highway, my pack on my back, and ahead I see the town I have never reached. Also within my view I see my fellow captives, women and girls and beyond them men holding scythes.

Light is what holds us here. Light gives life, but also imprisons it. Light is what makes pictures, and pictures are worlds.

But suddenly the moment moves, impelled by a wave of heat, and we are free. That light that comes from outside is gone, can no longer reach us. There is only the light of our own sun, and my foot goes down on the dust of the highway. Scythes sweep, cutting the standing grain. The women straighten, prop up the sheaves, then bend to gather more.

One of the girls smiles at me. I smile back, but there is no time to tarry. Eagerly I quicken my pace towards the town.

Life calls.

NICHOLAS ROYLE

The Sculptor's Hand

As a sculptor working exclusively within the realm of the classical ideal, I had never, to my knowledge, created anything that could be considered offensive. That and the fact that I was paying only a short, isolated visit to Scotland led me to believe that my involvement in the train crash just outside Glasgow was purely a matter of bad luck.

Two trains collided head on and although the speeds at which they were travelling were not great, one mounted the other, creating an image as absurd and inappropriate as caterpillars mating.

One of the drivers and one passenger bore the brunt of the crash, from which all I remember, because the whole thing was so completely unexpected, was the terrible sound of wrenching metal followed by an eerie silence.

I hit my head against a window and considered myself fortunate the glass did not break. Dazed, I climbed down from the train and sat on a grassy bank. A few moments passed before I had the near-presence of mind to re-enter the carriage and assist other passengers. Within a few minutes the emergency services began to arrive; I was draped with a blanket and helped into an ambulance.

I was detained in hospital until my lucidity returned and doctors had performed sufficient tests to make sure of that fact. It was just as I was leaving on foot by the front entrance of the hospital that I noticed the Premier arrive with an entourage of security men.

Her party made its entrance under the watchful lenses of television cameras and I slipped away, thankful to have escaped attention, since I was still somewhat shaken.

Without a second thought – for my faith in the safety of rail travel was not so frail as to be undermined by a single incident – I caught a southbound train immediately, my business with a television producer having been concluded before the accident and my visit to a former school friend in the northern suburbs subsequently postponed.

Several hundred miles south, back in the southern outskirts of London where I make my home, I resumed activities as normal.

I read the newspaper reports of the crash and felt quite detached from it. Even when I rang my agent and she said she had been worried for me, I still felt nothing. I gave her a report on my meeting with the producer, who had commissioned a series of sculptures for the set of a costume drama over a year ago and was now about to start shooting. I had made the journey to the studio at his invitation to advise on the lighting. The art director and lighting cameraman, clearly displeased at the producer's initiative, told me they were confident they could light the pieces with a degree of competence and they hoped I hadn't made a special trip.

My agent suggested a meeting at her offices in the city so that I could sign some papers for the television people and we could make some progress on the tangle of bureaucracy surrounding an upcoming gallery show in Northern Ireland. I was lucky, my agent needlessly pointed out, that classical sculpture, with or without the irony and self-awareness inherent in a 'revival', was currently enjoying great popularity.

I also rang Helen but didn't mention the crash to her. She hadn't known I was going to Scotland, so had no reason to bring it up herself. I drew out the conversation, hoping for an invitation to her house but none appeared to be forthcoming. As usual she was quiet and any conversational gambits were mine. Until she let me get to know her better I would not know if her dour telephone manner was just that or if it was an accurate reflection of her feelings towards me.

I told her I was working on a new series of figures and suggested she might like to come to my studio, where I could fix her a drink and she could see my new work before anyone else. I knew she liked my sculptures; possibly it was all she did find in me to attract her. We first met when she attended a private showing of my Illyrian project with some hack from a 'lifestyle' magazine.

'If you're going to be at the studio anyway,' she said, 'I might call by on my way into town. I'm meeting someone for a drink, you see,' she added.

'Oh?' I replied, betraying too easily the hurt I felt.

'Yeah, I dunno,' she said in her affected, lounge-bar drawl. 'It depends on the trains.'

I wanted to tell her that she didn't have to pretend, not for me. But I was too obsessed with the question of whom she was going out with and in what their relationship might consist.

'Yes, I'll be at the studio anyway,' I lied. 'So if you want to call in, fine. If not, no problem.'

I hadn't particularly felt like working that evening, so I was angry at myself for creating the situation. It was only a short train ride, but it was quite chilly and the waiting rooms lacked adequate heating.

At the studio I lit the gas fire and poured a drink. I picked up the hammer and chisel and put them down again; the wooden handles were cold and uninviting. I swallowed my drink and wondered if Helen would bother to turn up.

The three busts I was working on regarded me silently with blank eyes. Whenever I wasn't actually chiselling I always doubted the wisdom of the project in hand. In this instance, was I not wasting time and good stone on a project that was ill-conceived? My intention was to fashion Greek faces but in the Roman style. Even if it worked, my unfriendly critics – and they have always been around – would shout 'esoteric' even more loudly than usual.

By the third vodka I was digging even deeper: what was stopping me from addressing the concerns that really interested me? Why did I dwell on the past when what I most wanted to examine were the realities of contemporary politics?

Helen's arrival took me completely by surprise. The doorbell rang shrilly as an alarm clock. I let her in.

Her presence filled the small studio, her perfume my nostrils.

'I'm just passing,' she said.

I nodded as she noticed the three unfinished busts.

'I like these,' she said quietly, almost to them rather than to me, enfolding the first one in the palm of her hand.

I watched her hands move over the vague forms, her fingers dipping and stroking like a pianist's. Her fingers were long but not especially elegant. They moved, however, it seemed to me, with a kind of grace and not a little sensuousness. I wished my own head were made of stone.

She had a quick drink and left soon after that.

I sat down and had several more drinks.

When I boarded a train the next day to take me to the meeting my agent had proposed, I had not the slightest fear or premonition that it would later go through a red light and collide with another train. The points were set for the other train to cross from the slow tracks to the fast line. The final carriage of the crossing train slewed into the first two carriages of the train in which I was travelling. We knew none of this, of course, at the moment of impact.

I had been talking to an elderly lady who was coming up from the coast to see an old black-and-white film that had been revived at a repertory fleapit in the city. I watched her blue-veined fingers feathering lightly over the clasp of her snakeskin handbag. One minute we were swapping stories about old movies produced around the time when she was as old as I am now; the next, there were two loud knocks on the side of the train and we were lying down.

In the first instance it did not occur to me that this was the second train crash in forty-eight hours and that I had to be phenomenally unlucky to have been involved in both. Instead I just looked about me and checked to see that I could move, which was the case.

The carriage was on its side and sloping downhill. Metal door- and window-surrounds were twisted like Plasticine, windows smashed, seats uplifted and the ceiling buckled. The lady I had been talking to lay motionless. I crawled over to her, becoming aware of pain in my legs, ribs and head. I broke the silence by crying uselessly over her dead body.

I climbed out of the train, experiencing for the first time a genuine sense of *déjà vu* as I surveyed the scene. It seemed unreal. Five or six carriages had slithered down the embankment and lay strewn in suburban back gardens, pointing this way and that, like the sloughed skin of a snake. A greenhouse had been flattened as if it had been constructed out of matchsticks.

People began emerging from gaping doorways and empty window frames, looking as if they'd just woken up from a bad dream. They had blood on their foreheads and shirts. I stumbled across a piece of reflective glass and saw my own wounds were more severe than I had imagined. The left side of my face was covered with blood. I looked away and started to tremble. I knew I was going into shock.

In the hospital they didn't let me know what was happening, so I didn't have time to prepare myself before she appeared.

They had given me a bed, as I was to be treated for concussion in addition to my cuts and bruises. I was sitting up in strange pyjamas with a bandage around my head when she came around the corner into my part of the ward. Into my head at once came all my preconceived ideas and impressions of her, all the things I had planned to say should I ever meet her. They span round and round my concussed head as she leaned towards me, a three-dimensional version of her televisual image. Around the other side of the bed reporters and photographers jostled. She said something about being at an important conference but having to leave as soon as she heard. Was I in very much pain? she asked. I nodded, unable to speak. She told me I'd done well; as if it were a war and I'd been injured defending my country.

When I was back at home Helen called me every day for a week. I was offhand, since it seemed to me she was displaying a morbid interest; she had seemed less keen before I became a crash victim.

I finished off the three Greco-Roman busts in a frenzy of hammer blows and chisel thrusts. I studied them briefly, then stuck them on a top shelf, dissatisfied but unable to identify the problem. Only later would I discern the cynical curl to the lip on one face and the frowns of contained violence on the other two.

Helen stopped calling and I watched my level of alcohol consumption rise steadily. A student journalist rang me and politely inquired if I might let him do an interview. I was unnecessarily rude to the young man, pointing out that I already received sufficient coverage in the nationals. Two days later I rang back to apologize and offer my time; he graciously accepted my excuse of overtiredness but said the interview was no longer a priority as he had fixed a date with Lexington Przewalski.

I came off the phone in a foul temper. Although clearly a modernist, Przewalski had been, in my mind at least, a rival of mine for some time. I stalked around my rooms until I decided to vent my anger in an act of destruction. I took one of my Hellenic miniatures and propelled it at an unpapered wall. The miniature shattered and left a small dent in the plaster.

In an effort to normalize my life once more, I cut down the amount of vodka that passed my lips and launched into some new work. I had a large hunk of sandstone at the studio as yet untouched. With confident strokes I set to releasing from it a life-size male figure.

Work progressed satisfactorily until one night when I dreamed I was back in hospital. The Premier was coming towards me and I was paralyzed. Her hands fluttered over my arm. Before she touched me I woke up.

I couldn't do any work that day. With no expectations I rang Helen. To my surprise, she invited me round.

Although I made it clear I didn't want to talk about the train crashes, Helen persisted. She asked me if I felt resentment towards the railways. (She knew by now that I had also been involved in the Glasgow incident.) Did I blame the drivers?

No, I told her. If I blamed anyone, it had to be the bosses. And the buck didn't stop with the railway bosses, I emphasized. It went back to the government and those in it responsible for shrinking subsidies and squeezing cash.

We picked at our food and finished two bottles of wine. Almost in default of any direction in our moves, we ended up in her bedroom. As we undressed and climbed into bed I felt utterly miserable. Where was the excitement? Awkwardly I pressed my body close to hers; she kissed me on the nose and asked me what I was working on at the studio.

'A sandstone statue,' I told her. 'Do we have to talk about that?'

'It's just that I sense a lack of commitment,' she said.

'But this is the first time you've seen me in weeks,' I said, exasperated.

'I'm right, though, aren't I?' she pressed.

I was silent for a few moments.

'Well, I'm not exactly changing the world, am I?' I felt my former resolve to be inside her softening. 'Ultimately I'd like my work to change people's lives. But it's not going to happen with clichés plundered from ancient civilizations. I just feel I'm wasting my time.'

I turned over and stared at the wall. Some time later I heard Helen murmur that she would be grateful if I could leave at the same time as she left in the morning. I wondered what time that might be, then fell asleep.

If Helen hadn't wanted me to leave so early . . .

If she lived south-east of the city instead of south-west . . .

If I had turned down her invitation and spent the night at my home instead . . .

If I had not been depressed by a traumatic dream of lying paralyzed in hospital . . .

But I had the dream, phoned Helen, made the journey to her house, stayed the night and left at seven.

I don't know if I was on the train that was stationary or the express that crashed into it, since I was actually catching up on lost sleep at the time. It seems that there was a certain point at which the wreckage of the two became indistinguishable, as they had telescoped into each other.

I remember being crushed and, above all, feeling trapped. I may or may not have felt pain. Certainly I didn't entirely believe that the accident had happened. The moans and shrieks around me and the blood that was everywhere were part of a drunken dream. Someone said they were going to give me a shot to put me to sleep while they worked on freeing my arm. Drugged, I dreamed prophetic images and sequences that I would later bury at the back of my mind as they were far too horrible to contemplate.

Despite the best efforts of the hospital on behalf of myself and other victims, the media breached all defences, the Premier at their head as highest authority. I was the centre of attention, as a survivor of three rail crashes in as many months. It seemed to *me* incredible that there had been three major accidents in so short a time. But the media had a bigger miracle on which to focus.

I woke up to see the face of the Premier staring down at mine. Her hands floated like dead fish in the thick air above me. In the same instant I realized I had lost my left arm.

I believe I screamed, but cannot be sure. If I did, it was edited out of television reports and out of all but the few newspapers which, because they had a reputation for biting the ankles of the government, were taken seriously by only a minority.

Available time was used up in the Houses of Parliament by ministers who praised the Premier for her compassion. They declared the public enquiry open.

When I felt well enough, I agreed to talk to the media. Only two or three newspapers printed my comments about insufficient government money being pumped into the railways, about the discrepancy between the artificial prosperity and opportunities created in the city – which meant huge increases in the numbers of commuters – and the absence of significant improvement in the public transport services available.

In place of broadcasting my comments to the nation, television researchers dug into the files to reinterpret my early sculptures in terms of spurious prophecies.

I said that I would have preferred a visit from Royalty to those made by the Premier. I swallowed hard and said that I found it morally repugnant that she, as a party politician, exploited these situations to enhance her standing as a caring leader. Only one paper printed this without distortion, having made sure it was safely couched in the context of a much wider debate.

When I returned home I was besieged by the gutter press baying for gory stories. I listened carefully for telltale clicks when I lifted the receiver of my telephone and hoped I wasn't becoming paranoid. Helen sounded relieved to hear my voice. (I had already contacted her from the hospital, telling her to stay away.)

I hung on a few days, then left by the back door in the middle of the night, taking a cab to the studio. I uncapped a bottle of vodka and regarded my sandstone man, wondering how I would proceed with only one arm and half a mind.

The next morning, after a night in the armchair, I took up my sanding-saw but my one hand shook too much trying to support what before I had held in two. I left the sandstone man standing and turned my mind to other projects. Taking down the Greco-Roman busts from the shelf I deciphered their expressions, then swiftly dispatched them with my heaviest hammer.

Meanwhile, the hunt for a scapegoat for the most recent rail crash was well under way. The authorities and the media colluded more efficiently in such matters than in any other. And as luck would have it, the perfect scapegoat was unearthed: a senior technician who *might* have failed to dot a single *i*, and who in any case was *responsible* for the dotting of *i*s by himself and his subordinate.

I studied this man's stony face on the television as he posed for cameras on his way into the enquiry court. *You are charged with the role of scapegoat for the railway bosses and the government. How do you plead?*

This individual was guilty of working a seven-day week and all the overtime he could get in order to keep up with the spiralling cost of his mortgage.

I had my own scapegoat and it wasn't this innocent man.

I clipped a picture of him from the newspaper and tried to model his face in clay. Executed with only one hand, my effort was not wholly successful. His face was lopsided. But as I sat into the dusk, watching the changes effected by the fading natural light and the accumulation of shadows in the studio, I saw that my hand had accurately recorded the conflict between the unfathomable guilt the man felt and the suppressed sense of rightful indignation he also carried.

I called Helen to assuage her concern, but refused to give her my studio number in case she spoke to the press.

I drank more vodka.

When the television costume drama was only days away from its screening, one particular newspaper picked up on the fact that some of my sculptures were being used as set decoration. Since I was by now a *bête noire* in this and one or two other papers, voices were raised in support of a proposed cancellation of the transmission. Only one political magazine undertook to defend my position and attack the would-be censors. Being just one small, pulling voice, it was easily drowned out by the concerted efforts and dishonourable silence of the bigger boys in the playground, who were all rallying round the government during what was being referred to as a Difficult Time; rising interest rates were not popular, and inflation was on the way up again.

The programme was pulled at the last minute by the television company after, they said, taking advice from their lawyers on possible repercussions. A future date has yet to be set for transmission.

I rang my agent to see what she had to say about the postponement. I was shocked by her response.

'I'm sorry,' she said, 'it's not really convenient to talk at the moment.' Then she hung up.

The call from the gallery in Northern Ireland came the following week.

'How did you get this number?' I asked the man.

'Your agent. She said I should talk to you direct.'

'She's not my agent any more,' I said. 'But carry on.'

The man explained that he had received a request to cancel the show. But he had already placed the statues in his exhibition space as the opening was imminent. Now he wanted to know what he should do.

I told him to do nothing until I arrived.

'I'll catch a flight tomorrow,' I said.

Somewhere in the sprawling midriff of the country a family was sitting down to dinner when the news came on the television.

The man, who had just come back from another hopeless job interview, wondered what could possibly be featured on the news tonight. After all those train crashes, the air crash yesterday was scarcely credible. A jet flying to Belfast had lost both engines and failed in its desperate attempt to land at an airport en route. It fell short of the runway by only a few hundred yards.

His wife wanted to know what was causing all these disasters. It was a mystery to him as well.

The news tonight showed the Premier visiting the survivors in nearby hospitals. Among the survivors, the newsreader said, failing to conceal the disbelief in his own voice, was the sculptor who had survived the three recent rail crashes.

'It's him again,' the man said to his wife.

Her mouth dropped open. The children bleated for attention, complaining that their helpings were not big enough.

The camera now showed the Premier smiling as she approached the survivor, who in this accident had lost his right leg. His face was expressionless as the Premier came towards him. She stretched out a hand to touch his arm and his face began to break. Before the expression had properly formed, the camera angle changed and the Premier filled the frame, smiling at the poor man.

The man whose dinner was going cold felt tears come to his eyes. That she could be so compassionate even after the terrible things the sculptor had said spoke volumes. The man, who went out every day looking for work after foreign competition had forced the closure of the plant where he had worked for fifteen years, watched the television and knew for whom he would vote in the next election.

The rest of the news included a report on how badly the government had fared in the most recent opinion polls and a short item about the Opposition Leader's comment made in Parliament: that the public had lost its faith in public transport and were not likely to regain it on account of any example set by the Premier, who never went on public transport herself.

Although the television was still on, the man had switched off. He was eating his dinner.

At least, that's how I imagine it would have gone. I doubt I'm far off the mark.

The expression on my face which the viewers couldn't see was one of intense frustration at my inability to vent my anger. At that stage it was still difficult to move my facial muscles. The vicious, bestial rage within me was like a sculpture which screamed to be released from its block of stone and could not be.

The newspapers were almost unanimous in their praise of the Premier. The photograph of her smile was reproduced around the world, sustaining a legend. One leader-writer referred to a 'beatific mask bravely stretched over the tragedy'. Another described her smile as 'benign'. I thought of it this way too; benign like a tumour.

After that, things began to move more quickly. According to my psychiatrists, I came to terms with my loss faster than was expected and seemed to them to be a model patient. Could neither they, nor my surgeons, see that I was no longer of flesh and blood, but of clay? I had become the Premier's modelling clay and she a sculptress. The newspaper photographers and television camera operators had got it wrong: it was not her face that should have been beamed round the world, but her hands.

Her sculptures truly did change lives. In the same instance that I was her clay and the public her audience, the public, or a large part of them, also became clay.

I returned home before long and lived there under siege

from the press. This time I said nothing to them. My artificial leg represented the state of the art in prosthesis and functioned with some degree of efficiency. My major psychological problem stemmed from the fact that it was hollow; my old leg had not been.

The Opposition Leader had been encouraged by the amount of media coverage granted to his comments about the Premier's personal antipathy towards public transport. He saw there was a seam to be mined. With one eye on the government's poor performance in the opinion polls and urged on by his advisers, he challenged her to show faith in the transport systems she provided for the people.

When the reporters finally gave up on me and went back to their desks I put a call through to Northern Ireland. I spoke to the gallery owner; the statues were all still in place, the show remained unopened. I told the man to expect me the next day.

This time the flight went without a hitch. I purchased a sledgehammer and a stone-cutting saw from an iron-mongery and took a taxi to the gallery. Explaining courteously to the owner that I wished to make some modifications to the sculptures, I had him lead me to the exhibition space. It was to the gentleman's credit that he became greatly distressed by the orgy of destruction which followed. I could not expect him to understand.

I smashed every bowl, jug and figurine; I demolished every bust. The statues I left largely intact, severing only their left arms and right legs; these I crushed with the sledgehammer. The muscles in my arm ached so much I wept for them.

I thanked the gallery-owner and left him the hammer and saw as a small consolation. I had other business to attend to in Belfast before flying back home.

To my surprise, the gallery owner boldly opened the show two days later with the exhibits as I had left them. Newspaper critics spoke of my 'obviously deteriorating mental health' and 'all-round destructive attitude'. One defiantly avant-garde magazine said that I had 'bravely come to terms, in sculptural form, with extraordinary personal tragedy'.

The show was soon forgotten, however. The Premier monopolized the news again. She had spotted an opportunity in the challenge laid down by the Opposition and she used the front pages to invite me to take part.

The jet took off a quarter of an hour late; getting all the television cameras, lights and sound equipment onto the plane took longer than anticipated.

Seats had been booked for the Premier, her security men, the media, and myself, on board one of the larger jets belonging to a major airline. Only journalists and television reporters known to be sympathetic to her line of goverment had been invited.

The country would see the Premier using public transport and, furthermore, they would be moved to see that she had asked me to fly in the same plane. They would note the fact that despite all I had been through and the things I had said, I still trusted public transport and still supported the government.

They would not hear the complaints of passengers who had booked tickets for this flight and found they were switched to other flights to avoid security risks.

When I finally sat down in my seat and was able to relax before the cameras started rolling I thought briefly about Helen. I wanted her to know that I had loved her. Ironically, I probably loved her more than women with whom I had far happier relationships earlier in life. Perhaps I had just needed them less than I needed Helen.

I looked at my hand. It had created its last sculpture.

This flight will end in disaster. Millions will be watching the live coverage. Screens will go blank. The plane will be torn apart in mid-air. Debris will be scattered over a wide area. There will be no survivors. The accident investigators will show that there was a bomb. They will reveal that the explosive probably came from Northern Ireland. Finally they will prove that the explosive was hidden inside the hollow part of an artificial leg.

Notes on the Authors

Brian Aldiss, born in 1925, is one of Britain's most distinguished writers of science fiction and fantasy. His novels range from *Non-Stop* (1958) to *Dracula Unbound* (1991). He is also the author of many non-sf novels such as the highly praised *Forgotten Life* (1988), and non-fiction works such as the autobiographical *Bury My Heart at W. H. Smith's* (1990). 'A Life of Matter and Death' was his second contribution to *Interzone*, and represents his first appearance in one of our anthologies.

Phillip Mann, born in Yorkshire in 1942, works as a theatre director in New Zealand. He has written several sf novels, beginning with *The Eye of the Queen* (1982), and has contributed two short pieces to *Interzone*, of which 'An Old-Fashioned Story' was the second. His latest novel is *Wulfsyarn* (1990).

William King, born in Scotland in 1960, is one of *Interzone*'s more recent discoveries. 'Visiting the Dead' was his first professionally published story. He has also appeared in the anthology *Zenith* edited by David S. Garnett (1989). He now works as an in-house writer of fiction and 'colour text' for Games Workshop Ltd., Nottingham.

Ian R. MacLeod, born in 1957, is another of our recent discoveries and 'Well-Loved' was his second story for *Interzone*. He lives in Sutton Coldfield, West Midlands, where he is married to a solicitor and worked until lately as a civil servant.

Cherry Wilder, born in 1930, is a New Zealander now resident in West Germany. Her novels include *Second Nature* (1982), the fantasy trilogy which began with *A Princess of the Chameln* (1984) and *Cruel Designs* (1988). 'Looking Forward to the Harvest,' which is original to this book, represents her third appearance in an *Interzone* anthology.

Kim Newman, born in 1959, is the only writer who has appeared in all five *Interzone* anthologies to date. He is the author of *Nightmare Movies* (1984; updated 1988) and a novel called *The Night Mayor* (1989). He also writes entertaining horror novels and sf adventures as 'Jack Yeovil' – the first two being *Drachenfels* (1989) and *Demon Download* (1990).

Ian Lee, born in 1951, wrote 'Driving Through Korea', which we reprinted in our fourth anthology. He lives with his wife and two children in London. 'Once Upon a Time in the Park' was his second story for *Interzone*, and he informs us that since writing it his life has imitated his art: he suffered a bicycle accident near Buckingham Palace. Luckily, he was not badly hurt.

Richard Calder, born in 1956, is a new British author who continues to astonish. 'Mosquito' was only the second short story he ever wrote. (His first, 'Toxine', appeared as an original item in our fourth anthology.) Since then, he has written a third, 'The Lilim', which, for the time being at least, completes his cycle of automaton stories.

David Brin, born in California in 1950, is the author of *Startide Rising* (1983), *The Postman* (1985), *Earth* (1990) and several other very successful science-fiction novels. 'Piecework' was his second story for *Interzone* (his first, 'The Giving Plague', was the most popular item we published in 1988 and was reprinted in our fourth anthology).

Ian McDonald, born in 1960, is fast gaining a reputation as one of Britain's very best sf writers. His novels

Desolation Road (1988) and *Out on Blue Six* (1989) have been particularly well received in America. He lives in Northern Ireland, and 'Listen' was his first story to appear in *Interzone*.

Karen Joy Fowler, who lives in California, won the 1987 John W. Campbell Award for the most promising new sf/fantasy writer. Her highly-praised collection of short stories is entitled *Artificial Things* (1986), and she has since completed a novel called *Sarah Canary*. 'Game Night at the Fox & Goose' was her second contribution to *Interzone*.

Ian Watson, born in 1943, is one of Britain's most energetic sf novelists, and his many books range from *The Embedding* (1973) to *The Fire Worm* (1988). He hails from Tyneside, and now lives in Northamptonshire. He previously appeared in our second anthology, with a story called 'When the Timegate Fails'.

Neil Ferguson, born in 1947, was one of *Interzone*'s earliest discoveries, and his debut story, 'The Monroe Doctrine', was reprinted in our first anthology. Since then he has published three books, *Bars of America* (1986), *Putting Out* (1988) and *Double-Helix Fall* (1990). He lives in London, but travels frequently.

Barrington J. Bayley, born in 1937, is the author of sf novels ranging from *The Star Virus* (1970) to *The Rod of Light* (1985). He lives in Shropshire. A regular contributor to the magazine, his story 'Tommy Atkins' was reprinted in our fourth anthology and the piece published here, 'Light', is an original to this book.

Nicholas Royle, born in 1963, has sold over thirty short stories to magazines and anthologies as diverse as *New Socialist*, *Fear*, *The Fiction Magazine*, Dennis Etchison's *The Cutting Edge* and Chris Morgan's *Dark Fantasies*. 'The Sculptor's Hand' was his first contribution to *Interzone*, and we have since published other pieces by him.

Acknowledgments

We wish to thank the following people, who have assisted the magazine in various ways and hence have helped make this anthology possible: Paul Annis, Malcolm Edwards, Gamma, Judith Hanna, Simon Ounsley, Humphrey Price, Ann Pringle, Andy Robertson and Bryan Williamson.

Interzone is published monthly from 124 Osborne Road, Brighton BN1 6LU, UK. A six-issue subscription costs £14 (inland) or £17 (overseas). A twelve-issue subscription costs £26 (inland) or £32 (overseas).

All the stories in this volume were first published in *Interzone* magazine, except for 'Looking Forward to the Harvest' by Cherry Wilder and 'Light' by Barrington J. Bayley (which two are published for the first time in this book). Their original appearances were as follows: